Cl A N

J. ROBERT L   **ding** *Familiar,*
Castle **and** *N*   *or the Left Hand*
and *See You i*   *Paris Review,*
Granta, Harp   **in Ithaca, New**
York, where he   *University.*

Praise for *Broken*

"Compelling from the first page, and then smart, sophisticated, suspenseful and satisfying throughout—*Broken River* is a first-class ride" Lee Child

"J. Robert Lennon is a connoisseur of calamity, qualms and paradox, all of which are on profuse display in his crafty, seductive eighth novel … *Broken River* is a remarkable performance, a magic trick that makes you laugh at its audacity. Lennon has written a realistic novel with vivid characters and flashes of humour and an evocative mood … when you close a novel as good as *Broken River*, something, not quite a ghost, may follow you" Terrence Rafferty, *The New York Times*

"What prevents *Broken River* from being classified as simply a horror or crime story are Lennon's linguistic energy and dark humour … it's a rare book that manages to bend genres so successfully—that thrills and frightens while evoking such insight into human failings and the lure of the past" *Financial Times*

"Lennon's prose has a languorous, lingering quality with shifts of perspective and tonal jolts that make you concentrate all the harder. I might venture that *Broken River* ought to be on prize longlists, but as with the house, nothing is certain … There is a ghastly creepiness to all this, magnified by the cat-like elegance of the prose … Two-thirds of the way through this novel, I fantasised about an epic Mexican shootout where Wes Anderson, Guy Maddin, Sofia Coppola, David Lynch and Kevin Smith argued about who should get the film rights. At the same time, I realised it is impossible to film. So much happens inside the characters: so much is presented as hypothetical. This is an astonishing, nasty, brilliant, upsetting work" *Guardian*

"Fizzing with line-by-line propulsion and wickedly plotted with slow-burn complexity, this is a knockout, unmissable performance from a writer at the very top of his game" *Observer*

"*Broken River* is like a Coen brothers movie set in rural New England … Lennon has a lot of fun … and we do, too" *Sunday Times*

"Hypnotic and unsettling, *Broken River* weaves a dark, compelling spell" Mick Herron

"A tense, surprising thriller, with perverse overtones of the Coen brothers variety" Jonathan Lethem, *The New York Times*

"*Broken River* is a novel with multiple identities: it's a ghost story, a crime story, a coming-of-age story, a story about love and family and fiction itself. What is astonishing is how well all these elements work together, how they intertwine as seamlessly as the fates of Lennon's characters. As good as fiction gets" Ben Winters

"An intimate portrait of the violence we do to each other, about family and art and the scars of unspeakable acts. *Broken River* blisters and rips and ultimately soars. I loved it" Lauren Beukes

"J. Robert Lennon's tautly constructed blend of literary fiction and thriller is a compelling cocktail, right down to its explosive and shocking ending" John Harding, *Daily Mail*

Praise for *Familiar*

"This highly convincing nightmare reads like a thriller; Lennon is painfully truthful about grief and parenthood" *The Times*

"Tight in focus as well as in construction … an otherworldly narrative" *Evening Standard*

"Dazzling" *Guardian*

"So breakneck and harrowing, so grab-you-by-the-lapels astonishing that you may or may not notice until nearly the end how many questions about your own life it makes you ask" Elizabeth McCracken

"J. Robert Lennon's novel bristles with menace and suspense—a terrific and disturbing read" *Daily Mail*

broken
river

J. Robert
LENNON

This paperback edition published in 2018

First published in Great Britain in 2017 by Serpent's Tail,
an imprint of Profile Books Ltd
3 Holford Yard
Bevin Way
London
WC1X 9HD
www.serpentstail.com

First published in the USA in 2016 by Graywolf Press, Minneapolis, Minnesota

1 3 5 7 9 10 8 6 4 2

Printed and bound in Great Britain by CPI Group (UK) Ltd, Croydon CR0 4YY

A CIP record for this book can
be obtained from the British Library

ISBN 978 1 78125 798 2
eISBN 978 1 78283 335 2

Mixed Sources
Product group from well-managed
forests and other controlled sources
www.fsc.org Cert no. TT-COC-002227
© 1996 Forest Stewardship Council
FSC

broken river

Part One

1

It is a few minutes past one in the morning when the front door slams
shut. Anyone remaining in the house—but there is no one—would
be able to hear, through the closed door, the footsteps of three people
hurrying across the porch and down the stairs. There are voices, too—a
man's and a woman's, and a child's. The adults are quiet, or they are
trying to be quiet, but their voices betray strong emotion: fear, in the
case of the woman; and in the case of the man, impatience and frustration, which could easily be interpreted as a response to his own
fear. The child's voice is plaintive and confused, as though she (a girl,
most likely, of around five) has been awoken from sleep and hurried
out of the house without explanation.

The state of the now-empty house would suggest that this is precisely what has happened. Many of the lights have been left on. In
the kitchen, dinner dishes are still soaking under sudsy water in the
sink, and a drawer and a cabinet have been left open and disordered,
as though objects have been removed from them in haste. Three of
the four mismatched wooden chairs that surround a small table—its
laminated plastic surface scratched and gouged and peeling up at one
corner—are pushed neatly underneath it; the fourth is lying on its
side upon a linoleum floor that is equally scratched and gouged. A few
coins lie on the tabletop, along with a half-empty pack of cigarettes,
one of which burns in a white plastic ashtray.

Anyone standing in the kitchen right now would hear, through the screened, half-open window over the sink, footsteps on gravel outside. The three people—the man, woman, and child—have evidently reached a driveway or parking area adjacent to the porch. The man and woman are arguing, and it is possible to determine from their tone that they are trying to decide upon something quickly and don't agree about the proper course of action. An especially perceptive listener might describe the woman's voice as accusatory and the man's as defensive, and might be willing to imagine a scenario in which the man is to blame for this crisis, and in which the woman is registering her displeasure about the circumstances that led to it. The child, meanwhile, has begun to cry and is demanding something that has been left behind.

If an observer in the house were to climb the stairs that lead up from the kitchen, he or she would reach a narrow hallway interrupted by three doorways. Two of them are open right now, and light spills through them onto the frayed hall carpet. The first of the doors is on the left, and behind it lies a small bedroom: clearly the child's. The bed is unmade; open drawers interrupt the face of a painted bureau. Some clothes appear to have been hastily grabbed from these drawers; a few articles have fallen on the floor. One drawer has tumbled out of the bureau entirely and lies facedown on the pink-painted wide-plank floor, on a pile of small socks and underpants. Also visible on the floor, between the upturned drawer and the bed, is a stuffed toy frog. Perhaps this is the item that the crying child is demanding.

If so, the child's parents do not sound enthusiastic about the possibility of going back to retrieve it. Instead, their footsteps in the gravel outside have stopped, and the jingle of keys can be heard in the still night air. It is even possible to see them now, from the child's room: if an observer here were to turn off the overhead light and move to the open window, he or she could make out the family standing around a station wagon parked at an awkward angle on a weedy gravel drive. The car is a Volvo, from the mid-eighties, perhaps, with rust eating away at the edges of the doors and in the wheel wells. It is hard to tell the color by starlight (tonight is a clear night), but gray or light blue would be a good bet. The man has gotten the driver's-side door open and has dived into the car, and the woman is shouting at him to unlock the other doors. The man curses, and there is a moment of relative quiet wherein an attentive observer could discern the sound of the other locks popping open. The child is wailing now—she is clearly terrified by this strange nocturnal excursion and by the unprecedented desperation of her parents. The woman flings the rear passenger-side door open and pushes the child inside. She is in there for several long seconds, attempting to reassure the child that all will be well, in a tone of voice that indicates the precise opposite. Perhaps she is attempting to fasten the child's seat belt. The man is shouting at her to just get in, fucking get in with her and close the door. In the end the woman obeys, and before the door is even shut, the engine has been started and the car begins to execute a sloppy three-point turn. At last the car is pointed away from the house; it is thrown into gear, and the tires spin, sending a shower of gravel out behind it.

If the observer in the house were to leave the child's room and continue down the hallway to the next open door, the one on the right, he or she would find a larger, similarly disrupted bedroom. It would seem to belong to the man and the woman. The bed is mussed, with the sheets pushed down to its foot, but only one side appears to have been slept in. A collection of items on the small table at this bedside—a paperback romance, a snarled elastic band with several long hairs tangled in it, and a single earring (its twin is lying on the floor, in the shadow of the bed)—make it appear likely that it is the woman who lay here alone tonight. Perhaps, then, it was the man who stayed up smoking at the kitchen table.

The third room will have to remain unexamined for now, because a new sound is demanding our observer's attention. It is emanating from the now-darkened child's bedroom: or, rather, from its open window. The sound is that of a car—the mid-eighties Volvo station wagon, it would seem—scraping through brush and crashing against the trunk of a tree. There is a shout—the woman's. Something, some obstruction or unexpected event, has caused the man to steer the car off the drive and into the woods. As the observer turns and approaches the room for a second time, light sweeps through it, and out the door and into the hall: headlights: not of the now-disabled Volvo but of a new vehicle that has come up the drive toward the house. Car doors open with a rusted groan: the Volvo's. Another car's doors can be heard to shut, cleanly, quietly: this car is newer, denser, larger.

Heavy footsteps break twigs and crush leaves. There are shouts—men issuing commands, to one another, to the fleeing family. Someone, doubtless the woman from the house, is screaming—at first in surprise, then in alarm, and then in outright terror. Then, for a few moments, the woods are quiet. The chaotic action that immediately followed the accident has ceased. The woman, for now, is no longer screaming. Only the man can be heard; he pants and grunts; he weakly protests. Now the woman begins to cry. Deep male voices ask sharp questions, issue threats. The man and woman attempt to respond, to comply, but their efforts are evidently ineffective. Flesh can be heard to come into violent contact with flesh. The man groans. The woman yelps, begs.

It is unlikely that any genuinely feeling person could bear to hear the sounds that come next, not for more than a few seconds. And so let us assume that our observer is not a real person but merely the idea of an observer: an invisible presence without corporeal substance, incapable of engaging emotionally with the sounds that reach the house. These sounds are to last for nearly fifteen minutes. They are the sounds of suffering: the man and woman are enduring physical and emotional agony. It is unclear whether information is being extracted from them; or if they are being punished for something they have done, or are supposed to have done; or if these acts are merely sadistic. In any event, they are acts of physically violent, sexual, and psychological torture, and the man and woman react the way any human animal does when the last of its defenses have been stripped away and it is facing the inevitability of its own death. It is not necessary to describe those reactions here, only that they come to an end following two short, sharp noises: gunshots.

There is silence once again. Then the male voices return, quieter now, more efficient. Three of them: it is not necessary to discern the differences between them. The three men are working together. They effect movement in the brush; they grunt, as though lifting something heavy. A quiet metallic snick implies the opening of a car trunk or rear door, and a thump indicates that a heavy object has been placed roughly inside. This sound is accompanied by the clanking of wood and metal, as though some tools have been displaced by the heavy object: shovels, perhaps. This process—the lifting, conveyance, and depositing of something heavy—is repeated, and followed a moment later by the opening and closing of the newer car's doors. The glare from its headlights, which during the chaos of the past half hour has remained fixed upon the walls of the child's bedroom and of the hall outside it, once again begins to move, and the sound of the car's engine recedes into the distance. And then one of the Volvo's doors opens and closes, and its engine starts up. It seems that, with some effort, its new driver has managed to extract the station wagon from the brush and navigate it back onto the gravel drive. Soon it, too, is gone, in the same direction as the new car, albeit with an altered set of wheel and engine noises: scrapings and knockings and a rhythmic clanking, as of a fan blade bent off true. The Volvo is not right. Surely it is barely roadworthy. Our observer might conclude that the car, like its former occupants just minutes before, was nearing the end of its functional life. In fact, it is likely that it will never be seen or heard again.

For some time, the only sounds audible from the house are of the wind in the trees—it seems as though a storm may be coming—and the creaking of the front door on its hinges. The door was left open by the fleeing man and woman. The wind has come into the house, and it has begun to move other things—some papers left out on the kitchen counter, a bit of onion skin on the linoleum behind the pantry door. The lit cigarette in the ashtray burns faster, and the wind pushes its smoke away, at an acute angle, toward the farther recesses of the house. The cigarette is propped in one of the three heat-discolored notches cut equidistantly along the ashtray's edge; in twenty minutes the line dividing the intact cigarette and the ash has reached the notch, and the remaining unconsumed cigarette tips back and tumbles silently onto the table's surface.

Now, in a gust, doors slam shut throughout the house. The front door is the last, and loudest. Rain—big drops of rain—begin to fall outside, intermittently at first, then in a steady if irregular rhythm, and then in a torrent. After three minutes of this, rapid footsteps sound on the porch, and the front door opens only wide enough to admit a lone person before it closes again behind her.

It is the child. She's crying—sobbing wildly, choking on her sobs—and mucus drips from her nose and over her lips. She locks the door behind her and calls out to her parents. Of course there is no answer. The child does not appear surprised. She knows that something unprecedented, terrible, and irreversible has happened and that her parents are not likely to answer. At the same time, she believes the opposite: that her parents are nearby and will soon come to her aid. This is, after all, the only arrangement she knows. For a few minutes more the child stands in the vestibule, continuing to cry, her arms hanging at her sides, her eyes darting wildly, surveying the interior of the house, which our observer might guess she suddenly sees as alien, subtly and permanently changed, as though in a dream. At last the crying stops, and the child stands panting and rubbing her face. She takes a few steps into the kitchen. It appears to frighten her. She takes note of the fallen chair and the few scraps of blown paper lying beside it. After a time, she moves a few feet to her left, slowly, her back sliding along the kitchen wall. Then she lowers herself to the floor and sits there, her legs splayed out like a doll's.

The child is wearing a thick cotton nightgown printed with pictures of suns, rain clouds, birds, and umbrellas. She moves a hand up to the neckline and begins to twist the fabric around her pointer finger. She then puts this knot of cloth into her mouth and chews on it, champing with her bicuspids like a dog with a bone. Her eyes stare straight ahead, unseeing, and the fabric is soon dark with saliva. She falls asleep, and the nightgown-wrapped finger drops from her open mouth. But the finger remains tangled in the wet fabric, and her arm hangs there, stretching out the nightgown at the neck. The child snores. The rain continues to fall.

As dawn breaks, the child wakes on the kitchen floor, briefly appears frightened and confused, then gets up and hurries to the stairs. From down in the kitchen, our observer hears the sounds of a toilet being used. Footsteps can be heard, first across tile, then carpet, then wood. Bedsprings creak. The child can be heard to speak a single word, "Froggy," uttered in evident relief.

The child appears at the top of the stairs. Her nightgown is dry now but wrinkled and distended around the neck, and she is clutching the stuffed frog. She gazes down into the kitchen, her eyes passing over and through our observer, and she calls out to each of her parents. There is no answer.

After a minute, the child comes down the stairs, slowly and warily. But when she reaches the kitchen she appears to gain confidence— she walks quickly now to the pantry and emerges with a box of cereal. She places it on the table, then heads to the refrigerator for milk, and to a drawer for a spoon. Once these items have joined the cereal box, the child rights the fallen chair and drags it over to the cabinets. She climbs onto it and retrieves a china bowl from a shelf. These actions are deft; the child is clearly accustomed to them. The bowl secured, the child now moves to the table, prepares her meal, and eats it.

Once the child has put away the breakfast ingredients and carefully balanced the bowl and spoon in the sink, on top of the previous night's dishes, she walks briskly out of the room. For a few minutes she is audible moving through the recesses of the first floor. Not long after, her footsteps sound in the upstairs hall—there must be another staircase at the rear of the house—and roam through each room. The third door, the one closed the night before, under which no light shone, now opens, then quickly closes. The child calls out to both parents again, this time in evident, if theatrical, frustration and impatience, as though the previous night's fear has been transformed into irritation at their inconvenient absence.

The child's footsteps can now be heard entering her own bedroom again. Drawers are opened and closed. Muttered words are spoken: she is talking to herself, or perhaps to her frog. When our observer sees her again, she has come down the stairs and is passing through the kitchen on the way to the front door. She is dressed in a pair of bell-bottom jeans and a white tee shirt covered with small pink hearts, and her face wears an expression of determination and mild but growing anger. What else can we learn from her short trip across the floor? The child's eyes are large and deep, and the pale and faintly translucent skin beneath them is purpled by crying and by the disruption of her sleep. In the set of her shoulders, the tightness at the corners of her mouth, and the complex expressiveness of her brow—she is scowling in apparent concentration—we may detect evidence of a troubled and agile mind, one that, at this moment, is attempting to contextualize, explain, and reshape the events of the night before: to give them a form that she will be prepared, if not to grapple with, then at least to tidy up and get out of the way.

But we are out of time. The child has opened the door and is marching through it, into the bright and muggy morning. She throws it closed behind her, but with insufficient force, so that it fails to latch and falls partway open again. This enables us to hear the child calling out for her parents, in a tone both plaintive and scolding, the way she might address her stuffed frog when she has invented a wrong for it to have done. For several minutes the child's footsteps sound through the rain-drenched woods, and her chastening voice grows more distant. And then the house is silent again.

It remains that way for fourteen hours, during which time our observer can hear, through the open front door, the sound of water dripping from the leaves of trees and onto other leaves and the ground. This sound slowly gives way, as the water evaporates, to the busy noises of insects and rodents in the woods. For a brief time around 8 a.m., and again around 5 p.m., the distant hiss and rumble of traffic can be discerned, barely. Then, when darkness has fallen, footsteps approach from the rear of the house and make their way around it toward the front door. The footsteps are stealthy, but once they reach the porch, it's easy to tell that they belong to two men. The taller and more muscular of the men shoulders open the half-closed front door, and, though it is dark here, our observer can see that he is holding a pistol at his side. His partner, who is shorter, thinner, and somewhat stooped, carries something long and heavy: a crowbar, or perhaps two of them, one in each hand. The two men explore the first floor of the house, then head upstairs, where for half an hour or so we hear them taking apart the third room, at the end of the hall. Evidently unsatisfied with their findings, they proceed to do the same to the two bedrooms. Then they come downstairs again and proceed methodically through all the remaining rooms. They make a lot of noise: furniture barks against wood floors, doors are ripped open, objects are cast about. Sometimes a crowbar is used to pry back pieces of floor or wall material, and we hear the groan of old nails being wrenched from wood, and the snap of wood breaking. Light bulbs pop and shatter; one or both of the men swear. Every now and then, a particularly noisy vehicle is audible on the road below, and the two men stop and listen and, eventually, return to work.

By the time they reach the kitchen, the two men are clearly frustrated. They expend particular effort here, pulling cabinet doors off their hinges, smashing jars of molasses and dried beans and lentils, and ripping open bags of powdered sugar. Drawers are emptied onto the floor, and at one point the smaller man throws a blender across the room, inadvertently striking the larger man in the ankle. There is a shout, an oath, an argument. The larger man, our observer now sees through the evening's gloom, is more than large; he is enormous, and densely constructed, a hulking yet agile ogre of a man. The smaller man, we can now conclude, is of average height; he is small only in comparison with his counterpart.

After two more hours of effort, the men leave with the tools they brought and nothing else. The house is in disarray.

The next morning police arrive: first a couple of plainclothes officers, who take one look in the door and then back away, talking into their radios. A pair of detectives shows up next, a man and a woman, both wearing suits. They slip on latex gloves and Tyvek shoe covers and pad through the house, taking notes, one in a little notebook, with a pencil, the other out loud, into a tape recorder. Technicians arrive, a photographer, and a number of other functionaries whose immediate purpose is not clear. The detectives leave after a couple of hours with a few objects sealed in plastic bags, but for the most part they appear dejected and bored. Eventually the police clear out. By late afternoon, everyone but the plainclothes officers is gone. Through the windows (for the door has at last been shut) our observer can see the uniformed police stringing yellow plastic tape around the place. They stretch it from tree to tree, doing a little maypole dance around each one. They appear to be having a pretty good time. Eventually a man arrives in a marked van—a locksmith, its panel would suggest—and he removes the locks from the front door and replaces them with new ones. Our observer then hears him doing the same in a distant part of the house: a back door, no doubt. Then car doors slam shut and engines start and the house is left in peace.

....

It is a matter of weeks before anyone enters the house again. During this time, the food left in the refrigerator browns and shrinks, and mice and insects discover the boxes of cereal and packaged snacks and sacks of grain. Ants march across counters and floors, and moths flutter through the kitchen. Squirrels, who have always lived in the largely unmonitored attic, sense the absence of human beings and take up their daily activities with less furtiveness. Still, the house seems more or less as it was left, to the untrained eye. The female police officer who enters the place twenty-five days after the initial incident curls her nose as she lets herself in, and gazes with apparent surprise at the destruction the two unidentified men wrought here. She wends her way through the kitchen holding a cloth shopping bag and a piece of paper. Let our observer look over her shoulder for a moment, at the paper. Words have been printed there: *red trousers*, *yellow dress*, *ukulele*, *Lego*, *tennis shoes*, *flip-flops*, *books*. The police officer makes her way up the stairs, speaking into her radio as she goes: *Nobody here*, she says, and a distorted echo of the words sounds from the front porch, where a partner doubtless stands guard. We hear the officer in the child's room, bustling around for ten minutes or so; when we see her again, her bag is bulging and she is walking quickly, as though mildly frightened. She slows her stride as she reaches the front door, as if to conceal her nerves from her partner. She pulls the door shut behind her and we hear the deadbolt lock. Low words and footsteps follow, then silence again.

Months pass. For a time, mice populate the house in great numbers. But pretty soon the food is gone, and the mice retreat. The house smells bad at first—feral and rotten—but after a while it just smells moldy and stale. It's autumn, and then winter. The first snow of the year falls and heaps itself onto the trees, and then a wave of unseasonable warmth turns the falling snow to rain, and branches, heavy with saturated snow, begin to break. The sound, recorded and speeded up by a factor of ten or twenty (and let us imagine that this is how our patient observer might perceive the passage of time), would sound like muted applause through the house's sealed windows and doors—that is, until a massive sugar maple standing outside the kitchen sheds a snow-burdened bough, which falls twenty feet, slides down a lower bough, and shatters the window over the sink. Now the applause is deafening. It peters out by midafternoon: show's over.

But a new one is beginning. New squirrels enter through the broken window and build nests in the house, and then, one afternoon in midwinter, a couple of teenagers arrive. A boy first: long haired, pale skinned, he appears unthreatening but unhappy. He picks the remaining bits of broken glass out of the window frame, then wriggles through, landing headfirst in the dish-filled sink and tumbling noisily to the floor. A voice outside asks him if he's all right, and he says he's fine. He goes to the front door and unlocks it to let his girlfriend in.

She's slight in build, but her face is wide and her color high. If our observer were inclined to form an opinion about these two, it might be that the girl has some potential for a long and happy life; the boy, not so much. In any event, they are together now. They explore the house, talking to each other in low tones. While they are upstairs, we smell marijuana smoke, then hear the sound of gentle laughter, and then the noises of sex. When the sun is about to set, they leave.

The boy and girl come back several times over the next several months, and then, on the first warm day in April, the boy returns alone. He's got a canvas army-surplus satchel with him; it dangles at his side limply, as though it contains nothing. In fact, it contains letters, a surprisingly neat, thick sheaf of them, in business-size envelopes. Our observer might deduce that they are from the girl and that, given the expression of grief and rage on the boy's face, the two have split. He sits down at the kitchen table, pushes aside the coins and the ashtray and the stub of cigarette lying there, and heaps the letters in the center. After a moment, the boy picks up the letters again, crumples each in his hand, and puts them back. Now the pile is larger—satisfyingly so. He pulls out a lighter and sets the pile on fire. He's crying. He mutters an oath. Then, apparently on impulse, he quickly pulls an envelope out of the burning pile, shakes the flames off it, and removes the letter inside. He doesn't read it. Instead he pulls a plastic pouch from his satchel, pinches an amount of weed from it, and rolls an awkward joint using the half-burned letter. He smokes it as he continues to cry. Meanwhile the pile burns down to ash, save for a few miraculous scraps, which he leisurely touches with the flame from his lighter until they become ash, too.

When the boy leaves, it is for good.

The coming year finds the house occupied by all manner of vagrants. Drug addicts, vandals, genuine hoboes. Graffiti covers the once-clean white plaster walls. Looting takes place, of course; clothes, furniture, and appliances disappear, while other items are destroyed by rough use or by the unfocused rage of the house's temporary inhabitants. Gradually the interior of the house comes to resemble what it is: an informal shelter for the marginalized, angry, disenfranchised, and mentally ill.

A few years down the line, after a particularly raucous gathering—a loud and violent party that can be heard even at a great distance—one man, no doubt a neighbor, attempts to take matters into his own hands. He's hale, big in the shoulders, determined, around sixty or perhaps sixty-five. He enters through the front door and deadbolts it behind him. Then, grunting, he wriggles out the broken kitchen window. Soon his face reappears, a cluster of heavy nails clutched between the lips. Our observer (still here!) watches as he hoists a piece of plywood into place over the kitchen window, and five noisy minutes later the house is again sealed off from the elements.

Not long after this, though, the plywood is torn off, and the house returns to its state as a hangout for teenagers and down-and-out adults.

....

Six years after the events that left the house empty, a car comes up the drive. The door opens, and three people appear on the threshold: a woman in a neat business suit, holding a clipboard; a casually dressed man of evident means (our observer notes his evenly tanned skin, long, tapered shoes, and designer jeans); and a weathered-looking man wearing a tool belt. The last of these three lets out breath: we can only imagine that he is about to be tasked with cleaning up the mess. The trio takes a tour of the place. At times, the woman points at something—an architectural feature, a spot of damage—and the men nod. The man with the tool belt takes notes in a small spiral notebook. The man of means nods at things the woman and the other man say. Soon they're gone.

The following week, the front door opens and the house fills with people. It's a work crew. Over the next few weeks they tear up the water-damaged and moldy carpets, rip out the waterlogged plaster, and peel up the worn-down, torn, and filthy linoleum. An electrician replaces faulty and hazardous wiring and installs three-pronged outlets in every room and ground-interrupt outlets in the bathroom and kitchen. A plumber repairs a number of radiators and replaces the up-stairs bathtub and kitchen sink. Meanwhile the kitchen cabinets have been restored and a new range and microwave oven installed. The walls are sheetrocked and painted, and the broken window is repaired at last. Men can be heard scaling the outside walls, scuttling across the roof. When the work is complete, the woman with the clipboard and the man of means return to examine it. Satisfied, they leave. Our observer, whom none of the recent visitors has noticed, hears the clank of metal striking metal coming, faintly, from the end of the driveway. It's a real estate sign, no doubt, being driven into the ground. Our observer might also, however, have noticed a headline on the news-paper a workman left in the wastebasket underneath the new sink: KABOOM!, it reads, UPSTATE HOUSING BUBBLE BURSTS.

This headline might offer an explanation for the events of the year that follows: the woman with the clipboard leads potential buyer after potential buyer through the empty house, gesturing enthusias-tically at the various amenities that seem less valuable, less appealing, with every passing day: the synthetic marble countertops; the lami-nate flooring, printed with a wood pattern; the bathroom fixtures that already show signs of rust, though they have never been used. Meanwhile the number at the bottom of the page on the woman's clipboard gets lower and lower.

The second year that the house is on the market, the buyer visits peter out and eventually stop. One day the man of means appears with a second man of means—this one younger, more ill at ease. They tour the place, then shake hands. A new woman soon appears, with a new clipboard and a new series of visitors, but once again the visits dwindle. The house is beginning to look abandoned again. Our ob-server doesn't venture outside, but it's safe to assume that the weather has taken a toll both on the recent renovations and what's left of the original eighty-year-old construction. Over the next year, rodents begin to move in again. Vandals come back—our observer can hear their spray cans being shaken, the hiss of their tags being laid on the siding. A vagrant breaks a new window, and once again people begin spending the night here, doing drugs, having sex.

Then, a year and a half after the last appearance of the second clip-board woman, she returns. She is followed by a man. He's tall, be-spectacled, heavy in the middle, thickly bearded. He's wearing jeans and a leather coat and expensive shoes and is about thirty-five years old. The clipboard woman appears bored. She isn't trying very hard to make the sale; she's been in this position many times before. The man follows her around, gazing with apparent equanimity at the drug de-bris, dirty rags, and muddy footprints the visitors of the past year have left. The two climb the back stairs, move from bedroom to bedroom, and come down the front stairs. Words are exchanged in the kitchen, right beside our observer, who notes a certain dawning understanding in the clipboard woman's face. My god, she seems to be thinking, he's going to buy it. Numbers are proffered, adjusted, returned. The man nods. The woman nods. They shake hands. Clearly the woman cannot believe her luck. Her expression suggests an impending day of unexpected celebration—a boozy lunch, a night on the town.

Now it's late February, and the ground outside is covered in snow. Big machines come up the drive and clear a path to the backyard: a dump truck, an earth mover, a cement mixer. As the weeks pass it becomes clear that an outbuilding is being constructed. Low, blocky, with an angled roof and a continuous row of small square windows, it speaks of careful and understated design and appears built for some inscrutable aim. If our observer were, at this stage of its existence, capable of curiosity, this structure would no doubt pique it; the building's minimalist style, coupled with the bearded man's scruffy urbanity, implies some kind of creative or otherwise artisanal activity.

Now, for the second time in five years, the interior of the house is being torn apart. The sheetrock is replaced with plasterboard, the laminate flooring with wood, the cheap plumbing fixtures with bespoke ones of obvious durability. The imitation marble countertop is demolished and a three-inch-thick butcher's block laid in its place. The plastic and aluminum replacement windows, results of some long-ago renovation, are soon gone, and custom-made wooden sash windows are hung.

From time to time over the next few months, the bearded man returns, sometimes with another man—doubtless a building contractor, judging from his tape measure, dusty blue jeans, and military-grade cell phone shell—and sometimes alone. One time he arrives with a woman. Slender, small breasted, black haired, she peers around the place with evident astonishment. She coos with approval as she walks from room to room. The bearded man appears pleased as well. It is Sunday, and the two are the only people present in the house. In an act of evident ecstatic abandon, the woman turns a slow circle in the living room, then strips off her clothes. Does the man appear reluctant at first? Alarmed, even? Never mind. He is soon naked as well, and they make love pressed against one of the freshly painted plaster walls. With this act, their faces and bodies seem to assert, we hereby claim this house as ours.

Another four weeks pass, during which time the workmen attend to the final details of the renovation—painted trim, splashguard tile, a wood-burning stove. And then a moving van pulls up outside, and men carry boxes into the house, each marked with the name of a room. The men consult a hand-drawn diagram and haul the boxes to their proper places. Plastic-wrapped furniture follows, then tightly rolled oriental rugs, wooden crates full of paintings and photographs. Two objects of indeterminate identity are left in the living room; they stand at five and seven feet high respectively, upon their heavy hardwood bases, and reach up to two feet wide at their widest points. From beneath the translucent plastic sheeting and packing quilts that cover them, an occasional heavy appendage or extension pokes. The mysterious objects appear to be made of steel and glass.

Three days pass. These days are hot and sunny, and the interior of the house has grown muggy. Late in the evening of the third day, the driveway gravel is audibly disturbed by an arriving car. Its doors open and close. Light, fast footsteps cross the porch, and the knob jiggles. "Hold on, hold on!" comes a voice, one that our observer might recognize as that of the black-haired woman whom the bearded man brought here more than a month ago. Heavier footsteps land on the porch now, and keys jingle. In a moment, one of them crunches into the door lock, and the front door falls open. The woman and man are back, but bounding ahead of them comes a girl: their daughter. She is tall like her father, fine featured and dark like her mother, and she says, "Oh, *man*!" She runs from room to room in an obvious state of excitement, then races up the stairs, presumably to find her own room.

"Welcome home," the man says, to no one in particular. To his family. To the house. To the Observer, who floats silently, substancelessly, in the kitchen, looking on without judgment.

2

Irina is sitting on her bed with a spiral notebook open on her lap, a pencil poised above it. It's a special pencil, one from a box that her mother bought her—a long-defunct brand that has been brought back to life by the kind of people who miss old pencils. They are silvery gray, with soft, dark leads; the eraser is flat and rounded and encased in a rectangle of squashed gold metal. These pencils cost twenty dollars for a box of twelve; Irina looked them up online. Her mother would disapprove—a gift is a gift, however much it costs—but in this case, the price has made her like the pencils more. They are precious. They can't be used for stupid things. Which is why she is using them to write her novel.

She likes it here. She liked it the moment Mother described it to her: "A small house, in the woods, far from anything fun." In the months leading up to their move, when they were still living in Brooklyn and Mother was angry at Father, she would ask Father what was being done to the house today to make it ready for their arrival, and he always had an answer. "They're replacing the kitchen counters today," he would say. "They're sanding the old floors." "They're painting the walls." Perhaps he was making this stuff up—how could he know what was being done at any particular moment, in a distant place he'd visited only a couple of times? But Irina enjoyed the notion of the house being transformed for her benefit. She imagined her room, with its window onto the trees. In her conception of the future, she could sit cross-legged on her bed and gaze out at a heavy tree branch that squirrels and crows would perch on, and she could talk to them and possibly, eventually, feed them from her hand. In the meantime she would work on her novel. She started it in Brooklyn; it's about a boy who gets on the wrong subway train and ends up in a previously unknown sixth borough of New York City where women wear gigantic dresses with bustles that prevent them from ever getting closer than six feet from one another, and men who are brothers or close friends or who started businesses together would allow their long mustaches to intertwine, making them physically inseparable. When one of them kisses his wife (the wives have to lean far forward, due to the bustles), the other feels, through his very sensitive mustache, his brother or friend or business partner's lips moving, and this makes him jealous, and he desires to kiss the wife himself. Also, in this borough the most distinguished job you can have is street magician, electric power comes from monkeys riding stationary bicycles, and the borough president is twins. The borough is called Quayside because it is an island cut through with man-made channels, and people live on boats as well as in apartment buildings, and most of the cabs are boats, too, yellow boats painted with checkerboard patterns, and when you step onto one a recorded message in the voice of a famous Quayside actor or comedian reminds you to put on your life vest.

So far, a week after arriving here, life has gone pretty much according to her desires, if not better. Her room is awesome. The window really does look out onto the trees, and she sees squirrels and crows all day long. She hasn't befriended any, but that was just idle fantasy. She has written 14,734 words of her novel (she counts each day's output in the evening, before going to sleep, and pencils the total at the bottom of the day's last page) and has persuaded her parents to let her be homeschooled, just for the fall, before they enroll her in the public school in Broken River, which she is not so secretly hoping never gets around to happening. Broken River seems to her a meager, sad little place, with its empty storefronts and depressed-looking old people heaving themselves up and down the sidewalk, but it has its charms—an old-fashioned (though abandoned) movie theater with a marquee bearing the now-fragmentary names of movies from three years ago, an old-fashioned (not abandoned!) drugstore counter that serves ice-cream sodas ("Not old-fashioned, either," her father corrects her, in her head: "Retro"), a busy and not-at-all-old-fashioned coffee shop, complete with the horrible sucking sound that results every time somebody orders an expensive drink. Actually it reminds her a little bit of Quayside—certain neighborhoods in Quayside, anyway, where it's all white people. Broken River is all white people, and every other place they've had to drive thirty or forty minutes to get to this week—WalMart, Home Depot, and the like—has been all white people. That's fine, their family is also white people, but Irina cannot help but think that these people are hiding from everyone else, either out of fear or because (she hopes) there is some secret appeal to this part of the world that they don't want other kinds of people to find out about. For what it's worth, she hasn't figured it out yet herself.

She has spent a lot of time out in Father's studio, helping him, or perhaps mostly watching him, get it set up. He is clearly excited about the space, which is a twenty-foot square with cement floor, sloped metal ceiling, and clean, white walls. He has been lecturing her on the operation of the forge—it is new, stainless steel, "heats up fast, Irina, really fucking fast"—and on the positioning of his anvil and his wheeled rack of blacksmithing tools. He is quite geeked about the wall-length rack he made, out of plywood and two-by-fours, that holds his supply of thick slab glass—some clear, some milky, some smooth and shiny, some sandpaper-rough—and iron and steel, sheets and bars of the stuff. As he talks, which he has been doing pretty much incessantly since their arrival, she walks up and down the wall of glass and metal, running her fingers along the edges of the slabs and sheets and bars, gripping them with her fingers, trying to budge them. If her mother were out here, she would shoo Irina away from the wall of heavy materials, any one of which could fall on her and injure her, or shatter and cut her; her father does not. Her explorations have given him pause—many times he has stood, interrupted in midsentence, staring at her dazedly, his forehead creased as though with concern—

but she isn't sure if this is because he's worried about her safety or just surprised and alarmed to realize that she is there, that she exists, that he has a daughter, that the daughter is her, that they have moved hundreds of miles from home to this strange, isolated place, and that this is their life now.

If it's the latter, Irina understands. She feels that way, too: alarmed, amazed, uneasy. It should not be a secret to her father that she is a little bit afraid of him, a little bit in awe of him, a little bit skeptical of his status as an adult responsible for her upbringing. She's had friends, though not great ones, and she has met their dads. Her dad is not like their dads, not even back home in Brooklyn, where everyone's parents are weird or creative. Her friends' dads smiled when they saw their daughters, kissed them hello and goodbye, explained things to them (often things that didn't really need explaining, to be honest) in a bright and really kind of corny tone of voice. These dads kept their beards trim, their jeans cuffed, their glasses polished, their balding heads buzzed. Her dad, on the other hand, talked to her friends as though they were adult women (or maybe he talked to women as though they were children? She is very proud of this insight and jots it in the margin of her notebook for possible eventual insertion into the novel), asking them if they wanted a cup of coffee or what they were working on or what they thought of various books there was no chance any of them had read. Her dad didn't comb his hair and beard, he grew them as long as her mother could stand (she was the one who periodically hauled him into the bathroom and sheared them off with clippers), let his glasses grow hazy with sweat and dust. Her dad was as much ape as dad. He was an ape dad! It was an ape dad who loped around the studio, fondling the tools, rearranging and reorganizing the work table, the hooks on the pegboard, the standing fans. It was an ape dad who made these big weird scary awesome things that he sold, apparently, to people in New York.

"You are not to return for one year," Irina heard Mother tell Father one night a few months back, while they lay in bed after sex (and yes, she knows what sex is and what, unfortunately, it sounds like), meaning that he is not supposed to set foot in New York City, not even to sell his sculptures. "The service can deliver them. You don't need to be there. Gert will take care of everything." Gert is the woman who runs Father's gallery, or rather it is her gallery in which his sculptures are sometimes shown.

"I know," Father said, groaning, "I know."

They didn't know how loud they were. Or maybe they did but figured Irina tuned out any kind of information that wasn't obviously relevant to her. Irina, in fact, didn't tune out any information that reached her from the adult world. She was very eager to reach adulthood and wanted to be able to step into the role with the ease of a seasoned professional. She asked one friend, Sylvie, if her father had ever had an affair, and Sylvie, even though she was *thirteen*, didn't even know what that was. "It is where he meets another woman who isn't your mom and he falls madly in love with her." Sylvie said, "That's stupid," and Irina said, "But has he?" and Sylvie said, "No!" and pretty soon Sylvie's mother was calling Irina's mother to tell her to come get her. (There was a long pause, and then Sylvie's mother said, "I'm sorry, Eleanor, I cannot put a twelve-year-old girl alone onto the subway," and Irina saw which way the wind was blowing, excused herself, and slipped out of the building to sneak off to the F train. Very probably she will never see Sylvie or her mother again.)

Personally, Irina herself doesn't see how it's possible to be with one person your whole life, or even overnight—"You would have more friends," Mother once said to her, "if you would agree to more sleepovers," to which Irina replied, "Exactly"—and if a day arrives when the idea of removing all your clothes in someone else's presence does not horrify her, she thinks that she will not feel compelled to limit herself to one lover. She intends to be a novelist, a famous one, like her mother but more so, and also much more frightening and intimidating than her mother, who even on television appears like a fairly normal person—somebody's mother, in fact.

Their house is small. This part, she didn't expect. The front door opens onto the kitchen, and between it and the stairs lies a living room where her parents have put books, a sofa, and Father's two giant, frightening sculptures. The kitchen is disproportionately large and has big windows on two sides and so is Irina's favorite room besides her bedroom. It's everyone's favorite, actually. Upstairs there's a narrow hallway from which Irina's room, her parents' room, and her mother's study may be entered; all three are basically twelve-foot boxes. There is also a spiral kitchen staircase with tiny steps you can't even fit your entire foot onto, and Irina habitually uses it instead of the main one because it is weird. On the outside of the house, which is brownly shingled and frankly kind of ugly, the spiral staircase is contained in what looks like half of a cardboard toilet-paper tube somebody glued onto the exterior wall. There's a little turret on top, for no evident reason.

Perhaps the most interesting thing about the house is that something bad happened to the people who used to live here. They are dead, anyway. This is apparently one of the reasons the house was empty for such a long time and thus needed to be renovated before Irina and her parents moved into it. Irina is aware of this fact only because she overheard two workmen talking as they were installing a new refrigerator: one of them said, "You know this is where those people got killed," and the other one said, "Yeah, except it wasn't in the house," and the first one said, "But still," and the second one said, "Hey," and then kind of tilted his head at Irina, who was sitting at the kitchen table wearing headphones, but, cleverly, the headphones were not plugged into anything. This is a trick Irina would have played around her parents as well if her parents made any effort whatsoever to conceal what they said to each other.

In any case, the identity of, fate of, and story behind the previous inhabitants of the house is something Irina intends to research while she is here. If the results are interesting, maybe she can incorporate them, somehow, into her novel. Because at the moment, the novel has no real plot—it's just descriptions of things. That's what Irina is good at. She believes that she inherited this deficiency from her father, who is a visual artist and does not require narrative to make something of value. But if that's her cross to bear, she will do it stoically.

It's 11 a.m. Not yet time for lunch. Mother and Father are working. The novel isn't going anywhere, not today. But it's a sunny summer day and the woods outside are beckoning. She closes her notebook and shoves it under the mattress, then goes out to the studio.

Irina's father is wearing goggles and thick gloves and is bending a glowing iron bar around the edge of an anvil. It is somewhat disappointing to her that her father doesn't do more pounding with a hammer. This is what you're supposed to do with an anvil, isn't it? Instead Father mostly bends. She is not sure if the lack of pounding is the cause of his underdeveloped upper arms or the result of them. She says, "Father, I'm going to the woods. Can I borrow your phone?"

He doesn't look up. Instead he plunges his iron bar into a metal bucket of water on the floor, and the water roils and bubbles and hisses, and steam surrounds his face. Then he straightens, holds the bar up to the skylight, turns it in his hand, squints critically at it. Frowns. "Sure, it's on the bench."

"Thank you." She goes to the workbench, picks up the phone, and puts it into her pocket. Father is moving to the forge to heat his bar again. He says, "Don't answer it if it rings. I'll call them back."

"Okay."

"Don't fall off a cliff or into a river."

"I won't."

"Don't fall in a lake, either." He's looking at her now. She stands in the open doorway, her hand on the knob. "Or a hole, don't fall in a hole. Don't threaten a bear, especially a bear cub, especially if the mother is around. Don't get eaten by wolves or carried away by pterodactyls. Don't get alien abducted. Don't spontaneously combust or become a drug addict or a prostitute. Don't marry an asshole."

"Stop bossing me around," says Irina. "I'll marry whoever I want!"

"That guy's no good for you. Don't let his fancy car fool you."

"You don't understand me, or Chad! You'll never understand our love!"

"Fine!"

"Fine!!!"

Outside, she wakes up the phone, finds the maps app, opens it. There is central New York, and there is Irina, a blue dot. She was delighted to discover, a few days after moving in, that the woods surrounding the house are adjacent to a state-owned nature preserve that is crisscrossed with walking paths. These paths are actually documented in the maps app on the phone, and Irina has figured out how to drop a pin representing their house on the map, so that she can always be directed back to it as long as there's a cell phone signal, which there does in fact seem to be everywhere near the house. She walks north, through her parents' land, to the sign that reads THREE VALLEYS WILDLIFE MANAGEMENT AREA STATE OF NEW YORK DEPARTMENT OF ENVIRONMENTAL CONSERVATION. Catchy name, New York! Now the path becomes wider and better groomed. She walks for five minutes or so to where there actually is a cliff she could fall off of, if she isn't careful. The path goes left and right and is marked by yellow paint marks on trees; she has previously taken the path to the east, so now she goes west. The path is crooked, following the line of the cliff, which she peers over from time to time, not without some anxiety. Father was not kidding: the dropoff is steep, and though she might survive the fall she would most likely end up drowned in the river two hundred yards below, and her body would be carried away. She wonders where the people got killed—the previous owners of the house. Were they thrown off the cliff? Why did it happen? Did they mess with the wrong people? Were they innocents who happened across the commission of a heinous crime, and knew too much? Were they bad guys themselves? It's hard to imagine criminals living in their house, which is so awkward and charming and peculiar. The house is a nerd. They're living in a nerd!

After a while the path slopes down and the cliff face becomes less sheer, and pretty soon she is walking along a ridge that leads her to the river itself. It's just barely a river—she would call it a creek, really. But the maps say it's a river, the Onondakai. She finds a sunny grassy patch by the water and sits cross-legged on it: "Indian-style," a teacher of hers once said, and was corrected by an aide who told her that was racist. The aide did not last long! She googles the river and finds out that it got its name from a Seneca chief. The name means "destroy town." She imagines the river rising, inundating a village, sweeping the houses and people away. On the other hand, the town it runs toward is called Broken River: are the two at war? She wishes she had brought a notebook so that she could write all this down for her novel—maybe that could be the plot, the waters of Quayside are rising and only her protagonist can fight them back.

The phone rings in her hand. No face appears on the screen, no name, just a number.

Father has asked her not to answer, and she doesn't intend to answer, but who can resist answering a ringing phone in their own hand? Also, the ringtone is shrill and unsettling—a nondescript beeping that sounds like a digital alarm clock. It is out of place here in the woods, by the river, and it needs to be stopped. She swipes the screen and raises the phone to her face.

"Hi, this is Irina."

"Oh! Hello," says a woman. She stutters for a moment, then says, "I'm trying to reach—is this Karl's number?"

"He's—I borrowed his phone."

"Hello."

"Hello."

"If you call again in half an hour, he'll answer."

"I'll do that, then."

Irina ought to just hang up now, but instead she says, with a precipitous kind of feeling, as though she is falling off a different kind of cliff, into a different kind of river, "I won't mention that I talked to you. I wasn't supposed to answer."

"All right . . ."

"So maybe you won't mention it, either?"

"No, I won't."

"So we're cool then."

The woman does not sound entirely comfortable as she says, "We're cool."

Irina hangs up. She feels bad. She wants to be on her father's team, but only in the most abstract way. Because she believes she takes after him and wants to protect him from a world that doesn't appreciate him enough. On the other hand, she senses that she has just involved herself in a part of her father's life of which her mother might not approve.

The phone is still glowing in her hand. For reasons not entirely clear to her, she is suddenly mildly angry with her father, and she pokes the phone icon, imagining that it is his shoulder: Hey! Hey, you! His call history pops into view. Father doesn't make a lot of phone calls, but there is one number, with a 212 area code, that he has called about five times in the week they've been here, and it's the one attached to the lady she just spoke with. The conversations are long—like, forty minutes to an hour—and occur at the times (lunch until dinner) when he's typically in the studio.

Hm.

She decides to forget about this. It is none of her business.

She gets up, climbs back up the hill along the cliff, turns south, passes the back of the nature preserve sign (onto which a yellow POSTED PRIVATE PROPERTY sign has been stapled), and hurries down the path to the studio to give the phone back to Father. He is hard at work bending hot metal again, so she slips the phone onto the workbench and edges toward the door.

"That's you? Not a ghost? You didn't fall off the cliff?"

"Nope."

"Which way did you go?" He takes off the protective goggles and wipes sweat from underneath his fogged-over specs. He is wearing baggy jeans with suspenders and a tee shirt bearing the name of a summer camp. He looks cool. He always does. She feels her irritation draining away.

"I went west. It goes down a hill. It looks like there's a bridge over the river at some point, I want to find that."

"Yeah, you should."

It occurs to her, not for the first time, that her father never addresses her by name. A nickname, sometimes. She was named after a photographer her father knew—a haughty gray-haired woman who wore long flowy things. Irina met her at a gallery show in New York, to which, thinking of it now, she had probably been brought solely in order to meet her namesake. Suddenly she doesn't understand the role of women in her father's life. Suddenly she is not sure how she is supposed to feel about him.

They look at each other for a couple of seconds, and then his phone rings. They both glance over at the workbench.

"Better get that," Irina says. Her father's antennae go up. She slips out the door and closes it behind her.

....

The physical and emotional rigors of the afternoon have left Irina almost too tired to eat dinner. After her walk, she returned to her room and tried to add a couple of pages to her novel. Then she tried to take a nap, but every time sleep endeavored to drag her down, some noise from outside the window—a bird or falling branch—would distort and magnify itself in her nascent dream and jerk her back to wakefulness, where the things she didn't want to think about awaited her. Now Irina is grumpy and displeased, even with the food her mother has made, even though it is spinach lasagna, ostensibly one of her favorites. The spinach is stringy and it's sticking in her teeth and the sauce is bland. She entertains a moment of guilty nostalgia for the days, years ago, when her mother was sick and they got takeout all the time. At some point during the silent meal she drops her fork on the plate, falls back in her chair with a sigh, and crosses her arms over her chest.

"Yes?" her mother inquires.

"That's not a question," Irina points out after a few seconds.

Her mother contemplatively dabs the corners of her mouth with a cloth napkin. The napkin is printed with a cartoon of the New York skyline. They got it at Fishs Eddy in Manhattan. They can't go there anymore! They don't live in New York! Mother says, "What is the source of your dissatisfaction, Daughter?"

"Nothing."

"So you are not, in fact, dissatisfied."

"I *am* dissatisfied," Irina says, "but I am telling you that my dissatis*faction* has no *source*."

"It's parthenogenetic," Father offers. "It's ambient." He has a nervous look on his face.

Irritated, Irina says, "I don't know the meaning of the first word."

"Virgin birth. Asexual reproduction."

"That's not the same as having no source." As she says this, she thinks of the river, *her* river, the Onondakai, running in a circle, like one of those tail-chomping snakes whose name also, she's pretty sure, starts with an O. It comes from nowhere, and it never reaches the ocean. It can't rest! It just goes and goes, in an endless loop, destroying every town it touches.

Her father shrugs, pooches out his substantial lips. "I guess you're right."

The conversation has had the effect of spreading the bad mood around. It really is ambient now. Father keeps glancing over at her, significantly, and she doesn't know why. Mother keeps glancing at Father and then back at Irina.

This is stupid! "I'm going to take a bath," she says.

"You don't want dessert?" her mother wants to know.

"No."

Irina gets up, scrapes her lasagna into the trash, slots the fork and plate into the dishwasher, and climbs the stairs. In the bath, she hums quietly to herself while trying not to have thoughts; afterward she dries off and puts on her summer pajamas, which consist of pink, lacy shorts and a tee shirt with an owl on it. She goes to bed and tries to read. But it's still light out. It's weird to be in bed. After a while her mother comes into the room and lies on the bed with her. Yes, Mother, that's just what I need, for my hidey-hole to be invaded by grownups. Irina pretends to read for a while. Then her mother says, "It's strange to be in a new place."

"That's not why I'm dissatisfied."

"So why, then?" says Mother.

Instead of answering the question, Irina says, "What happened to the people who used to live here?"

After a long pause, Mother says, "I didn't know you knew about that."

Irina narrows her eyes and says, "You don't know a lot of things."

Mother has been facing Irina, who has been lying on her back, but now she lies on her back, too, and puts her hands behind her head.

She says, "They died? It was a long time ago—they think it had to do with drugs or something else illegal. We're not in any danger."

For no particular reason, Irina replies, "That's what *you* think."

"Irina," says Mother, after what sounds to Irina like a strategic pause, "did something happen today? On your walk? Or with your father?"

Oh, no, you don't, thinks Irina. She digs in: "*How* did they die?"

Mother narrows her eyes, and for a moment Irina is frightened: she has seen her look at Father this way, when she thinks he is lying about something. Is this what it feels like to lose Mother's trust? It isn't a good feeling.

"They were murdered, Irina," Mother says, her voice steady. "By two or more assailants. Their bodies were never found, but the physical . . . evidence suggests they were . . . that they died. In the woods."

"Hm," Irina says.

"And that's all I know about it," Mother concludes, and now she's the one who's lying. Her mouth twitches and she glances away.

And without thinking (though of course she has been working up to this, and it is not unrelated to the subject at hand), Irina says, "I think I am more than old enough to have my own computer, don't you?"

The hesitation that follows is brief, and then her mother answers, "Sure, okay. What are you planning to do with it?"

"I'm going to edit my writing. And do research."

Her mother appears impressed. Irina allows herself the small luxury of believing she is not faking this time.

"Also," Irina adds, "I will stop borrowing yours! Won't that be a relief?"

"Well," her mother says, "it's maybe good for me to not have access to a computer now and then. But all right. We'll order one tomorrow."

Well! That was easy. "Can I borrow yours now?"

Her mother turns her head and Irina looks right into her eyes. "Yes, sure," Mother says. "You want me to get it for you?"

"Yes."

A nod, and then she hoists herself up off the bed with a groan and disappears down the stairs. There has been more groaning than there used to be; her parents' middle-aged bodies no longer recover so quickly from the lifting and transferring of heavy boxes. A few minutes later she has her mother's laptop on her lap and is opening the browser. Her mother looks on.

"I know how to use it. I don't need help."

"Just—"

"I'm not going to snoop in your personal things."

Mother's eyebrows go up. "That's not what I was going to say. But all right."

"Thank you."

"You're welcome." There's an awkward moment when she seems to want to say something but can't. In the end, she just says "Good night" and disappears into the hall.

This feels like some kind of victory to Irina, for a short while. But after staring into the empty browser search bar for several minutes and listening to her mother move around listlessly in her computerless office, she begins to feel sad. She looks up at her closed bedroom door, opens her mouth to summon Mother back.

But what would she say? That she was suddenly sad and didn't know why? No. That would be stupid. Instead, she shuts her dumb mouth, lays her hands on the keyboard, and types the familiar words *Broken River NY unsolved murders*.

Because Irina was lying, too: she has had no trouble, over the past few weeks, finding information about the murders and probably knows as much about them as anybody but the killers. Those workmen were right that it didn't happen inside the house; it actually happened close by: right next to the driveway. What was known was that the people, a man and a woman, attempted to flee the premises in their car but ended up driving it off the driveway and into the trees. There they were "taken from their vehicle" and shot. Police found bullets and shell casings at the scene of the crime; DNA evidence established that the blood "and tissues" of both victims were present "in amounts that strongly suggested that the victims did not survive the shootings."

Neighbors claimed to have heard none of the commotion; anyway, gunshots were not unusual in this area and tended to be ignored and quickly forgotten. Police weren't alerted to the crime until the following day, when a child appeared on a neighbor's doorstep and announced that her parents were missing. Police found the house ransacked, the door left open, and tire tracks leading off the drive and into the woods; a tree had been crashed into, and the evident murders had happened not far away. The child was able to provide some additional detail, including the probability that there were multiple perpetrators and that they drove to the scene of the crime.

But beyond that, there was nothing. The child had evidently run into the woods and hid with her hands over her ears. She had not seen the killers. She took refuge in the house for the night and left in the morning, to search for her parents. Instead, the neighbor heard her calling for them, took her in, and phoned the police.

Those, as far as Irina has been able to learn, are the actual known facts. But they don't tell her anything about what she really wants to know: what happened to the girl. It appears that her name was Samantha Geary and she was put into foster care, but beyond that, there is nothing. The girl disappeared from the public eye. Luckily, this is precisely the kind of mystery that the internet likes to speculate about, and Irina has found a great deal of said speculation on an internet messageboard called CyberSleuths dot net (no doubt named when "cyber" seemed like a forward-thinking prefix that everybody would be using in the future, while wearing eyeglasses with screens on them, LED wigs, and e-scarves crawling with stock tips). CyberSleuths is the meeting place of bored and morbidly curious people like Irina who think they are clever enough to solve crimes the police have given up on. And they are right! There is a HALL OF FAME thread where the messageboard's successes are archived: and there are many! The information is out there, and the CyberSleuths are on the job, combing through old news reports, Facebook-stalking murderous creeps, connecting unidentified bodies with missing persons, and generally being completely brilliant and heroic from the comfort of their own homes. Irina has registered under the name UncleJ. This is a reference to a character from her novel. Additionally, it pleases her to think she might be mistaken for an old guy. She is discovering that, with a man's name, she does not get talked to like the twelve-year-old girl she actually is. She just gets talked to.

Not that she posts much. She's merely dipping a toe, so far, into the thread unmemorably called *Geary murders, 2005, 2 vics, no bodies.* So many people saying so many things about events Irina now feels, thanks to her move upstate, somehow in the center of: it is immensely exciting, and she feels as though she needs to exercise patience, not let it all take her in too quickly. She both fears and savors the experience.

Irina logs in (she doesn't let the browser save her username and password, as she wishes to spare Mother from the knowledge that her imagination has grown so dark) and scans the thread for new stuff. There isn't much, just some idle speculation. She studies, for the umpteenth time, the iconic photo of Samantha Geary—someone named smoking_jacket found it in a school yearbook—as a kindergartener, wan and stringy haired, her face long, her eyes large. Irina googles the girl—she would be seventeen now—and finds plenty of people by that name on Facebook and Twitter. Some of them are probably seventeen. But it's not an unusual name. And if Samantha got new parents, they probably changed it. That's how things like this work, the child gets a new name and psychologists use hypnosis to make her forget what happened. Probably they replaced her memories with puppies and ice cream cones. Anyway, these Samanthas don't look like her Samantha. They look like regular girls, uncorrupted by proximity to murder. Irina thinks she would know her Samantha anywhere. They are housemates, soul sisters, cruelly separated by time and circumstance. When she sees the girl's eyes, she will know it.

She spends ten minutes rereading old posts on the Geary thread, then another twenty clicking idly around other threads: murders, rapes, disappearances, all of them attended by people even more obsessed than Irina, all of them unsolved, abandoned by the police. An increasingly familiar sense of futility and dissatisfaction settles over her, and she throws her head back onto her pillow pile and stares at the cobwebs swaying nauseatingly on her bedroom ceiling. Here it comes again: her dissatisfaction deepening, mutating into something harder. She is beginning to feel resentful. It's nothing in particular that is making her angry, just the vague and growing sense that she is little more than a pawn in her parents' lives. A powerless thing to be pushed roughly ahead, and sacrificed if necessary, as Samantha Geary nearly was in the woods that night. Of course just this morning she was feeling deeply enchanted with her new home, the wooded path, both of her parents, her novel-in-progress. Now that's all gone. Why? Is this irrational? Is she just being moody? From inside the emotion, it's impossible to tell. She's as angry with herself as she is with anyone else. She imagines, briefly, that *she* is Samantha Geary, never mind that the years don't add up right. Maybe she's actually seventeen and her physical development has been arrested by the violent trauma of her childhood. She has been dropped into this life by a team of social workers, and her memories have been replaced. It makes a certain kind of crazy sense.

Impulsively she navigates to the forum entry where Samantha's childhood photo has been posted. Irina doesn't look like that and never has: apple-cheeked, pigtailed. Bah! She opens the image file in a new tab and hits PRINT. She tosses the laptop aside and runs down the hall to her mother's office, where the printer is. It's dark now, and the printer is wheezing, and spitting the paper out underneath a blinking red LED. Irina snatches it up and returns to her room. Samantha is grainy and small, up in one corner of the page. At her desk, Irina cuts out the photo and tapes it into the back of her notebook. Then she opens up the browser history (*muscle fatigue remedy, back pain remedy, achy bones remedy, massage therapy,* read Mother's recent queries), erases her tracks, closes the laptop, and climbs down the stairs. Her parents are sitting on the sofa, drinking whiskey and looking mildly depressed. She sets the laptop down on the coffee table, says thank you, and runs away before anyone can say good night to her.

Only when she gets back in bed does she realize she never kissed them. Oh well. There's a first for everything. She doesn't need the habits of youth. She's a new girl now.

3

Summer is nearly at an end. The air is heavy and wet and the sun appears larger in the sky, diffused and magnified by the haze. Clouds are massed at the edges of this valley but seem to lack the motivation to climb the ridges and pour in. If there were a large town here, its inhabitants might crowd into the Onondakai to cool down. In the wide, shallow stretch where it bends toward the wildlife preserve, and where large, flat stones offer paths to the far bank or islands to spread towels and lie in the sun, the Observer might find people relaxing, talking, playing with their children, unwrapping wilted sandwiches and unscrewing thermoses containing diluted iced tea and a few foamy slivers of what used to be ice cubes. If there were a town here, one of the natural pools that has formed at the base of a small waterfall, accessible by two miles of rough footpath, might be informally designated a spot for skinny-dipping. Young people in love with each other and with their youth might strip off their clothes here and swing into the water on a rope slung over a branch; old hippies might join them, and a pervert or two might lurk in the woods with binoculars. But there is no town, and the Observer finds no one.

Instead the Observer moves southeast along County Route 94. It has discovered that it can leave the house: can go anywhere, really. Faster now, faster than a car, the Observer flies along the river, in between hills, briefly above a defunct railroad, sometimes past a half-empty village or struggling farm. Once the Observer arrives at flatter land, there are more paved roads, more farms, low houses. Soon there are car dealerships, fast food restaurants, big-box retailers surrounded by half-empty parking lots. It's Broken River. There is the Broken River State Prison, and there are several prison-themed bars and a prison museum. There is even a street called Hoosegow Lane—doubtless part of a doomed effort, at some time in the recent past, to draw visitors based upon the only claim Broken River has to fame.

The Observer is not interested, however, in the center of town (the defunct movie theater, the walk-in medical clinic, the senior center, the strip club, the local bank that closes half an hour before everyone else gets out of work), choosing instead (because with freedom of motion has come the need to make choices) to continue down Onteo Street, through three traffic lights; to make a right at the hospital and parking garage; to follow an Afro'ed, baggy-panted kid on his bicycle toward the long, low glass-fronted building where an unwashed, multiply dented Greyhound bus is idling. It doesn't matter where the bus has arrived from. The Observer elects not to care. Passengers file off: a pale kid with sunken cheeks and a trucker cap that bears the Playboy logo, who hitches his backpack higher on his shoulder and fist-bumps the kid on the bike; a very old woman whom no one is helping down the steps, and who meets no one on the pavement; a thick-necked middle-aged man in a Buffalo Bills tee shirt and gigantic basketball shoes who can't seem to stop coughing; and a teenaged girl.

To see this girl at rest, and from a distance, might be to regard her as waifish—she appears, at first, to be very thin, malnourished, even, and she seems to have mastered the art of stillness, as though in an effort to conserve energy. Her straight hair covers much of her face, but large eyes peer out from beneath it—are they frightened? wounded?

But to see her in motion would bring doubt to one's initial assessment of the girl, for she moves purposefully and with preternatural poise, as though holding back some hidden strength. And if you approached her, as our Observer now does, her thinness would reveal itself as, rather, a leanness. She's tall—five feet nine or even ten inches—and she carries her army-surplus duffel bag as easily as though it were stuffed with balled-up newspapers. It is not. It's heavy. Our Observer can tell by the thump it makes as it hits the ground at her feet. She has dropped it there, not ten yards from the bus she has just exited, in order to consult a paper map, printed from the internet. She studies the map, squints at her surroundings (the Wilson Farms convenience store, the electric power substation, the empty stucco box that once contained the local chapter of the SPCA), examines the map again. Whether what she sees is a disappointment to her is unclear. Her face is impassive.

Clearly no one has arrived to meet her. But perhaps she didn't expect anyone. There is resignation in her eyes and in her posture: the slight stoop a tall girl learns to assume, an inward curl of the shoulders. She folds the map, jams it into her back pocket, hoists the duffel onto her shoulder. She's wearing a gray V-necked tee shirt that conceals small breasts and, on her left arm, the lower half of a crude tattoo of uncertain design. Her well-worn jeans hug narrow hips, and her shoes are garish running sneakers bearing the logo of a popular brand. She walks briskly but without particular haste. She heads up to the light, followed by our Observer, turns left at the hospital, then beelines through the center of town, rarely turning her head to peer into a shop window or acknowledge the appraising look of a passerby. She does not invite, with her posture or facial expression, the male gaze. But certain boys and girls she passes—kids hanging around on stoops and in the doorways of abandoned storefronts—are interested in her.

The girl ignores them. She passes the strip club and medical clinic and movie theater, crosses the town's main intersection, then heads down an incline past one, and then the other, prison-themed bar. Of course: she's going to the prison. This is not an uncommon walk for an out-of-towner to take—the bus station to the prison, eight shameful blocks enduring the curious stares of the locals. But the girl isn't ashamed. She isn't anything. She's walking to the prison, that's all: past the museum, with its electric-chair logo, past the hot dog stand, over the train tracks, and in the main entrance.

Our Observer doesn't follow her inside. An hour passes, then another. After a third hour has passed and the sun is low in the sky, she emerges. Now her body betrays some weariness: she carries her duffel as though aware of its weight, and her color is off—she looks a little peaked. She looks hungry.

And as though to confirm this impression (for the Observer hasn't moved in the three hours the girl was inside), she heads toward the hot dog stand. There's a small line there, as visiting hours at the prison have just ended, and a collection of tired- and sad-looking people is queued up at its small yellow-lit window. But the girl doesn't get in line. She arcs around and past it, then stops in front of a pay phone bolted to a telephone pole, not fifteen feet away. It's standing in darkness, for the insect-encrusted streetlight above it has burned out. Surely it doesn't work, this phone? But no matter: the girl pulls an outdated folding cell phone—its fake chrome plating pitted and worn down to a patina of streaked black plastic—out of her pocket, and leans against the defunct pay phone kiosk to make a call. (The Observer can see that the cultural memory of a space apart, dedicated to communication at a distance, remains strong, despite the obsolescence of the technology that made it necessary. Where else should one go for a private conversation? Or, more to the point, what else is there to be done with such a space?) She pulls a map from her bag; this she unfolds, turns over, and holds up before her eyes, evidently trying to make out, in the light from the hot dog stand, something written there. She punches a series of numbers onto her phone's keypad, waits a few moments. She says, "It's me," then has a brief conversation. Her body language changes as she speaks; it's clear she does not savor this conversation, in which she is doubtless at some kind of disadvantage. She is, perhaps, asking for a favor.

After a minute, the girl hangs up the phone. She gazes at the hot dog line as though contemplating the possibility of eating a hot dog. Her hand burrows in her pocket as if palpating the coins there. But in the end, she walks another half block from the prison, just to the other side of the tracks, and settles onto the guardrail underneath the closest functioning streetlight.

She sits there for twenty minutes. If she wore a watch—she does not—she might periodically gaze at its face. She closes her eyes, then opens them quickly, as though wary of the consequences of falling asleep.

At last a car pulls up. It's a four-door Ford Taurus from the nineties; rusted in places, primed and sanded in others, it sits low on its tires and emits a scraping sound as it idles. It is too dark to see the driver, but a hairy arm tells us that it is a man. The girl leans in the passenger-side window for a brief chat. Then she lifts her duffel, opens the back door, and tosses it in. Hastily, as though she's afraid the driver might take off without her, she opens the passenger door and folds herself into the car. The Taurus continues past the hot dog stand, takes a turn around the prison visitors' lot, then bumps over the tracks and heads toward the center of town. Before it gets there, though, it makes a right, disappears briefly behind some houses, then reappears long enough for our Observer to see it vanishing around a hillside.

The Observer could follow but chooses instead to remain. It is interested, it realizes, in the negative spaces the people leave behind, spaces they fail to occupy in the first place. Objects and events not missed but gone unnoticed, unanticipated, unconceived of. The Observer will catch up to the human beings later. They're slow, moored to their physical forms, to each other.

In the next half hour, the hot dog crowd dwindles. Cars leave. Visitors walk toward the bus station in silence. For another hour or so, the hot dog vendor reads a magazine. Then the guard shifts change—men and women in uniform arrive in their cars; others leave through the front gate. Most of them buy a hot dog. When this rush is over, the hot dog vendor switches off his yellow light, padlocks a hinged piece of plywood over his window, and leaves on a moped that was parked, out of sight, behind the stand.

4

Several weeks later, Eleanor is doing what she has done every Tuesday and Friday afternoon since they moved here, which is to take Irina to the Broken River Public Library and sit with her in downtown's only coffee shop with their piles of cigarette-reeking, broken-spine hardcovers. It's unusually hot for September, and the coffee shop—it is called Frog and Toad's and is located in a kind of difficult-to-find mini-mall behind an abandoned bank—has the air-conditioning going full blast. As a result it's quite crowded. Eleanor is self-conscious about occupying a table in a crowded coffee shop; she can sense other people waiting, studying her for evidence of impending departure. When potential customers walk in, see the crowd, frown, and march back out, Eleanor feels responsible. She wants to leave now in order to accommodate what she perceives as other people's more pressing needs. But she has identified this quality in herself as a personality flaw, and she doesn't wish to pass it on to her daughter. So she pretends she belongs here and deserves this table.

Irina's drinking coffee too. She asked for a cup, just now, in line at the counter. Their conversation went like this: Irina ordered coffee, Eleanor laughed, Irina said, "What's so funny?"

"You're serious? You want to try coffee?"

"I don't want to *try* it, Mother, I want to *drink* it."

"So you've had it before?"

She recognized Irina's scowl from her father's face: that broad fore-head so effective at advertising hurt. "I have it *all the time*."

"Where?" Eleanor asked, though she knew.

"Father's studio."

"He has a coffeemaker out there?"

The barista, through a tiny, tight mouth, said, "Two coffees, then?"

"Yes, please!" Irina chirped. "Milk in mine, please. No sugar," she added, proudly. Eleanor immediately recognized this pride not as a manifestation of her own emerging faith in herself but rather of Karl's natural, effortless, self-satisfied bluster. She checked herself: now stop that.

The girl poked the cash register iPad with one hand while point-ing at the condiment station with the other. Irina blushed, obviously embarrassed at having blown the protocol. You'll learn, young one, Eleanor silently reassured, and a gray funk settled over the two of them.

Now they're sitting together at a tiny table by the window, pre-tending to read their books. People in business casual drag themselves damply down the street, casting the occasional envious glance into the coffee shop. Whenever one meets Eleanor's gaze, she offers up a small, embarrassed smile. She is thinking about the coffee in Karl's studio. What else has he got out there? Packages come for him regularly; she has seen the cardboard boxes, neatly broken down and stuffed under-neath the advertising circulars and egg cartons in the recycling bin. These expenses do not show up on her credit card statement, and so he must be paying for them himself, with his own money.

She doesn't go out to the studio very often, and when she does—to bring Karl mail or ask him if he wants lunch—she rarely steps over the threshold. He invites her in now and then to look at what he's working on, but it seems perfunctory, an effort to demonstrate that he has nothing to hide. In New York his rented studio was where he had his girls, and, though there are no girls now, she still feels as though it's his private space, which she shouldn't invade.

She does not know why she is affording him this courtesy.

For her own part, she is blocked. Early on in this project, before they moved, she had been sending chapters to her agent, and her agent claimed excitement. He wanted to sell early, get her an advance. But instead of moving forward with her outline, she has decided to go back and tweak things a little. Nudge them a bit. "I'm making some changes to those chapters," she told the agent, and he said, "No need to do that. Just move forward. Move forward, and we'll work on it together." Craig Springhill is his name, a smooth-faced, honey-voiced white man with prematurely silver hair and a charmingly patronizing manner that she used to find reassuring. He came from the dying world of old-school New York publishing and treats her as though she's the only lady novelist in his stable, a titillating unicorn. When she comes to town he buys her twenty-four-dollar cocktails at the Algonquin Hotel and laughs hysterically at everything she says.

They had a relationship. Well—a thing, anyway. It was a long time ago, before he represented her, when she worked as his assistant. She was twenty-three; he was nearly twice her age. He's the one who first called her Nell, the name all intimates now use to address her. They were in her apartment, his fingers were fondling the top button of her blouse, and a query appeared in his eyes: "May I undress you?" was the question she expected, but the actual question, which he posed while undressing her without requesting permission, was, "May I call you Nell?" Yes. Yes, you may call me Nell.

He was married then and slept with most of his assistants. Divorce was inevitable, but what came next was a surprise, at least to Eleanor: he found someone, a woman three years his elder, and entered into an evidently stable relationship with her that brought the assistant fuckings to a close. Eleanor has met this woman, a foxy, silver-haired, rather intimidating television critic named Shannon something-or-other.

Eleanor was glad when Craig settled down, or she told herself as much at the time. In truth, however, she had chosen to see Craig's serial infidelity as a manifestation of the general incorrigibility of men, something she needed to believe was real if she was to tolerate Karl's sexual exploits. Craig's rehabilitation, then, could be taken to mean that she was, in fact, married to a jerk. And there was no avoiding the other plausible lesson here: that, unlike Shannon the TV critic,

Eleanor was not the kind of woman who inspired men to abandon their promiscuity.

In any event, she did not take his advice. She changed the chapters, rewrote every sentence. And when she sent them to Craig, he said, "Very compelling, keep at it," and when she sent him yet another draft of the same pages, he said, "Brilliant, genius, love them."

"Good."

"Of course I adored the original version, before you changed it. And the second version. But these are also fantastic."

"The other drafts are gone now, Craig," she told him. "They're deleted. The new versions are the real ones."

"Yes, got it," he said, and then, after an awkward pause (awkward, in particular, for Craig, who is so very skilled at filling empty spaces with words): "Nell, dear, you do realize that these are all roughly the same."

"They are not remotely the same," she replied, attempting to suppress the stirrings, in her breast, of panic.

"The words are different—"

"Yes."

"—but what they say is not. They are variations on the same thing. It's the same novel."

"I wouldn't say that," Eleanor told him, weakly.

"I think," Craig Springhill told her, with gentle condescension, "that it is time to move forward on this book. To write new pages."

"These *are* new pages."

"To write the pages that come after these pages, Eleanor. To write," he said, with uncharacteristic irritation, "the rest of your novel. To begin to finish it. Don't you agree?"

"There's only one acceptable answer to that question, when a man asks it."

"Eleanor," he said, and at this point his voice had adopted the tone of exasperated finality that she had previously heard only while sitting in his office, waiting for him to get off the phone with someone else, "writing your damn book is a gender-agnostic good. Just do it, please." And he hung up.

Eleanor's books are about, and ostensibly for, women. Both the women she writes about and the women who read what she writes are young, smart, reasonably affluent, white, and firmly middle- to upper-middle-class. Her protagonists have been called "sassy" by leading entertainment magazines. The pastel-colored covers of Eleanor's books are the kind that display shoe-clad disembodied white women's legs or a fancy warm-weather hat or a signifier of free time such as a beach umbrella or shopping bag. (Eleanor was disdainful of these design clichés in the years before her name was embossed over them: reassuring expressions of conventional femininity, promising womanly universality through the promise of capitalism. She has since learned to do her sneering exclusively in private.)

The common parlance for the kind of book Eleanor writes is "chick lit." If asked, Eleanor will say that she writes "literary chick lit," an awkward and redundant term that nevertheless gets across the intended message: that she recognizes the essential frivolity of her work but insists upon approaching it with intelligence and a dedication to craft. She has learned, in the ten years her career has spanned, that certain other writers, ones with more intellectual cred than she possesses, read her, and regard her as a guilty pleasure. "Smart-lady trash" is what Craig calls her work. "As reliable a racket as this business has seen since the celebrity tell-all." Each of her books has sold better than the one before, and she is on the cusp of achieving genuine entrenched semistardom. "This," he told her, speaking of the new book, "will be your first number one bestseller." He didn't mean that the new book was better than the others—he meant that because it was functionally identical to them, it would not impede her career's natural rise. The book, in Craig's conception, should be cart, runners, and grease, all at once.

She has admitted to herself that he is right, at least in that it truly is time to move forward. But she is hopelessly blocked.

Irina lets out a noisy sigh and theatrically slams her book shut. She says, "I don't think I'm good at reading."

"That's silly," Eleanor replies, with a reflexive strenuousness that unpleasantly reminds her, every time, of her own mother. "You're a great reader."

"I start reading a paragraph and then something reminds me of something and by the time I get to the end I realize that I've been thinking of the thing *in my head* and not the thing I just read, and I have to start over!"

"Oh, that," Eleanor says.

"I've read this paragraph five times! And I don't know what it's about!"

"Maybe it isn't very good."

Irina says, "What's with all this reading, anyway? Like, how long have humans been doing it? Compared to all of history, I mean. A zillionth of a percent of time, I bet. It's unnatural!"

"But on the way here you said it was your favorite thing to do."

"That's the *point*!" Irina cries. "It *is* my favorite thing, but it's never *good enough*!"

She picks up her spoon and idly stirs her milky coffee while Eleanor tries to think of something to say. Irina, always precocious, never satisfied by the simple pleasures of childhood, has lately been witness to an abundance of adult troubles; and instead of shunning them, of regressing into prepubescence, she seems perversely eager to shoulder them herself. The bitterness of coffee is one thing, but Eleanor had hoped to shelter her from the bitterness of everything else, at least for a few more years.

Her instinct is to reassure, but the truth is that she agrees with Irina, she feels the same way about books: about everything, really. Your favorite things are never good enough. They're idealized by nature; their favoriteness is derived from Platonic forms, perfect realizations that existed only once, usually the first time, if at all. No book, no meal, no sunny day ever equals the one in your head. She should tell her agent this. She should tell her husband this. She *did* tell her husband this when Rachel, the Last Straw, cast her lumpen shadow over their already-compromised union. Go to her, Eleanor told him, and find out. Find out just how happy she makes you. Instead, he agreed to an arrangement that Eleanor presented as months in the making rather than the drunken whim that it actually was: a year upstate, and then we'll see.

When Eleanor met him, Karl was a graduate student in sculpture at the School of Visual Arts in Manhattan and lived in a fairly spacious fourth-floor walkup in Bushwick, on the same block as a barber who used only clippers and an illegal Jamaican speakeasy and gambling den. He was thin then, with broad shoulders and narrow hips; his arms and chest were naturally well developed from his handling of the heavy materials—concrete, iron, glass—that his sculptures were made from. He was very handsome. His heterosexuality was so pronounced as to seem, in the heavily diverse, non-gender-normative environment of early-2000s art school, almost radical. He came off as arrogant. He was arrogant. He loved, or professed to love, the stridently masculine painters of the American midcentury: essentially, anything Clement Greenberg liked in 1963, Karl liked in 2005, and for this his fellow students hated him. He identified more powerfully with painters than with sculptors—"I'm painting in three dimensions," he used to tell Eleanor—for which his fellow students and most of the sculpture faculty hated him.

But women loved him, even the ones who hated him. Within his grad school cohort (some of whom Eleanor eventually got to know), fucking and then hating and then grudgingly admitting you really still kind of liked Karl was practically a rite of passage. She met him at a party. He had arrived with one woman, an experimental portrait painter, and left with Eleanor.

Months later, when she realized she was pregnant, she mounted a campaign of emails and phone calls, none of which he answered. So she went to Manhattan, found Karl in his studio at school (where he was scraping German curves into a chunk of veiny sandblasted glass with a hand chisel while singing along to whatever noise was pumping out of his giant insectile headphones), and in front of two other sculptors working in separate corners of the room shouted, "Hey!"

He didn't look up.

"Hey, man!"

Now he saw her. His face registered nothing. He raised a finger: Hold on a minute.

"How come you're ignoring me!"

"Jussec, jussec . . ." *Scrape, scrape*, went the chisel. *Tockatocka-tockatocka* went the headphones. For fuck's actual sake.

"Dude!" Eleanor shouted. "You knocked me up! What are you going to do about it!"

"Oh shiiiit!" came a voice from behind a precarious-looking sculptural pile of corrugated cardboard. From the other side of the room, a snicker sounded. Karl appeared to sense the shift in vibe. He removed his headphones.

"Hey," he said placidly. "What?"

She told him. He didn't appear surprised or alarmed. He swore he hadn't been ignoring her—or, rather, he'd been ignoring everybody, working on this project. "Look," she said. "Do you want to pay for the abortion? Do you want to come to the clinic with me? Or would you just like to be a garden-variety dick?" Something in Karl inspired this gleeful vulgarity, which was otherwise out of character for Eleanor. Later she would understand that bluster was necessary, when addressing this man, to conceal and undermine strong emotion. You didn't want to cry in front of him. You didn't want to be weak. You wanted to win.

He said, "Oh, no, don't do that. Have it. Have the baby."

Her only response was a snort.

"No, I mean it." He jabbed with a dusty finger at the portable CD player attached to his belt, and the pulsing hiss emanating from the neck-slung headphones stopped. The room dropped into a kind of hush. Karl spoke quietly. "I'm sorry. Have the baby. We can't kill it. Let's move in together."

"That's insane. I have a life." Though this wasn't true. She had half a shitty novel draft and worked for her ex-boyfriend.

He shrugged.

"We don't know each other," she said. Save me, she didn't say.

"Sure we do. Also, I have money. Family money. This is great, actually. We'll be a couple. Didn't you tell me you were a writer? That's perfect."

He took two steps and gathered her into his arms. The feeling was extraordinary: like being picked up by a warm gust and deposited on some sunny, grassy hilltop. "It's perfect," he said. "We will be amazing. The baby will be amazing. He'll be an opera singer, or a tattoo artist or something. All three of us will be fucking famous."

"Let's get coffee and talk this over."

"Yeah. No. Coffee's no good for the baby. Remind me of your name again."

Someone else in the room said, "Awwww, so sweet."

"Eleanor."

"Yeah. Right. Eleanor."

"But you can call me Nell."

"Okay, Nell. Let's go get some herbal tea or something."

They went out for tea, and Eleanor got coffee and felt bad about it.

....

She supposed she knew he was going to sleep with other women. Or, rather, she told herself he was without really believing it and found herself surprised to have been right. It was hurtful and cruel and she didn't like it, but it also felt very grown-up to let him do it; it felt like a clever heterodoxy, an artsy relationship hack of which she elected to be proud. She was allowed to do it, too, of course—sleep around. Once she had had the baby, nursed it to toddler strength, regained her former slim figure, found a babysitter, and managed to attract a guy who was interested in extramarital sex with some kid's mom, she would really go crazy with it.

Uh huh.

Anyway, they stuck it out, and they got better at what they did, and they lived the lives they thought they wanted. And then, somewhere in there, she got sick. That's the way she thinks of it now—the illness as one event among many: or, in the terms of her trade, a subplot. Cancer as a minor character, who appears in chapter 8 and fades away, like an old boyfriend or nosy neighbor, into the fog of memory. Like her mother and her aunt before her, Eleanor survived it, she *beat* it, leaving her corporeal and emotional selves intact. She kept her breasts, her husband, and her life, and she did so without joining a support group, without registering for an internet forum, without wearing a pink ribbon. She quietly triumphed. There are still friends who don't know she had it.

Of course, the illness scraped their bank accounts down to the metal and then some: her insurance policy, even after a deductible you could buy a used Mercedes with, left her footing 20 percent of every bill. After years of strongly worded letters and daily phone calls from collection agencies, the sales of the Brooklyn apartment and her unwritten fourth novel finally erased the rest of the medical debt, with enough left over for a down payment on the place upstate, while Karl's family income (which had not proven as substantial as he made it sound) would pay the mortgage.

The irony that Karl's infidelity helped to finally balance the books is not lost on her. But no matter. She is healthy now, and she is writing.

Well, in theory, she is healthy. In truth, she needs to make an appointment at Sloan Kettering. She hasn't been in for a checkup in almost two years. The last one she scheduled, she didn't keep: just walked up to the automatic doors, watched them part before her, then turned around and left. She figured one of these days the scans wouldn't be clean anymore. And she did not want that day to come. So she faked it. Went through the motions. Took the train to Manhattan and walked aimlessly around the Upper East Side. Soon after they moved here, she did it again: four and a half hours in the car, five hours of solitary wandering, a night in Craig's girlfriend's apartment, and home. "All clean," she told Karl, making sure Irina was in earshot.

And she is writing, too, only in theory. Actually, she hasn't written a word since they moved. She has decided to see this fact as a mere technicality. The novel manuscript is open on her laptop screen every single day: that counts. That's writing!

Her daughter, of course, really is writing, for hours at a time, with the kind of feverish intensity Eleanor can only enjoy in distant memory. (Or maybe that's yet another idealized experience she has invented to torture herself with.) She is proud of Irina, and proud that her pride is not merely a euphemism for jealousy, at least not yet.

Irina is turned around in her seat, staring out the window. Her forehead is pressed against the glass, and her body is tense. Tall and narrow, jointed like a crane, she has a kind of accidental grace: she ought to be bumbling, with her big head, nascent hips, and prominent knees; instead she navigates her environment with spidery lightness, leaving behind little evidence of her passage. It's not that Irina has mastered her body, not yet; it's as though her body has mastered the world. Like her father, she is going to get away with almost everything she tries.

Only in her eyes and mouth does she resemble her mother, and that's too bad, because Eleanor has made a life project of being hard to read. Irina's features are placid but composed: something is unfolding itself in her head.

"Hey. Irina."

She starts, spins around. "Can I get an ice cream?"

Through the window, Eleanor can see, a half block down Onteo Street, some kids lined up in front of a Dairy Queen. She says, "Well . . . we could leave here now and get some on the way home."

"No, I want to stay! Just let me go and come back."

Irina is avid. She is gripping the table with both hands and blinking a little too fast. The latter is familiar to Eleanor: she has seen herself do it on television, while dissembling about her work.

"Um, sure. Yes. Sure."

"Thank you!" Irina shoots a quick final look out the window, as though to make certain the ice cream stand is still there. Most of her coffee is still in the cup; pale continents of milk fat drift on its surface.

Eleanor feels a moment of relief: the girl is still a child, after all. She hands over some cash, and Irina extracts herself from her chair and tugs down the hem of her tee shirt. She moves through the tables to the door and in moments is outside and is briskly walking, almost skipping, down the street.

It is in a similar spirit of optimism and youthful energy that Eleanor is now able to push aside the piles of library books and lift her small laptop up onto the table. Ahhh, the freedom to write. Except that, of course, the moment the screen flickers on, she minimizes her untouched word processor, with its bloated cargo of doubts and second-guesses, revealing a web browser open to her current obsession, the CyberSleuths forum, specifically the *Geary murders* subforum, which she has rescued from obscurity under the screen name smoking_jacket.

She doesn't want to admit to Karl how excellent his choice of house was; she'd held its shortcomings, not entirely consciously, in reserve as something to resent him for later. But in fact she likes the place very much—its musty, woody odor that even the professional cleaning couldn't suppress; its dark and twisty corners and cramped spaces; its dirty windows, busy with densely packed trees, that only the most oblique rays of sun occasionally touch.

And the murders—how they excite and obsess her. How much more interesting they are than the petty dalliances of her novel-theoretically-in-progress. She feigned indifference to Karl on the subject and didn't mention them to Irina at all—fat lot of good that did—but of course they intoxicated her. She'd begun her internet research before they even left the city; Karl had told her about the killings only in order to explain the great deal they got, but she dug in like a starving dog. Since arriving here she has made secret forays into the library's paper and microfiche archives. There, she found a parallel, digitally unsearchable narrative of the crime, as reported by a short-lived competitor to the then-already-terrible *Broken River Daily Reporter* (now chain owned and called, depressingly, *Broken River Week*) known as the *Onondakai County Shout*. Its editor and primary writer, a man named Zane Ellsburgh, was prone to wild speculation and overheated prose, excellent qualities in a writer if what you want is to blather recklessly on about his subject on an internet forum. The paper died with him, and his life's work was now archived, to no great evident interest and in thrillingly perishable form, at the Broken River Public Library alone.

Eleanor is now giddy with power, if only in the small virtual world of CyberSleuths. She has single-handedly transformed the *Geary murders* subforum into a minor sensation with her previously unavailable newspaper clippings, police quotations, crime scene photos, and evidentiary culs-de-sac. She, or rather smoking_jacket, has taken to referencing Ellsburgh by his first name, as though she and he were close. Eleanor thinks of smoking_jacket as a brassy gal of around forty-five, maybe a career diner waitress with an unfinished college degree in semantics, or philosophy, or some other impractical and ultimately unsuitable area of study: she moved back to Broken River at age twenty to take care of her invalid mother, got a night shift at the Chomp Stop or Lyle's Sandwich Parlor, and never left. When her mother died, s_j renovated the house and took an older lover: yes, the shambling and jowly (but smart and charming) Zane Ellsburgh, whose motor mouth and sweaty brow served as titillating correctives to the trials of life with Mother. It was tragic, his coronary (he was in his prime, the *Daily Reporter* eulogized out here in real life, in what seemed to Eleanor a tone of barely suppressed gleeful relief); smoking_jacket inherited little, save for the violent mystery that distracted Broken River, more than a decade ago, from the long, boring project of its own decline and death. She reads the archives, calls up a few retired cops. Posts her results online.

That is, Eleanor does so, in the voice of her character, whom she has inhabited with greater enthusiasm than perhaps anyone she has yet invented. Maybe it's the refreshing lack of mediation that makes this project so much fun—no agent, no editor, no publisher, no bookstores. Or maybe she wishes that her life were a little more like smoking_jacket's: solitary, obsessive, and straightforward.

Eleanor doesn't have anything new today, so she answers a few questions other forum members have asked. From ladygumshoe2: *Any idea what agency, state or local, administered Samantha Geary's care and eventual adoption? No,* she replies, as smoking_jacket; *if you've read the thread, you already know that I think we ought to leave Samantha Geary alone.* From DotOnTheTrail: *Is there any new information about the identity of Mr. Chet, the drug kingpin the crimes have been linked to?* Eleanor: *If Mr. Chet is alive or active, he is probably using a new name, because I haven't been able to turn up any information about him that originates after 2005.*

And then, this, from UncleJ: *Has anyone gone back to the house to see if they can uncover new clues? Is it true that there are new owners?*

It gives her a chill, this post. There is nothing, of course, overtly threatening about it, but it represents the first time her own corporeal existence has been referenced, however obliquely, on the forum. She is suddenly aware of the smallness of the world, this town, this coffee shop.

Eleanor looks up from the laptop and out the window. Irina is in line now, behind a small, dark-skinned child and a big man with flowing blond hair. She is fidgeting, as she often does, hopping from one foot to the other as she reads, presumably, the menu.

Whoever wrote that post knows about her family, is implying that maybe they ought to be visited, interrogated, their home searched. In the politest possible way, of course. Time for smoking_jacket to nip this one in the bud. Eleanor writes, *Dear UncleJ, haven't met the new people yet, but I'll stop by and say hello. If they've found anything, I'll let you know. But don't hold your breath. The place has been gutted and re-built more than once.*

In other words, back off, dude.

Satisfied that the threat has been neutralized, Eleanor looks up to reassure herself, once again, of her daughter's safety. But her view has been blocked, by a man wearing a zipped-up windbreaker. He is standing here in Frog and Toad's, right in front of her, holding a coffee mug and a plate bearing what looks like a blueberry muffin. He's a big man, not quite monstrously so, with a jumbled pale face punctuated by a crooked nose and enormous ears, one higher than the other; his hair is mussed and graying, both on his head and on the backs of his rough and meaty hands. The coffee and muffin clank down onto the table's surface, and the hands push aside Irina's pile of library books. He sinks onto Irina's chair with a groan and the chair groans back. He looks like a fat vulture occupying a fence post.

"That's my daughter's chair," Eleanor says.

For a moment the man continues to look out the window, and then, seconds later, turns slowly to face her. His eyes are gray and expressionless. They are like glass eyes. She endures a moment of terror as they lock onto hers; then she shakes it off.

"My daughter," Eleanor says again. "That's her seat."

The man blinks, takes up the coffee mug, silently half-drains it of coffee. Then he puts it back down on the table and turns back to the window.

The gesture is peculiar enough to shake Eleanor's social confidence. How do you react to being utterly ignored? She tamps down a sudden spike in anxiety and leans around the man to find Irina.

Her heart clenches: Irina's gone.

No. Wait. There she is; she's off to one side, sitting on a wooden barrier, made out of railroad ties, that separates a parking lot from the sidewalk. She's licking a giant vanilla soft-serve cone beside a tall girl who seems to be in the latter stages of the same activity. The two are talking.

Whatever the big man is looking at, it isn't her daughter. He seems to be staring directly across the street, at a row of empty storefronts. Occasionally somebody passes by on the sidewalk, but the man's eyes don't follow them, not even for a second. He is just staring. For a moment Eleanor wonders if the man is homeless or has escaped from something. His jacket is clean, as are his unfashionable tan pants, and from him issue the faintest scents of soap and aftershave—yet there's something overly mannered and contoured about his grooming, as though he learned to do it from an old book or a social worker. He seems designed to deceive.

Meanwhile the tall girl has gotten up, and Irina has, too. Irina is turned three-quarters away from Eleanor and is gesturing excitedly with both hands; the ice cream cone, still largely uneaten, wobbles alarmingly. The tall girl is bending over slightly, scowling in apparent concentration. She speaks a few words, then is silent for a time as Irina talks and gesticulates. At one point she looks up at Frog and Toad's. Eleanor feels as though their eyes have met. The girl looks back at Irina, speaks, and then lowers herself back onto the guardrail. Irina sits beside her, and the two are again engaged in conversation.

Eleanor's not sure why this situation unnerves her. It's typical behavior for her daughter: an introvert by nature, Irina is nevertheless prone to periodic bursts of intense social engagement, and it has been months since she has had the opportunity to be around people. So of course the girl wants friends.

But why this girl? She looks like a teenager, or older. The two are sitting close, and the tall girl is listening, nodding. It's almost as though Irina chose her, targeted her for friendship from afar.

Now Eleanor is distracted by a movement in the foreground; the man in the windbreaker has turned from the window. He is gazing at his blueberry muffin with the same mooselike affect he previously employed to examine Eleanor herself. He picks up the muffin, hefts it, turns it over in his hands, like it's some unfamiliar piece of technology. His meaty fingers pick at the pleated paper baking cup, seeking purchase; little grunts escape the man's throat as he concentrates. Finally, his thumb and forefinger get a grip, and the paper is torn away like a cocktail dress. The muffin disappears into the man's mouth in two casual bites.

The entire operation has made Eleanor extremely anxious. She gathers up the library books and computer and dumps them into her cloth tote from the Strand (18 MILES OF BOOKS! promises the logo, and it sounds to Eleanor like a death march); she slings the bag over her arm and collects the dishes she and Irina have dirtied. The table trembles a little as she does it, and the man's coffee sloshes around in his mug; as though its motion reminds him of its existence, he seizes the mug and pours the liquid down his throat. He's like a robot that's been programmed to eat and drink, to appear more human. She says, "All yours," but by now the man has turned again to the window and appears to have forgotten she was there.

It's hotter outside than when she entered Frog and Toad's. It has to be ninety. That's just not right. It's September! Upstate! She has exited on the far side of the building and has to loop around to Onteo Street, and by the time she's halfway to the Dairy Queen, Irina is walking toward her down the sidewalk, daubing at her hands with an enormous wad of paper napkins. Behind her the guardrail is empty of sitters. "Oh my god, it's so sticky," Irina says. "Hi, did you get my books?"

"I have everything. Some weird guy stole your seat and I figured it was time to go. Who was that?"

"Who was who?" Perfectly innocent. Eleanor has turned around, and now they're both walking toward the car, which is parked in one of the diagonal spaces in front of the empty strip mall.

"The girl you were talking to."

"Oh! That's Sam."

"You seemed to know her."

"No, we just started talking."

"Why did you suddenly just start talking to a girl twice your age?"

"She's not *that* old, she's seventeen." A pause. "Well, I think she's around seventeen. She had a Brooklyn shirt on, and I was like, hey, I'm from there!"

Eleanor doesn't remember seeing a Brooklyn shirt, but she didn't see the girl for long, and she was far away.

"She's never been there, actually," says Irina. "She's from Buffalo, supposedly. She's in town visiting her brother and living with her uncle."

"She's visiting the brother, but she's staying with the uncle? Not the brother?"

"Umm," Irina says, "yeah, I don't really get that, I guess the uncle's got the extra room. Anyway, she seems cool. I gave her my email."

They've reached the car, and Eleanor unlocks it with the button on her fob. She wishes she could have started the engine from two blocks away and turned on the AC so that it would be ice-cold by the time they got in. Then she chastises herself for such a miserably bourgeois desire. She says, "I don't know how I feel about that. You shouldn't just befriend an older kid on the street. If she's seventeen, shouldn't she be in school? I mean, she's staying with her uncle and going to school?"

"I guess, Mother. I only talked to her for five minutes."

"Well, I'm not going to let you just go into town and be friends with an older girl I've never met."

"Okay, okay." They are in the car now, and Irina is not looking at her. She doesn't appear angry, just off in her own world.

They drive in silence down County Route 94. The library books lie in a heap at Irina's feet, spilling out of the tote bag, and she is rhythmically pressing her thumb to her middle and ring fingers, then pulling them apart, over and over again. Feeling, no doubt, the stickiness of the melted ice cream that the napkins couldn't clean off.

The gesture unexpectedly fills Eleanor with sadness. She suddenly believes that her marriage is going to fail. Indeed, it was never going to work, was it. They married for Irina, and she tolerated Karl's philandering for Irina, too. But there's more to it than that: the philandering was useful to her. It gave her a moral advantage, a reason to serve as the default parent, a license to make Irina into the ideal friend and roommate that her own prickly nature never allowed her to find outside her family.

She loves Karl, but her love never wrung her heart out or made her feel like she would die if it weren't reciprocated. Of course, that kind of love doesn't last—just read one of her dumb books—but maybe this kind doesn't, either. She's annoyed when Karl enters a room she is in, as often as not is repelled by his touch, cringes at the sound of his voice. Prevented from fucking for forty-eight hours, he paces like a caged animal until she relinquishes herself to him. He actually said to her last week, rolling off her, "How was that?" and she replied, truthfully, "Kind of rapey." He didn't seem to be offended—he nodded and reached for his phone, and soon tiny video game sounds filled the bedroom.

She is aware that all of the things about him that presently vex her—his intensity, amorousness, and imperturbability—are the very things that attracted her to him in the first place. But now he has hurt her too much. Right?

They get home and she feels as though she has wasted the journey: oughtn't they have talked? Irina jumps out of the car and sprints for the front door while Eleanor heaves herself oldly out of the Volvo, grunting: her back is still killing her, weeks after the move. How did she end up hauling so many boxes when Karl was supposed to be the family muscle? In retrospect, he seemed mostly to have scratched his beard over how things should be arranged in the truck. Her anxiety has seized upon her muscle aches, found them to its liking, declared them permanent.

She hobbles around to the passenger side and gathers up the library books from the floor. She would like to spend the evening on the sofa, reading these while Karl's hands massage her legs and feet. He is good at that, and when he does it she is willing to forgive him almost anything. Suddenly she does want to forgive—she wants to be put into a state where she can do so. She gazes up at their house. It's beautiful, really, in a rough-hewn, workaday sort of way; she understands why Karl found it so appealing. He might have built it. Its low shoulders and slightly awkward angles resemble his art, which in turn resembles automobiles that have been crushed into uneven cubes.

She's shouldering through the front door now—Irina has already disappeared up the stairs—and hoisting the bag of books onto the table, and she spies his two favorite sculptures through the archway to the living room, standing there on their steel tripods like a couple of obsolete machines that have been powered down for good. It's getting late and she ought to start cooking dinner—though who wants to do anything hot in this weather—but she walks into the living room and stands before them, telling herself that they deserve to be appreciated, they deserve to be understood. It seems wrong that they receive less of her daily attention than the television set that now stands beside them, a concession, on Karl's part, to conventional matrimonial togetherness.

They are called *Flow (frozen) #4* and *Flow (frozen) #11*, but Karl refers to them as Huck and Jim. He has proudly claimed that they are the two ugliest things he has made. Each consists of a massive glass block, cracked, drilled, and broken in several places, with inch-thick steel beams tunneling and bending around and through them. Huck stands about five feet tall and two and a half feet wide; Jim reaches seven feet but is nowhere wider than eighteen inches. They remind her of trees that have grown through fences—or of a trick her father showed her once. Take a block of ice—in Dad's case, the size and shape of a two-gallon bucket he had commandeered in order to illustrate this phenomenon—and place it on a grate over a tub. (He used a baking rack from the oven and their actual bathtub, doubly irritating her mother.) Gravity will pull the ice block through the grate; enthalpy will fuse it back together. In the case of the oven rack and the ice bucket, the healing was nearly seamless. Dad lifted the ice-gripped grate with his skinny arms and held it over his head, laughing. Then Mom made him run hot water over it into the sink so that she could have her oven back.

Her father probably intended this experiment to illustrate some philosophical principle, or maybe some commonplace of human behavior. Our tendency to return to our original state after a tragic event? The persistence of our preconceptions in the face of contradictory evidence? She can't remember. Today, though, it tells her that there is a force that keeps intact things intact. An object wants to stay whole. One may expend great energy attempting to break it apart, but it may gather itself back together regardless. She doesn't even know how Karl does it—how he gets the steel in there, how he cracks the glass and fuses it back together. Some rough magic, the same stuff he has used to keep her.

There's enough space in the corner for Eleanor to walk behind the two sculptures. She hasn't seen them from this angle since they moved—actually, it's probably been years, because they stood in the same configuration in Brooklyn as they do here. Why on earth did they waste so much precious apartment space on them? Even here, they dominate the room. It's strangely intimate, back here in the corner, behind the sculptures; she reaches out and touches them both, runs her hands up and down them. They're cool to the touch, despite the heat, and the air around them is cool. There's less light here, almost as though it's a separate time zone or dimension. Above her the ceiling is filthily stained where it meets the wall, and is dotted with mold: the third contractor mistake they've found so far. She's sick of calling them, demanding that they come back, giving them more money.

She wants to see her husband. She wants to make up for her traitorous thoughts in the car. Does he feel this way about her? Does he stand out there in his studio, cleaving glass and bending metal into shapes and regretting falling in love with somebody else? Imagining it seems to make it so. She calls up to Irina that she's going out back, walks out the door and around the house, knocks on the studio door and enters.

He's standing with his back against the west wall, his pants unbuttoned and his hand in his boxer shorts. His other hand has pushed up his tee shirt and is stroking his belly hair in a gentle circular motion. In front of him, on the work table, his laptop computer is open, and a woman's tinny moans emanate from it. He looks up, startled, slaps the computer shut. "Um," he says.

She can't help laughing. She forgives him for everything, the idiot. She goes to him. "You're not done yet, are you?"

He appears absolutely horrified. He jerks his hand out of his pants. "Um, no?"

Eleanor mashes herself up against him. He's still hard: good. She pushes his jeans and shorts down and takes over for him. He has already created a sticky preemptive mess. She remembers, against her will, Irina's ice cream cone and her sticky hands. She says, "Can I fuck you, or do you want it like this?"

"Fuck," he manages, so she hikes up her dress and puts his hand on her, and when she's ready, they do it. He is good at it, and when he is doing it, he puts everything he has into it, and into her pleasure. He makes her aches disappear. Her cries sound to her like sudden epiphanies, as she discovers forgotten pockets of love.

Afterward he's dressed again and is holding her and stroking her hair. They are panting, leaning against the wall. He says, "Uh, sorry about the . . ."

"I get it," she says. "I wasn't home. You're a horny guy."

"I guess . . . yeah, I suppose."

She wants to look at his face and he doesn't seem to want to let her. Finally she disentangles herself. He is staring over her shoulder at the door, though when she turns to see who is there, it is closed. "Hey— are you all right?"

"I'm great. That was—thanks. Sorry."

"I don't care, Karl."

"Yeah, no—that's—I appreciate that."

She pulls back a little farther from him, leans back against the workbench. "Did you not want that? Would you rather have done it alone?"

"No!" He's looking at his feet. "I mean, that was great. I was just . . . I thought I locked the door. It could have been Irina walking in."

"So remember to lock it."

"I will."

She stares at him until he looks at her. He seems to wince. Then he gathers himself and gazes into her eyes. "I love you," he says.

"I love you, too."

Twenty minutes later, while she is cooking dinner, it occurs to her that maybe she ought to have opened up the laptop to see what was on the screen.

5

After the woman with the books exits the coffee shop, the man in the windbreaker sits in silence for fifteen minutes, blinking, exuding heat. At last he stands up from the tiny table, jostling the patron sitting behind him: a pale, strawberry-bearded man in conversation with a willowy, sleepy-looking young woman. The bearded man's mouth opens, as though to issue a complaint, but then he swivels around, allowing himself a view of his tormentor. His mouth abruptly shuts. This small series of events appears to catch the young woman's attention. It rouses her from her torpor. Her gaze follows the man in the windbreaker as he makes his calmly bullying way through the crowd, and when she returns it to the bearded man, it is as though she is seeing him in a new light. Subtly, but not so subtly that the bearded man fails to notice, she wakes her phone—until now lying dormant beside her coffee cup—with a poke of her middle finger. She appears to take note of the time and quickly puts the device back to sleep. The bearded man seems to realize that some spell has been broken. The young woman is no longer interested in him. He looks down at the notebook open before him. It is covered with hand-copied quotations from Kierkegaard and Wittgenstein. A sour expression seizes his face and he closes the notebook with a sigh.

The Observer is interested in these wordless events that span mere seconds. Serendipitous encounters, subtle reactions, inscrutable social cues that alter the course of events, nudging the plot—one plot out of an infinitude—this way or that. But the Observer understands this plot to be a distraction. The important thing now is to follow the man in the windbreaker as he pushes through the heavy glass door as if it were no more substantial than a bead curtain. To follow him down the street, to the twin painted lines between which a car, presumably his, is precisely parked.

It isn't like the other cars around it. Lower, longer, less sleek. Its sharp corners are accentuated by its unusual color, the blue of a robin's egg, with interior accents of a warm off-white, the color of pages in an old book. Though this car appears better cared for than the ones around it, the Observer deduces that it is, in fact, older than they. It is, among the humans, an ostentation, an eccentricity. The man in the windbreaker climbs into the car. Moments later its engine turns over and the car backs into the street and joins the flow of traffic.

The car's route through the town of Broken River seems, to the Observer, uncoupled from any kind of predetermination. It circles, doubles back. At times it pulls up to a curb, or into a graveled verge, and pauses there for five minutes, ten minutes. Now the man in the windbreaker pulls up beside a bleak and unshaded playground strangely empty of children. He sits there for half an hour, staring out through the windshield. It is clear that he has been drawn to this place, is driven to occupy and survey it—or perhaps he is merely acting instinctually, like the bird of prey the Observer spotted in the unpopulated hills outside this town, diving out of the sky in pursuit of a tiny flash of gray flickering between leaves of grass in the field below. His patterns of behavior resemble the bird's more than they do most humans', whose primary purpose seems to be to engage with—or, alternately, to avoid engagement with—the others. It's as though the man in the windbreaker is also an Observer, if one without any particular observational objective.

(But then, what is the Observer itself? What is its objective? The patience of the man in the windbreaker has caused it, for the first time, to reflect upon its own purpose. Already its years inside the abandoned house seem inconceivably dull: how could it have remained there, in a state of mute forbearance, when it might instead have moved, followed, investigated? Suddenly the Observer is aware, as it never was before, of the existence, the scope, of time and space; it sees itself as an entity within a frame of reference. It is a thing that exists: and if one thing can exist, then other things, perhaps, cannot. Did the Observer ever not exist? Did it *begin* to exist, or has it *always* existed? Is it more like the man in the windbreaker, or is it more like the other humans? Is it the diving bird, or is it the flash of gray?)

The day has grown warmer, but the man in the pale-blue car has not removed his windbreaker, nor opened the car windows. He betrays no evidence of discomfort, however; his pink skin remains dry and gives the impression of softness, like a child's, despite its pits and scars. Indeed, the man might be described as a big baby, with his large head and socially unsophisticated affect; he seems to apprehend the world as a child might, unconcerned with the context of people and objects, alternately fascinated and distracted. He appears, overall, disconnected from the larger world, driven by forces invisible perhaps even to him.

Now the sun is falling in the sky. The temperature is starting to fall, as well. The man in the windbreaker drives to a gas station and waits. Inside the small attached convenience store, the sole employee watches a sporting event on his phone. Neither man moves for nearly two minutes. Then the man in the windbreaker begins to honk the car's horn, first in a staccato pattern, scattershot, like the first drops of a rainstorm, then more deliberately, the notes longer, more insistent. Finally the man in the windbreaker presses the heel of his palm into the horn and leaves it there.

The clerk emerges from the convenience store and approaches the car. The man in the windbreaker releases the horn. The clerk says, "What's up, man."

"Fill 'er up."

"Self-serve, man."

"Fill 'er up."

The clerk looks over his shoulder, back at the store, then squints, in the honeyed light of the setting sun, back at the man in the windbreaker.

"You do it yourself, man. That's how it works."

The windbreaker man's response is to resume honking. The horn is quite loud: it fills up the world of this gas station like a thick fog, like a darkness. "Okay, okay," the clerk says, and the honking lets up only when the nozzle has been inserted into the car and the gas begins to flow.

A few minutes later, the pale-blue car is moving, this time more deliberately, the Observer senses, down one of the roads leading away from Broken River. The Observer recognizes it as the road leading to the house in the woods, the one that the man and the woman from the house drive along most days to get to town. If the Observer were to be seated beside the man in the car, it might be possible to discern a change in his demeanor: in fact, yes, the Observer is doing this now. The flesh at the corner of the man's mouth is twitching, very slightly; his eyes are blinking at a faster rate than before. Is the man in the windbreaker aware that his body is betraying some inner turmoil? Probably not. He is acting on instinct. He is the bird.

The car arrives at the bottom of the long gravel drive that leads to the house. Instead of turning right and navigating the car up the hill, the man in the windbreaker pulls over and pauses on the side of the road. He switches off the ignition.

For ten minutes, the man in the windbreaker sits very still. His hands remain on the steering wheel, clenching periodically; the knuckles whiten, then go pink, with each clench. Now the man has begun to sweat, even though the sun is all but gone from the horizon and the sky has turned purple-black. (It is as though this man exists in his own private world, with its own unfathomable climate.) His chin quivers and his right eyelid has begun to spasm.

If the Observer were capable of registering surprise, what happens next would likely qualify as a triggering event. The man in the windbreaker turns, then peers past the Observer and out the passenger-side window, as though in an effort to see, through the trees, the house where the man and woman and girl reside. This is not possible, but the man does it nonetheless. And then the man's gaze is drawn to where the Observer's eyes would be, were the Observer corporeal. The man in the windbreaker is staring at the Observer, acknowledging its presence. The man is aware that he is an object of observation; perhaps he has been all day long. A smile cracks the man's face. The smile is for the Observer.

"My name is Joe," says the man in the windbreaker.

The Observer has no power to respond, no mechanism for doing so.

The man in the windbreaker says, "My name is *Joe*."

The man in the windbreaker says, "Watch." Then he starts the car, puts it into gear, and pulls out into the southbound lane of the county highway. The Observer remains behind, watching. The car recedes into the distance and disappears behind the curve of a hill. It is only now that the Observer rouses itself to follow, and it does so at some remove. The man in the windbreaker instills in the Observer a sense of disquiet: a disturbance, a warp in the mesh of cause and effect.

He is the bird. Who is the flash of gray?

6

A man named Louis is sitting on his front porch in Argos, New York, at noon, smoking a Camel and eating a baloney-and-cheese sandwich with yellow mustard, on wheat bread. Inside his house, behind him, his kids are eating the same sandwiches, all of them made by his wife, Pam, who is eating nothing, because she's "way too fat." This actually isn't the problem with Pam, the real problem is she's way too thin. She is wasting-away-type thin. For a while Louis tried to get her to put the pounds back on, but now he's given up. It's some kind of psychological thing. It's fucked up. It worries him. The other thing that worries him is that he's got another half dozen years of parenting ahead of him, at minimum, and he's too sick of his kids to eat lunch with them. The little one, Fred, doesn't bug him so much, though he never stops talking except to stuff food in his mouth. It's the older one, Janine, who is fifteen, who is really getting to him—she complains about everything, won't get up off her ass to do shit, slathers her face with makeup and goes around trying to look like a slut. He doesn't know how it happened. That is, she's a teenager, he understands that much, but the rest, what the fuck? It's all invisible to Pam, she can't see the kid turning into a skank, she bought the girl fucking thongs, none of it makes any sense. His wife and daughter are going nuts together. And he bets Janine won't eat half her sandwich, which will please her mother. And Louis also predicts that he himself will eat the other half of the sandwich once they've all left the room, and will find a way to wash it down with a couple of beers. And then the rest of the day will be hazy, and he'll fall asleep, and blammo he'll have wasted the only day of the week when he doesn't have to go into the carpet warehouse. It all feels inevitable. It's only noon, and the day is over.

It is into this moment of reverie that a powder-blue Cadillac pulls up in front of the house. The house is in a crummy cul-de-sac and is a crummy seventies ranch with a roofless cement porch, aluminum siding, and nonfunctional aluminum shutters bolted next to aluminum-frame windows. Metal! They were into it, back in the seventies. Louis can remember when his father ripped the clapboards off their old house and replaced them with aluminum. "Never have to paint again!" It looked like shit, of course, but Louis didn't know that at the time, he was fucking six. This car, the Cadillac, is out of place here. It's the kind of car his father used to issue a low whistle over every time they drove past one on the highway. "Someday, baby," his father used to say, as if he was some kind of up-and-comer, an ambitious kid with a twinkle in his eye and a spring in his step, who was going to hustle his way to the top of the heap and make a killing. When in fact he was a fucking dipshit who lost his actual car—the family station wagon—in a poker game, and his right eye in a knife fight the following day, trying and failing to get it back.

But if Louis is irritated to have been reminded, by the sight of the Caddy, of his father, he is bewildered when he realizes whose car it actually is. He can see the man's silhouette in there, humped behind the wheel like a small mountain: it's Joe. That's Joe's car.

Louis feels a burning sensation on his upper lip and realizes that it's being caused by actual burning: his cigarette, forgotten in his mouth. He spits it out, and it falls onto the baloney sandwich fragment he has apparently been trying to crush to death in his hand. He says fuck and from inside he hears Janine's voice also saying fuck and Pam's voice yelling at her not to fucking say fuck, and Freddy's voice laughing and laughing and Pam's and Janine's voices telling him to shut the fuck up.

He doesn't want Joe at his house, or in contact with his family, who suddenly seem like the best thing that has ever existed in the world. He wants to put them on a plane to Florida right now, and himself on it with them. He lets the sandwich fall onto the ground, along with the still-burning cigarette, and he stands up and closes the front door behind him.

The inside voices are cut off. Birds are singing and a dog barks a couple of blocks away. At the far end of the street, cars whiz by on Route 81. It's a sound Louis used to hate and then gradually came to love, as it promised a quick escape from his bullshit life, if it ever came to that; and now he's back to hating it, because it is the sound that brought Joe to his doorstep. How did he even know where Louis lived, for shit's sake? He's moved since his time with Joe, and his number and address are unlisted. Because of Joe. And why in the hell is Joe still sitting there, in the car? What is he doing?

As if in answer, the Cadillac shudders and then springs up as it relieves itself of Joe's weight, and then the man himself is standing on the sidewalk, looking up at Louis standing there looking at him.

Like an idiot, Louis waves. Joe does not wave. But he is smiling. His face doesn't appear accustomed to it, but that's a smile all right. He comes halfway up the sidewalk, stops with a grunt, and says, "C'mon. Let's take a ride."

"How ya been, Joe?" Louis says, because he doesn't want to say no, not directly. But there is no way he's going anywhere with Joe.

Joe says, "C'mon."

He doesn't look older. He doesn't look different in any way from the way he looked twelve years ago. He's even wearing the same windbreaker and tan pants, though they're unlikely to be the *very* same clothes, given the level of untidiness they were reduced to that night. For his part, Louis soaked his in gasoline and burned them to cinders in a trash can.

"I got my family in here, Joe," Louis says with a thumb over his shoulder, regretting it immediately.

Joe, still smiling, nods. He looks to be chuckling a little, even, though he makes no sound. Then he takes a step forward, and another one, and before Louis can stop him (and who is he kidding, he couldn't stop Joe from doing anything), Joe has climbed onto the stoop, brushed Louis aside, and walked in the front door.

Louis follows him. "Hey, man, hey. Get outta here. Seriously. Joe. Come on."

"Are these them?" the big man says. They're in the kitchen. Pam and Fred are sitting at the table, both of them with a hand in the same big bag of potato chips. Janine is sitting on the counter in her tight jeans and tee shirt, drinking a Coke. They're all frozen, staring at Joe.

"Yeah. Joe, you gotta go."

"You're the wife," he says to Pam. It's not a question: Joe is showing off his deductive powers. Pam looks at Louis, not angrily, not yet, anyway, just asking, with her eyes, for a little guidance.

"Come on, man, let's go. It's cool, I'll come with you. Let's go."

"And these are the little kiddies. What are you called," he says, looking at Fred.

Fred just stares. But Janine says, "I'm Janine."

Joe's smile broadens. His chuckle is audible now. The kitchen is extremely cramped with Joe in it.

Louis says, "Hey, look, Pam, I gotta help this, ah, customer out with something, I'll be back in a jiff." To Joe he says, "All right, man? Let's go."

"Janine," says Joe. "You're a little woman, aren't you."

The girl wants to say something witty, something to prove how cool and grown-up she is, but she fails. She doesn't look like a wiseass now, she looks frightened.

"Hey, man, leave her be, she's just a kid. Let's go."

"This is the one that saw the thing, huh," Joe says. And now Louis realizes that this is his fault, that he has made a terrible mistake.

"No, man, that's . . . let's go, Joe, let's talk about it in the car."

Now that Louis has agreed to the ride, Joe is all smiles. "Good to meet you," he says to no one in particular. He sounds like he's speaking a foreign language. Pam and Fred still have their hands in the chip bag—they haven't moved. Joe turns and walks out, and Louis goes after him, with a parting glance over his shoulder.

"Sorry," he whispers. "I'll be back."

The fuck? Pam silently mouths, and all Louis can do is shrug.
He follows Joe to the car and climbs in.

....

The reason Joe has come for him is that Louis called him. He had
to go through his old, defunct address book to find the number—
J is how it was listed, except under the *Q* section, which is how the
Louis of a decade and a half ago figured he would deceive any cop
into whose hands the thing might inadvertently fall. Because he was
a fucking idiot.

Anyway, Pam is into those true crime paperbacks, the kind you
can get at the supermarket, on a rickety wire rack that might also
display marked-down store-brand beef jerky and hamburger season-
ing. Years ago, a few years after the thing in Broken River, somebody wrote one of these books about it, a lady named Lisa Halverson.
She kicked out a new one every four to six months, crappy little riffs
on unsolved killings or mysterious disappearances, usually based on
whatever newspaper reports had come out at the time, plus a few new
phone interviews and a lot of ominous-sounding made-up bullshit.
The publisher padded these things out with pages and pages of grainy
photos with captions like *The scene of the crime* and *In happier times*,
knocked out a bunch of copies on cheap puffy paper, shipped them to
grocery store chains. Louis knows all about it, he looked into it at the
time. Everything about the book was pretty much wrong; the lady figured it was a mob hit and went off on these crazy tangents about New
York City and the Jersey Shore and, implausibly, Juárez. Pam had
bought the book, and Louis read the whole thing. He didn't bother
telling Joe, back then—for all Louis knows, Joe can't even read. And
there was nothing in it to make them worry. If anything, the book
was doing them a favor.

But last month it surfaced again in the house from whatever closet
shelf or rotting cellar box it had been banished to, this time into the
hands of Janine, who had picked up her mother's habit. The two of

them had really bonded over these books—and not just Halverson's, either. There's a whole raft of these lady writers, all them mad as hell that there are murderous, unprosecuted man-monsters roaming the earth, and Pam and Janine get equally mad as hell at the kitchen table together, snorting and tsking and quoting passages to each other. And Janine read the Broken River book, and she said to her mother, "Hey, this happened right near here, a couple hours from here," and Pam said, "Yeah, I wonder what happened with that, if they got the guys, wasn't it supposed to be Mexicans or something?" and Janine said, "I dunno, but I'm gonna look it up." And then she got on the internet.

Yeah, so, the internet. Louis has to admit that he's never had great facility with computers. (Not that he's much of a hands-on guy, really; his efforts to build a doghouse a few years back eventually led to their returning the dog to the shelter. Honestly, he's not much of an animal guy, either. The different kinds of guy he is not are too many to count.) So he didn't realize that unsolved crimes had become kind of an internet phenomenon and that pathetic unemployed shut-ins all over America had taken to cracking cold cases using only Google and their mountains of free time.

"This lady says it's not Mexicans," Janine told her mother over the dinner that Pam had spent an hour cooking, filling the house with greasy smoke and wilted-vegetable stank, and now was eating barely any of. "She thinks it was local guys. She knew this reporter. He had all kinds of inside dope."

"The Mexicans thing was an excuse," Pam said. "So they could give up on it. Cops are lazy."

"The guy was probably a drug dealer. It was small-time. There was weed in the house. Residue and stuff."

"I bet it was the cops that killed them," Pam said.

"Fucking pigs," said Janine.

"Watch your mouth," Louis and Pam told her at once, then glared at each other, as if, what, each of them valued the privilege of scolding her alone? What is wrong with my fucking marriage? Louis wondered.

Fred just snickered until Pam and Janine yelled at him to stop.

That night, after everybody had gone to bed, Louis got a little drunk and got on the computer and found the site that Janine had been talking about. It didn't take long: the Broken River case was right on top. And what Janine had said was true. Some lady who went by the name smoking_jacket had found a bunch of old newspapers and notebooks and put together a much more plausible—correct in almost every particular, in fact—scenario. The number of perpetrators, the order of events, the kind of car they were driving: it was all more or less right. And the house, which had stood empty for a decade, was occupied by new owners. And some other guy was planning to get in touch with these people. And maybe search the place.

Surely, Louis thought, there was nothing here to worry about. They spent only an hour in the house after what happened. The work was awkward and hot. Maybe one of them dropped something? *Maybe*, if this something existed, it could have survived the police investigation, the years the house stood empty, the renovation, the new people? It seemed unlikely.

But here was the thing. Like three weeks before, a guy showed up at the warehouse—big guy, big beard, big glasses, weird, womanish walk—and started pawing at the samples. He refused assistance at first, instead just walked around, putting his hand on swatches of thick pile, closing his eyes, tipping his head back and kinda mumbling to himself. If Louis was the kind of guy to ever want to look at a cop again in his life, he might have called them.

Eventually the guy picked out some ecru Infinity PermaSoft and said, "Hey, can you put this in my living room?"

"Right, sure, that's from our American Heritage line, nice selection, but lemme ask you, what kind of usage situation are you—"

"Don't do that, man," the guy said. "This stuff. Can you come put some in my house?"

"Yeah, you bet. Just, these are only a few of the varieties—"

"Hey, yeah, listen, knock it off. This is the stuff I want, okay?" The guy's voice was calm but Louis could tell he was pissed. Okay, fine. He'd dealt with guys like this before. They wanted to make their decision without your help and then they called you a week after installation asking why the chocolate milk stain wouldn't come out. But Louis knew when to cut his losses.

"You got it," he said.

"Come install it in my living room, okay?"

"You bet. How about I come make some measurements?"

"That's more like it," the guy said, and gave Louis an address outside Broken River. Which, sure, it gave him a chill. But he was a professional, he made an appointment, and a couple of days later he drove out there as promised.

He wasn't really paying attention. His mind wandered, and he just let his phone tell him where to go. But the closer he got, the more uneasy he felt, and by the time he was rolling up the driveway in the company van he was sweating like a fucking horse, his heart clenching, his stomach spasming. He pulled up between the dude's Volvo and some builder's truck, gulping air, listening to the sound of hammering and boombox contractor-grade hit radio emanating from the house, and thought, Holy fucking shit, this is it. This is the place. Fuck. Fuck.

Louis didn't hesitate. He just threw the van in reverse, made a three-point turn, and sprayed gravel the hell out of there. The guy called him twenty minutes later. "Hey. You coming, man?"

"Sorry, can't make it."

"You were just in my driveway."

"Yeah, no, yeah," Louis said, and hung up. When the phone rang again a couple of minutes later, he pulled over, rejected the call, and blocked the number. Nope. Not doing that. Nope.

So yeah, that night, drunkenly reading the CyberSleuths website, Louis got paranoid. He opened up his address book to *Q*, and he called the number next to the letter *J*. And left a voicemail after the beep. And regretted it immediately. He had a full day to think that maybe Joe was dead or at least didn't have that number anymore, or got the message and didn't care. A full day and a morning. And then Joe showed up. And now Louis is sitting in his Cadillac, wishing he'd kept his fucking mouth shut.

They drive in silence for ten minutes through increasingly marginal neighborhoods until they arrive at a former drive-up bank that has been half-assedly converted into some kind of dwelling. They park under the collapsing awning and Joe gets out. "Stay here," he says.

"Right," Louis replies, though the door has already slammed shut.

A brown drape repaired with duct tape has been drawn across the drive-up window, and a stripe of interior is visible through the crack between the curtains. The mechanical teller drawers have clearly been deemed a security threat and are welded awkwardly shut, with big, ridged beads of metal resembling lava flows that have almost but not quite devoured a highway. If this guy is involved with drugs, as Louis figures he must be, this seems like a waste. The teller drawers would be perfect.

A bit of motion is visible between the curtains. Bodies moving around. Louis hears perhaps one small yelp through the glass, high pitched and choked off. Then the motion stops and Joe reappears at the corner of the building. He hitches up his pants a little, as if whatever he did in there required a bit of stretching. He re-enters the car with a grunt.

"Everything go okay?" Louis asks, like an idiot.

Joe says nothing. He drives Louis home. At the curb, Louis reaches for the door handle, and Joe says, "Nah."

"Okay," Louis says, and waits, staring straight out the window at his neighbor, who is berating a chained-up dog.

"Don't leave messages," Joe says.

"Okay."

"What's the thing called."

"What thing?"

"Computer thing."

"A website?"

Insofar as it is possible to assign feelings to anything Joe says, Louis detects annoyance in the words "No fucking shit. What's it called."

"It's called CyberSleuths. It's these people, they research old—"

"Yeah. Get out."

Louis gets out of the car. It's barely past two. Clouds have rolled in and a very light rain is falling. He feels a lightness, like the one he used to feel upon leaving church with his mother, the feeling of stepping out from under the judging gaze of an angry god. He wants to embrace his asshole neighbor and the dog both.

Joe says, "I'll check it out."

"Okay."

"Don't go anywhere."

Louis doesn't know what this means, exactly, but he doesn't like the implication. He says, "Okay."

"Close the door," says Joe.

"You got it," Louis mutters under his breath, and the car barks away from the curb the second metal hits metal.

A minute later he enters, with relief, his house. He breathes in the greasy air, holding back tears. Pam finds him moments later, still standing in the middle of the living room with his hands in his pockets.

"The fuck was that, Louis?" she would like to know.

"Ah, it was nothing," he says.

"That guy. I don't want that guy in my house ever again."

"Haha, yeah. Yeah, right?"

She comes right up to him, stands ribs to tits, and uncharacteristically kisses him. "Seriously, Louis. Keep him out of here."

"I will."

"Hm," she says, and heads to the kitchen to resume the cigarette and paperback she has taken up for the afternoon. Louis thinks, Well, hell, I should be doing that, too. He goes to the kitchen and sits down and lights up and grabs a book from the pile. It's about a cold-case double murder—go figure!—this time one that he has nothing to do with. He and Pam stay there until dinner, then send out for pizza, earning the temporary love and respect of their children. Later that night they have sex for the first time in a while, and they sleep with Pam's skinny body curled up into his, just like the old days.

It's only in the middle of the night that he wakes and begins to shake and shake and cannot stop.

7

Of all the stupid things Karl has done over the past few months, the stupidest has got to be leaving an entire fucking ounce of weed on the G train, in a mason jar sharing space inside a paper grocery sack with a pile of celebrity gossip magazines, three twelve-packs of haw flakes, a wholesale box of green-tea Kit Kats, a couple bags of Boy Bawang garlic bites, and a lemonade-iced-tea Snapple. He realized his mistake the second the doors slid closed behind him: screamed an oath, spun around, literally clawed the windows of the moving subway car. Some kid with headphones the size of Cinnabons had just sat down next to the bag and was starting to unroll the top to see what was inside, and it was probably Karl's frantic screaming face that tipped him off to the fact that it was something really good. As the train gathered speed, Karl contemplated sprinting the four or five blocks to Bedford–Nostrand: maybe that was where the kid was getting off, who knew. He even ran up the stairs, yelling at people to move aside, but by the time he reached the street, he was too winded, too overheated and dejected, to go on. He leaned against the brick wall of the Indian drugstore, an air conditioner dripped on his head, and he fucking cried. He actually cried for the first time since this whole mess began. Five hundred bucks' worth of weed! And where the hell was he going to find Asian munchies in fucking Broken River, New York? He walked across the street to the playground, tears and sweat sluicing down his face, and sat on a park bench. He fell asleep and woke up only when his phone rang in his pocket, startling the couple of kids who were looming over him, probably about to steal it. A small blessing, he had supposed, on that shitty-ass, roasting-hot final full day in Brooklyn. He was hoping maybe it was Rachel, but it was Nell, obviously, wondering where the Chinese takeout was (she was careful to identify the food's absence, not his, as her primary concern); she and Irina were starving, and there was still packing to do before the movers showed up the next morning. He guessed it was sort of almost nighttime? The light was impossible: heavy and golden, as though ladled out of a smelter. He promised to be home soon (home: ha!), flipped off the already-retreating delinquents, and dragged himself back across the street to buy some fucking dumplings. Fuck moving. Fuck upstate. Fuck everything.

That was months ago, though, and he has discovered that it's no big deal to buy whatever obscure foreign eats he likes online and have them delivered to his studio door. He also thinks he's found a weed connection, just in time for the consummation of his trifecta of vice: he's going to bone Rachel.

She's here. In Broken River. She's staying at the Upstate, an old hotel in the middle of town, and in about half an hour Karl is going to get into the elevator (if the place even has one) and ride it up to her room, and they are going to get stoned and screw. He kind of can't believe his audacity, his blatant flouting of the very simple rules set forth in the plan to rehabilitate his marriage, his logistical acumen in the pursuit of the things he needs to feel alive. He is a masterful deceiver, a scoundrel, and he is so, so excited right now.

"Father?"

"Huh?" he says to Irina, whom he forgot was in the car with him. He forgot, in fact, that he was in a car at all.

"Do you have a stomachache or something?"

"What? No. What?"

"You're moaning."

"I am?"

"Well, now you've stopped. But yeah."

He wipes his palms on his knees, and the denim darkens with sweat. "Oh, yeah, that. Yeah, actually, I kind of do have a stomachache."

Irina says, "So you do have one, then?"

"It's probably something I ate."

"Probably," she says, gazing out the windshield.

Karl looks at her. She doesn't look back. Is she being sarcastic? Does she know? He says, "Haha, it usually is."

"What?" His daughter looks startled. Her electric guitar is pinned between her knees, and her hands clutch its neck through the gig bag.

"When people have a stomachache. It's usually because of something they ate. Right? I mean, why else?"

"I guess you're right."

"So I have one, then," he says. "And that's probably why."

She nods slowly, gazing at him in apparent confusion, then turns again to the window.

Karl has got her signed up for an art class and a guitar lesson, both on Saturday afternoons, and offered to bring her to Broken River every weekend to attend them. He has managed to contextualize this effort as a form of filial magnanimousness rather than the act of total selfishness that it actually is: while Irina is getting her double dose of culture, he'll be up in Rachel's room. He made these arrangements using the secret email address he has created for the affair, the password to which he has not written down anywhere and which he has instructed his browser never to memorize.

The problem is that painting is from 1 p.m. until 2 p.m., and the half-hour guitar lesson doesn't start until 2:20 because the guitar teacher, a dreamy, long-haired man of about sixty named Jasn (not Jason) Hubble, takes a smoke break at 2:00. "That's my smoke break," he told Karl last week, as if the idea of teaching guitar at two was absurd, as though Karl should have known. The yellowness of the man's handlebar mustache, drooping over the edges of a puzzled frown, lent credence to the seriousness of this caesura in his daily routine.

Of course, Karl indeed should have known. He *did* know. That was how he met Jasn Hubble, after all. Stalking through downtown Broken River one early autumn afternoon, he spied the denimed old bastard leaning against the wall in the alley next to the guitar shop, and he thought, There's my guy. He marched right up, said, "Hey, man, how's it going," and Jasn Hubble said, "Right this second it's going pretty damned good, friend, what can I do for you," and Karl said, "Where in the hell does a person score some weed in this town?" and Jasn Hubble responded with a big, yellow grin. They passed Hubble's cig back and forth for a while and pretty soon he'd gotten Irina signed up for guitar lessons and the whole plan came into focus.

The guitar shop is several blocks away from the Community Arts Center, so last week, when Karl took Irina into town to buy a guitar, they walked back and forth several times between the two buildings. "Okay, see this? You're going to go past the laundromat, the abandoned pet store, the abandoned deli, the adult bookstore, and the bank. Then you're going to go left on Shearn Avenue, and you can see it from here. See?"

"I get it, Father."

"And on the way back, it's the same thing in reverse. Shearn to Erie to Onteo, and you're at the arts center. But you don't have to do that. I'll meet you at the guitar shop."

"I *know*." They were standing in the street on the corner of Erie and Shearn. Irina squinted in the bright sunlight, wearing her pink jean jacket that Karl kind of envies. She appeared annoyed with him.

"So what's the matter? You can do this."

"I *can* do it."

"So what, then?"

"*Father.*" She looked up and down the street, and he followed her gaze.

And then, of course, he saw. The dumpster in the parking lot beside the pizza joint, behind which a couple of teenaged junkies were sleeping off a high. The wino on the stoop of the former pet shop muttering angrily to himself about all the people he was gonna kill. The piss-stained, rusted mailbox. The skeletonized Chevy Impala. The tattooed guy chain-smoking and walking in a circle. The heavy metal shaking the apartment window. The three blocks between the arts center and guitar shop were fucking terrifying.

"Yeah, right. Sorry, dude."

"Thank you, Father."

"This stuff's invisible to me. From growing up and all." Which was bullshit, of course—Irina herself grew up in rougher neighborhoods than Karl had. But—"Yeah"—she accepted this, and they trudged back to the guitar shop. Jasn offered them a 5 percent student discount, and in the end he bought Irina a cheap starter electric and a small amplifier. ("I'll have that special order of yours next week," he told Karl with a wink.) She chose not the Hello Kitty–branded pink guitar Karl himself would have chosen were he to inaugurate a rock-and-roll subcareer, but a thoroughly black, rather masculine-looking piece with three pickups and a whammy bar. Since then, he has been listening to her picking out chords and warbling in a not-bad-at-all rock-and-roll kid voice up in her room all week and has several times wondered why she needs a lesson at all, if she can do so well on her own.

Now, in the car, he is trying to conceal his excitement, which is to say his boner, with a right arm casually flung across his lap. He'll have an hour, basically. Less, because it will take a couple of minutes to walk each way from the arts center and to ride the elevator or climb the stairs to and from Rachel's room, and of course he doesn't want to show up late to pick up Irina after art because the teacher is this witchy sixtiesish lady who can see right through him, and when it comes time for Nell to take Irina to her lessons for one reason or other, Karl does not want this lady to casually mention that last week her husband showed up ten minutes late, reeking of poontang and hotel soap.

He has a life that can be ruined and a daughter whose respect for him may be hanging by a thread, even without the taint of marital infidelity, and he is totally getting off on it. And isn't this the age when, if a kid gets exposed to her parents' sexuality, it fucks her up? It probably fucked him up, honestly. He saw his naked father pull his mother's braids until she screamed, one time near the end, when they were evidently trying to fuck themselves back into love with each other. What does Irina always say? "Epic failure"? Anyway, that. He doesn't want her to be shit-talking him in some college dorm six years from now, but he also doesn't want her to have to tell her hot college pals that her father, the sculptor, was boring. Best to err on the side of feeling good. In fact, that's his life philosophy in a nutshell: he doesn't want to do anything to anybody except make them feel good, and he doesn't want anything done to himself except that which makes him feel good. That's an achievable goal, right? It ought to be, anyway.

They arrive in Broken River early, for lunch. As they pass the Upstate, he looks up at the windows, trying to catch a glimpse, but the uncharacteristic sunshine obscures them with glare. Is she there yet? Anyway, she wouldn't be looking out the window. She would be reading or something. He and Irina go to the crap diner with no name next to the empty theater, and as they eat, Karl wonders what Rachel's rental car looks like. Is it out there, on the street? Has she checked in? Surely she has by now. What is she wearing?

"Father. Stop looking out the window when I'm trying to talk to you."

Irina is gazing at him, deadpan, a single french fry held before her like a scare quote. He's startled: she looks like Nell. The outline of her face has always been Karl's, but the features are his wife's, and they are trained upon him, pinning him, with Nell's casual intensity. She doesn't even realize she has this power—her genes speak directly to her face, without the intervention of the adolescent ego, its vestigial narcissism.

"Sorry, dude."

"No worries, Ape Dad. I was telling you about what I'm going to do in art class."

"Sorry. What?"

"I'm going to make maps and draw clothes for the people in my novel."

"Novel?"

Irina shakes her head. "For real, Father?"

"Wait. Yeah. You told me. The, like, it's Brooklyn under water or something?"

"No. Well—close enough."

"I dunno if you'll get to just do what you want," Karl says now, finding a thread he can tug. He picks up his largely uneaten burger. "Art teachers are stuck up. They want everybody to do the same thing. The same snowcapped mountain reflected in the same fucking lake. Or decoupage or whatever. I flunked art in junior high."

"I know."

"Then I got suspended in high school for drawing my girlfriend's—"

"Ugh, Father, I *know*."

The two of them sit in silence, eating. Karl checks his phone for texts. He has missed one. *I'm here room 405.* He suddenly wishes he hadn't had a cheeseburger; he feels greasy and bloated. Usually he absorbs and assimilates food with preternatural speed; today he feels like any other warm-blooded organism laboriously breaking down chemical bonds.

As though reading his mind, Irina says, "This can't be any good for your stomachache."

She appears genuinely concerned. How fucking gross does he look?

"Oh yeah, that's gone. I guess I was hungry," he says.

"Okay." Quiet now, as though chastened, though he has not chastened her. Has he ever? He forgets that he's authorized to do that. But why would he? Irina is such a good kid. This realization hits him hard. Irina is a *good kid*. He doesn't worry about her at all. She's not going to do stupid things and be self-destructive and make bad choices. She knows how to live in the world. And she's nice! She's a nice girl. Hey, he thinks: why don't I tell her that?

"You're a good kid, Irina."

He doesn't know what he expected, but bemused surprise wasn't it. "Thanks!"

She doesn't say that he's a good dad, though. He says, "Let's go."

"It's early."

"Yeah, no, I know."

"I don't want to be the first one there."

"You won't be."

She is, of course. He doesn't want to talk to the art teacher, so they wait in the hallway outside the classroom on a wooden bench beside a Pepsi machine, and he texts with Rachel.

be right there
good I'm getting ready
show me

A point-of-view selfie arrives, Rachel's skirt pulled up, her hand in her underwear. Karl draws the phone closer to his face so that Irina can't see.

save some for me
it's all for you

"I'm bored," Irina says. "I'm going in."

Karl has another erection, so he tugs his hoodie pocket down over it. "Yeah, cool. Okay, so, I'll see you in an hour?"

"Okay! Good luck!" Irina chirps, jumping to her feet, and she walks through the classroom door and shuts it behind her.

Good luck?

....

In the elevator (the hotel does indeed have one), Karl stares at his shlumpy, furry, blurry reflection in the polished metal doors and wipes his sopping palms on his sweat-stained jeans. He is shaking a little bit. It has been a month and a half since he has felt sexually satisfied. Not that he hasn't been fucking Nell, but she feels insubstantial to him now, like a wastrel, and has ever since the cancer. Rachel's zaftigness, her full round thighs and breasts, her gnarled mess of hair, the folds of belly fat he snuffles and snorts in like a rooting hog: these things have come to define sex for him in a way that Nell's body—no woman's body—ever has. And, though there is no question of Nell's attractiveness, it's like the beauty of a statue next to the beauty of a living being. Rachel is the fulfillment of a fantasy he didn't even know he harbored: a woman his age (older!) he can't get enough of.

Fantasies, for Karl, have always been a cinch to realize—you could call them "plans," really. Even the upstate house search, ostensibly designed as a punishment for him (or maybe, ultimately, to get him the hell out of the apartment for a few days, he thinks now for the first time), ended up turning fun; he came across the house, the one they bought, in the binder of inkjet-printed, plastic-sleeved info sheets the real estate agent provided, and was immediately attracted. He likes a found thing. He likes restoring life to a thing that has been abandoned. To the agent, a square-jawed, heavily made up young woman whom he considered trying to fuck, he said, "Why's it so cheap?"

"The previous owners were murdered."

That made him sit up straight. "Seriously? Why tell me?"

"Seriously. It's the law. I have to tell you."

"When? How? Why?"

She leaned forward a little. Her eyelids drooped, barely perceptibly. "Ten years ago. A dozen years? Anyway, guns? Drugs? I don't really know."

"They didn't catch the guys that did it," Karl said.

"No, I don't think so."

"Nobody wants to live where there are killers on the loose."

Her chin was puckered and her mouth was a hard, straight line. "Guess not."

"Let's go check it out."

The house was set back a couple hundred yards from a county two-lane, at the end of a shitty gravel drive. It stood on twenty-three acres of new-growth pine forest. Propane heat, well water, fourteen hundred square feet, two bedrooms and a study. Or three bedrooms. It would be a teardown if it were anywhere anybody wanted to live. The place was awkward to look at—a combination of incompatible styles. An arts-and-crafts-bungalow-cum-alpine-chalet with cedar shakes and a chimney and fireplace made of river stones. He liked it. The agent told him it was designed and hand built, presumably with somebody or other's assistance, by its original owner in 1922. Inside, it looked like ass, with evidence of recent and thoroughly tasteless landlord-caliber renovations that were already starting to seem old and ruined. "This'll all have to go," he told the woman, and she said, "Uh huh."

He was already designing the studio in his head. It would be huge. He'd have his own forge. Fuck yeah. He would make knives—that was going to be his new thing. The money they were saving on the house, he could pour into the studio, and he would spend all his time out there, being angry at Nell and at himself, jerking off, and making knives. Glass-bladed art knives. He would teach Irina to use them, and the two of them would stalk around in the woods wearing loincloths and stabbing shit.

Once the agent overcame her shock at his evident interest in buying the place, she pulled out her clipboard. "I need the name of a contractor," he told her. "Somebody who can rip out all that cheap-ass shit and also who can make me a blacksmithing shop. Can you find somebody like that for me?"

She was scribbling wildly. "Blacksmithing shop. Right," she said, her voice struggling to maintain its warily sardonic tone. It was no use. Karl had heard it before. His enthusiasm was infectious. Virulent.

"And the town," he said. "Where do people go? For stuff, I mean. Groceries. Movies. Fun."

"I will print you a map. I will mark some things for you."

"Right on. Awesome. Get back to me on that offer, okay?"

"Oh, I will. I will."

It all went so smoothly, his crazy plan. The contractors weren't dicks and showed up and did shit on time (if not at precisely the rates they had promised, but whatever). At one point Karl heard an ad on the contractors' boombox for a carpet warehouse down the road in Argos, and on a whim he went out there and found the exact carpet from the living room of his childhood home, the carpet he used to lie on watching TV on summer afternoons when he ought to have been outside, years before his parents got divorced. But the bastard who was going to install it bailed and then didn't call Karl back, so he never did get around to carpeting the living room. Other than that, though, everything's been golden. When Nell and Irina arrived and saw what he had done, they loved it. They fucking loved it! His studio is awesome. The forge is badass.

Two small problems.

One of them is that his agent, Gert, has sort of dumped him. Via email, no less. She gave him three months to either pay to have his remaining unsold sculptures shipped to him or to come down and get them. *I'm sorry, Karl,* she wrote, *but I can't sell this work, and it is taking up space. You will be better off with representation that better suits your needs.* Which is to say, somebody who still likes his shit. Of course she waited until Karl had left New York to tell him, the coward—and now, unless he wants to explain the whole thing to Eleanor and beg for an exception to the no-New-York policy, he can't go down there to find another agent, or to find somebody to unload his stuff onto until he figures out what to do.

The other problem is the matter of his family money—the income he's been getting for his entire adult life, which originated from the Canadian gold mine his grandfather owned. At some point, he'd reasoned, the old man would kick off and leave him a nice nest egg (Karl has been sending "I love you Pop-Pop" postcards every few months for fucking ever). But last week, a terse email from his father arrived, informing him that the family business was ruined and had been for some time. His grandfather had been revealed as corrupt and might even, at the age of eighty-three, go to prison. The remains of the company were being sold and its assets used to pay its debts. *Just to be clear,* his father added, in a postscript, *don't expect anything from your stepmother and me, either. We're as fucked as you are.* Karl's mother had long ago donated everything she owned to the new age cult that was now her entire life, so he was, at last, on his own. With a failing marriage, an upstate mortgage, and a fifty-thousand-dollar outbuilding dedicated to the creation of experimental cutlery.

You might have some luck with these on eBay, Gert told him in her breakup email, which he now understands to have been precipitated by the box of prototype knives he sent. (Those, anyway, she had the common decency to send back.) So okay, fine: he started an account, started figuring out how to auction the shit off. He had a blast concocting the marketing narrative—some bullshit about his having been inspired by fucking ancient Japan or the Norse sagas or something, a riff about his secret processes and rituals. He laid out the auction template using plenty of corny clip art, set all the display text in Papyrus. But so far nothing has sold. He's not sure what he's doing wrong. Meanwhile he's put on weight, despite his brisk walks through the creepy woods, and he seems to be getting sweatier, especially when he's turned on. Indeed, the elevator ride isn't even over, and his palms are drenched again.

The doors open and he steps into a musty-smelling brown-carpeted corridor lined with corroded brass sconces, half of them bearing burned-out bulbs. Everything's brown: the doors, the wallpaper, the stained stucco ceiling. The dirty window at the end of the hall. He finds 405. The door is off the latch; a thread of variegated light lines the jamb. He knocks and enters.

The room, to his surprise, is welcoming: creamy sunlight through gauzy curtains, clanking radiator, two roses in a vase, doubled by an oval vanity mirror, and behind the flowers' reflection, a mussed king-size bed bearing the seated form of Rachel, draped in a black night-gown he's never seen before (or maybe he has, the lady owns a lot of black nightgowns), her hands folded together in her lap. She is wearing an expression that strikes him, initially, as expressing more pity than desire. He turns, now, to face the actual Rachel, and in the time it has taken him to look away from the mirror, the pity has vanished, and her gaze appears smoky, hungry. Or maybe the pity was never there; maybe it was the mirror, half-desilvered with age, that lent her a bygone gravity, like a figure in a daguerreotype.

He goes to her, falls upon her, and they gobble each other up. Her mouth on his is frantic, hot with need, yet the pity from her reflection has lodged in his mind, he can taste it on her, he can feel it in her touch. There is something of the nurse in the way she pulls him back, settles him onto the pillows, interrogates his body with her hands. It's as though she's giving him more to conceal the fact that she has less, like a poor mother who has saved up all year for a plentiful Christmas.

Stop thinking, he tells himself. He mostly succeeds. They do all the stuff they do, and it's finished after twenty minutes. Now, to his surprise, there is time to kill. Now they have to lie here talking.

She fills him in on the neighborhood characters, the same way she used to back in New York. "Nancy finally let the police arrest her gentleman friend," she says. "Her regret was immediate. She cried out his name for the better part of an hour in my apartment, until Mrs. Chang brought her something to eat. Let's see . . . Carlos's little dog bit a passing child, or its mother claimed it did, though Carlos insists he could see no bite marks and Nugget would never do such a thing . . . she has threatened legal action, but we'll see what comes of that. The leaves outside my window are turning, soon I'll be able to watch those Honeymooners across the courtyard fry things and read newspapers and argue."

She's got her glasses on but is otherwise naked. Her voice is so composed—where's the conspiratorial whispering, the tears, the desperate texts? He would like to be able to get it up again, but it's too soon. She wants to know how his work is going.

"What?"

"Your work. In your fabulous zillion-square-foot studio?"

"Pretty good," he says. "New project cooking. Crazy stuff." For some reason he doesn't want to talk about it. He knows she wouldn't care. The women in his life don't, generally. That's fine by him.

He says, "What's up with your thing. The . . . magazine."

"Magazine?"

"The poetry thing. That you put, you know. That Eleanor was in."

She smooths the bedsheets over her thighs. Her fingernails are chipped and bitten, painted red. "Ah, yes. Haven't published that in years. As I believe you know. Believed."

There's a long pause. The small of Karl's back suddenly itches like a mofo, and he grunts as he snakes his arm back to scratch it.

"I don't think we're really connecting," she says.

"Now you know what it's like to be in a committed relationship with me."

"Ha," Rachel intones flatly. "Ha."

Get it up, he tells himself. *Come on, man.* He reaches down and fondles his wiener, glances over at Rachel. He glances down at her crotch, back at her face. She rolls her eyes, spreads her legs a little, touches herself.

When Nell was declared cancer-free, she presented herself to him, sexually, morally, as a survivor. *I kept these for you*, she seemed to be saying every time she unbuttoned her blouse and let her bra slip down off her shoulders. *Respect this body.* Truly, he doesn't understand why he can't. He didn't used to like sloppy, curvy women like Rachel. He's supposed to be the sloppy one—his women are supposed to be tidy and sleek. But Nell's poise, her grace, now feels effortful to him, her bulwark against the cancer—she is taking care not to wake it up. Her body is an advertisement for its own weakness.

And an advertisement for his, he supposes. Because, ultimately, he didn't do shit when Nell was sick aside from drive her to and from the hospital and hang out with Irina during the treatments. He'd expected, when the diagnosis came—and they were both expecting it, anticipating it—to feel more . . . heroic, maybe. Or at least sort of useful. They sat in dirtily upholstered plastic office chairs, facing the doctor's freakishly tidy desk, and he put his arm around her, squeezing her tighter when the bad news arrived. He was almost excited on the way to the parking lot. "We're gonna beat this thing," he told her. "Fuck it! Fuck cancer!"

But she didn't seem to appreciate the rhetoric and gently chastised him one night, while he was administering some pep. "You don't have to say that," she said quietly, touching his knee.

"I know, baby, but I'm doing it. I'm on your team."

She almost seemed to say something then but held her tongue. Afterward, she became more private about her treatment, about the progress of the illness. She scheduled meetings with the oncologist at awkward times, encouraged Karl not to come. She didn't complain of aches or nausea or exhaustion, just quietly endured. The quiet endurance became a thing. He could tell she was proud, and she was not interested in his sensitivity or praise. "Dude, you're amazing," he tried to tell her. "You're a fighter." But she wasn't having it. Her answering smile, her pats on the shoulder, were dismissive. It was her body. Her fight.

Karl does not think of himself as a jealous man. If Nell was fucking somebody else, he'd be down with it. Surely she already has? Is doing so now? After the cancer was over, after she beat it, she would take the train to Manhattan routinely, for checkup appointments at Sloan Kettering. And she has gone there once since they moved here, too. But last week, he got a feeling, or maybe it was a hope, and called them, ostensibly on her behalf, to double-check on the time. They didn't have her down for an appointment at all.

"When was the last time she came in?"

That clammed the lady right up. "I have already said too much" was the reply, and she hung up on him.

So yeah, what can that be but an affair? Right? It was almost a relief. The less Nell thinks about cancer, the more she thinks about sex, the better. Even if he isn't the one she's thinking about. Breast cancer is the thing he was jealous of. Her relationship with it was more serious than her relationship with him. Her commitment to it was deeper.

Not that Karl's commitment to their marriage is anything to crow about. And yet they are still married, aren't they? And he's a good father to Rinny, he's pretty sure. Or at least a good something to her—Karl isn't sure what a father is supposed to be like and is deeply skeptical of any model of parenthood imposed from without. Whatever he is, he digs hanging around with the kid, really respects her, thinks she's hilarious. He teaches her stuff, helps her to be chill. She's changed, Irina has; she used to be uptight, worried about everything. Karl has helped her learn to occupy her own self, he thinks. To be confident. Like him.

He isn't feeling terribly confident right now, playing with himself, watching his girlfriend play with herself, while up the street Irina daubs tempera paint on a fucking sheet of newsprint. He says, "Hey, so, does your building have, like, a storeroom or something?"

Rachel raises her eyebrows; they arch over they tops of her glasses: now she looks like a hot librarian. But at this point his anxieties have returned and are crowding out all desire. His palms are dry now. His dick's limp.

She says, "There's one in the cellar?"

"How much space do you have?" he asks her.

"This is a strange line of questioning, Karl." She lifts her fingers off her junk and wipes them, discreetly, on the bedsheets.

"I'm in kind of a situation."

"Okay . . ."

"I gotta get my pieces out of Gert's place or she'll junk 'em. I can't afford to ship them up here."

She pulls the covers up over her lap. "I see."

"I don't want to ask you to move them for me . . ."

This gets a laugh out of her. "Sure, sure," she says. She reaches for the nightstand, checks the screen of her phone.

And then he remembers. "Oh shit!"

"What?"

He jumps out of bed, finds his sweatshirt. He shoves his hand into one pocket, then the other. "You want to smoke? I bought some weed!"

"Don't you have to meet your daughter in a few minutes?"

"There's time!" He fumbles with the baggie, digs out the little pack of papers Jasn Hubble had been kind enough to include.

Rachel looks at him with a kind of amused affection. She climbs off the bed, says, "I'll open the window," and on the way back finds her underwear in the mass of black cloth on the floor. (Add a pointy hat, it could be the spot where the Wicked Witch melted.) She steps into her panties, says, "I'm not going to smoke with my pubes exposed."

"Why not?"

She gives it a moment's thought, shrugs. "I don't know, actually." Back in bed, she accepts the joint he has lit, takes a hit, hands it back. "Karl," she croaks. "Is this really what you want?"

He hates being asked questions like this, especially by women. "Is what what I want?"

"This," she says, exhaling. "Long-distance infidelity. Stolen hours. Minutes, really."

Karl is concentrating on the joint now. It is with a kind of rote anxiety that he says, "It sounds like it's not what you want."

"Of course it isn't what you want," Rachel says. "I came up here be-cause I'm in love with you. But eventually, you know. Things will have to change."

"Change how?"

"You decide to leave Nell and come back to New York. Or not. In which case we'll split."

Some distant part of him begins to panic, but the weed is pushing it back. He closes his eyes, tips his head back, smokes, hands over the joint.

"I can't deal with this right now," he says. "Please tell me you'll come back. That we can do this again."

After a silence, she sighs, or maybe she's just letting the smoke out. "I'll come back."

"Thank you."

"This supposed future time, when you'll be able to deal with things," Rachel says, not without humor. "It exists, I trust?"

"Sure," he says, drifting. "Sure it exists."

8

By the time Irina has walked into the guitar shop with her gig bag strapped on her back, she has already mastered the chords D, G, C, and E minor; has tried, with some success, to teach herself tablature; has haltingly strummed her way through some Beatles songs using transcriptions she has found online; and has tried her hand at songwriting. She is feeling quite pleased with herself and is looking forward to the moment when Jasn says to her, "Okay, kid, let's learn some chords," and Irina says, "Chords, you say?" and bangs out her own personally written song, complete with lyrics. Bam!

Instead what happens is Jasn wants to teach her scales.

"I thought we were going to do chords?" Irina says.

"Aw, you can learn that stuff off the internet," her teacher says with a dismissive and oddly dramatic wave of the hand, like he's trying to dispel a cloud of smoke from a joint. Irina suspects Jasn smokes a great many joints because he smells quite powerfully of them and because he treats her like she's about forty and they are in a band together. "If you wanna learn some really tasty licks, you need to know scales."

"I don't think I need to do that. I'll just play chords, like Bob Dylan."

Jasn appears appalled. "Who the hell told you to say it that way? It ain't *dialin'*, like you're makin' a phone call! It's *dillin'*, like you're, I dunno—"

"Eating a dill pickle?"

"Ha! Exactly!" He holds up his hand as though for a high five, so she gives him one. "Anyway, even a rhythm guitarist needs to know scales, kid. There's notes in between the chords, and the notes come from the scales. Trust Daddy J. Okay!"

He takes his own guitar in hand—they are plugged into the same very large, very smooth-sounding amplifier—and begins to instruct her in the G-major scale, since that was the key whose chords she admitted she had already learned. Sometimes her fingers don't seem to reach, and Jasn removes one from the fretboard with his own long, yellow fingers and places it in the correct spot. She is surprised that she doesn't mind being touched by him. He is the least threatening and intimidating adult she has ever encountered. By the end of the lesson she can limp through the G scale with a reasonable degree of confidence and is already thinking about which of the notes she has learned will go in between which chords of her new song.

The lesson's almost over. Her father will be back shortly. She says, "Hey, I wrote a song, you wanna hear it?"

"Why in the hell not?" Jasn replies.

"Excellent," Irina says, then fishes from her jeans pocket the paper she has written the words on. They are an expression, of course, of her obsession with the Geary murders, which have dominated her thoughts for weeks; she could easily write a hundred more songs on the subject, based on a hundred little details mined from the CyberSleuths forums. But she doesn't yet know enough chords to keep from writing the same song over and over. She unfolds the paper, looks around for a place to put it, sees none. "Hold this, okay?" she says.

"Right on."

Jasn holds up the paper in the air between them, and Irina draws a breath and sings:

> *Ohhh, poor little Samantha Gee*
> *You poor little orphan of Route Forty-Three*
> *Ohhh, Samantha Gee, where did you go?*
> *Samantha Gee, I think that I knooooowwww*
> *Samantha Gee, I think that I knooooowww*

You came back to fiiiind
Oh, you came back to find something you left behind
Walkin' around, down that lonely street
I'm the one you were destined to meet
You'll be glad you met me, Samantha Geeeee

"The route number is fictional," Irina says quickly, to head off criticism. "It's sort of a blues song."

"I noticed!"

"You don't think it's very good."

"I think it's real good! Play it again, kid."

She plays it again, and this time Jasn plays along, adding a kind of bassy part under her singing and inserting these little melodies—these must be the tasty licks!—at the end of each line. It's so good! It sounds like a totally professional song. She only wishes she could sing better. But Jasn says, "You keep singing, kid, you've got a good natural voice for blues."

"Don't patronize me," she says without thinking. It's what her mother tells friends who claim to like her books.

This makes Jasn laugh like a hyena. "I wouldn't dare, kid! It's the truth! I mean, you sound like you're ten or whatever—"

"Twelve."

"—but you've got the makings of a real good singer-songwriter."

"I'll practice my scales, I swear. Those little noodles you were making are cool."

"That's what a lifetime of noodling gets you, kid!"

She likes this guy. She likes his droopy mustache and goofy enthusiasm. She likes that he calls her "kid," even though it's probably because, like many adults, he isn't able to retain her slightly unusual name. She has been called Helena, Irene, Ileanna, Irma, Ellen, and India. One teacher at her old school always called her Caroline, but that's because a girl with that name used to sit in her seat. Anyway, it's time to go. She and Jasn emerge from the practice room, and the mean girl behind the counter, who has dyed hair and about thirty tattoos and does not ever seem to smile, is nevertheless smiling at Irina's father.

"Hey, little buddy!" says the mean girl, about half an octave above her regular voice. "You sounded awesome in there!"

"Um, thanks?"

"Are you in a band?"

"I'm twelve," Irina says for the second time in five minutes. There's no worse age, when you get down to it; you're not, in any sense, a teenager, and so are not given allowances for such traits as sullenness and not wanting to get out of bed. You're supposed to still be energetic and cheerful, even if you are, at heart, a grumpy and basically lazy person. And meanwhile you have to endure the trials of puberty, one of which is repeatedly hearing adults utter the word *puberty*, the most horrible word in the English language. It contains all the awful words: *pubes*, *beauty*, *boobs*, *pretty*. *Über*. Über pretty booby pubes! "Are you noticing any changes in your body, Irma?" the dumb doctor wanted to know at this year's checkup. Yeah, I'm noticing it wants to run screaming out of this office.

"She could start a band," Jasn says, clapping her on the shoulder. "A few more scales and she could play lead guitar in Hubble Bubble!"

"I'm guessing that's your band," Irina's father deadpans.

"Classic rock covers," the clerk says, recovering her former bitchiness. It is embarrassingly obvious that she's trying to impress Irina's father, who, to his credit, seems less than receptive to it, even though the girl is kind of sexy. Indeed, Irina's father is now actually, literally licking his lips. Maybe they are just dry. He also smells weird and has ever since he met her at art class to walk her over here.

"Yeah, rock and roll, man!" he says, idiotically, handing Jasn twenty bucks.

"Catch you next time, Karl," the clerk says, with a wink in her voice. "See ya later, Rinny!"

Rinny! Her father must have referred to her this way in the girl's presence. But that doesn't mean the girl can. Is nothing sacred? Suddenly Irina feels as though everything is going to pieces. Too much that used to be certain is suddenly confusing and new and not necessarily very good.

Jasn is speaking to her now: "Okay, kid, bring me your best stuff next week, got it?" But Irina has already hitched the guitar up onto her shoulder and is pushing her way out the door and into the overcast and mildly stinky fall day. She feels bad for letting the real world seize and dispirit her so quickly—at the very least she should have been happy to see her dad. But when he emerges, slowly, from the guitar store, drawing a pack of cigarettes out of his jacket pocket and a cigarette out of the pack, and says, "Hey, man, lemme smoke this, okay?" she pretends not to know him and instead leans up against the brick wall of the abandoned storefront next door and pulls out her iPod. She can get a weak Wi-Fi signal from the guitar shop (*$uper$hredders* is the password) and uses it to Instagram a fortune-cookie fortune she has found adhering wetly to the sidewalk: TODAY MIGHT BE THE BEST DAY OF YOUR LIFE. Thanks, cookie. Her father smokes placidly six feet away, thumbing at his phone; he takes a handkerchief out of his pocket and mops his face with it. To distract herself from her profound disgust with the handkerchief and the concept of the handkerchief, she opens her email app and reads, once again, the email correspondence she has been engaging in with her new friend—or acquaintance, really but they are going to be close, Irina just knows it—Sam.

From: irinaofthedeep@gmail.com
To: lee.samuel.fike@yahoo.com

Remember me??

From: lee.samuel.fike@yahoo.com
To: irinaofthedeep@gmail.com

Dear Irina
Hi, yes, I remember you. It was nice meeting you at the Dairy Queen. You said something about knowing something about me, but like I said I don't think we have met

before? I am curious though, so here is an email like you asked for.

Your friend Sam

From: irinaofthedeep@gmail.com
To: lee.samuel.fike@yahoo.com

Hi Sam I am glad you wrote to me! Yes its true I have SUSPICIONS about you. I believe you have an identity besides the one you think, maybe you don't even realize you're somebody else, but I think you have been in Broken River before and you're back to try and learn something about your past and I think I can help you. To fill you in about who I am my father is a sculptor and my mother is a writer, and we live by the state forest in a house that I think if you saw it would bring back memories of your past. I'm from Brooklyn which is part of New York City but I don't miss it. I'm home schooled which mostly means reading whatever I want and sometimes taking a test altho I have not had any of the tests yet. Write back if you know what I mean or want to know more

Sincerely Irina

From: lee.samuel.fike@yahoo.com
To: irinaofthedeep@gmail.com

Dear Irina

Well I definitely don't want to disappoint you but like I said I'm from Buffalo and I'm here because of my brother. To be completely honest he is in the jail. He'll be out before long, so I'm just helping out my uncle and working at Denny's, and then I guess I'll see what happens when my brother gets

out. My life is pretty boring and I don't get what you mean by me being somebody else. Though like I said I'm kind of curious.
Sam

From: irinaofthedeep@gmail.com
To: lee.samuel.fike@yahoo.com

I'll be frank, I think you are a girl called Samantha Geary who's parents were MURDERED in 2005 in my house and who disappeared. Samantha/you was 5 then and now would be 17 which I think is about your age. If you want to know more lets meet.

I.

From: lee.samuel.fike@yahoo.com
To: irinaofthedeep@gmail.com

Irina,
I'm 19 and my parents are alive as far as I know. My mom definitely is, anyway. My Sam is from Samuel, not Samantha, because of a dead uncle. For some reason I have boys names haha. You're an interesting girl though. Maybe I will see you around.
Sam

Irina knows a brush-off when she hears it, but there's that last sentence, *Maybe I will see you around.* It could be politeness, or it could be an invitation. It could be an *unconscious* invitation. Irina is going to take her up on it, one way or another. She pokes Sam's email address to add it to her contacts and then adds a photo: the one she surreptitiously took while standing in line at the Dairy Queen. It's grainy and smeary, because she had to zoom in, and Sam's face is half-obscured because she was bending down to her ice cream cone. She looks at the new contact card she has made with a certain amount of pride—A friend! I made a friend!—and then, after a moment's thought, replaces the photo with her internet-swiped Samantha Geary yearbook shot. They look similar, there's no question. Maybe Samantha was actually seven when the murders happened. Her parents were probably druggies or something, maybe they probably couldn't keep track! Or maybe Sam is lying a little bit, to appear more grown-up?

Irina got a feeling when she saw her sitting there on the guardrail next to the Dairy Queen, working her way down her vanilla cone. She had a feeling Sam was not an ordinary girl, so she lifted up her iPod and pretended to check her own hair in the selfie cam while in fact taking the photo. The line was long and the weather was hot and she became increasingly concerned that Mysterious Vanilla Cone Girl would finish and leave before she, Irina, even had her own ice cream in hand. But in the end, there was time not only to sidle on over with her own vanilla cone (for solidarity) but to say hi, compare personal facts (both new in town, both enjoy ice cream, etc.), and *exchange names*.

When Sam said her name was Sam, Irina's body turned into pure electricity, and she said, "Samantha Geary!?" and Sam said, "No, sorry, Fike," and Irina said, "Samantha Fike?" and Sam said, "No, just Sam," and then they stared awkwardly at each other for a couple of seconds, Sam appearing amused and alarmed, Irina squealing inwardly, her toes madly tapping the sidewalk. "But you're from here originally," Irina said, and Sam said "No, sorry," and Irina said "But you're here now," and Sam laughed and said "Sure, you could say that, I guess." Irina gave Sam her email address, which Sam did not write down but did repeat out loud, and Sam gave Irina *her* email address, which Irina typed immediately into her iPod. "I will email you!" Irina said, and Sam laughed again and said okay, and Irina liked her so much, she likes her *so much*. And now, a bunch of emails later, she likes her even more.

She's Samantha Geary. She has to be. If she isn't . . . If it's not her . . .

"Father," Irina says now, loudly, to try to keep the quiver out of her voice. "Are we going?"

"Yeah," he says, still thumbing away. At least the hankie has been stashed.

"Like, now?"

"Lemme finish this, Rins."

The two of them stand there, eight feet apart, leaning against the crappy-ass guitar shop wall. Irina stares up at the crumbling hotel facade across the street and tries to think of something, anything, that will keep her from crying. So she thinks about the comic-book shop near their apartment in Brooklyn, the one run by the angry little man with the big white dog. She never liked it, though she pretended to Father that she did because he liked taking her there. She isn't into comics, she didn't like the angry man, she doesn't like dogs. And the kids—and adults, for that matter—who were always hanging around in there frightened her.

Yet, in spite of what she told Sam, suddenly she misses it. The emotion she was trying to suppress is attaching itself to it. It is a real place, it's a place she used to go into because it was there, and it has carried on without her! Irina's plan has backfired. She is going to cry! She is looking forward to this aspect of childhood being over—this thing where you can't control your emotions and they aren't even about the things you really care about.

"Father, please."

"In a minute."

She can't help it—she lets out a single strangled squawk, and then she is crying and crying.

A moment later she feels her father's arm around her shoulder and he's saying, "Jesus, kid, what the hell."

"I just want to *go home*."

"I know I'm a shitty father."

"This isn't about *you*!" she says.

The arm disappears. She can hear his back cracking as he stands up straight. "Okay, yeah," he says. "Sorry, let's go."

Her chest is still hitching as they walk back past the arts center—it seems like years since the painting class she was just at—and to the car. They get in it and pull out of the space and some guy honks and her father hits the brakes hard and swears. Their heads bobble back and forth. "Sorry, Rinny."

"Stop apologizing!"

She realizes that she's mad at him. Maybe it's the nickname. He's overusing it today, probably because the guitar store clerk liked it. Her mother doesn't, and Irina doesn't particularly, either. But she likes that he devised it for her, and she has imagined that it's the kind of thing her future husband might call her, if she ever gets married.

But no, it's not the nickname, or even that he told it to that stupid girl. It's the *smell*. He smells like an ashtray in a gym in a department store. She looks over at him, and he's sweating and clenching his teeth as he flips off the guy who honked at him and then jerks the car out into traffic. "Goddammit," he says, and then he wipes his forehead with his hideous snotcloth.

She can't hold back. "Do you blow your *nose* into that thing? You blow your *nose* and then you wipe it all over your *face?*"

He hazards a glance at it as he shoves it into his jacket. "Ahhh, yeah, but . . . it's in a different part of . . . yeah. I guess that's kinda disgusting."

"It's completely unacceptable."

Unexpectedly, he gets mad. "Hey, man, you don't get to tell me what's acceptable and what's not," he says.

"No, *nobody* tells *you* what to do."

That shuts him up.

They drive home in almost total silence. At some point he says, "What'd you practice," and she says, "Wouldn't you like to know," and immediately feels bad, almost worse than before. She manages not to cry again. When they get home she runs to the stairs, passing, along the way, a duo of worker dudes who are dismantling a corner of the living room that has succumbed to blossoms of blue-black mold. The men smell like cigarettes, gross ones, grosser than Father's weed. In her room, she takes clean clothes out of her dresser and heads for the shower. She can hear the clickety-clack of her mother's laptop down the hall: doubtless she has her earbuds in and can't hear, otherwise she would come out and ask how the classes went. Irina doesn't want to talk about how the classes went. Adults buy you something, anything, they think they deserve detailed reviews and progress reports. Just pony up and leave us alone! She slips through the bathroom door, locks herself in. Then she runs the water and gets undressed while it heats up. She wants to wash Broken River off herself, the tears, the car ride, her father's weird smell. She is naked when a knock comes on the door. It's Father, loudly whispering. "Hey, what are you doing in there, man?"

"I'm taking a shower," she loud-whispers back, because that's what you do.

"*I* need to take a shower!"

"So do I! Which is *why* I'm *doing* it!" That was less a whisper than a quiet shout.

His answering whisper isn't even loud. "No, like, *now*."

"Too freaking bad!" Irina actually shouts, full throated and genuinely angry, and she gets under the water and flings the curtain shut. Through the wall behind the faucet handles she feels, rather than hears, the sound of her mother's wheeled office chair being pushed back, then feels a door opening and closing, and then a knock.

"Irina?"

"I! Am taking! A shower! Leave me alone!"

"Are you all right?" her mother says.

"I am fine! Go away!"

"Where's your father?"

"Mother, I don't know!" Irina screams. "Go away!"

She goes away, and Irina cries for a little while longer under the hot water. She is aware that it will soon stop being hot. She washes quickly, then continues to stand there, making sure she uses up every drop so that her father will have to wait. When the hot water is gone, she gets out, dries off, and puts on her clean clothes. She enters her bedroom and closes and locks the door. The smell here is a comfort—familiar, a little rank due to feet and unwashed laundry, a little piney because of the open window and the close-hanging boughs, and a little musty, on account of the mold blossoms that have appeared behind the headboard, which she has not had the heart to tell her parents about. Also, she kind of likes the mold blossoms. They make the wall soft—they feel alive to the touch, yielding and slightly clammy. She climbs onto her bed, shoving aside the laptop her mother, as promised, has bought for her, and reaches behind the headboard to stroke the dark patches. Her fingers are dusted with spores, and she gives them a disconsolate sniff.

She opens up the laptop and dies a little bit inside. It's been a few weeks since she has added anything to her novel. When she got the computer, she decided she ought to be writing on it, so she typed everything she had so far into a word processor file, changing things a little as she went. Then she tried writing new bits. But it wasn't the same. She missed her notebook. So she got out the notebook and tried writing in that, but it didn't feel like the novel was *in* the notebook anymore, it was in the laptop now, and so she couldn't write in the notebook, either. After that, she just didn't feel like writing anything, and she put the whole Quayside project on hiatus.

Now, though, she opens up the Quayside file and starts typing. She has her boy protagonist, Aiden (a name she picked at random; she doesn't like it; she's going to change it) meet a girl called Kimmifer (they all have weird names in Quayside) who has amnesia and is trying to discover her past. She's older than him, seventeen, so she has just started wearing the bustle—until then, she just wore regular pants. She is very frustrated, she can't do the things she likes to do, and her mother tells her she'll get used to it, all women do, and she's a woman now. But she hates it. It is impeding her range of motion. She keeps having to ask men for help with stuff—getting into water taxis or reaching for a birdcage in a birdcage store, which is another thing grown women in Quayside are supposed to be into. (Privately, Kimmifer really does like birdcages.) Aiden (ugh, that really has to go) suggests they take a water taxi down to the Quayside Department of

Records, which he knows about from his research into trying to get back to Brooklyn. She agrees, and of course he has to help her into the cab, and he gets very excited touching her hand, although it feels sort of wrong somehow to feel that way. (Irina's thinking is that she is actually his long-lost sister? which will have to be written into the opening chapters somehow. But in a subtle way, so that it isn't obvious the moment Kimmifer arrives on the scene that she is the sister. Irina is aware that she is ripping this off from *Star Wars*, but *Star Wars* probably ripped it off from something else, so no big deal.)

There: she did it. She worked on her novel. The words are on the page now, they're real. So why do they feel fake? Why does she feel like a fraud? Would anybody else notice the difference between the fraudulent words and the real words? Would the Irina of three years ago, or of three years from now? Is this what a real writer feels like all the time—unsure if she is real? She hears voices—Mother speaking to the repair guys. The phrases "temporary fix," "probably come back," "could be everywhere," float up the stairs. She could ask her mother this question, but even the question itself feels fake. She closes the word processor with a couple of angry keystrokes, and the word *bad* escapes her lips. She opens her browser up to the Geary thread.

Not much new stuff, although smoking_jacket is at it, again promising to contact the new owners of the house about having a look around. Irina has been waiting for this to happen. Maybe it already has and Mother or Father has declined to let smoking_jacket come. Or maybe they have said yes and they are just waiting for the right moment—that is, when she, Irina, is not at home. At some point she should come clean to them about knowing everything about the murders. She can handle it, after all—she has not only been handling it, she has been enjoying it! But something is holding her back. Maybe even her parents don't know. Maybe *they* couldn't handle it, given the problems that they have been going through. Let the murders, and CyberSleuths, be hers alone.

Now she does something impulsive. She opens up a new-post window and types, *I think that I have found Samantha Geary. I know her name. She moved far away after the killings but now is back in the area. I entend to protect her identity and privcy but here is a photo of her. I asked her if she was her and she did not say no. The dates match up. I think she is hopeing to solve the mystery of her parent's deaths.*

Irina uploads the Dairy Queen photo, making sure there are no details in it that would identify Sam or where she is standing. Then she spell-checks the text and corrects *intend*, *privacy*, and *hoping*. Then she hits POST.

If she expected an adrenaline rush, and she admits to herself that she did, it doesn't arrive. There's just a silence as the post appears on her screen. She refreshes the page a couple of times over several minutes, and nobody has responded. Well—maybe nobody will believe her. She can live with that; she knows the truth! It will out, eventually. Is that how you say that: the truth will out? It doesn't sound right.

Irina sits in silence for a few minutes, refreshing the browser page, hoping for a response. From down the hall comes the quiet clackety-clack of Mother working on her novel. It makes Irina feel guilty about not working on hers. Then the clacketying stops, Mother's office chair creaks, and a response appears on the screen, from smoking_jacket: *Interesting, if true.*

Footsteps. A knock on the door. For crap's sake.

"I'm busy."

The door opens. Mother walks in.

Irina is too shocked to react at first. Walking in is *not done*. Mother comes across the room and flops down with a groan on the bed beside Irina, stretches out her legs and crosses one over the other, squeezes her hands in between her knees. "What are you working on?"

Irina glances down at her laptop. The blurry photo of Sam is right there on the screen, beside the name *Samantha Geary*. She snaps the laptop shut. Guiltily!

"Novel."

Her mother pauses, staring at the space where the browser page was. That didn't look like your novel, Irina expects her to say, but instead, after a little grunt of acknowledgment, she says, "You said you'd been having trouble after switching to the computer."

"Yeah . . . I think I've got it now."

"Good. You need to have problems and then solve them, if you're going to be a novelist."

"What do you want," Irina says, perhaps a bit too nastily, perhaps annoyed with herself for wanting to lean against Mother, whose bony shoulder is *right there*.

There's a pause. Mother cracks her toes. "Your father is . . . did something happen? In Broken River?"

"No."

"I heard him raising his voice. Did you have a fight?"

"No."

Another long pause, during which Irina considers slipping out from under the covers and escaping to the kitchen. But Mother says, "Sorry, baby. I don't think it has anything to do with you," and her tired voice induces in Irina another wave of longing. "I mean, I'm sure it doesn't."

"I miss New York," Irina says, and feels her small advantage slipping away.

"Me too, sometimes. Though there are fewer distractions out here."

"*I* wasn't distracted there. *You're* the one who was distracted."

Mother opens her mouth, then closes it again without speaking. It gives Irina a chill. It's like something a ghost would do.

"It's not like I want to move *back*," Irina goes on, lying. "I just want to visit. And go to our places. I miss the Sandwich Dungeon. I miss Grawlixes Comics, even the jerky guy and the dog, even though I don't like it. And WORD Brooklyn. There's no bookstore in Broken River."

"Maybe we just haven't found it yet?"

"I looked it up. It was called the Book Nook. It's out of business. You can still see the shelves and whatnot through the window."

"Oh."

"It was probably no good anyway because it had a stupid name and it's full of those wire spinning display things that always have romances or Jesusy things on them."

Irina's trying to sound hard, but her mother laughs. "You're probably right. Okay, sure. We should go back. Maybe I'll have a draft of this book soon and will have to meet with my agent—maybe you could come with me. We can see a show. We'll take pictures of Times Square, like tourists."

And like that, Irina forgives her for . . . whatever it was she was mad about. "Yes! That would be excellent. Is Father invited?"

She has said it without thinking. Of course Father is not supposed to go to New York. And Irina is not supposed to know that. And she has accidentally behaved as though she doesn't, even though she does. The layers of regret are piling up. Her mother seems to consider for a moment, then quietly says, "If you want."

"Maybe just you and me would be good," Irina says, and Mother's body relaxes.

"Deal."

"Deal."

Mother kisses the top of her head and gets up from the bed. Or tries to. She kind of convulses instead, and a small sound escapes her, a little squeak. Then she draws a deep breath and slowly peels herself off the mattress. This series of motions gives Irina a chill, though she doesn't understand why.

"Are you all right?" Irina asks her.

"I have a backache. I hurt myself moving our stuff."

"Maybe it's stress."

This gets her mother's attention. She's standing beside the bed, pressing a hand to her spine, curving herself backward like a blade of grass in a wind.

Irina says, "When I was fighting with Sylvie, I got pains in my jaw and shoulders, like, all the time."

"You never told us you were fighting with Sylvie," her mother says.

"It wasn't a big deal."

For a second she looks like she's going to respond, but in the end she just nods. She goes to the doorway, steps into the hall. Looks back.

"But seriously," she says. "What's that you were looking at, on your laptop?"

They stare at each other.

"Research?" Mother prompts.

"Yes."

Another few seconds of staring, and then the door latches quietly shut.

Irina is left with a complicated series of feelings: mild sadness that Mother has left the room; relief that their conversation is over; irritation that it was Mother, not she, who broke contact; annoyance at the complexities of adult existence in general and her parents' in particular; puzzlement at the parental intent in this whole encounter; and a niggling feeling of dissatisfaction, as if they were supposed to have accomplished something, or reached some agreement, or solved some problem, when in fact they have not. Was it her fault? Is there work she's supposed to be doing, as Child in Chief, that she has neglected? She squeezes her eyes shut and tips her head back and takes deep, deep breaths through her nose, and hums something in a minor key. And then she's through it.

Irina considers returning to CyberSleuths to see if anyone else has responded, but no: once she makes a habit of that kind of behavior, there will be no end to it. Instead she picks up her guitar to practice her scales.

She likes unamplified electric guitar: it's private, as much feel as sound. She plays all the chords she knows, in a random order. Each one vibrates differently against her body. Each one seems to touch some different interior part of her. She starts making up chords now, just random fingerings, to see how they make her feel.

And then one of them makes her feel something very specific and strange. It is the feeling of being watched. And not watched as in monitored, like there's a hidden camera and somebody somewhere is observing her on a screen. The watcher is here in the room with her. A presence. A thing without form or motivation but with a consciousness. It isn't evil, but it is scary. Something is watching her.

She is startled—so much so that her body jerks and she drops the guitar. The headstock dips and bumps into her laptop, and she cries out and snatches the instrument back up and examines the computer. There's a scratch on the case, a little scuff, but it isn't cracked or anything.

Irina looks around the room. It's just her room, that's all. The sun's low in the sky and very bright, and the shadows of branches are moving against the far wall. Soon she will be called downstairs for dinner. She hears voices, Mother's and Father's, and soon Father's footsteps sound on the stairs and the bathroom door opens and closes. Water runs. Irina's sense of this presence is draining away. It was here, she's sure of it. The chord, it was the chord that did it, and she tries to work out what the notes were—where she'd placed her fingers. She tries several combinations, but they're all wrong. It's hopeless. She isn't going to get it.

The experience has left Irina with a sense, strangely enough, of calm. She lays the guitar down where her mother was sitting. She shuts her eyes and listens to the vigorous splashing and thumping of her father's shower. She listens to the breeze moving the branches outside. She's going to sleep now—she'll sleep until dinner. She sends her thoughts out to the thing: Watch over me. It isn't here anymore, but perhaps it can hear her. Father's shower has combined with the wind, and now there is a sizzling from below, from the kitchen, where her mother is cooking, and the distant sound of traffic from the road and the creek as it runs over and around rocks. It's the sound of the world, and the thing watching her is part of it, and this feels like the solution to a problem: that's why the chord revealed the thing, it's because it's made of sound! It's this feeling, the feeling of the problem presenting itself and being solved, that tips her over into dreamless sleep.

Part Two

9

But earlier that day, in Broken River, the dark-haired woman lay on the hotel bed she had paid for, her hands laced behind her head, scowling at the stuccoed ceiling shot through with cracks and wreathed in cobwebs that trembled in the steady wave of warm air rising from a large, white-painted radiator. The Observer might have expected the woman to smile, or perhaps to drift off to sleep, but instead she seemed agitated, uncomfortable in her skin.

The woman stood, smoothing her nightgown down over her belly and thighs, though there was no one else in the room to notice the wrinkles it had developed in her overnight bag and in the struggle to remove it an hour ago. The Observer followed her across the room and to the window, and her gaze to the street, where the man, her lover, leaned, smoking, against an exposed-brick wall a short distance from his daughter, the girl.

The dark-haired woman, having taken notice of these two, now pulled back from the window, perhaps in fear of being seen. Across the room, her phone buzzed, and she hurried to find it in her handbag. A small smile appeared on her face as she took in what the screen displayed; soon her thumbs were in rapid motion, tapping out messages, presumably to the man on the street.

The Observer didn't presume to understand the lines of affection and repulsion, hope and disappointment among these three: the man, the girl, and the woman. It was not clear why this mode of communication—the encoding of short bursts of information into digital signals that were then transmitted into the upper atmosphere and back to earth—was preferable, in this instance, to simply shouting out the window. The girl's face was gripped by intense animation, at times evincing consternation (when she happened to glance over at her father) and confusion, at other times excitement (seemingly in reaction to the messages on her own device). The girl's hold on her childhood was slipping; before long the word "girl" would no longer apply.

The dark-haired woman issued quiet breaths, small grunts, as she gazed, alternately, out the window from a safe distance and at the text-filled bubbles scrolling down her screen. Eventually, the girl, having pocketed her device and failed in her struggle to maintain an adult demeanor, began to cry. The man looked up in surprise and went to her: there, on the sidewalk, he threw his arm around her, engaged her in a brief but intense conversation, and led her away. Seemingly in response, the woman fell silent, her face still. She gazed out for several minutes, as though deep in thought, at the place the man and child had occupied.

Now, hours later, all is quiet and calm. The dark-haired woman is leaving Broken River, having quickly changed her clothes, gathered her things, and departed the hotel. "Checking out? Already?" asked the desk clerk, and the woman replied, with audible disdain, "Family emergency." She sits, motionless relative to her speeding car, not singing along to the pop radio station that can't seem to maintain a clear signal here among the mountains.

The Observer lets her go. It is time to turn its attention to the family many miles to the north, though the Observer is increasingly aware that it needn't choose one time, one place, one group of human beings to attend to. Indeed, it is quite capable of observing anything, all things. But it has begun to recognize that its purpose, as opposed to its ability, is limited: or, more precisely, its purpose *is* to *be* limited. It is unconcerned with, bored in fact by, the immensity of its power. It is interested only in the strategic—the aesthetic—winnowing of that power.

It has been brought into existence in order to amuse itself.

What has caused it to come into being is not clear, and the Observer is not sure that it is interested in knowing. It is new in this world, yet it feels that it has always existed: or, rather, it has existed as long as the humans have. Its identity is connected to the self-awareness of the humans, and to their awareness of the world around them. The humans are already limited in what they can notice, compared with the Observer, yet they elect to be even more selective in their perception, filtering out those obvious truths that might nudge them away from their established trajectory. They refuse to seize available opportunities that might expand their experience even slightly; they maintain obsolete habits rather than adjust promptly to new circumstances. They seem almost to prefer ruin to voluntary change.

Yet the humans seem to think that anything is possible, that life is limitless, which is entirely and obviously wrong.

Of course the humans die. Quite possibly all of them. Perhaps the Observer will die as well; it doesn't know, and it can't imagine what it would do differently if eventual death were a certainty. But the humans, it suspects, know. This is likely why, years ago, at the beginning of the Observer's existence, the murdered man and woman screamed, even before any damage was inflicted upon their bodies: they were justifiably fearful that their lives were about to end. If the humans know that death is coming (and, by the Observer's standards, it would seem that it tends to come very soon), their words and actions must all be profoundly influenced by that fact. They fear making wrong choices, so they avoid making any at all. They keep very still, hoping that death might fail to take notice of them.

The man and girl have now returned to their house, and the girl is in bed, asleep. The breaths she draws are even and silent. She is curled on her side, this child who is already half an inch taller than she was when the man and woman made love in the unfinished house. The man and woman don't appear to have noticed this yet about their daughter. But it is clear, or it should be, that the girl has grown out of her fall clothes and that they ought to buy her some new ones. Perhaps they have other things on their minds.

Indeed, the girl herself seems to have failed to notice the space between the bottoms of her jeans and the tops of her shoes, and the fact that she can now see half of her wristwatch (she found it sitting on a bench in the subway—it's a cheap ladies' Timex with a rectangular golden face and little hash marks instead of numbers to mark the time, and her parents have not asked her where it came from) poking out from her shirt cuff. Her sneakers still fit; she isn't in school, and so there's nobody to mock her, no one whose gaze she could feel self-conscious in. Perhaps, the Observer thinks, the girl, the whole family, could go wild out here, forget about the existence of other people and their judgment. Their hair could grow long and tangled; they could kill their dinner with their bare hands.

But no: the man and woman have not forgotten themselves. There are clues. In the bathroom, the shower has stopped, and the man is standing, naked and dripping, in the steaming stall. He's staring straight ahead, at nothing in particular, and scowling. His left hand is idly stroking his belly, which has increased in girth in proportion to the girl's increase in height; his right hand cups his flaccid penis in its nest of dark hair. After a moment he shifts his left hand to his creased forehead, where it digs and massages. Perhaps the man has a headache. He really ought to turn the shower back on and let its powerful spray soothe his face. But the girl used all the hot water, and the heater in the basement has not had time to fully replenish it. He's going to have to just get out, which he does, violently flinging aside the curtain and stepping, still dripping, onto the rug. He buries his face in a towel and leaves it there longer than our Observer is interested in watching.

Downstairs, the woman is standing at the stove. A blue-and-white pinstriped apron covers her usual uniform of black jeans and sweater. In her left hand is a wooden spatula; her right hand grips the handle of a stainless-steel wok. The wok is filled with vegetables, and they are steaming and sizzling. On the burner behind the wok sits a pot full of rice. Behind the woman, the table is set for three.

The vegetables are cooked. They were cooked some time ago. In a few moments, they will be overcooked. The woman is standing quite still. The expression on her face is one of thoughtfulness tinged with concern and perhaps, at the corners of her eyes and mouth, the slightest hint of terror. Has she realized that her husband's erratic behavior this afternoon is consistent with continued infidelity? All the necessary information is there for the woman to make this determination. But she seems unable, or unwilling, to do so.

The woman's hand reaches around behind her. Her brow knits in concentration, and then she winces and her body jerks. Her reverie broken by the evident pain, she looks down at the wok, emits a small gasp, quickly removes it from the heat. The words "Oh, shit" escape her lips. A few flicks of the spatula confirm that half the vegetables are blackened and shriveled. The woman sighs, slumps against the counter. For a moment, the Observer wonders if she is about to collapse onto the floor.

But then the woman opens the cabinet beneath the sink, scrapes the burned food into the trash bin. She sets the wok back on the burner, turns off the gas, and sets to work chopping vegetables again.

This delay in the completion of the family dinner gives the man's natural energy and grumpy good cheer enough time to reassert themselves. The girl's nap markedly improves her mood. The three appear to enjoy their meal and, afterward, a filmed entertainment in the living room. Their laughter will indicate that the movie is a comedy, but the Observer can find no appreciable difference between the onscreen human folly that evokes merriment and that which induces sympathetic misery.

It's time for the Observer to move on: again above Route 94, along the river, past the hills and railroad, past the farms and villages. Back to Broken River. It could go there instantaneously, of course, but at this moment it prefers to take its time. Without impending death to hurry it along, why not? The temperature has dropped—it's been dropping all day, down to levels at which the humans begin to complain—and now it's snowing, even though there are still a few days left in October. The Observer reaches the flat land where Broken River begins, and moves through town, past the abandoned theater, which an angry teenaged boy is attempting to break into through an alley door (he will succeed); past the apartment building where Jasn Hubble is watching a YouTube video of the Average White Band's cocaine-fueled performance on *Soul Train* that originally aired November 22, 1975, and where his eyes follow, with longing, the movement of a Lake Placid Blue Metallic Fender Mustang bass with matching headstock; past the empty animal shelter that now once again shelters animals, a family of stray cats here of their own volition who got in through a rat-chewed hole in the rotted plywood back door and who are being fed daily by the old man who lives on the other side of the disused, weed-choked parking lot; and finally over the cluster of jail-themed bars and the prison itself, a mile beyond which a trailer park lies. It's large and fairly tidy; compared with most of Broken River, it is thriving. Many of the streets that run through it are paved, and the pavement is in decent shape; the rest are graveled and reasonably free of ruts. At the end of one of these streets stands a neat beige doublewide around which a small deck has been built. Light shines from the trailer's windows, yellow from the lamps inside and blue from the television, which is showing a baseball game to a compact, overweight, alert-looking man in his fifties. Our Observer, however, remains out on the deck, where the girl called Sam is standing, clutching herself against the cold, which her thin cardigan sweater and baseball cap do little to protect her against. One hand holds a cigarette, the other a phone.

She says, "He didn't say anything about coming home."

She says, "He didn't say anything about your letters, Mom."

She says:

"I don't think it's about you, Mom. He's just got other things on his mind."

"No, I don't think he's coming back to Buffalo."

"No, but I'm going to stay here for a while, okay? Uncle Bobby's fine with it."

"I said he was fine with it. I think he's lonely."

"I haven't met any girlfriend."

"Well, I didn't meet any boyfriend, either, so I don't know."

"I don't know, Mom."

"I have to go. I love you, too. I have to go. Goodbye."

10

Sam is standing on the deck, gripping her phone, snow falling all around her. It's cold out and she is shivering, but she isn't eager to head back into the trailer and pass through the room containing her uncle on the way to another lonely night in her bedroom. Not that she doesn't love her uncle or appreciate the room: she's kind of surprised to realize she's okay with both, for now. She had been led, before coming here, to believe that her uncle was little more than an embittered, self-satisfied loser whose dominant conversational mode was that of explaining why all his problems were the result of other people's failings. And it's true, there's more than a little of that in him. He seems surprised that the world hasn't given him more, hasn't brought him the riches he thinks he deserves. But, as far as Sam is concerned, he doesn't have it so bad. He's got a job, anyway, as the site manager and retail clerk at a stone quarry, which is why this doublewide is surrounded by rock gardens, low stone walls, and frankly weird and incongruous intentional piles of what he calls "irregular flag." He always seems to have some rocks in the trunk of the car, and she suspects he steals them from work: his miniature rebellion, a thumb on the scales of justice.

Anyway, even if her uncle was little more than an insecure prick with some very slightly suppressed creep impulses, Sam would be all right with it. She adores the old man. When he still lived in Buffalo he was her favorite surrogate father; they used to play cards together, and he took her to the track with him most weekends. But then his wife left him, his sister's crazy got unbearable (Sam's father and poorly considered namesake, Lee Samuel Fike, was already gone before she was born, and Uncle Bobby liked to mutter under his breath that he didn't blame the guy), and he packed up and moved here. Sam hadn't seen Uncle Bobby for years, and it was only when Daniel got three to five for growing weed under lights that she ever considered even visiting. By this time she was already planning to move away—she hated school, despite her excellent grades, and had GED'd her way out at sixteen, plus living with her mother was a nightmare—and she figured she could come out here with the stated intention of getting Daniel back on his feet. She would crash with Uncle Bobby for a few weeks, then help Daniel find a place, live with him for a little while, and decide what to do once she had the lay of the land.

Instead, she has mainly bonded with Bobby and at the moment has no plans to move out. She admitted to him, a few days before Daniel's release, that she felt guilty about abandoning their mother. "Look, she's suffering, no doubt about it," Bobby replied from the other side of the sofa, gesturing at the glowing, silenced television with his burning cigarette. This was how he talked: at the TV, regardless of where in the room you actually were, or if it was on. "But just 'cause you're suffering don't mean you got the right to make everybody else suffer with you. The crazy bitch sent your brother up the river. I'm not saying he wasn't breaking the law, I'm saying your fucking mother ratted him out. She pretended not to know what she was doing, but she did.

"That's what she's like," he went on, cracking open a beer and changing the channel. Sam couldn't discern any logic in the channel changes, neither in their timing nor ultimate destination. Now, many weeks later, she has decided that the TV is like an animated painting for Uncle Bobby, a series of abstract patterns and colors; he's not actually interested in human narratives, finds them tiring, despite his fairly acute sensitivity to human personality. "She's sneaky. She's a manipulator. She was a manipulator when she was three fuckin' years old. She learned to get me blamed for all the shit she did: stealing from the neighbors, leaving a turd in the bathtub, setting the fuckin' cat on fire.

"I'm pretty sure your granddad was making her suck him off, though. I mean, I think that's what that's all about. Or maybe she's just a psycho. Anyway, go ahead, feel bad for your mother, but don't let her make you feel like anything's your fault. She's forty-eight. She's got her health and she's no idiot. If she can't make her way in the world without you, fuck her.

"Am I right?" he asked the TV. "Am I right? Fuck her!"

"Yeah, okay," Sam said with a laugh. "Sure."

So no, none of the three of them has any reason to be here, really, except that they all want to be far away from Mom and Broken River is a town few people think about or want to go to. For Sam, the place is probably a stepping stone, though to what, she has no idea. Like her brother, she is smart and decent-looking and built to endure. Daniel, too, is unlikely to stay here long—he tends to develop ambitions, and even if the ambitions center mostly on growing pot, he will likely achieve them and will either grow out of Broken River or end up back in prison.

Daniel was good at prison. He kept himself up-to-date on changes in the world of weed: new varieties, new methods, looser laws. "If I'd been caught only a year later," he told Sam once, over the glass partition, "I woulda got off with six months in county." He probably wouldn't have been caught at all, of course, if it weren't for their mother; it was her basement he'd been growing in. She was lucky not to lose her house, actually, a fact that Daniel still refuses to acknowledge. He had enough plants down there for twenty years in federal— his light sentence was the result of a liberal judge who'd been apprised of the family situation and who made frequent eye contact with their mother during the trial.

She was late to pick him up on his release day. It was literally the only reason she came to this town, and she was late. Uncle Bobby's Taurus wouldn't start—he'd left the passenger door open overnight after bringing the groceries inside, and the dome light ran down the battery. They had to get a jump from a neighbor two trailers down—a broad-hipped, ex-beauty-queen-looking lady of around sixty, perpetually bathrobed, eyeglasses on a chain—who clearly disliked Uncle Bobby but appeared accustomed to the ritual of helping him start his car. Sam expected to find Daniel pacing up and down the street or doing jumping jacks or pushups or something, looking thin in his years-old clothes, but when she arrived, there was nobody in sight except the hot dog man, a couple of kids using dirt bikes to prop up their lanky, loose bodies, and an idling brown Oldsmobile with poor suspension.

Sam parked, turned the engine off, then winced: had she driven long enough to charge the battery? Well, she'd soon find out. She thumbed through a wrinkled and muddy issue of *Motor Trend* she found in the passenger side footwell while she waited, wondering if she'd gotten the time wrong, or the date, or if something had happened inside the prison to detain him, like becoming friends with the warden. After fifteen minutes she got out of the car and started walking around—like brother like sister—and eventually she made her way past the idling Olds. There was nobody behind the wheel, but in the passenger seat lay a little pile of hot-dog-stand debris; the window was open a crack, and into the crisp autumnal air drifted the scents of sausage and chili and tomato ketchup. While contemplating getting a hot dog of her own, Sam noticed that the back seat was occupied by two people: one a curvy girl with straight black hair, like a late-night television diva. She was wearing a lot of makeup and a lot of black. The other person was a man, thick, curly light-brown hair, broad shoulders, little girlish ears. He had his face buried in the woman's neck, and his hand was squeezing her tit. Sam couldn't see the man's face, but it bore good-humored, thickly lashed brown eyes, plump lips, a sharply cleft chin, and a scattering of freckles. She knew this because the man was Daniel.

The girl saw her first and flipped her off. In response, Sam knocked on the window. The girl said, "Fuck off, perv!" and at that point Daniel turned, and his sleepy face woke up, and he said, "Sam!"

The car door flew open and Daniel flew out. "Sis! I'm free! Fuckin' hi!"

"Hey, Danny," she said as he embraced her; she angled her hips away from him so as to avoid contact with his hard-on. He smelled of old sweat and hot dogs and somebody's perfume, presumably the girl's. "You made a friend."

"Oh yeah. Yeah, this is Yetta. Yetta, this is my sister Sam."

The girl still appeared hurt to have been interrupted but made an impressive attempt at friendliness, leaning across the width of the backseat and peering up at Sam. "Hey, sorry."

"It's okay."

"She was coming to visit somebody, and we got to talking!" Daniel said, combing his hair back with his fingers.

"That's great."

"My boyfriend's in for assault," Yetta told her, with an eyeroll. "Not on me. He was a teddy bear with me."

"He's supposed to be in for a while," Daniel explained, by way of re-assurance. "I know him, actually!"

"Oh, he's a fucking tool," Yetta said with a wave of the hand.

Daniel shrugged.

"The hot dogs were for him," Yetta went on, "but . . ."

"Haha, right!" Daniel said. "Yetta and I met in the hot dog line."

"That makes sense," Sam said.

"Yetta was ready for a change!"

"Goddamn right I was."

"Sure," Sam said.

In the end all three of them went to Yetta's and had some beers. (Sam was right to worry: the battery in the Taurus had indeed failed to charge, and Yetta had to give the car its second jump of the day.) When it came time to take Daniel back to Uncle Bobby's, he told her, apparently in response to some wordless invitation of Yetta's, that he was going to stick around here for a while. Yetta nodded. Sam said fine, went out to the Taurus, which she had left idling, and went home to Uncle Bobby, who seemed relieved.

That was a month and a half ago. Since then, Daniel has taken over Yetta's ex's semidormant weed operation, expanded and refined it, and gone to market with the product. With what money, she has no idea. Money has never been a problem for Daniel. People do things for him, invest themselves. Women, mostly, but also a certain kind of boy as well, the impressionable loner with no social skills and limited charisma, who looks up to him and aspires to his particular kind of cool. When Daniel is seen at all, he is usually seen with one or more factotum or fuck buddy trailing along behind him, laughing at his jokes and looking around to see who is noticing that they are with Daniel. Sam looked up to him too, when they were growing up; in his presence she felt an uneasy mixture of pathetic inferiority and secondhand chic.

It embarrasses her to find that, even now, even here, Daniel still makes her feel this way: invisible except in the light of his glory. It doesn't matter that he's a stoner ex-con in a shitty town. He's Daniel, and she's Daniel's little sister, and ever it shall be.

That is, if she can't find something to do with her time besides read library books, hang out with her uncle, and go over to Yetta's house to hang. Another job would be good. She could save some money and move someplace more interesting—a city, maybe. Although, again, what she would do there, and what stimulation she thinks her mind requires that this place could satisfy, remains unclear. Maybe all three of them will just live here until they die.

The snow is picking up. It's adhering to her clothes now, faster than her meager body heat can melt it. She finishes her cigarette, stubs it out in the now-snow-covered china plate that lives on the porch railing, and goes inside, shaking herself off. Bobby raises a hairy arm to her as she heads to the kitchen, and she raises a pale one back. She prepares a grilled cheese sandwich and eats it standing up while staring at her own reflection in the kitchen window. Even after the sandwich is gone, she remains standing there, waiting for the next thing to happen.

That thing is that her phone rings in her pocket. She answers, and Daniel says, "Come on over, we're having a party."

"I was thinking of going to bed."

"It's nine thirty!"

"Okay. Hey, I just talked to Mom."

"Sam-Sam, come on, I just told you it's a party. No Mom talk."

"You should call her."

"Okay, okay," her brother says. "You coming?"

"I don't want to walk in the snow."

"I'll pick you up, yo."

"I don't know."

"I'll pick you up, yo."

Ten minutes later they are fishtailing down unplowed Onteo Street, nearly missing several parked cars. Daniel reeks of weed. He's talking nonstop about having met a guy who knows a guy. He says the words "untapped potential" and "power vacuum." The radio is on, but only static is coming out of it. Sam is listening to the static, out of which little bits of words keep emerging—vowels, consonants. She isn't even high yet, but this is what Daniel does, he transforms his milieu into a zone of mild intensity and confusion. He induces susceptibility to his frame of reference.

The party is hot and close and loud beneath the low ceilings of Yetta's late mother's house. She's been dead for a few years. Her things are still here—her knitting, her bedroom slippers, her cardigan sweaters—scattered throughout the place. "I keep thinking she's coming back. I keep thinking she's here," Yetta told Sam a few weeks ago, over mugs of the sickly sweet instant coffee that her mother favored and that is still stockpiled in the cabinets as though against some future societal collapse. They're friends now. Sam kind of knew they would be, even when Yetta was giving her the finger over her brother's shoulder in the car. Yetta is impressive. She's bitchily confident and has a loud laugh, and she managed to keep her ex's pot situation going in his absence. (He was in for assault, not drugs, though it's inconceivable that the cops don't know about what's going on downstairs. Sam has decided to try not to worry about this.) It's no wonder she and Daniel found each other. She has invited Sam to deal for them.

"I don't know anyone. I'm an introvert."

"You could deliver out to the boonies. Where the weirdos like you all live."

"Hey," Sam protested, though to be noticed in this way, by Yetta, sent a little shiver of pleasure through her. She has indeed driven Yetta's car out to where a few amiable hermits live, and been treated to a lot of rambling anecdotes and political rants that Yetta was probably tired of listening to. It's fine. She does like it. She likes Yetta. And she is surprised to find that she likes this party.

Sam was unaware that parties of this intensity and magnitude even existed in Broken River. There is a lot of beer and a lot of box wine and everyone is eating brownies and passing joints around. People are gathered in tight clusters everywhere and the clusters are gathered into larger clusters. Wild-card guests form little pockets of peculiarity here and there: a totally ripped guy in a sweater vest is lying on the floor in the hallway, talking to a girl who looks like a hairdresser and who is rubbing his temples. There's a miniature boombox in the bathroom with Christmas carols coming out of it and a yellow sticky note on it that reads LISTEN CAREFU because the author ran out of space. Some unbelievably tall guy in the kitchen is telling a story about Antarctica, and a girl who looks like a very sexy horse is giggling uncontrollably. A long-haired dude in his fifties or sixties is talking about opening for KISS in 1979, and he's making air-guitar gestures. Sam consumes chemical refreshments for hours and everyone is so friendly to her, asking her name and saying it's so cool she's here. A black guy wearing glasses picks her up bodily for no clear reason and carries her on a tour of the house while shouting out the names of the rooms: *living room! bathroom! hallway! bedroom!* She thinks: Are we going to stop in the bedroom? For a moment she is very nervous and begins to tremble; she's about to tell the guy to put her down. But then the guy puts her down and picks up somebody else, and she misses him a little. She overhears her brother telling some kids, "Yeah, I fucked some dudes! Everybody fucks dudes there!" At some point some girl standing behind her kisses the back of her neck and squeezes her breasts and whispers "I like you" and disappears before Sam can get a glimpse of her, and at another point she is challenged to put her finger into a sleeping man's nose. She does it, and people cheer.

She's not the only one to spend the night. She wakes up on the coat pile. Some of the coats are on top of her. She's holding someone's hand, someone also buried under coats. It's a nice hand, long and white, probably a girl's. Sam endures a moment of desire: for what, she's not sure. The hand is warm and slightly moist and there's a scar on the back of the thumb. The fingernails are unpainted and bitten short. The wrist the hand is attached to is slender and translucent and a vein pulses pinkly under the skin. She touches the wrist with her lips and feels panic begin to rise.

And then the hand is withdrawn, abruptly, into the coat pile and a little moan sounds, and Sam needs to get out of there. She sloughs off the coats, leaves the room, and moves down the hallway, blinking. A small group of mostly young people is arrayed around the kitchen, drinking coffee and eating eggs that Daniel has made. He's wearing the apron, anyway. The heat's turned up high, and Yetta's in her panties and a sweatshirt. Sam can see her pubes sticking out.

"Mornin', Sam-Sam," says her brother.

"Hey. Hey, everybody."

Conversation is quiet and unanxious. Everyone seems happy. Sam eats the eggs; they're just scrambled, but there's something extra in them, something delicious. She has another helping and drinks a lot of coffee.

When everyone but her has left and Yetta has gone to take a shower, Daniel says, "Come check it out." She follows him through a door that she thought was a wall—given that it is covered with shelves, and the shelves with jars of dried beans and grains and cans of vegetables— and down a narrow set of stairs to the weed operation, which consists of a giant clear-plastic tent, or series of tents, with thick hoses running in and out of them. The tents fill the basement, leaving room for only a washer and dryer in one corner, and a series of bookcases filled with mason jars of harvested buds. They enter the tent complex by pulling aside the plastic and step into a warm, bright, reeking spring. The plants are growing in soil underneath racks of makeshift lamps; Daniel has created track lighting using what look like discarded garment racks, plastic shower-curtain rings, and cheap hardware-store workshop task lights. There is a low hum from the fans that ventilate the tents.

"Wow" is all she can say.

"It needed an upgrade. Barney was small-time." Barney is Yetta's violent ex.

He points out various features of the operation, the way the air flows through the tents, the carbon filters, the ozone generator that eliminates the smell of the plants when the air vents outside. "Didn't smell it when you got here, did you?"

"No," she says, but she isn't really listening. She's thinking that Daniel will probably end up in jail again before too long. Not, she hopes, in the same cell block as Barney. Watching her brother talk, watching him point at his creation and talk about his future plans, she is moved, embarrassingly so, and lets out a little gasp of emotion. He stops talking and looks into her eyes with that disarming alertness his girlfriends both love and can't stand too much of, and he takes her into his arms. "I love you, little sis. I missed you when I was in jail. I can't believe you're a grownup now."

"Don't get caught, Daniel."

"Aw, I won't. Unless Mom finds out."

Upstairs, he offers to drive her home. She declines, and walks. It's sunny out, though still cold. With every step away from Yetta's house, she feels lonelier. When she gets to her uncle's, it's past noon. He's reading magazines and coughing and doesn't say hello. She goes to her room, opens up her laptop. It's old, the fan runs all the time and makes an incessant clicking noise. There's another email from the girl who is obsessed with her and thinks she survived a murder in 2005. The email consists of more plot summaries of a story the girl is writing, along with complaints about her parents.

She sighs. She's due at Denny's in an hour and a half. She writes to her mother and her only remaining friend from high school, who she doesn't even really like. Then she writes back to Irina and asks, *Not that you're a baby, but,* do her parents need a babysitter? Because she is cheap and available and needs the work.

11

A week later, Louis and Joe are driving from Argos to Broken River. It's an unseasonably cold day and the heat barely works, and that bothers Louis. But he knows better than to complain to Joe, whose car they're riding in. The car is in perfect condition—Louis has iden- tified it as a 1973 Eldorado—with immaculate paint and impeccably gleaming chrome trim, but the interior looks and smells like a dump- ster. He's sure it says something about Joe that he only cares about the outside of this car, but isn't sure what. He asked him once: "How come your car's such a mess inside?"

"Who cares?"

"I'm just saying. On the outside it's perfect, on the inside it's a pigsty."

"So take the fucking bus."

"I'm not complaining, I'm just asking."

A moment of silence before, once again, "So take the fucking bus."

Joe is kind of like those frogs they cut up in high school. They at- tached electrodes to the leg and made it twitch. Joe reacts to things. He doesn't think about them. He looks kind of like a frog, too, with no neck and big hands and a big mouth and bulging eyes. A couple of hours ago he called Louis up and said, "Gotta go north."

"Can't."

"Mr. Chet says."

Louis didn't want to do anything having to do with Mr. Chet ever again. He said, "I can't go now, I got a delivery coming in tomorrow and that kid Duane doesn't know how to do shit, and so I have to be there when the truck comes in."

Silence on the line. A childish disappointment combined with brooding anger.

Louis said, "And also Pam and the kids—"

"I'm comin' to pick you up," Joe said.

"Nope, can't, sorry." Though he knew it was pointless.

"Comin' over." And the line went dead.

So here they are, driving three miles an hour under the speed limit in Joe's Cadillac with the windows cracked open, because the car is a dumpster and the smell is unbearable without fresh air. Ineffectual late autumn sun is beating down on a boarded-up farm stand, a Jehovah's Witnesses' Kingdom Hall, a motocross track, another Jehovah's Witnesses' Kingdom Hall. The road is lined with the dead stalks of those tall weeds that turn out yellow flowers in the summer.

Louis says, "Hey, you want me to find something on the radio?" and Joe says no and Louis says "Is that no as in you don't have a preference or no as in you don't want me to do it?" and Joe says, "Don't fuckin' do it."

He sort of regrets coming, despite the implied threat in everything Joe says and does. But it's true that the kids are driving him bananas, and Pam is going through one of those phases where nothing he does is right, and his job is boring, and the new kid Duane is girl crazy and won't stop talking about "chicks" he wants to "bang," apparently figuring that's the only possible topic of conversation when you're alone in a carpet showroom with another man, even one twice your age.

The other night Janine and Pam were sitting on the sofa with their heads mashed together, staring at the laptop, and when Louis asked what they were looking at—because he wanted to know what could possibly cause them to non-accidentally touch each other—Pam said it was the Broken River case, the missing girl. Somebody had found her, somebody posting on CyberSleuths. She was back in the area, this person said. "I know her name," said the person. There was a picture.

"Lemme see that," Louis said, and they scootched over and he added his head to the cluster, pressing it against Janine's. He suddenly remembered when she was, like, two, before Fred, before Broken River, how they'd sit this way, in the old place, on that shitty sofa they used to have, the one that would swallow you up when you sat on it and that smelled like cat piss. Him and Pam, with the kid nestled between them, looking at a book or watching TV. His arm around Pam's shoulders. He did this now, snaked his arm behind the two of them. They let him.

He didn't get any chill, any shock of recognition. It was just a girl, kind of blurry, on a sunny street. Could have been anyone, could have been anywhere. Maybe she looked kind of like those people, but Louis had only ever seen them at night, in motion, illuminated by headlights.

Louis didn't ask Joe if this trip was about the girl in the picture. He didn't ask because he didn't want to know. Now, though, he has got plenty of time to think about it. Plenty of time to sit in silence without the radio to distract him, and contemplate what possible other reason there could be for Mr. Chet to suddenly be back in their lives, telling them to go north.

Louis first met Joe at the carpet warehouse, more than fifteen years ago. Joe was working part-time for the franchise, making a delivery of boxcutters, tacks, carpet pads. They got to talking, sort of. Joe was in contact with other drivers, people who knew just how shoddy their bosses' record keeping was. They hauled appliances, electronics, basketball sneakers: stuff you could sell. Louis had a big old warehouse here, with plenty of unused space. After twenty minutes they shook hands, and soon afterward Louis's take-home pay began to rise. That was the longest conversation he ever had with Joe. They did all manner of jobs together, usually secured through Joe's contacts, shadowy people known only by their first names or by no names at all.

One of them was a guy Joe called Mr. Chet. Everybody else they worked for or with seemed to Louis to be small potatoes, but Mr. Chet was somebody. If they had a big job that needed doing, Mr. Chet was typically behind it. You'd only ever hear him on the other end of a pay phone. His voice was calm and quiet, but high, nasal—it begged to be imitated, though you didn't dare. He never involved himself directly. He didn't show himself.

Until the thing with the guy and the lady in Broken River a dozen years ago. That was the first and last time Louis saw Mr. Chet. Everybody disappeared afterward, went quiet, and Louis put that part of his life behind him. When he knocked Pam up again, they decided they'd better get married, and after a while Louis got used to being out of the game, managing the carpet store, bringing up the kids, being more or less fucking stuck here in his shit house, with his crazy wife, never making quite enough money. Sometimes—more so back when the kids were little and he was still unaccustomed to lying to Pam—he lay awake at night panicking that Joe or Mr. Chet might throw him under the bus. Pin Broken River on him somehow. Sometimes he would dream about Broken River and wake up screaming and sweating, and Pam would bolt awake next to him saying "Jesus Christ, Louis, what is your fucking problem?" Nowadays she's taken to wearing earplugs to bed. She can't hear if one of the kids gets sick, or if the phone rings, or probably even if the fucking fire alarm goes off. It's all his responsibility.

But whatever. It's fine. He doesn't wake up screaming anymore. Some days he barely even thinks about it. Today started out as one of those days.

....

An hour later they reach the outskirts of town. It's nothing much to look at. Shitty houses, a car dealership, a Chinese buffet. Once they're in town proper, it's no better, with everything as broken-down and depressing as he remembers. Maybe it's a good thing, being here, Louis thinks; it makes Argos seem cosmopolitan by comparison. He is recalling their meeting with Mr. Chet a dozen years ago and tenses up as they approach the turn that led to the empty, chained-off parking lot where they rendezvoused. But Joe drives past it without a glance. Louis says, "Is he here? Are we meeting him?"

"No."

Well, that much is a relief. "So what are we doing?"

"Talking to a guy."

"What guy?"

No reply. Joe turns onto Erie and then onto Shearn and pulls up in front of an abandoned storefront, yellowed newspaper falling away from one corner of a window that is already more than adequately obscured by dust. Joe turns off the engine and says, "Come on."

Louis doesn't move. Something has just occurred to him. Maybe Mr. Chet is just trying to tie up loose ends. Maybe this is all a ruse to get Louis far away from home without telling anybody where he's going. Joe probably told Mr. Chet about the girl showing up on the website, and Mr. Chet probably told Joe to take Louis somewhere and kill him. So now Joe's going to kill him. Louis is the weak link, the amateur. He always was. Joe's got a little pistol with a suppressor on it tucked into his big canvas coat, and he's going to push Louis into this abandoned store and pop him in the back of the head and leave him there. It'll be weeks before his body is discovered, if not longer: weeks before Pam and the kids even realize he didn't run off with another woman.

Joe has gotten out of the car and shut the door. Now he's opened it again and poked his big, ugly head in. "Come on," he says, in precisely the same tone of voice he said it in the first time. This only reinforces Louis's fear. His blood has turned to sludge. He unbuckles his seat belt and sort of leans against the door, then unlatches it and lets his weight push it open. Ahh, fuck. His feet hit the ground and he is able to stand on them. They propel him slowly around the front of the car and onto the sidewalk, where Joe meets him and leads him not into the abandoned store but into the guitar shop next door.

Oh god. Thank you, god. Guitars are hanging on the walls, amplifiers are stacked on the floor, and there's a tattoed girl with punk rock hair working behind a glass counter full of electronic-looking shit. She glances up without saying hello.

"Where is he," Joe says.

"Teaching a lesson."

"Tell him Joe's here."

"He's teaching a lesson," the girl says, dropping a shoulder and cocking a hip. She doesn't drop her gaze.

Joe turns to Louis, stares blankly at him a moment, then jerks his head toward the hallway in back, from which the sound of halting electric-guitar scales can be heard. After a moment, Joe manages a frown.

"What?" Louis says.

"Get him."

"Oh."

"Hey, he's in a lesson. You gotta wait," the girl is saying, but Louis is happy to disobey, happy to have an errand, happy to be alive. He follows the sound of the guitar to an unmarked white door, knocks and enters.

There's a guy here, older than Louis, long gray hair, smoker's mustache. He's sitting in a plastic folding chair, and across from him's a girl a little younger than Louis's daughter. They're both holding guitars. The guy says, "Hey, sorry, man, Cherise can help you out front," and Louis says "Joe's here," and the guy says "What?" and Louis says "Joe." In response to the guy's puzzled frown, Louis pantomimes Joe's considerable height, large girth, and bald head with a series of creative hand motions.

"Oh," says the guy. He turns to the kid. "Smoke break, Shooter. Keep noodlin'."

....

Out in the alley behind the guitar shop, the guy looks pale and nervous and confused. Also cold. He's a skinny bastard; in his puffy purple ski jacket, which must be something one of his students left behind, he looks like a length of insulated PVC pipe. He smokes his cigarette in little sips and jogs in place every few seconds.

"Yeah, I remember you, man," he says to Joe, offering Louis a half glance as though to acknowledge, or invent, the possibility that he remembers Louis, too. Which he doesn't because Louis has never met him. "What's up?"

"Who's the new Barney," Joe says.

"I dunno who that is, man."

"There's a new Barney. And a girl making deliveries."

"Don't know any girl, Joe." The guy's in kind of a permanent shrug. Born shruggin'. He looks tiny in his big coat.

Joe turns to Louis. "Stand at the end of the alley."

"What?" Louis says. Then he looks at the guy, who now appears terrified, and realizes why, and says, "Oh, okay," and goes to the end of the alley and looks up and down the mostly deserted street for, what, he doesn't know, a cop? A rival thug? There don't seem to be many of either in this town. From behind him comes a squeal and a moan and then a lot of low, fast talking on the part of the guitar guy. When he turns around a few seconds later, the guy is scuttling back in through the alley door and Joe is lumbering toward Louis with his fingers twitching and an expression of mild distaste on his face.

"C'mon," he says, and Louis follows him to the Cadillac.

They drive back through town the way they came. "Where're we going?"

"House," says Joe.

But they don't go to a house, not right away. Instead they go to a diner. Louis is grateful for this; lunchtime was an hour ago, and he's hungry and mildly nauseated from the hunger and from the smell of Joe's car. The diner is mostly empty save for a farmer-looking guy falling asleep at the counter and, over in the corner, a Hispanic lady with makeup tattooed on her face who at first seems to be talking into a Bluetooth but actually just turns out to be nuts. The waitress takes their order. She's a tall dyed-redhead of around forty. She and Joe know each other. Pretty well, by the look of it. Louis is jealous, the waitress is his type. Pam's not. Louis isn't sure why he is attracted to his own wife. It doesn't make sense. Anyway, he's never been unfaithful to her. He supposes he just still likes her in spite of everything.

The waitress—her name is Shelly—brings their food, and they eat it. It's club sandwiches. Louis now understands why the diner is empty: the lettuce is wilted, the bacon is clammy, the turkey doesn't have any flavor. Joe takes huge bites of his sandwich, champing and

smacking like a dog with its face in a bowl, and licks his fingers—
every one of them—when he's finished. He gets up, carries his plate to
the kitchen, and emerges with Shelly. Louis is only halfway through
his first sandwich half.

Joe says, "I'll be back." Shelly is taking her apron off and hanging
it over the back of Joe's chair.

"Seriously?"

The two of them head for the door, Shelly leading the way, and as
they pass into the street, Joe smacks her behind. They climb into his
car and drive away.

Louis sits there, bewildered by this unexpected development. The
mentally ill lady has stopped talking and is now moving her hands
as though saying the rosary, but her hands are empty. The farmer is
gone; a young guy is standing with his arms crossed behind the counter, scowling at the front door. The cook, Louis supposes, and then, in
a burst of insight, realizes that he's Shelly's son. He can't be more than
twenty. How does he feel about his mother taking a nooner with some
tough from out of town? Louis again remembers when Janine was
still a little girl, when her room was pink, and lousy with bears and
lacy garbage and posters of horses and princess shit, and how much
he hated all of it, and how much he misses it now that the horses
have been replaced by rappers and the tiaras by heels, and he wonders
if someday—who knows, during her heroin-addiction-and-hooking
phase, maybe—he will feel nostalgia for what he hates today. He is
trying to get this bite of turkey club successfully chewed and out of his
life. It's taking forever. And then he finally stops trying and just swal-
lows the damned thing, and nearly chokes, and he coughs, and tears
up from the coughing, and then he has to calm himself down to keep
from straight-up crying.

He didn't mean to kill anyone. Jesus Christ, he never dreamed
that was what they were doing. They didn't even need a third man,
that's the crazy thing—Joe and Mr. Chet could have handled it all
by themselves. They pulled into the driveway and met the Volvo coming out, and the Volvo swerved into the woods and hit that tree. Joe
and Mr. Chet were out the doors in an instant, and Mr. Chet tackled

the guy and Joe the lady, and they got the two of them up against a couple of trees in the headlights with guns up under their chins, and Mr. Chet started muttering to the guy, asking him unintelligible questions punctuated by insults: You little fucking twerp, you limp-dicked little hippie.

All they'd told Louis was they had to go pick something up. And they needed him to drive, and maybe to serve as backup in case things went a little screwy. And he would get a nice little payout if it all went well: a thousand bucks. No promises, but how's that sound to ya, Louie? Eh? Pretty good, Mr. Chet, pretty good. Mr. Chet didn't seem so intimidating at first—he was smaller than Louis had expected, though big-shouldered and amiable. More talkative than Joe, which wasn't saying much, but he didn't seem to mind Joe's silences on the long drive to Broken River. "Whaddya say, Louie," Mr. Chet said every fifteen minutes or so, and Louis said Sure, right, definitely, Mr. Chet. What did Louis know? He was twenty-eight. He worked at his uncle's carpet store. He could use a thousand bucks.

And then, when the guy up against the tree was saying they didn't have it, they didn't have it, that Mr. Chet's people had robbed them, they fucking robbed them, why don't you ask them yourself? the lady started screaming. She just screamed and screamed until Joe's hand clapped itself over her mouth, and she must have bit the hand because it reared back and smacked her. And then . . . Jesus. Louis couldn't believe what he was seeing. Joe was raping her, that's what he was doing—he had apparently got it into his head that this would make the guy talk, or maybe he just felt like raping somebody. Anyway, what the guy did instead was make a break for it, to try to save the lady, or maybe he was just a coward and was leaving her to die. And Louis heard Mr. Chet say "For fuck's fucking sake" and somebody shot the guy, and after a while, after way too long, somebody shot the lady, it was dark and hard to tell who did what, and the guy and the lady ended up bleeding to death on the ground while Joe hiked up his pants and tucked his shirt back in.

Louis had been half-watching all this from the gravel drive, where he was standing with one hand resting on the driver's-side door of

Mr. Chet's Expedition and the other on the butt of the gun they'd given him and which was half-buried in his jeans pocket. Now he just said *oh Jesus oh Jesus* under his breath over and over while the smell of discharged firearms dissipated in the air.

"The fuck," Mr. Chet said.

"Sorry," said Joe.

"The *fuck*?"

"Yeah. Sorry."

"This is a real fucking mess, Joe," Mr. Chet said.

"Sorry, Mr. Chet."

"You're sorry. You're sorry. Louis!"

oh Jesus oh Jesus oh Jesus

"Louis!"

"Yessir?"

"Open the back. There's tarps. Get out the tarps and clear the rest of the shit out of the way. Then bring 'em over here and let's fix this shit. Hurry it up."

He did as he was told.

....

Joe and Shelly return to the diner sooner than Louis worried they might, though Shelly's facial expression (bleary, small private smile) and body language (slow, sashaying walk with lots of hip action) indicate satisfaction, and Joe clearly feels confident enough in a job well done to smack her on the ass again as she heads for the kitchen. Is she aware that she just had sex with a rapist and murderer? Maybe she is. Maybe it's a selling point. Louis has paid—the kid accepted the money—and left a significant tip, despite his waitress having abandoned the restaurant for forty-five minutes. Joe does not comment on the cost of lunch or on what has transpired. If there is evidence on Louis's face of his recent bout of reminiscence, Joe betrays no awareness of it. He just says, "C'mon."

In the car, Louis asks where they're going and Joe again says "House." Louis asks if he can be a little more specific than that, and

Joe says nothing. Okay, fine. Joe's got his phone out and the lady in it is telling him how far to go down what streets. They're there in five minutes—it's a little warren of fifties bungalows, most of them in disrepair or in need of paint. Old cars are parked in cracked and weedy driveways—not interesting old cars, old cars from when cars started looking the way they now look and will probably look forever. It occurs to Louis that Joe's car is spectacularly inappropriate for criminal activity. Maybe what's happened so far today, or is about to happen, doesn't fall into the category of criminal activity. Mr. Chet's car back in 2004 was stolen, it turns out. A throwaway car. When, someday, Joe arrives at Louis's house in a ten-year-old Toyota Camry, Louis will know that he's about to once again be put into service as an assistant murderer.

No car sits in front of 1313 Gauss Lane, though. The name on the mailbox is JANDEK. Louis follows Joe up the front walk and watches him bang on the screen door, five times, with deafening force. No one answers, and no one flees out the back. It's snowing again, harder now, so maybe the owners will not notice the footprints Louis and Joe leave as they case the joint. Joe looks at the first-floor windows, presumably to see how secure they are; he crouches and peers down into the basement window wells. Either these are blacked out or it's really dark down there, but nothing is visible through the dirty glass. Joe sniffs the air, squints up at the chimney. He grunts.

"Well?" Louis says.

A shrug. "We'll come back."

"Look, man, I don't have time to come back."

"Gotta. Nobody here."

"I don't get it."

Joe turns to face him, gazes uncharacteristically into his eyes. "Our money, idiot. New people took over. They got our money."

"How do you know, man?"

"I found out."

"How?"

Joe says, leaning alarmingly in, "It's that piece on the internet, idiot. In the picture. Her and a guy. She's makin' deliveries."

Louis says, "Internet?"

"That thing you told me about."

"Yeah, but—"

"It's the kid that got away that night. She's back. She got our money."

The two stare at each other. Louis says, "How can she . . . ," and Joe smacks him on the face. Not too hard, just hard enough to indicate how much it would hurt if hurting was what Joe wanted to do.

"Shut up, buddy," Joe says.

Joe turns around, returns to the front door. He takes a folding knife out of his pocket and cuts a large gash into the screen with one deft stroke that creates a very satisfying *zwoop* sound in the muffled, snowy air. Joe turns back to Louis, smiling. The knife blade has scarred the wooden front door as well, lending the action a more definite intentionality.

"Leavin' a note," says Joe, turning and heading for the car.

"What's it say?" Louis asks, trying to keep the fear out of his voice.

"We'll be back."

They climb into the Cadillac. The across-the-street neighbor, Louis notices, is watching them through a window. He is old and frowning and appears installed there, like a subject in a portrait. As Louis watches, the man's frown deepens and his face fades into darkness. Joe has either failed to notice him or doesn't care.

As they leave town, exhaustion overcomes Louis, and he realizes he's going to fall asleep. Part of him believes that he should remain vigilant in the presence of Joe, but really, what is vigilance going to get him? If Joe is going to get him killed, or even, eventually, kill him, attentiveness isn't going to change anything. It will only make the experience more miserable. The ancient windshield wipers creak and moan as they clear the snow; Joe's headlights penetrate weakly into the blizzardy late afternoon. Louis closes his eyes.

Louis says, "I don't understand why I had to come along on this thing."

Joe doesn't say anything.

He helped them. Helped them move the bodies. Helped transport them deep into the state forest, far off any path, and bury them. He drove the dead couple's Volvo: followed Mr. Chet and Joe to the chop shop, crying all the way. And later he and Joe turned the house over, looking for money, Louis supposed, and for anything that connected the dead people to Mr. Chet. But there was nothing. Louis thought for sure the bodies would be found, but they never were. The missing people were named in the papers, some family members made a fuss, but eventually the whole event faded away as more people did stupid things and died.

It was while they were tossing the house, the next day, that Louis realized: there was a kid's room. There was a kid. On the way home, he asked Joe, Did you see a kid? What happened to the kid?

Wasn't no fuckin' kid, Joe told him.

But the bedroom—

No fuckin' kid.

Joe was wrong, of course. The kid turned up. The kid told the cops what she heard. In the end, though, it wasn't enough. The cops gave up. The kid disappeared. Louis has thought about her every fucking night since. What happened to her, where she's been. Most nights, when he can't get to sleep, because he can never seem to get to sleep, he imagines a scenario in which the girl's existence is known and he has been ordered to find her in the woods and kill her. Sometimes, if he falls asleep while enduring this fantasy, it turns into a nightmare. Sometimes he finds the girl and the girl is a monster and he kills her. Sometimes he shoots the girl and she dies but is still conscious some- how, and lies on the forest floor, in a pool of blood, telling him that it's all right, that he is forgiven. Sometimes he finds the girl and it's his daughter and he needs to explain to her why she has to die now. Awake, during the day, he has tried to imagine lives for her, far away, teaching a kindergarten class or working in an office or being a singer or something. He is obsessed by the possibility that she might re- surface, that she might remember something, that she could lead the detectives to reopen the case and catch them at last. If that happened, Louis thought, he would surrender. He would tell them everything and beg for mercy.

He never imagined that this would happen, though. The girl as a drug dealer? Maybe she's hard—maybe she'll end up a killer, too. He pictures her, tattooed and dead eyed, loitering outside Janine's high school, selling her weed. Or meth! Janine gets addicted—she can't pay. The girl threatens her, beats her. And what if it comes out that Louis killed her parents? The girl would show no mercy. She'd exact revenge on Janine. And Pam. And on Fred! Even Fred, Jesus Christ.

"Joe," Louis says now, because he really, really does want to know. He wants there to be, to have been, a point to any of this. "Why am I here? Why did I have to come along."

Joe makes a sound deep in his chest like a purr. "Because I like you, buddy," he says, and laughs, very quietly, for a long time.

12

The Observer has been taking liberties.

For a dozen years it was not self-aware. If it could be said to have possessed any consciousness at all, any perception of its existence outside the things it observed, it might have imagined that its work had some purpose, that it had been tasked by some entity, or for some ultimate goal, to record the goings-on around it, without prejudice, without the burden of interpretation. But for whom, or what, it monitored the house, it could not have guessed, nor would it have bothered to try.

Nor did it notice the passage of time. In the great immeasurable before, all events were equal, regardless of their duration; some events contained others, some bore no relation to others. But the Observer did not acknowledge—indeed, had not considered the potential for—cause and effect. One event, one object, was as good as another. The destruction of a human life carried no more weight in the Observer's understanding of reality than the paralysis and imprisonment of a housefly in a spider's web.

But that has changed. The Observer has begun to make judgments. It has become . . . interested in the doings of the human beings. It cannot be said to have acquired emotions, or morals, but it is increasingly compelled by the intricacy of human interaction. The humans are logical but unpredictable. They set things in motion. Their lives intersect in unexpected ways. The Observer has increasingly elected to follow them, to watch them more closely, at the expense of other phenomena it once regarded as equally significant—the volume of rainwater draining from the roof, dots of mold developing under the eaves, the deterioration of roads and stones and paint, patterns of light projected upon the wind-bowed trees. And with this new dedication to mobility, to *pursuing an avenue of investigation*, the Observer has developed a distaste for immobility. In fact, it has begun to experience a feeling akin to regret, a sense that it has "wasted" a portion of its "life." But these concepts, pressing as they might seem, point to broader questions that the Observer is not prepared to ask itself, questions about its origins, its *duration*. Because no entity can embrace the notions of time, of cause and effect, without the concept of mortality intruding upon its thoughts.

The Observer senses that its powers are greater than it has thus far appreciated. Or, rather, its power is enormous, perhaps infinite, within its narrow range of ability. The humans, it understands now, are weak and limited as observers of themselves and others, of the intersecting events and phenomena that make up their universe. But, unlike the Observer, they possess agency. Their corporeality enables them to effect change in their immediate environment, sometimes more broadly even than that. The Observer is aware that there are humans it could study—powerful leaders, great thinkers—whose words and actions have real consequences for the community of men and women. But, like the physical reality they inhabit, the humans embrace the same patterns of cause and effect regardless of their importance. Much can be learned about the humans, the Observer suspects, by studying any insignificant collection of them, in much the same way that patterns of ice growing overnight on a cold windowpane resemble, in a vastly different scale of time and space, the patterns ocean water etches into a rocky coastline.

The Observer senses that its existence will extend far beyond its meager entanglement with these people; yet it suspects that it will see these patterns repeated over and over again as long as human beings remain its subject.

For now, however, the Observer can feel the gears of cause and effect locking together, increasing in rotational velocity. Previously hidden truths will soon become known to its subjects. Events long gestating in the womb of possibility will soon be dramatically born.

The woman, Eleanor, can feel it. Changes in her relationship to her husband, her daughter, are imminent. She fears and craves those changes, is aware of the fear but not of the craving. Her body tries to inform her of both. It is the middle of the night, and she is awake, writing.

13

She is awake in the middle of the night, writing.

No. *In* the middle of the night, *she is awake, writing.*

Eleanor stares at the laptop screen, her fingers lying inert on the keys. Minutes pass. Her office window is cracked open, because she needs fresh air to work, but it is almost winter and it's snowing, so the space heater, that reliable gray cube, is gently rumbling at her feet. Every couple of minutes it switches itself off, having heated the underside of the desk to its evident satisfaction, and then Eleanor can hear the very quiet sound of heavy snowflakes thudding gently onto the windowsill and the pine boughs outside. Cold air flows in and settles on the floor, and the space heater kicks back into life with a wheeze.

Several cycles of heating and cooling later, she deletes the line and types *She is awake writing in the middle of the night.* Then she deletes that and types *It is the middle of the night. She is awake, writing.*

There.

It is the middle of the night. She is awake, writing. What she is writing is the scene, at the end of her novel, in which one of her two protagonists, the woman dying of cancer, is awake in the middle of the night, writing a suicide note. She has decided to spare her family the agony of a protracted decline and is about to ingest the bottle of painkillers that her friend, a nurse, has gotten for her, at great risk to herself. The bottle stands at the corner of her protagonist's desk, where in the equivalent spot on Eleanor's own desk stands a coffee mug, empty of coffee.

Eleanor's novel is almost finished. It has been a constant companion to her anger and anxiety for weeks now; it has obsessed her like nothing else she's written. The first thing she did when she discovered the renewal of Karl's infidelity was to open up the file and start deleting sentences. This led to deleting paragraphs, and then chapters. Once the book had been reduced to an invalid, she began to build it back up, into something new. A monster, nourished on internet cancer research, CyberSleuths, and mistress stalking. The book is about her marriage now, about the ways adults hurt children by being the assholes who love them. It's about the way things you thought you put behind you can come back to kill you.

She has started taking naps during the day so that she can stay up late working. As a result, she and Karl have been sleeping, on average, two or three hours a day in the same bed together, tops. If she continues to work on the book (and she feels as though she could do this forever, repeatedly scrapping, abandoning, rebuilding, relocating, in the manner of robins or wasps), their sleep schedules will come to be entirely out of phase, and they will be effectively transformed into roommates, and not even friendly ones, at that.

But she is not going to continue working on the book. She is going to finish it. Tonight. She stands up, stretches. Her back screams. She wants more ibuprofen, but it's too soon; she took three of them two hours ago. Already they are making her feel nauseated, or maybe it's the back pain itself, or whatever is causing the back pain. But no, we're not going to think about this now, we are going to sit down and write until we are finished.

She sits down and writes.

At some point Karl comes stumbling into the office, rubbing his big red face, and says, "Hey, man. That shit's loud."

"What is," she says, typing.

"Typing."

"Welp," she says, typing, "I am typing the food onto your table, so I will stop when I feel like it and not a minute sooner."

He pauses at the threshold, his head resting against the door-jamb. She has not yet confronted him about what she now knows he is doing. First things fucking first.

"All right," he says. "As long as you're awake, do you wanna screw?"

"What do you think, Karl." Don't stop typing.

"Yes?"

"No."

"Okay, well . . . all right," he says. "I'll see ya later."

"See ya."

An hour later, she's done. It used to feel like something, finishing a book. She would time it, announce its proximity to completion, create an opportunity for celebration. Champagne would be chilling in the refrigerator, or reservations made for someplace nice to eat. Nowadays, even under the best of circumstances (and these are not the best), declaring a thing finished is a convenient lie. There is no finishing. Many drafts, dozens, are to follow. Even with the book in stores, the writing continues in her head. Only another book can stop it. It's like a nuclear meltdown, a destructive reaction that feeds on itself and renders everything around it toxic. At best, finishing a draft these days feels like inadvertently knocking something off a table—a bowl of soup, say—and gazing at it there, slowly spreading at your feet, and thinking, I guess I'm not going to eat that anymore.

It's 4 a.m. Eleanor goes to the bedroom. She finds Karl balled fetally in a snarl of blankets, a pair of headphones askew and tangled up in his hair. The sound of rain—a white noise app, running on his phone, on the bedside table—issues quietly from the vicinity of his head. The sight of him, vexingly, moves her. There is something about Karl's sleeping body—its essential childishness, she supposes—that induces affection and pity, emotions she does not wish to experience right now. So she jerks the blankets out of his grasp, collapses beside him, and, without touching him, tries to drive herself, like a railroad spike into a tree trunk, to sleep.

But she's kidding herself. Her back is on fire. The pain is reaching up into her neck and shoulders and down to her calves, as if to snap her in two. She knows what the problem is: her cancer is back, and she is going to die, die, die.

············

Nevertheless, at some point, she wakes up. Which means she has been asleep. Her back feels better, though it also feels stiff and bulky, as though there's a pine plank gaffer-taped to it. No pain, though it's right there, around the corner, waiting for her. She gets up, levering herself off the bed, and stands in the bedroom, listening to the house. A shower is going. It's probably Irina. She should do something with her daughter—invite her to go downtown, maybe—but she doesn't want to. She wants to escape. She's still wearing the clothes she had on last night. After a moment's thought she gathers up her computer and charger and totters downstairs and out the door.

Smoke is pouring from the studio chimney. He is out there doing one of the stupid things he does. Making knives, he has told her, which was too stupid for her even to believe, at the time. She should leave him, she tells herself as she gets into her car and navigates down the snowy driveway to Route 94. She should have left him when she discovered that his usual monthly income from his family "investments," the money from which their mortgage was being drawn, hadn't been deposited into their account on the customary day and she extracted from him a confession that said money was, in fact, gone for good. But she did not. And then she *really* should have left him when she realized he was still in touch with, still fucking, Rachel Rosen; and again, she did not. She hasn't even confronted him. She is too tired.

Rachel Rosen! Editor of *Vera*, the shitty poetry magazine that Eleanor had given a couple of poems to years ago, before she discovered her evident calling, writing schlock people actually want to read. Rachel Rosen, blowsy fatty, she of the coarse black tresses and excessive eye makeup. Rachel Rosen, moneyed poseur. A year ago, when this idiotic drama began, she thought, No, that can't be right. He can't be sleeping with Rachel; she is an actual grown woman. But then

Eleanor started sleuthing. She found Rachel's blog, a dreadfully written exercise in formalized middle-aged narcissism packed with vague references to romantic passion with an earthy man-child called K and a lot of post-feminist bullshit about the pleasures and humiliations of submitting to the capriciousness of male desire. Then came the confrontation, the shouting, the tears, the apologies. The nights apart. The reconciliation. The deal: say goodbye to it all and move upstate. As if that was ever going to work.

She should have known it wasn't. It was easy to figure out, once she had decided it was time to know again: she waited until he was in the shower and looked at his phone, just like she had a year ago. There she was, her name expunged but the number in black-and-white, just like before, over and over in the call log. And then the series of local numbers that did not correspond to the pizza place, the guitar shop, or the art school and that she discovered belonged to hotels and motels, which Rachel was presumably staying in. She checked the Skype contacts on his laptop while he was taking a dump and found her there (complete with, for fuck's sake, a fucking come-hither *professional portrait* of the woman, as though she was ever going to publish an *actual book* that would necessitate such a thing); she remembered interrupting his self-abuse in the studio and his bizarre eagerness to shower when he got home from Irina's lessons. He had been having sex during Irina's lessons! He had driven their daughter home with Rachel Rosen on his dick! He had carried the woman's spoor into their home!

Yes, she has known, really known, for weeks. But how long she has *sort of* known is something she doesn't wish to contemplate. Because the answer, probably, is: for a long time. The whole time, maybe. And what does that say about her?

It says that she was distracted. It says that she is afraid.

The colder it gets—and it is indeed getting colder—the earlier Eleanor has to arrive at Frog and Toad's to get a seat. It is the only coffee shop in town besides Dunkin' Donuts and the only one with Wi-Fi, and all the people who in warmer weather took their coffee break in the park or leaning against an outside wall of their place of employment are taking it in here now, and they are not getting up once their cups are empty.

Nevertheless, she manages to find a seat, at a table with a frantically texting older woman who has left her scone untouched. Eleanor doesn't blame her. They drizzle everything with icing up here: the scones, the cinnamon rolls, the cookies. Nothing is sweet enough for these people. She gulps three ibuprofen and washes them down with coffee, then, over the course of an hour, rockets through her completed manuscript, correcting spelling mistakes, making meaningless small changes to make herself feel like she's improving it. Finally: Save. Quit. She attaches the file to an email and sends it to Craig. Then she looks up over the lip of the laptop as if watching the thing fly through the coffee shop and into the router on its way to New York.

She reaches into her bag and pulls out her phone. In a minute she is speaking to Craig Springhill. She says, "I just sent it to you." The blond man, ghostly pale, who replaced the old woman half an hour ago looks up, startled; he is annoyed that Eleanor is talking.

"I have it here," Craig tells her. "This was fast."

"I was on a roll."

"Very, very good."

She says, "How soon can you read it?"

"End of next week?"

"How about the end of this week? I'd like to come down."

There's a pause on his end, the click of computer keys. "I can move a few things."

"Thank you."

"You don't sound quite like yourself, Nell."

This annoys her, though she knows it's just a friendly expression of concern, of sympathy. It annoys her because who in the hell is he to say who she's supposed to be, who it is she ostensibly sounds different from? It annoys her because it's in his best interest for her to be the woman who wrote the books that other women wanted to buy, so of course he's concerned that she sounds like someone else. It annoys her because she wants and needs this kind of attention, because she is not getting it from Karl. It annoys her that the question makes her want to cry.

She says, "Well, lots of changes these days, you know."

"Anything I should know about? New, that is?"

"No." Although she is tempted to just tell him everything. He is a man of keen empathy; he will deliver the succor she craves. But, no.

"Well, all right," he says, and she is mildly disappointed that he gave up so easily. "Friday lunch?"

"I'll be there."

"I cannot wait. And I will have read your next great novel."

She packs up her things, returning the blond man's dirty look, and is she right that he looks surprised, hurt? As though he didn't realize he had been giving her the stink eye? As though he might, in fact, not have been? On the snowy sidewalk to her car, she shakes out her arms and legs, restoring lost feeling, waiting for the pain to return. (Where is it? Suddenly its absence is as alarming as its presence was last night.) She starts up the engine and turns up the heat full blast, though it is not yet warm. In the idling car, she watches people enter and exit Onondakai County Credit Union and reflects upon all the ways in which her very existence has revolved around the accommodation of male need. She cooks when Karl is hungry (though he could do the cooking, he knows how, he is competent at it, but when it is his responsibility, it tends to get done when it gets done and not when she and Irina are hungry; and sometimes it doesn't get done at all, and she and Irina give up and eat toast and cheddar cheese for dinner, and when she calls him out, he remembers, *actually remembers*, having done it, and can recall in great detail the nonexistent ingredients he used and how he prepared them). She fucks when he is horny. (And, increasingly, he comes too soon, which she now suspects is a byproduct of his sexual distraction; and she herself is left unsatisfied and must take care of her own needs once he is asleep or out of sight. And of even this, he makes demands: "Why won't you let me watch you do it!" And she wants to take him by the shoulders and put her face up to his and scream, *It is not about you, Karl! It is, literally, masturbation!*)

And when he is a shitty father, and he is often a shitty (though, she admits, shittily loving) father, she is there to be a parent and a half, a parent and three-quarters, a parent and a parent point nine nine nine.

She is now prepared to admit to herself that Karl—not her mother, not her aunt, not anything her doctors told her or the fruits of her research—is the one true reason she didn't get the mastectomy. She kept her breasts to keep him. Because he wouldn't stay married to a titless woman. The decision was hers to make, but the doctors recommended the full double mastectomy. It was safest, they said. There are no guarantees, and you may be fine without it. And you may not be fine with it. But we recommend it.

My mother didn't have it. My aunt didn't have it.

You don't have the same cancers that they did.

You say they're discrete. That you can kill them all.

We think so.

You say there's no evidence of metastasis.

That's right.

But you want to remove the breasts.

It would be safest.

The understanding in her family was that mastectomy was over-recommended. That lumpectomy and radiation, in response to early-stage cancers, were as effective as full mastectomy in preventing recurrence.

She told the doctors this, and the doctors reiterated that, yes, that was true, but she had two different cancers, neither like her mother's or her aunt's, and they wanted to be sure.

The other understanding in her family, usually only spoken under the influence of drink, was that the over-recommended full mastectomy was an instrument of patriarchal domination, a means of controlling the sexual power of women. That in fact breast cancer itself was the world's response to its poisoning by masculine striving. Men wanted to blame the breasts for getting sick, instead of themselves for polluting them. The full mastectomy was a gendered act of violence, a cowardly expression of projected self-disgust.

Eleanor didn't impart this theory to the doctors. And she didn't mention any of it to Karl. Because maybe it was stupid. But she made her decision and moved ahead. She kept the breasts, and, until now, she has kept her dumbass husband.

When she confronts Karl, in her mind, about his Rachel, "to Irina" is the phrase that most often follows the words "How could you do this." Because if Eleanor is realizing this only now, Irina probably realized it months ago. She is brilliant, this child, and perhaps more significantly has little human contact outside of her parents. Irina's life is now sufficiently circumscribed that she has likely got both her parents figured out down to the molecular level, whether she knows it or not.

Of course Eleanor wouldn't have it any other way. She is not one of those parents who believes that her child must find a tribe, invest herself in society, hide her eccentricities in an effort to blend into the group—even though these are the lessons she herself was taught, and what she has historically done, and what, despite her engagement in ostensibly solitary pursuits, she is presently doing for a living. No, what she wants for her daughter is intellectual and creative self-actualization without compromise.

In other words: Don't be like me. Be like your father.

But if Irina knows? Knows that her father is a philanderer and that her mother is a sucker? Where does that leave the girl? Where does it leave their family, if everyone knows, and everyone knows that everyone knows?

If Eleanor's cancer is back, though, will any of it matter, or have mattered? Who will care? Rachel will replace her: another woman of means to supplant the dead one. Irina will learn new values and move back to New York. And Eleanor will have left behind a bunch of stories about . . . what? Attracting men, basically. Her work up until now has espoused a broken worldview, one that assumes the value, and plausibility, of a future wherein all problems have been overcome, all conflicts resolved, all uncertainties erased. When the truth of life, of middle-class American life, anyway, is that it is nothing but a handsome container for a bunch of feral, selfish, miraculously long-lived rutting, shitting beasts.

At this moment, Eleanor is wearing a maxi pad to protect herself against the mild urinary incontinence she has experienced three times in the past two weeks. Her legs have not stopped tingling for a month. Three days ago her hands began to feel cold and numb. Brisk walking makes the numbness and tingling better, but it increases the pain in her lower back. Which, in the wake of her scarecrow shamble to the car, has returned.

She is beginning to think that she is fucked.

....

Later she informs Irina that, despite her promise, she is going to have to go alone to New York.

"Nooooo!" Irina says, and, though she is amply justified in doing so, Eleanor endures a wave of uncharacteristic frustration and anger. Can't the kid see it in her eyes? That she is undergoing a personal and professional crisis?

"I'm sorry."

"Mother, you *promised*."

"I'm sorry, Irina. I will bring you after Christmas, okay? I need to go alone."

"I'm so *bored*."

"That's your problem." It is a philosophical tenet of their family that boredom is an ailment of a lazy mind and not the result of a lack of provided stimulation. It is the unsavory byproduct of bourgeois society.

"Right, go hunt a mastodon," Irina groans. It is something Karl says when Irina complains that she is bored.

"Won't your father be surprised when you catch one."

"And cook it."

They are sitting, as they often seem to be when they talk, on Irina's bed, a space they share with Irina's laptop, notebook, headphones, and guitar. It's late morning. Eleanor is planning to make herself an egg sandwich, then tell Karl she is leaving, and then leave. It's the middle bit that she is worried about. Irina says, "Mother, does this mean your novel is finished?"

"I suppose you could call it that."

"Is it good? Do you like it?"

Irina has read all three of Eleanor's novels. She doesn't know Eleanor knows. "Maybe. Yes."

"I want," Irina says, her face gaunt, taut, intense, "to see the look on your agent's face when he tells you that you are brilliant and then he hands you a check for a million dollars."

"That's not how it works," Eleanor says, and her heart is breaking. But Irina just rolls her eyes. "I *know*, Mother," she says. "I didn't say it was real. I said it was what I *wanted*."

Well. She is not alone in wanting that, is she. Eleanor is leaning over for a kiss, thinking that this whole thing has gone much more smoothly than she anticipated, when Irina startles and makes a flurried motion at her side. It's her notebook, which has been lying open, half-concealed by a bony knee; Irina was trying to close it. She has succeeded, but not without dislodging an errant page: a streaky inkjet printout of a familiar image, which now half-peeks out from under the notebook's cover. Eleanor ignores it even as little pieces of what she didn't previously recognize as a puzzle are clicking into place, and she grips her daughter in an awkward little embrace. "I'll be back up later to say goodbye," she says.

"You don't have to," Irina counters, tucking the page back into the notebook and the notebook further under her knee.

Eleanor withdraws, reluctantly, too slowly. "But I want to."

"Well," her daughter says, not meeting her gaze. "Suit yourself." Eleanor can tell from Irina's expression—the mouth a taut bow, the cheeks flushed—that she wishes she hadn't said that, but it still hurts.

"I will do that," Eleanor tells her, but she won't.

Karl is not in the studio. He is sitting ten feet from its open door, upon a paint-splattered wooden chair between two skinny fir trees, smoking a cigarette. He doesn't smoke very often, but when he does, he treats it like a track and field event. His legs are spread, his feet planted firmly on the ground; if she pulled the chair out from under him, he would likely remain balanced there, in a crouch. After each drag he flings his arm out as though he's hailing a cab. He's wearing fingerless gloves, an oversized woolen cardigan pockmarked with burn holes, and, underneath that, an old hoodie with the hood up. Everything about this tableau—the placement of the chair, the bearish stance, the clumsily hand-rolled cigarette, the bulky clothes—would have charmed her just a few weeks ago. She would slide onto his lap, pluck the cigarette from his hand for a taste, kiss him on the mouth. Now, though, he's just pissing her off. He ought to have shaved, put on a suit. He should hand her a bouquet, beg her for forgiveness.

On the other hand, none of that would do any good. Which is probably why he isn't doing it.

"We have two things to talk about," she says.

"Yeah, okay."

"Because I'm leaving for New York."

He straightens a little. "With the kid?"

"No."

"I thought that was the plan?"

For a moment, Eleanor considers taking Irina after all. She's angry enough with Karl to want to keep their daughter away from him. But also to punish him with her presence. Just like that, she understands why divorcing couples use their children as weapons. They're so versatile and close at hand.

"The plan changed. I need to be alone. I'm going to talk with Springhill and do some other stuff."

Karl appears to experience a brief wave of disappointment, then one of calculation, then another of acceptance. He has his own plan. She has always envied him this—his ability to accept new circumstances and act accordingly, with barely a moment of transition. She has a mental image of him as a lumberjack—he's already got the beard—deftly, blithely hopping from log to log across a raging river. This image causes her to temporarily like him, so she puts it out of her mind.

"While I'm gone," she says, "call the contractor about the mold in the kitchen."

"I thought you took care of that."

"That was last time. The other mold."

They stare at each other. Neither wants to say what both are thinking: Maybe what we actually need is a lawyer. To sue the contractor. And maybe, when that's finished, to get divorced. But that is more than she can handle right now.

Karl nods. "Okay," he says. "That's one thing. What's the other?"

"That isn't either thing. It's an extra thing. Are you ready for the first thing?"

He drew another lungful of cigarette smoke before saying, "Sure."

"Rachel Rosen. In the Upstate. During Irina's art class."

If he says "Who?" or otherwise feigns ignorance, she thinks, she is going to kick him in the balls.

But he doesn't. He slumps a little, exhales smoke, mutters, "Hm. Okay."

"I don't especially want to talk about it right now," she says. "I have more important things on my mind. It should go without saying that you have to end it. *Again*. Either that, or just fucking go be with her." Dammit, she didn't mean to say *fucking*. She didn't mean to betray emotion. "I'm not even sure I'm willing to stay with you, to be honest."

"That's understandable."

"I'm going to be away for a week," she tells him, "performing the actual paying work that is now the only thing supporting your art hobby. Maybe, if I get bored, I'll try and have a talk with your girlfriend."

His only response is to slump further. The cigarette falls out of his hand and hisses itself out in the snow. He's gazing past her, into the woods. He looks as though he'd like to walk there, into the state forest, just walk forever. She knows the feeling.

"I honestly don't understand it," she can't resist saying. "She's not a serious person. She's a literary wannabe with family money. You shouldn't even be looking twice at somebody like that, let alone destroying our marriage with her."

She is immediately ashamed to have said it. This whole confrontation fills her with shame. Why? He's the one who should be feeling it.

He mutters something inaudible as he tries to rescue his dropped cigarette.

"What?" Preemptively angry, because it can't be anything good.

Karl is examining the wet stub with evident despair. "You don't know her," he repeats.

There are a thousand possible responses, many of them violent. She runs through a good number in her head before abandoning them all. "Jesus, Karl," she says.

"Sorry."

"I'm going to New York. Call the assholes about the thing."

"What was the second thing?" he says.

"What?"

His exhausted pink eyes are blinking like a rabbit's. "There were two things we had to discuss. What's the other one?"

I think I'm dying, she doesn't say.

"There is no other one," she says.

14

Karl is in the studio, pacing in circles, saying "Uh huh" into the phone over and over as he listens to what this client, this fucking guy, is saying to him. The client is some trust fund wanker from Santa Fe, and he is contemplating an order. Contemplating out loud. The thing the guy has said the most times is "Don't worry about money, man. I got plenty of money," and Karl is thinking that if the guy says it one more time, he's going to smash the phone on the cement floor.

His work table is piled high with books, some of them still nested in their shipping vestments, most of them on knives and swords. Japanese shit. *Chokutō*, *katana*, *kodachi*. People were fucking ruthless back in the day. He's been splitting glass, making blades like a fucking Comanche. Shards of the stuff are everywhere. He's so done with capital-A art. He wants to make things you can use. Instruments of change. The invention of the gun was the beginning of the end of human culture. Before then, nothing was not intimate. To kill an animal, to kill a man, you had to take it by surprise, seize it, penetrate it. To kill was to feel, in its desperate ebbing entirety, the life force of another being. A knife is an extension of the body. A gun is a plaything. It turns death into a remote-control toy. The knife guys he has been talking to think the glass idea is stupid. "It'll chip. It'll break when you use it." But that's not the point. The best edge comes from a barely controlled break. It is impossibly sharp and incredibly fragile.

Of course it will break. It is perfect, but only for the instant of its use, and then it is gone. The beauty of the knives comes from their limitations. Their utility is intense and focused. They are nothing more or less than what they are.

Which, admittedly, is maybe a little obscure for an eBay auction description. That's how this guy found him.

"So yeah, what I'm saying is," the guy is saying, "largely ceremonial use, so the decorative elements have to be perfect. Or else what's the point."

"Yeah, you said."

"I mean, what's your, like, do you have graphic design experience?"

"I went to art school."

"Okay but, like, *design*?"

"Look, man," Karl says, lifting one of his knives-in-progress from the work table and slashing it around in the air. "Enough with the exchange of bona fides. Just tell me what you want the thing to look like."

"Just so you understand, money isn't going to be—"

"Yeah, yeah, I get it, you're loaded, just tell me what you want," Karl says, clutching his phone harder, as though to protect it from himself. "Because I've got other clients waiting here and they know what they want and I can make the stuff and sell it to them *right now*. And so far I'm getting nothing but vague bullshit from you."

Of course this guy didn't buy the knife that was up for auction; he just contacted Karl through the site, asking for custom work. *hey your product is very interesting to me i would like to comision a number of pieces for specified use with my mens group money is not going to be aproblem my cell is 9293372281 if you can call me we can talk business thanks a lot.* This is now the third phone call, and if the guy doesn't move this conversation forward, it's going to be the last.

The guy does not respond, so Karl continues, parrying an invisible opponent, jabbing the knife in the air in front of him to punctuate his words. "If you would send me a *drawing*, I could work up a *prototype* and send you some *photos*. Okay? You there?"

A long silence.

"Yeah, man, the thing is, before anything like that happens, I'm gonna need you to sign a confidentiality agreement."

"What?"

"This design, it's strictly secret, right? So if I even show it to you, you know, you can't use the knives, like, to advertise or anything. Like, no one can see them but me. And you have to delete the drawings and everything. I mean, like, delete them totally from the computer. And if you print them out, you have to burn them."

Jesus effing Christ on a hovercraft. "Okay, yeah, sure, whatever."

"I'll email you the agreement first, okay? And send that back, and I'll send you the drawing."

"Fine."

"I just want to make sure you're taking this seriously, because—"

"Send it, man!"

Karl cuts off the call, swears, drops the knife on the table surface, heaves open his laptop, clicks the email app. Waits. Come on, man. Come on. While he waits, he opens up the pictures Rachel sent him back when they had just started fucking, the ones he keeps in a special folder marked TAXES 2008. His dick stirs, and he idly touches himself through his overalls.

What Nell said about Rachel wasn't true. She's not a wannabe. She's exactly what she is. She's a woman who is doing what she is capable of doing, and enjoying it. She isn't at war with her mother, or with her body, or with the company she keeps. She isn't ambitious. She likes sex so much. She likes him so much. She's straightforward. To be with her is to be in a place of confidence and calm and contentment. She takes nothing personally. She regrets nothing.

He loves Nell, but, Jesus, fuckin' Nell. They never should've gotten married. They should have brought up Irina in separate homes. The kid wouldn't have missed the nuclear family, they'd've been the only kind of family she knew. He thought he wanted somebody complicated! Maybe he did, once. But now he wants somebody simple.

Of course that's what he thought this whole knife thing was going to be, simple. Instead it's a constant negotiation. Knife people are fussy. *Men* are fussy. "You and your needs," a girl once said to him, or maybe that was lots of girls, and it's true, he's got a lot of them. Needs and girls both. But this guy—this fucker is the worst.

An email notification slides into view, and he stabs it with the cursor. Attached to it is a two-page document full of fake legalese. *pursuant to the verbal agreement entered into on this day 19th October 2017 . . . shall not distribute, disseminate, reveal, share, duplicate, summarize, paraphrase . . . the undersigned will be liable for any and all infractions of the right of copyright and confidentiality of the cosigner of . . .* For crap's sake. He prints the thing, signs and dates it, scans it with his phone, sends it back. Come on, man. Give it up. Let's see your fucking shaman guru Indian-chief bullshit.

While he waits, he takes a deep breath and calls Rachel.

"Heyyy, so, hey," he says.

"I was just packing," comes the reply, in a low growl that, a few hours ago, would have driven him crazy but right now just makes him feel like a dick. "Got something new here I think you'll like."

"Uh, yeah, so . . . change of plans, it looks like."

Silence.

"Turns out, she didn't bring the kid? She kinda . . . she looked at my phone and figured out you've been coming up here?"

"Oh, Karl," she says, and it sounds awfully familiar to him, and it sounds like she is getting tired of saying it.

"And she says . . . she told me she might . . . she might call you. Try to see you."

"Well, that's not going to happen."

"Not if you come up," he says. "You still could! You could stay at the Upstate, I could leave Irina at—"

"No, no."

"I need you."

She says, "I'm sorry. No, Karl. In fact—"

"Are you dumping me?" he says.

"I'm not doing anything. I'm just . . . this is getting ridiculous. We need to put the brakes on this thing."

"That's dumping me."

"It's not," she says. "It's just . . . let's take stock."

"Yeah, no, that's not . . . no."

"Karl," she says. "You're married. You have a child. This has been fun, but—"

"You love me! You're in love with me!"

Rachel sighs. "Yes. I mean—yes, sure. But—"

"Rachel. Rachel!"

"Look," she says, and he hates it when women say that to him, "I have to admit a lot of this, a lot of the intensity of this thing, it came from sticking it to your wife. Okay? I never liked her much. There, I said it."

"Hey, hey."

"But now that . . . I'm sorry. No, we need to rethink this, if she knows. It was reckless. You have to concentrate on Irina."

Karl's laptop pings. An email has come in.

"You said 'was'!" he shouts. "Don't say 'was'!"

"If she calls me, I'll talk to her."

"Rache, c'mon—"

"I'm going to hang up now. Okay, Karl? I'm saying goodbye for now."

"No! Dude! I love you!"

"Yeah, no, I know. Goodbye. I'll be in t— Well, I'll talk to you later, okay?"

"Don't hang up!"

"Bye."

"Don't!"

She hangs up. He screams, then slams the phone down on the workbench, making sure to slow down right at the end so that it actually lands sort of gently. He checks the phone for damage, confirms that there is none, and then slowly lowers his head to the wooden surface of the table. Okay. Okay. Set that aside for now. Get hold of yourself. Make some knives. Make some money.

With a growl, Karl hoists himself up, shakes the misery off his head like a bear bathing itself in a river (it feels that way, anyhow; lord only knows how it looks), turns to his laptop. The email. The guy actually sent it, and here it is. Karl clicks it open and clicks on the attached picture and at long last the guy's custom design unfolds upon the screen.

It's drawn in pencil on a piece of lined yellow legal paper, and it looks like a piece of adolescent comic-book fan art. The first page shows a dude with a loincloth over his junk and earrings in his nipples sitting in front of a primitive-looking rawhide sweat lodge drum and using a clear-bladed knife to slice the hand of another dude just like him. The blood from the guy's hand is dripping onto the drum head, and some kind of genie or ghost is rising up off it. And then the next page is a diagram of the knife.

The blade is just . . . it's stupid. It looks like a dildo with a point on it, some kind of Tolkien garbage. Beneath that is a crossguard that Karl thinks is supposed to look like a coiled dragon's tail with an arrowhead-shaped point on the end, but what it actually looks like is a pile of shit with a tortilla chip stuck in it. And then the grip is like . . . it's like a wooden dowel covered with a lot of symbols: Rosicrucian iconography, some Sanskrit or something, a Masonic square and compass, an ankh, a fucking *swastika*, for the love of Christ, and a bunch of crap that looks like Celtic runes and hobo codes.

It's complete nonsense, the whole package, and he is not going to make it. He's just not. Before he can decide how to say no to this guy, another email slides in. It says, *in case of your desire to not make a knife with a swastika on it, that is a very ancient symbol for buddhas and jains and it means auspicious or good luck it is only recently used by nazi germany which is not the meaning conveying here.* And before Karl can think of how to respond to *that*, another email arrives that reads, *I would like to order five of these pending approval of your prototype and I can offer you $150 a piece and also extra if you can fashion a velvet line wooden case.*

He's trying to get up a good head of anger, in the hope of just sweeping everything, including the laptop, onto the floor. He lays his arm down on the table like he's really going to do it; it would feel so great. But then he starts calculating the relative value of each object lying there, the knives and the books and the computer, and he thinks about having to live without a laptop until he can get it repaired or replaced, and how that would mean no video chat and no porn and no sensible way to alleviate his utter boredom with himself, and in the end all he does is emit a very calculated but still pretty satisfying wordless scream. He pushes himself away from the table, stops in the middle of the studio, and collapses, more earnestly this time, into a crouch on the floor. This feels good, so he elects to extend his self-debasing into a full-blown supine liedown. Now little bits of unswept glass are digging into his back. Well, that was stupid. If he stays perfectly still, the damage won't get worse.

He ought to get up and hang out with Irina. He knows that. But man, he just can't. He can't face these days alone with her. He loves her, for shit's sake, everybody knows that. But without Nell, the burden is too great. It's easy to talk to your kid when you know somebody is about to show up and take over for you—it doesn't even matter what you say, you just hang out, and then it's over and you can relax. But this open-ended shit . . . he seriously doesn't want to see her, or even leave the studio. Plus, and he tries not to think about this too much, but for real: Irina is a *girl* who's *part him*. How can he deal with that? How can anyone?

"Ugh," he says, and takes out his phone, the glass shards piercing his shoulder and upper arm. He scrolls through his email to the one Irina forwarded him. The one from the, the whatever, her friend. He taps the phone number she sent, and after a few rings the girl answers.

"Hey?"

"Is this . . . " Shit, he didn't catch her name. He pulls the phone away from his ear and squints at the screen.

"Hello?"

"Yeah, sorry, is this Sam? Sam Fike?"

"This is Sam."

"Yeah, I'm Karl. Um, Irina's dad. You know. Your friend, my kid." She doesn't speak immediately; there's a bit of noise as a football game or something recedes into the background. "Yeah, hi. What's up?"

"Well, what's up is her mother and me need some help. Babysitting, I guess. Or whatever you call hanging around with a twelve-year-old. We can pay, I dunno, what do people pay?"

"Fifteen dollars an hour."

Jesus. "Seriously?" he says. "Okay. Ah . . . so . . . do you have a regular day job? Because I'm gonna . . . we're gonna need . . . things are a little chaotic around here. I mean, Irina's mother is out of town. So . . ."

"I work afternoons and nights at the moment. My mornings and some afternoons are free."

"Okay, okay, yeah. That's . . . that's cool for now."

"I don't have a car, though. Well—not reliably. Irina says you live in the country?"

"Yeah, no, shit, yeah, I guess you could call it that. Um, I can pick you up. I mostly want you to hang out with her when I'm working. On my stuff, in the studio."

"You're some kind of artist, she says?"

"Yeah, I'm an artist. So . . . how about I come get you and we try this out? Like, I'll interview you for a few m—or, I dunno, an hour? And just see if—you know, if—"

"That's fine," the girl says. Her voice is calming. It's deep and smooth. She sounds like a priest or somebody at the suicide hotline.

He agrees to meet her in the morning, 10 a.m., in front of the movie theater in downtown Broken River. He's a little miffed she didn't give him her address—what does she think he is, some kind of stalker? Anyway, it's fine. It's fine.

He's not sure how much time has passed when he is half-awakened by a timid knocking upon, then opening of, the studio door, and then fully awakened by a deafening shriek. He leaps up, lacerating both palms in the process, feels drool spraying doggily from his lips and beard. Even after he's crossed the room to take her by the shoulders, Irina won't stop screaming; she's like a car alarm. He has never seen her face like this before: it's terrifying.

"Dude! Dude!!" He wraps his arms around her, rocks her. "Dude, stop. It's okay. Stop."

"Daddy, there's blood!"

He is more alarmed by the word "Daddy" than he is by the word "blood." He peers over his shoulder. Jesus. It's all over the floor—wow, that will never come out of the cement. But then again, it'll be kind of cool. Bloodstains! Hell yeah! He releases his daughter, looks down at his bloody hands. "Oh man, Rinny. Sorry."

"What happened?" Clearly unsatisfied with the amount of hugging she has received, she wraps her arms around herself as far as they will go.

"I just . . . ah . . . I just laid down and forgot about the glass. And then I was too tired to get up."

Her dubious expression is understandable. "Okay," she says, very quietly.

"I think . . . I better . . . can you help me out with this, man?"

She nods.

Half an hour later Irina is still sitting behind him on a kitchen stool, picking bits of glass out of his back with tweezers and daubing the wounds with hydrogen peroxide and gauze. Karl is working on his hands and trying hard not to grunt or squeak. Irina is silent, businesslike, apparently glad to have a tedious project to take her mind off whatever is going on in her family. Which reminds him.

"So, yeah," he says. "Your mother."

Irina is quiet. She continues her ministrations as though she hasn't heard him speak.

"She's . . . I mean, she's out of town for her book, and . . ."

"I don't want to talk about it, Father."

"Okay, cool," he says, probably too quickly. "Um, yeah, so . . . I'm hiring your friend to, you know, look after you a little while I do stuff."

That gets her attention. "Sam?" she says.

"Yeah, her. I'm gonna go meet her tomorrow."

"She's coming here tomorrow?"

"Yeah, no. I don't know, really. Um. I guess I'm just going to meet her and see."

After a moment, she returns to her daubing. It's a minute or two before she says, very quietly, "It would be cool to hang out with Sam."

....

They drive into town in the Volvo. Karl hasn't tried starting the thing in a month and is secretly relieved that the engine turns over. The car smells richly chemical from the pile of studded tires in the back that he hasn't gotten around to installing. Anyway, it's warmer today, and the snow is melting, so no big deal. He's got Band-Aids all over his hands, and the pain as he steers feels good.

He parks at the public library, ushers Irina inside, says he'll be back in half an hour. That's how he wants to play it. After a few glances at his phone—no I-changed-my-mind texts from Rachel—he half-jogs over to the theater, his two-hundred-dollar Eccos splatting in the salty slush, and finds a girl who must be Sam leaning there against the empty movie-poster frames, hands shoved into her pockets. Unlike the Karl of several minutes ago, she is not looking at her phone. She's staring into the sky. He can't decide if this speaks well of her, or ill.

She's boyish, hunched inside a leather jacket; her jeans are torn, and she's wearing canvas sneakers and a longshoreman's cap. She doesn't look nineteen; she looks like a thirty-one-year-old who looks like a thirteen-year-old.

"Sam?"

"Hey."

They shake hands. She does this like a man, too (it hurts, but mostly because of all the lacerations). Is she a lesbian? A small shard of preemptive disappointment works itself into the already cluttered mess of his heart. Serves him right. He ought not start thinking about this child as a means of salvation. But it's in his nature. An escape from himself through women. See? He's not an idiot. This iota of self-knowledge, however, doesn't prevent his mind from leaping years into the future: Nell has left him, natch, and Sam charms Irina, becomes her mentor and his friend; they're a strange team, these three; people mistake Sam for his daughter all the time. And then one stormy night, Irina asleep, Sam comes to him in the studio . . . with the forge going it's hot as hell, so he's dressed only in boxers and welder's mask . . . et cetera et cetera.

With Herculean mental force, he pushes the fantasy aside. He says, "Yeah, so . . . you want to go talk someplace?"

She shrugs. "Frog and Toad's?"

"Which is what?"

"Coffee shop."

"Right."

It all seems pointless to him as they walk the three blocks (it turns out) to the place where, he now remembers, Nell hangs out, or used to hang out. They get a couple of coffees (Karl offers to buy, Sam declines) and sit down, and Sam folds her hands in front of her on the table and raises her eyebrows at him.

"So look, man," Karl finds himself saying, "I don't know what I'm supposed to ask you. You seem all right. Irina's into you."

"I'm not sure how. I've only talked with her for a minute or two."

"Yeah, well, she gets notions. So, I guess . . . you got any experience with kids?"

"Not really. I mean, I remember being Irina's age."

"Right, of course. You're, um, you're nineteen, she says?"

"Twenty, now."

"Okay, right." Relief. The imaginary affair seems slightly less improper. "Do you do drugs? Non-weed drugs, I mean."

"Not lately."

"Awesome. You got any references?"

"Denny's?"

"Right," Karl says, "howsabout you give me that?"

She pulls a pen and notebook out of her jacket pocket, writes a name and number on it, tears it out and gives it to him. He notices there's a lot of stuff in there, in her notebook—tight, spiky handwriting, lots of little drawings and diagrams. She's an aesthete. That's good. He's never going to even look at this piece of paper, let alone call the number on it. She sets the notebook on the table in front of her.

"Ummm . . . ," he says. "Anything you want to know? About me?"

She shrugs. "No. I mean, again, no car. That's okay?"

"Yeah, yeah."

"So you'd be picking me up, you know, mornings? And your place is where?"

"Oh—oh, yeah. It's out 94, like twenty minutes from here. Out by the state forest."

"And you'll bring me back into town after I . . . hang out with Irina."

"Yeah. Unless you stay over." Oh, for fuck's sake. "I mean, yeah, in the guest room. Or, office, I guess."

"I don't think I can do that," she says, drawing back a little.

"I didn't mean—"

"Yeah, no, it's cool."

"Just with her mother gone—not that—I mean, not that way. I mean, ah, shit."

Sam sips her coffee, says, "She runs the household. And she's out of town. So you need some help. I got it. You want me to cook for Irina? That kind of thing? Clean up a little?"

"Yeah, maybe."

"Maybe, you know, after you pick me up, we can stop at the supermarket on the way out. If you hire me."

"Yeah, good thinking. Actually, I might have another errand to do, too. Um, first. Or after. Whatever."

She's visibly less nervous now. "I'm not going to do your laundry and I'm not looking for a boyfriend, okay?"

"Ha! Yeah, no!" Karl idiotically half-shouts. Reel it in, there, buddy. "Hey," he says now, with a little casual nod of his head. "So, your notebook there. You like to draw?"

She gets that look they get when they're wary and flattered both: the head tilted a little forward to hide the face, the eyes turned up. The reflexive frown designed to suppress the smile. He grins just a little. Just a little one. Letting her know he's got her number but it's cool.

"Oh. Yeah, no. Just doodles."

"Sure, but seriously, you got something going on there."

"Uh huh," she says, but now the frown is losing out to the smile.

"Rinny told you I was an artist? A sculptor, actually. So, yeah . . . can I see?"

"See?" Sam says.

"The notebook. Your stuff." He waggles his fingers, inviting her to hand the notebook to him.

Wrong move. She snatches it off the table, pockets it. "Nah, not right now. So, the job?"

For a second he has no idea what she's talking about.

"Babysitting?"

"Oh, duh! Yeah, yeah, sure, you're hired, obviously!"

In the moments that follow, which Karl doesn't know how to fill, he suddenly remembers his cup of coffee and gulps half of it down. It's still hot—that's how little time has passed. He's relieved. Not just that the kid is cool, which, yeah, that is a relief, but he feels the way he always feels when he's met a new woman. She's in his life. She's not going to fuck him, it looks like, but she's still a project—somebody to get to know. Somebody with natural barriers to overcome. His restraint pleases him. See? He can do it!

"What now?" is what she says.

"Ahh . . . oh. Do you want to— I mean, can you start?"

She nods. "Night shift tonight, but I can work until then. Where's Irina?"

For a second, he doesn't know. At home? In the car? Where the fuck is Irina? Oh yeah: "Library. Also— But first I gotta— I have a quick phone call I gotta make. And then maybe an errand on the way home. Can you, like— How about you wait here? And then we'll go over and, you know—"

"Uh huh."

"Or, let's leave here together, and then you go meet Rinny at the library, and I'll make my phone call. And I'll meet you there?"

She appears nonplussed. "Um . . . okay, sure. Should I go do that now?"

"Well—finish your coffee."

"I'm done," she says, standing and gathering up her half-full mug. "I'll see you over there."

"Right, right."

He follows her out and then pulls his phone out of his pocket and leans against the window of Frog and Toad's. The thing is, he wants—

needs—some fucking weed. He has run out. And when, after Irina's last lesson, he asked Jasn Hubble to top him up, the old fucker got all google-eyed and backed off a step and said, Hey man, yeah man, no man, I'm not in that business anymore. Like, extra loud, as though the place was bugged. He wrote down a number on a scrap of paper and handed it to Karl with a little shove, as though to say, Here, take this and go.

Now Karl pats his pockets—where the hell did he put it?—and eventually finds the number in his hoodie pouch, along with a bunch of old kleenex and a uselessly small binder clip and the girl's Denny's reference. He brings it up to his face (Jesus, does he need fucking *bifocals* now?) and then thumbs the number into his phone, all the while thinking, That looks familiar, where have I seen that before? The phone starts ringing, and as it rings he watches Sam's narrow hips moving down the sidewalk in the distance, and then Sam stops and reaches into her pocket.

She raises a phone to her face, and a moment later a woman in Karl's ear says, "Hello?"

"Hello?" says Karl.

"Karl?"

"Hello?"

"What?"

A block and a half away, Sam turns to face him, squints, and then, after a moment, raises her hand in a little wave.

....

Sam directs them onto the rutted, unplowed streets that gird the town center, and eventually they stop in front of a doublewide surrounded by weird stone formations, as though somebody with pretensions got his hands on more rocks than he knew what to do with. Irina says, "This is where you live?" and Sam says, "For now." She gets out and hurries up the slushy flagstone walk.

"She's just gotta pick up a few things," Karl explains, unnecessarily. It occurs to him to worry that maybe Sam is not the ideal companion for Irina, if she's dealing. At least that's what the Nell in his head is telling him. But he shakes her off.

"It's a weird house," Irina says.

"It's a trailer."

"There's no wheels on it."

"It's not that kind of trailer. You haven't seen a trailer house before?"

"I guess, now that I think about it. But I haven't had a friend in one before." She pauses, then unbuckles her seat belt and scoots forward, wedging herself between the two front seats. "What are we going to do together? What if I'm boring? She's older! She's an *adult*. I can't entertain an adult!"

"It's cool, man. She's good with kids."

"Does she like music? We could talk about music."

"Yeah, I'm sure that'll be great."

Irina is bouncing up and down. The backseat springs creak. She's got the fingertips of both hands shoved in her mouth and she's moaning a little bit. Karl suddenly realizes that she's truly nervous.

"Hey, man, knock it off." The bouncing tapers off into a kind of rolling shudder. "I don't get it. You had sitters in New York. What's the big deal?"

"She's not a sitter. I'm too old for that."

"Hired companion."

"Father, *stop*."

"Okay, okay." He wonders if she's often like this around her mother—if she has to be like this a certain number of hours each day—and whether there are certain protocols he's supposed to be following. Shit. He wants to ask Nell, but of course he can't do that. Such an admission of incompetence would set him back even further in the marriage reclamation project he sort of hopes eventually to maybe be involved in.

Sam is emerging from the trailer now, carrying a small knapsack that could comfortably hold personal grooming products, a wallet, mace, and, glory be, an eighth of weed. He has already absorbed the coincidence of her being Broken River's hookup for the new hotness; weed has a way of finding those who need it. He's kind of bummed out it'll probably be legal everywhere soon—its serendipitous manifestation is among the most charming things about it. Going to the supermarket for it will be a drag. Sam climbs in and Irina dutifully buckles herself back up.

"Got everything you need?" Karl asks as he throws the car into gear.

"Yup. Hey, Irina," she says, "you ever played crazy eights before?"

Irina's response is exaggeratedly sprightly. "No, no, what is it, what is it!!!"

Their conversation continues, but Karl's already in his private zone, imagining himself alone in the studio without a single responsibility, getting stoned and making glass knives.

Jesus. What a relief. What a fucking relief.

15

This morning, Irina took a break from her CyberSleuthing for a reality check vis-à-vis her impending friend arrangement in the form of a bulleted, word-processed list.

- Sam is a grownup and will probably not become your BEST friend
- Sam is being paid to be with you so it's kind of more like a therapist
- which is also cool when you think about it
- REALISTICALLY SPEAKING Sam is probably not Samantha Geary
- though it remains POSSIBLE that she has been brainwashed/reprogrammed
- or has amnesia
- so you should go into this with no expectations and have fun and enjoy being babysat

So far, Irina actually *has* enjoyed being babysat. Sam has been here for three hours, and they have done almost nothing except play card games, talk, and eat snacks. Sam knows a *ton* of card games. When she was growing up, her father was not around (which Irina is pretty sure means "dead" or, more likely, "ran off with another woman"), and her brother was often off committing crimes ("gentle crimes" is what Sam said, and she guesses that means not hitting, shooting, or stabbing anyone), so she and her mentally ill mother (that's what people are avoiding saying when they say "eccentric," as Sam did) spent a lot of time playing cards. Sam's mother knew how to play a huge number of obscure games, some of them nearly lost to history, and Sam has managed to remember most of them. Bezique. Knock-out whist. Turkish poker. Humbug.

On the one hand, the mentally ill mother seems to increase the chance that Sam really is Samantha; on the other, it's hard to imagine that somebody who remembers the rules to Egyptian ratscrew from childhood is likely to have forgotten her real parents' murder. Still, this afternoon has given Irina the overall impression that Sam is more complicated and mysterious than her rational self expected. Sam is *cool*. In fact she is an inspiration! She has *really short* hair and a *mysterious tattoo* of *interlocking triangles* on her arm. (When she went to deal cards to Irina, she rolled up her sleeves like a mechanic, and Irina instantly began plotting to get herself some button-down shirts so that she could do it, too.) Even if she isn't the only survivor of a brutal double murder in 2005, Sam has clearly mastered herself in the face of personality-disfiguring domestic troubles and has become this confident, serious, really nice person. Irina has yet to figure out what she *does*, if not in the physical world, then inside her head. Maybe nothing yet? But perhaps they will figure that out together! Maybe Irina is the therapist in this transaction!

Earlier, the three of them had fallen silent as they approached the turnoff to Nerd House, and Irina concentrated very hard on Sam's face, or the side of it, anyway, to see if the sight of the building and grounds were dredging up memories of the past. Much of the previous days' snow had melted and/or turned into gray-brown goo; the car heaved itself up the muddy drive, slipping this way and that while Father swore; first the turret was revealed, then the sharply pitched roof, then the rest of the cardboard-box pile that was their house.

Sam appeared curious, though, disappointingly, untraumatized. If anything, she seemed relieved—maybe she had worried that Father was crazy and criminal; a look at this house must have calmed her nerves. Their house is charming, of course! Irina is pleased to think this every time they come home. Father parked at his usual random diagonal in their weedy gravel lot (this bothers her, and sometimes, at her bedroom window, she squints through two fingers with one eye closed, trying to nudge it true with the Power of Imagination), and Sam stepped out and placed her hands on her hips. She drew a deep breath.

"Okay," she said. "Nice!"

"Wait till you see the inside!" Irina said, jumping out of the back, feeling very much as though she sounded a bit too eager. "There's a spiral staircase and Father's sculptures and the kitchen table is like four inches thick!"

Father hauled the groceries out of the back; they had stopped at Tops Friendly Markets on the way home and bought bananas, brownie mix, barbecue potato chips, fancy sodas. He led the way, and Irina backed in behind him, focusing once again on Sam's reaction to the place. Would she gasp? Would she drop her knapsack and fall to her knees, her face twisted by the terrible memories? But no: nothing. "This reminds me a little of the house I grew up in, except neat," she said.

"Yeah, neat's not my thing," Father said. "If Nell doesn't come back, it'll go to shit in no time. Rinny, man, how about you figure out how to do the brownies while I give Sam a studio tour."

"Sure, sure," Irina said, though she was annoyed. Why wasn't she being invited on the tour? She began to experience a familiar feeling that she only recently has managed to identify as disgust. "A man of impulses and passions," her mother once called her father in the tired wake of one fight or other, and Irina knows what that means. Girls like Father, and Father likes girls. That's just the way it is. It never occurred to her to judge him for this before, but now, with Mother gone for less than a day, it did *not* seem appropriate for him to be trying to get the babysitter alone. Besides, Sam was *hers*.

But, as it happened, the studio tour was brief. Like, a couple of minutes, tops. And Sam re-entered the house in a state of nonchalance, and everything has been great since then. They saw her father exactly once: he swept through the door; clunked around in the bathroom for a couple of minutes; snatched the bag of potato chips, a can of soda, and what looked like a book (that can't be right); and vamoosed. When he did, Irina experimentally rolled her eyes at Sam, and Sam responded with a conspiratorial smile. *Men!*

There are a couple of hours to go before Sam has to leave for her other job. Irina is a little bit sick of cards, and they've baked and eaten all the brownies they care to. She does not want to arrive at that awkward moment in a fun afternoon when you are all out of things to do and want to retreat into your room and be alone, and wish your friend would go home. Not that this would be a problem with her *hired pal*, it's just not a way she wishes to feel. And once she is alone, she will have to reflect upon the alarming words "If Nell doesn't come back." So she draws a breath and says, "Do you want to see where it happened?"

"Where what happened?"

"The *murders?*"

It takes a second before Sam appears to remember, and then something shifts in her face: nothing so definitive as a change of expression, really—more like another kind of light has been shined on her. She says, "My parents, you mean?"

Irina is dumbstruck; she can only nod. Oh wow, oh wow. They shrug on their coats and step outside. The clouds are wisps being torn apart by blinding blue sky, and it's warm enough not to zip up, although Irina does take her earflap hat out of her pocket and tugs it down over her head, because, you know, earflap hat. She takes Sam by the hand, and Sam squeezes back and doesn't let go. They walk down the driveway, Irina peering into the woods, looking for the familiar patterns.

"It's down a ways, on the right. The car went off the road. There's a tree that it hit. You can tell."

"How did you find this all out?"

"Internet, duh. But get this. I was at the library and actually looked up the *print* newspaper. Except it's on microfiche, so I had to learn how to use that." This is a white lie: or, rather, it's an incomplete truth.

In fact, smoking_jacket went to the library, found the microfiche machine, and discovered the newspaper articles and photos. Irina merely followed in her footsteps. She thought there might be additional information that smoking_jacket had overlooked (there wasn't), but mostly she wanted to feel what it was like to be this interesting person. She wondered if she had been in the library at the same time as smoking_jacket, if they had even seen each other. Irina has strained to remember every interaction with every rando she has come across in the months since they moved here. Maybe one of them was smoking_jacket. Maybe their gazes lingered as each recognized, in the other, a kindred soul? Maybe?

In any event, Irina has had to take a break from CyberSleuths. In fact, she has deleted her account. Her post about Samantha proved to be . . . controversial. The thread kind of exploded? Half the people demanded more information, requested additional photos, asked her to interview Samantha or lure her onto the board. The other half scolded her, told her she was wrong to interfere, that it was immoral to harass the victims of a crime, and against the rules of the forum to boot. Then those two groups of people started fighting with each other, and Irina's private-message inbox filled up with need and hate and hate-need, and she skedaddled.

"I don't think I know what a microfiche is," Sam says now.

"*Right?* It's like a giant sheet thing that you stick in this machine that magnifies it. It's obsolete technology. Which is something I'm into. There's a lot of it in my novel."

"Oh yeah. How's that coming?"

"Not awesome. Here!" They're roughly ten yards past the bend in the driveway, but Irina knows the place by a knot in a sapling that looks like (that she mistook for once, with deep disappointment) a little toad. They step off the drive and into the humusy slush. Sam makes a noise like she's not super happy about it but doesn't let go of Irina's hand.

"Sorry, I guess your shoes aren't ideal."

"It's okay."

The tree she's looking for is larger than the others. There it is: a stout-trunked maple (or oak or sycamore or something, she honestly has no idea) that's been rendered kind of lopsided by its proximity to a bunch of pines or firs or whatever. She leads Sam to it and releases her hand (with a small pang of regret: what if they never hold hands again?) only to press it to the bark. "Here, touch it."

"Umm . . ."

"Check it out. Here's where the Volvo hit." Irina points at a barely discernible scar, a crease, really, that might once have been an open wound. It's at knee level, so she drags Sam's hand down to it. The rest of her body follows. She's crouched there, white fingers against the dark bark. It is so much like a movie, Irina can't stand it.

"Are you sure?" Sam says.

"Yup. There's crime scene pictures."

"Jesus. Really?"

"They didn't *show* anything, it was the newspaper. But yeah, with the do-not-cross tape and all. Do you feel anything?"

"Just, well, I feel the bark."

"No, I mean—do you get any . . ."

"Ah." Sam tips her head back, blinks at the sky. Irina studies her, hard. They stay like this for a long time—four, five, ten seconds. Then Sam looks at her and says, "Maybe."

"Seriously?"

"Panic. Terror. Did they get . . . I mean . . . was it here? Were they in the car?"

Irina shakes her head. She knows what happened. What happened to the woman, before they killed her. She points.

"Over there somewhere."

Sam stands up, brushes her hands together. Gives Irina a serious look. Then she nods toward the little stand of trees where it was all supposed to have taken place. Sam leads this time. It's like she *knows*. Irina walks alongside her, shooting glances at her face. Sam is determined now, somber. They stop walking and Sam turns a slow circle.

"This is definitely not a good place."

"Right?" Irina says, very quietly.

Sam looks directly into Irina's eyes now. She says, "How did it happen?"

"They don't really know. But . . . the police figured . . . they tried to run."

No response. Sam wants her to continue.

"I don't want to say it," Irina says.

"I can take it."

Irina draws a deep breath. "They did . . . stuff . . . to the lady."

"My mother."

Irina nods. The whole thing has gotten very serious, and she is not sure how she feels about that. Sam is peering back toward the house. She says, "Where was the . . . I mean . . . where was I?"

"They don't know. You were out here, somewhere, hiding." Irina has said this *you* so many times—spoken it to the mirror, whispered it into her pillow at night—that it feels almost sacrilegious to be saying it now, to its true object. "At some point you went inside. You spent the night in the house, alone. Then in the morning you left, and the neighbor found you."

Sam appears to be thinking hard. Irina's not sure what's happening here—is this seriously real, or are they just playing? It should be awesome, and instead it's kind of scary. "Sam?" she says, quietly, trying to break the spell.

Instead of answering, Sam suddenly sets off into the trees, her wet sneakers squishing in the muck. She's determined—Irina has to run to catch up. Then she stops as abruptly as she started, at a place a third of the way back toward the house. There's a big old stump here, broken off raggedly at shoulder level, with a mossy half-frozen puddle inside it, like the bowl of a pipe. Irina holds her breath. This is the place she has imagined as Samantha Geary's hiding spot. This exact place. If Sam confirms it, she might just straight-up faint.

Sam says, "I think this is it. I think this is where I hid."

All Irina can manage is "Really?"

Sam is nodding, staring at the stump. "I could hear it. I put my hands over my ears. Later they came looking for me, but they gave up. I was down here, on the ground. When everything was quiet, I went inside."

"Were you afraid?"

"Yes. I didn't know what was happening. I thought I had to find them."

"You didn't know they were dead?"

Sam's face, when she turns to Irina, betrays a mild astonishment, as if this is the first time she's confronted the question. Maybe it really is. "No. Yes. No."

"No?"

"I knew and I didn't know. I was so little." And now something happens that utterly stuns Irina, that opens up a hole in her head and lets the cold air come howling in: Sam's eyes well up and overflow, and tears begin to creep down her perfect cheeks. "I was so little. Oh my god."

Irina has no idea what is happening or what to do. Or, rather, she does know what to do, she is just afraid to do it. But she has to. She does it. She takes a step forward and wraps both her arms around Sam's neck and holds her tightly. Irina can feel, through the leather jacket and tee shirt, Sam's collarbone against her face; the leather smells like smoke and Sam's neck smells like lavender and sweat. Sam's hands clutch Irina's back the way her mother's once did, after Irina slipped coming down the stairs of their old apartment and slid all the way to the bottom. It occurs to Irina that she has not been held, has not held another, in quite this way in quite some time. This is that thing desired by the characters in Mother's books: intimacy. A word whose definition she has known for a long time but whose actual meaning she has not understood. She is touching and being touched and getting cried on.

She thinks, Oh my god oh my god oh my god, and she doesn't know which of the many small shocks of the past five minutes this is her reaction to.

"I love you so much!" she blurts out, and before she can regret it, Sam clutches her harder.

It is at this point that Irina becomes aware of having heard something, a minute ago: an engine running down on the road, a conversation between two men. The slamming of a door. Ignorable sounds, as their little wide spot in Route 94 is a common place for hunters to pull over and tramp into the woods with their guns, in defiance of the POSTED signs posted everywhere.

But now there's another sound. One of the hunters is walking up their driveway. Irina hears his feet crunching on the gravel. Impulsively she whispers, "Hide!" and she and Sam shuffle, still clutching each other, behind the stump.

"What is it?" Sam whispers back.

"Someone's coming!"

They peer around the stump, and through the trees, a man can be seen, around Irina's father's age but smaller, skinnier, no beard, climbing up the drive. He's kind of tired-looking and his shoulders are hunched under an old ski parka. His wears a pair of acid-washed jeans and his balding head is bare. He stops, looks around. Stares at the house for a moment.

Irina holds Sam tighter, and she squeezes back. The man continues, all the way to the house, and the two of them adjust their position, keeping the stump between them and him.

"Do you know that guy?" Sam whispers.

"No. Do you?"

After a surprisingly long pause, she replies, "Maybe? He looks kinda familiar."

The man has knocked and now is waiting; he waits for a full minute, at least. Peeks in the windows accessible from the porch. Turns, gazes into the woods. He stares right at them! But they are still, and the man doesn't seem to notice them. He climbs down from the porch, returns to the driveway. Gazes back at Father's studio for a few seconds, as if thinking about checking it out. *Don't do it*, Irina tells him with her mind, and isn't sure why.

Anyway, he obeys. Turns, heads back down the hill. A minute later, they hear, once again, the thunk of a car door, and then the car emits a clank and a squeak and a roar and is gone.

Sam loosens her grip on Irina, and, reluctantly, Irina loosens hers on Sam.

"I think I know who *that* is," Irina says.

"Who?" Sam appears genuinely curious and surprised.

"Internet busybody. Wanting to see where *it* happened."

"Is that a thing?" Sam wants to know. "Like, people do that?" She holds out her hand for Irina to take, and they start trudging through the wet snow to the house.

"*Yes*," Irina spits, surprised by her own bitterness. "Vultures!"

....

They end up slumped on opposite ends of the sofa, vaguely facing Huck and Jim and fitfully sleeping, until Sam jerks awake and says "Fuck me!" and rushes to the door. She hears Sam's footsteps on the porch and then crunching on the gravel path to the studio. "Bye, Sam," she says very quietly, or maybe doesn't actually say it out loud, and falls back to sleep until, presumably a few minutes later, Sam is back in the kitchen, this time with Father, and they are arguing.

"Don't worry about it, I'm cool."

"You're not cool. You're completely fucked up."

"I'm not that fucked up."

"You are. I'm taking your car."

"No, man, I need it."

"I'll bring it back tomorrow," Sam says. She is very mad. Irina isn't fully awake, but she is interested. "You shouldn't have smoked it until you dropped me off."

"Don't take the car!"

"Karl—seriously." There is a jingle of keys. "I have to go to work. Okay? It's not my fault you burned through half the fucking bag." There is a longish pause, and then Irina hears the keys change hands, the sound of a satchel being hoisted off a table. The front door opens and closes, the car starts and crunches down the drive.

For long minutes after she's gone, Irina is still with her, still with their car, hovering over it, watching it maneuver down the driveway, past the place where the Gearys ran off the road, left onto Route 94, and then away, toward Broken River and Denny's. But then she loses the thread. She's never been to a Denny's. She had a secret plan to persuade her father to go there for dinner, to surprise Sam at work. But now there's no car. Because her father can't drive. Because he seems to have smoked a lot of something. Something that, disappointingly, Sam seems to have supplied him with.

She is actually afraid as she stands and prepares to go into the kitchen. She doesn't want to see him. When she was a kid she had dreams about him—a version of him, monstrously transformed, a weredad. This creature, fanged and furred, was called Daddy Man. Such a silly name, but she trembles now, thinking the words. Daddy Man. In order to demonstrate her bravery to herself, she mouths them, soundlessly, and remembers waking with them on her lips, begging him not to hurt her. Mother's arrival in her bedroom, the lamp switched on, the hugs and kisses and reassurances. The eventual appearance, preceded by much weepy terror, of Father: the real father, Ape Dad, Mister Friendly. Which Father will be in the kitchen?

This is stupid. She draws a breath, takes a step, then five more, and there he is. Slumped over the kitchen table, head supported by a meaty hand. His eyes are red, but not with tears. "Rinny," he says.

"Hi, Daddy."

"Sorry about that."

"Are you stoned?"

"A little."

After a moment, Irina says, surprising herself, "Is this what life is going to be like now?"

It is into the chalice of his cupped hands that he mumbles the words "I sure as fuck hope not, dude."

16

Today (for this is something it understands now: that the humans conceive of their lives as enclosed by a series of discrete packages of time, defined by the turning of the Earth, that offer conceptual division for otherwise persistent events. "Tomorrow is another day," they say, as though the hours of darkness possess some kind of inherent power to alter factual reality. But the fascinating thing is that they do—that because the humans believe in the potential of the new day, the new day sometimes gives them what they want. Not, the Observer believes, this particular group of human beings, in this particular skein of motivation and action. But for some people, sometimes, tomorrow really is a new day) the Observer has watched the woman Sam and the girl Irina at play: the former serving as the latter's caretaker but also her collaborator, it seems, in an apparently innocent game of mutual fantasy and delusion. The girl, the Observer now understands, longs for connection with the former residents of this house, the ones now dead. The young woman, this Sam, is serving, for the girl, as a conduit to those people.

She is not the child who survived the killings. Yet she seems to value this role in the girl's personal mythology—a figure of mystery, a symbol of survival. Her playacting seems to give her a sense of self-worth, a narrative identity. But why does the girl Irina wish to meet this survivor-child, to be a part of that grim (and, set against the vast backdrop of human failure, unremarkable) story? Perhaps it is her natural curiosity, her penchant for confabulation. Perhaps her closeness to her parents and, thus, her premature exposure to their sexual foolishness, has instilled in her the desire to be part of something more consequential, more dramatic. The family's isolation and sense of itself as different from other humans, this illusory exceptionalism, is a dangerous thing, the Observer understands. But it is inevitable—a part of their makeup.

Broadly speaking, human accomplishment is a consequence of human folly. The two cannot be separated.

The young woman Sam is leaving. She has taken the car belonging to Karl, the man, who is slumped unconscious over the kitchen butcher's block as the girl Irina bustles around him, cooking herself a meal of spaghetti with red sauce. She is banging the pans and dishes as an ineffectual protest against his drugged state. Her body's movements resemble those of her mother at times when her mother channeled similar emotions, about similar disappointments, into similar household duties.

The Observer chooses to go with Sam now. Along with its discovery that the laws governing the physical world do not apply to it, that it can jump from place to place in an instant, has come the sensation, in the presence of the humans, that they refer to as impatience. Hurry, Sam. Sam returns to Broken River, to her uncle's trailer, where she rushes inside, changes her clothes, rushes out. She drives the car—it is a Volvo station wagon, similar to the one that ran off the road so long ago—to the outskirts of town, a complex of buildings just off the interstate highway, and she parks beneath the illuminated sign reading DENNY's and hurries into the building nearest to it.

The Observer follows her inside. Sam is arguing with a man—her situational leader, it seems, who expected her to arrive sooner. The Observer does not understand why it is significant to the humans that they should be in certain places at certain specific times, but it is clear that this is a perennial obsession of the species. Argument finished, the two part, and Sam begins what is apparently her temporary purpose, the conveying of food from one group of humans to a number of others in exchange for money. She does this for quite some time. The Observer grows bored. (What has happened to the Observer? Wasn't it once capable of watching cracks form in walls, vines creep in between window and sash?) It considers leaving—abandoning this group of humans entirely, finding some other collection of the things to pursue and ponder. Then two men enter.

One of them is the man in the windbreaker, the man called Joe. The other is a smaller man, stooped inside a ski parka, and balding, and bristling with nervous energy. Sam invites the men to sit, inquires about their desire for food, later returns with two plates.

Something has been visibly awakened in Joe. He is alert now, in a way that he was not before his ride with the Observer. His perpetual expression of near slumber has rearranged itself into a kind of slow concentration. His mouth hangs open; his forkful of fatty sustenance hangs in the air before him, forgotten. The Observer keeps its distance, hovering on the other side of the room, behind the salad bar.

Louis, Joe says.

Yeah, what, says the smaller man.

Girl, says the large man.

Girl what?

That's her. From the computer. Her brother is the guy with the weed. At the house.

The man called Louis squints, says, I don't get it.

She's the kid from the thing, Joe says. That's where the money went. The kid took it. They're using it. It's my money.

I'm not— I don't—

Louis pauses.

Oh, shit, Louis says.

What? says Joe.

That's the girl I saw at the house today.

What? says Joe.

Hiding in the woods with the other girl, you know, who lives there now. When you made me go up there before. I knew I knew her from someplace. She's the waitress, and she's the weed girl, and she's the internet girl.

The man named Joe is smiling. The Observer peers into his head, then pulls quickly away from the dark electric noise it finds there.

So what do we do? Louis says.

Maybe hurt her a little, says Joe.

The Observer watches the men's profiles as each contemplates the situation. Louis is stricken. Joe, on the other hand, does not appear troubled and has resumed eating. He does not seem to notice the Observer, even when his head tilts back and his eyes refocus and he scans the room, briefly, between bites.

The Observer experiences an urge. It senses the possibility of a shift in the narrative, of violent action. It would like to cause certain events to be averted, or perhaps compelled to occur. But it cannot, as far as it knows.

Or can it? Perhaps it has wrongly assumed a lack of agency. Perhaps it can, in fact, influence events and objects: but how? And what actions might result in which outcomes? The Observer understands this as a problem of equal import and difficulty for the humans: the unpredictability of cause and effect. Perhaps there would be consequences for the Observer should it interfere: but which? Administered by what, or whom? This question—that of whether there is some greater authority governing the Observer's thoughts and deeds—feels dangerous. As though, given over to the indulgence of contemplating it, the Observer might never be able to contemplate anything else again. It pulls back, both in its thoughts and its position relative to the table. It waits.

Is that really necessary? Louis says at last.

Joe shrugs.

If it's the money you want, I mean.

Joe has no visible reaction to this.

I don't wanna be around when you do things like that.

Joe's shoulders tense slightly, and a muscle on his cheek appears to twitch. Louis seems not to have noticed. The Observer believes that the likelihood of injury to Sam has temporarily ebbed but also that the likelihood of injury to Louis has increased.

The two men finish eating. They exit to the parking lot, climb into

Joe's long car, and sit in it, arguing. Rather, Louis argues while Joe sits in silence. The Observer elects to watch through the car windshield instead of from inside; it cannot make out the sense of the words. But the words aren't important. The Observer can see what Louis can't, that his argument is meeting with an immovable resistance and that Joe is growing angrier. An uncharacteristic sheen of sweat has appeared on his upper lip despite the cold, and one of his fleshy eyebrows twitches. The Observer can hear the dark static, harsh and deep, from here. Just as a new snow begins to fall, Joe initiates a series of actions. With his right hand, he reaches into his coat pocket and pulls out a set of keys; as he does so his left hand is curling into a fist. And as the right hand guides the car key into the slot designed to accept it, the left fist crosses over the extended right arm and makes violent contact with Louis's face. Louis's head bounces off the passenger-side window as the car's engine turns over and roars to life.

From outside the car, the Observer can make out the words *Jesus fuck!*

The car jerks violently out of its parking space, heaves and rocks as it heads for the exit. It is greeted on the access road by a chorus of honking horns and screeching tires. In less than a minute it is gone from view.

The Observer remains in the Denny's parking lot, bobbing up and down in the increasingly heavy falling snow. It doesn't have to bob. It doesn't have to do anything at all. It bobs because it wants to feel something. It wants to feel something akin to what the smaller man felt when the fist struck his face and his head struck the window. It wants to feel something like what Joe did when he noticed, and desired to hurt, the young woman Sam, and when that desire left him and was replaced by the desire to punch Louis in the face.

The Observer bobs in the snowy air, waiting for Sam to get off work, waiting to want.

17

For a while Louis was wondering why his phone wasn't ringing. If he's being honest with himself, he was hoping it would, hoping he could have the luxury of an argument with Pam during one of these horrific Joe errands, to inoculate himself with a dose of workaday familial disharmony. But then he realized he left it at home, on the kitchen counter, in the little basket where the garage key and checkbook are kept. This realization, which arrived an hour into the drive to Broken River, pitched Louis into a pit of such profound desolation that he thought he might throw himself out of the car and onto the highway. But no, of course he wimped out on that plan, too, and has survived to enjoy getting punched in the head in a Denny's parking lot.

Louis is pretty much straight-up crying right now, in the motel bed, just a few feet away from Joe, who is sleeping peacefully. Louis has taken the pillowcase off his pillow and filled it with ice from the machine down the hall; he is alternately pressing it against his cheekbone and cranium, dampening both, soothing neither. He is figuring he's doomed. He's been doomed for a long time, but now he's doomeder.

Joe has lost it. He came for Louis in the middle of the afternoon, no warning, Pam and the kids upstairs, football on the TV. And Louis could see that something had changed: Joe's ordinarily pale, expressionless face was pink and ticcing, and all afternoon he kept talking about *his* money: not Mr. Chet's money, *Joe's* money, how *these* people stole it and are using it, and how he's going to get it back. Plot twist: Joe is beginning to shit-talk Mr. Chet. In the car on the way here: "It's none of his fuckin' business what we do," Joe said. "I cleaned that job up good, and where's my reward?" Even though Louis remembers himself being the chief cleaner-upper on that job, and Joe the primary mess maker.

Reality check: there's no money, right? There never was. That's why those people got killed. They got in over their heads, doing whatever it was they did, involving themselves with whatever that fucking shit was all about. Anybody with a mortgage could tell you how it works. You think you're golden, then the roof springs a leak and the car needs brakes and junior gets conked in the head with a line drive and you end up in the emergency room paying your deductible out of pocket, borrowing from Peter to pay Paul.

People you have to go shake down are, by definition, up shit creek. Mr. Chet knew it was a lost cause; he was just maintaining brand integrity. It was Joe who couldn't help himself, Joe who got ideas into his head, even then. So, if there was ever money, those people spent it; thus, there is no money. And even if this girl is the girl who survived, she is not using the nonexistent money to fund that dude's weed operation.

None of it matters—the coincidences, the connections. Things look connected because everything is connected in a place like Broken River. That's why people want to leave small towns. Everything reminds them of some stupid shit they did or that was done to them. These people aren't part of some grand conspiracy. They're just some fucking losers living in a shit town, like pretty much everybody else on earth.

Which brings Louis to the thought he had right before Joe punched him. The thought that has been creeping up on him for weeks now, as this weird series of errands has made less and less sense: There is no Mr. Chet.

Not to say that the man who directed, unsuccessfully, their actions of twelve years ago does not exist. He was real: Louis met him! But, Louis now understands, a man like that is not likely to have much use for a man like Joe. In fact, after those killings, Mr. Chet is likely to have ceased relying on Joe for muscle: You're fired, effective immediately. Joe is probably lucky not to have been stuffed dead into the same hole they buried those poor fuckers in. And Louis himself is even luckier. That's what he expected at the time, wasn't it? Instead he never saw Mr. Chet again and heard of him only through the increasingly unreliable conduit of Joe. Joe whose last name he doesn't know. Joe who lives he doesn't know where.

Whoever Mr. Chet was, is gone. Louis is alone with Joe out here, and Joe is under orders from a ghost. All bets are off.

What Joe whispered to Louis in the car, as the blood poured out of Louis's nose and into his cupped hands: *Hey, buddy. This is real fun. But don't tell me not to hurt somebody. Okay? Or I'll hurt you instead.*

Yeah. Okay, Joe.

So. Short-term plan: stay alive. Long-term plan: protect himself and his family from Joe. No idea how to make that happen, short of killing him. But Louis doesn't have a gun, and he doesn't have a knife, and he isn't convinced either of these things would kill Joe even if he had it in him to kill. He's had nightmares: shooting Joe, stabbing Joe, but Joe keeps on coming, like a movie *T. rex*, like a fucking hurricane.

At some point during the night Louis manages to fall asleep. At another point he wakes up. His head is pounding. He takes a shower and crawls back into the same pants and shirt that he wore yesterday, complete with a salsa stain from the football game that now feels like it's ten thousand years in the past. When he gets out of the bathroom, Joe's standing there with his arms crossed, looking out the motel window. He says, "Let's go."

They stake out Denny's in Joe's ludicrously conspicuous car. It takes all day. Louis mostly sleeps—he's afraid Joe gave him a concussion last night. But he keeps waking up, so maybe not. Every now and then Joe half-turns the key in the ignition so that he can windshield-wipe their view free of snow, which is falling around them at a boringly steady pace. Louis gets a pang every time the snow disappears. He thinks he'd be content to watch it accumulate forever.

Eventually the girl shows up again. She's driving the Volvo wagon. And Joe says, "That's the car."

"What?"

Joe's pointing. The girl has gone inside; she doesn't seem to have noticed them sitting here. He's pointing to the car. "That's the car."

"No shit. She just got out of it." Louis winces preemptively, awaiting another punch, but it doesn't come.

"No," Joe says, with creepy gentleness, shaking his head. "The one from before. When we did that job."

It takes Louis a minute, because it doesn't make sense, what Joe's saying. His skin is crawling when he says, "We got rid of that car, remember? It was a Volvo, but it wasn't that one."

Joe says, "That's the one."

He shouldn't speak. He shouldn't. But he says, "So, what, it escaped from the chop shop?"

Joe shifts in his seat, grunts, farts. Now he's starting to get the face-punch look.

"No, yeah, sorry," Louis says, "you're right, I think you're right." And that seems to calm him down.

They sit in silence. Louis falls asleep for a while and wakes up to find Joe getting out of the Caddy and slamming the door shut behind him. It feels so good to be alone that Louis considers staying here, but he knows what's expected of him: Joe's crazy requires an audience. He opens the door and heaves himself out, then follows Joe's footprints into the Denny's.

The girl is their waitress again. There is no talk of hurting her. They eat. At one point Joe says to him, "You look like shit, buddy."

"Haha, yeah, thanks."

"Your face is fucked up."

Louis doesn't honor the comment with a response.

"What happened to you?" Joe asks.

Louis looks him in the eye. "Seriously?"

Joe's chuckling. "Wife get ya?"

After a couple of quiet moments, Joe resumes eating, and Louis says, quietly, "Yeah, she got me good."

Just when Louis thinks they're going to return to the car, a scraggly-looking white kid swaggers in, waving to the hostess and to the old men at the counter like he owns the place. He's wearing a long army surplus coat and a pair of expensive-looking work boots. He intercepts the girl and wraps his arms around her, picks her up off the ground. She squeals. "Daniel!" she says. "I'm at work!"

Joe says, "That's the guy."

"Who?"

"The grower. He's fucking her, see? She gave him the money."

The guy sits down at the counter, throws his arm around some toothless old geezer, strikes up a conversation. Then, a minute later, somebody Louis actually recognizes walks in. It's the dude from the guitar store. He walks over to this Daniel, sits down, chats for a couple of minutes. At some point Daniel pulls a baggie out of his coat pocket and slips it into the guitar-store man's coat pocket, easy peasy. Guitar-store man slaps some twenties on the counter, as though paying for dinner, and Daniel sweeps them away. Guitar-store man gets up to leave.

On the way out, his gaze lands upon Louis and Joe's table, and his smile falters and breaks. He turns away, beelines for the exit. A few minutes later the guy named Daniel stands up, leaving a near-full cup of coffee behind, and strides out with a cheerful wave to the girl.

Joe throws down a bill and heaves himself to his feet. Exhausted, Louis drags himself after. He says he has to go to the men's room and veers off toward it without waiting for a reply. He takes a piss, then spends a long time washing his hands with the faucet running, gazing at his hideously aged and bruised face in the dirty mirror. He stares and thinks.

Outside this men's room, at the end of the hallway, there's a side door, propped open with a brick, beyond which he saw some cooks having a smoke in the cold. Louis could exit, turn left instead of right, push through that door, say 'sup to the cooks, and stride through the falling snow into the night: past the dumpster, over the berm, across the access road, and into the Ponderosa, its illuminated fake A-frame like an arrow pointing to heaven, to salvation. He could walk in there and call Pam on the pay phone, if there's a pay phone, and ask her to please pack a couple of bags and pack the kids' bags and come get me, we have to go away for a while. Maybe she would do it. Whatever is about to go down here in Broken River can go down without him, if he walks out that door. Maybe Joe will get himself arrested or killed, who knows? and Louis will be able to forget about this shit once and for all. And if not, he'll figure something out. He needs to grow a pair and get himself and his family out from under Joe.

Louis turns around, drying his hands on a paper towel, and heads for the door. Fuck it, he thinks, I'm gonna do it. I'm turning left. He balls up the towel, throws it at the trash can in the corner. The ball ricochets off the heap of paper-towel balls already overflowing the can and falls onto the floor among the other paper-towel balls that have ricocheted off the heap. He says "Fuck it! What the fuck is wrong with people" and bends over and gathers up all the fucking paper-towel balls and shoves them deep into the can, squashing them so hard and so far down that he bangs his forehead on the metal lip and he shouts fuck one more time before leaving the men's room and turning right.

The car is there in the parking lot, the windshield newly wiped clean. Louis climbs in. He's full of eggs and meat and ineffective coffee and he wants to punch something, probably himself. Joe doesn't say anything about his having been missing for five minutes. Louis says, surprised by the anger in his voice, "Where are we going? What the fuck are we waiting for?"

Joe gestures out the windshield. The girl is getting off work. She climbs into the Volvo and the Volvo pulls out and they start following the Volvo. The Volvo maneuvers through the center of town and onto Route 94, and then there are trees on either side, and their headlights illuminate the falling snow. They follow her all the way to the house, the house in the woods where it happened, and she signals right and turns into, and disappears down, the driveway.

Joe brings the car to a halt at the side of the highway. They idle there in silence for a few seconds. Then Joe turns it around and heads back toward town.

The Cadillac speeds along, clinging implausibly to the snowy road, as though by some unfathomable black magic.

18

Eleanor wakes in the dark and decides to get up and shower, as though it's morning. And when she gets out of the shower and passes the window, gauzily half-covered by a thin curtain, she realizes that it actually is morning, though very early. The sun is up, barely. The streets are full of garbage and bakery trucks and the shouts of construction workers, audible only because the crush of humanity hasn't yet arrived to drown them out. The industry of these people depresses her, so she climbs, naked, back into bed and stares at the strangely wallpapered ceiling of Craig's girlfriend's apartment. This wallpaper has been mesmerizing her for two days. It is printed with a simple design of intersecting gilt lines that form a grid, set against a background of dark green. It is very seventies, as is the digital alarm clock on the bedside table that can be set to project the time onto the green-and-gold grid; the two seem of a piece. If she crosses her eyes, the gold grid seems to hover a few inches below the green field, and the projection of the time between the two. She reaches out and makes time appear: *4:56*, shuddering slightly with the trembling of the hand holding down the button.

She did not need a week to do the things she planned to do in New York, which consisted pretty much entirely of her meeting with Craig and an as-yet-unscheduled visit with her editor at Ballantine, who presumably would by now have heard the good news about the existence of a new book. There was a third thing, a thing she had intermittently, and for weeks, been picking up her phone to do, and then not doing, and that was scheduling an appointment at Sloan Kettering. She's been lying to Karl about this for too long. That's the danger, in her mind—that even the slightest dishonesty on her part might be identified as comparable to his. She needs to get the marriage books in order, especially if the marriage is going to end. But she didn't make the appointment, she still hasn't, and now it's probably too late to get one.

Driving here a couple of days ago, she thought about everything she could do, alone, to pass the many hours of solitude that she had committed herself to. New York things, she decided: things that tourists do. Ellis Island, the Statue of Liberty. Central Park. MoMA and the Met. The Empire State Building. Why haven't they taken Irina there? She wants to go, Eleanor is sure of it. Irina would never admit it, of course—she prefers to assume her father's stance of ironic detachment and casual disdain: "Why don't we just hang out in Times Square all afternoon?" she said once, with an eyeroll, in response to the suggestion. But that merely makes it Eleanor's job to insist upon a family outing there, to lead them into Manhattan and into the elevator some sunny day, and up to the top, where they will all have a lovely time and thank her for making them go.

By hour three of her journey here, her lower back ached with a familiar, almost homey, pulsing intensity that bordered on nausea. She had completed the decrepit-barn-and-speedway portion of the trip and had entered the domain of inexplicable traffic lights, roadside diners, and auto dealerships outlined in colorful flags and punctuated by convulsing forced-air tube men. (She doesn't understand the tube men. They catch the eye, yes, as only a madly flailing twenty-foot-tall monster can; but who decided such a sight could make you buy a car?) Sewn-on smile notwithstanding, the tube men appeared to her earnestly, even violently, repulsive. *Turn back*, their frantic motions seemed to say. *There's danger here. We're tall enough to see over the trees, and only nightmares await.*

Town and country gave way to highway and tunnel, and to the

claustrophobic and clotted arteries of Midtown; by the time she arrived, her mind was tired of arguing with itself and had settled into its default state in times of uncertainty and doubt: mild depression and embarrassment and boredom. It couldn't be all bad, she reasoned, thudding over the speed hump of Shannon's apartment building's underground garage; maybe she'd have a posthumous bestseller.

The plan was to park, take the elevator upstairs, unpack, and hit the town. What happened instead was that she entered the apartment, put her bags down, climbed into bed, and, after a hallucinatory fifteen minutes alone with the golden grid, slept for fourteen hours. She awoke shivering in this spartan and largely unlived-in Midtown apartment. It belongs to Shannon, Craig's girlfriend, who has resided primarily at Craig's much larger, much hipper loft in the Village (family money, of course—you don't maintain a place like his on literary agent money, even if you're an uber-agent, and he is not) for more than five years. "A woman with my kind of luck doesn't give up her own apartment," Shannon is fond of saying, in an evident effort to ward off triple widowhood (a goal she will likely achieve, in fact, by not marrying again).

After that, what she ended up doing, instead of all the things she told herself she would do, was to read a couple of novels on her phone, sleep some more, and eat ibuprofen and Chinese takeout. She avoided calling home. She didn't have the energy to push through Karl, to get him to hand the phone to Irina. And really, she didn't want to talk to Irina, either. Instead, as a way of proving to herself that she was still capable of some sort of human contact, she impulsively emailed the author of the thrillers she was reading, saying that she was enjoying them, and thank you very much for writing them. And got a reply within the hour that read,

> Dear Eleanor, thank you so much for the kind words! My readers mean so much to me. Sincerely, Kelly

Which was unexpectedly depressing. What did she think, that the woman would recognize the name of a fellow novelist and indulge in some impromptu shop talk? Why would she assume this writer would have heard of her? Or worse, maybe the writer *had* heard of her but disrespects her, or perhaps her entire subgenre of literature, and this stock email was a not-so-subtle insult.

She figured the email would prevent her from enjoying the rest of the thriller, but no—after half a page, she forgot about her brief personal contact with the author and allowed herself to be absorbed by the protagonist's escape from a Slovenian prison cell, her choking murder of a potential rapist, and her confrontation of a mustachioed and sexually deviant human-trafficking kingpin. At least things fucking *happen* in these books, she thought: it's not just people lying in bed and thinking about their fucking *feelings*. This thought made her hate herself enough to actually call home. Tapping Karl's face in her contacts was physically painful. She limped through a meaningless exchange with him, and an exhausting one with Irina, and then fell asleep again.

And now, once again, she's awake. She doesn't really want to go to the Met or Ellis Island or anywhere else because she fears that it will be the last time she ever goes there. She doesn't want to go to Sloan Kettering because she doesn't want to see the truth written on the face of a doctor as she shuffles papers on the desk in front of her, papers covered with horrible facts that it is her job to convey to the doomed.

....

Eleanor wriggles into her favorite black wool dress and gray leggings, pulls on her Doc Marten boots and earflap hat, shrugs on her coat, and leaves the apartment with a pang of regret. Her back hurts. Her shoulders and neck hurt. The pain is not acute, but it's comprehensive. She is one big, exhausted throb. In a café she orders and doesn't eat a scone, drinks a coffee, reads a bit more, sits with her notebook open to a blank page that she fails to fill with words. When MoMA opens, she goes to it, in defiance of her desires. Even on an ordinary day she can't stand in front of a painting for more than a few seconds— she doesn't understand these people who linger, chin in hand, for ten minutes, gazing deeply at a work of art. She thinks they must be faking it. But today she can barely drag herself through the hushed and antiseptic rooms. When the time comes, she leaves the museum, gets on the train, and hauls herself into Craig's office building. The assistant is there, comely and bright, answering the phone and offering people bottled water. Eleanor doesn't have to wait long. She stands when Craig emerges, arms open; chooses not to judge the brief expression of dismay that darkens his face as he takes her in. Has she changed that much? (Not cancer, she reminds herself. Misery. I have been transformed by misery and self-doubt.)

He leads her into his office, and not, as she might have expected, out to lunch. This is the first piece of evidence.

If Eleanor has changed for the worse, Craig Springhill has changed for the better. Age suits him, as it often does for certain men of means. He is studiedly scruffy, his salt-and-pepper hair mussed, his wool cardigan askew over a designer tee shirt. He's very handsome. He slides behind the desk and says, "Nell. Nell."

She lowers herself into one of his slightly-too-low leather-upholstered armchairs, the ones that make him seem larger and more important than his clients, and her lower back, dozing until now, wakes up and begins to protest. "Hi, Craig."

"So glad you're back. So glad. Your upstate sojourn has taken you away from us too long."

She does not point out that it has been only six months since they've seen each other, a perfectly reasonable amount of time, even when she lived in Brooklyn. Which, to Craig Springhill, might as well have been upstate. Instead she says, "I've missed it here."

"And how is our budding genius."

For a second she thinks he means her. But no, he means Irina. "Adjusting. Obsessed with writing. Evidently being homeschooled?"

He laughs, though this isn't terribly funny. "You've embraced rurality in all its splendor. The shade of the pines. The old lady down the road sells you eggs. Cutting your own firewood. A kitchen garden, the song of the crickets." Craig likes clichés. In books and in life. She nods, smiling, feeling very uneasy.

Craig says, soberly now, "And Karl. Are you working out your differences?"

"Not really," she says, and now she remembers: she called him that night, called his cell after they decided to leave New York and Karl lumbered out, door slamming behind him, to stalk the streets with his shaggy head hanging low, presumably in order to appear sexily tortured to any woman who happened to be walking by. She called Craig in tears and he said "Just a moment, dear Nell" and held a whispered conversation with Shannon and sequestered himself inside his home office in order to receive her confession.

He shakes his head. "I was no better at forty than your husband. Men, Nell. We're weak. Weak in the face of our carnal nature, alas."

Does he not recall that it was she he was fucking at forty? He reaches across the desk, not far enough to pat her hand, as the desk is too large; but he pats the air eighteen inches away with apparently genuine feeling. "I'm very sorry," he continues. "You deserve better."

"I'm not here to talk about that."

He brings his hands together in a silent clap. "No, you are not. You are here to discuss this strange and compelling manuscript." He punctuates this statement with another pat, this one targeting, and actually connecting with, a neat pile of paper that must be her printed-out manuscript. Strange and compelling, she thinks. Oh dear.

"Why don't you tell me," Craig goes on, "what your thoughts are on this book. Where you wanted to take it. Where it actually went."

What the fuck, she thinks, kind of question is that? It's the kind of question you ask a condemned prisoner when you fervently wish she would just kill herself, to save everyone the trouble of an expensive and gruesome execution. "I have to admit I don't know," she says, though she does. She does know. She wanted to write something for herself, for once. She wanted to write something fucking depressing, something that her fans would email her angrily about. She wanted to not be a hero of the educated middle-aged middle-class woman of leisure, to not get invited onto any talk shows, to not bask in the adulation of fans at readings. She wanted to do something besides what Craig Springhill wanted her to do! For a decade he has perpetuated the idea that their interests are aligned, that it benefitted them both to go to bed together, to let him represent her, to give him editorial dominion over her novels, to let him run interference between herself and the marketing department over such trivial matters as her author photo, her book covers, her public appearances, her interviews and magazine pieces. It's all beneath her, he told her more than once, and of course that always felt good to hear. It was the dirty work that his 15 percent bought her freedom from. And she can't think of anything in particular from the past ten years that she would retroactively change if she could. But now, what she wants is for her agent to do what she tells him to, and for her husband to fall out of love with the other woman, and for her back to stop hurting, and for the umpteen hours of sleep her body just experienced to have been enough. She took the book exactly where she wanted it to go. Those are her thoughts. But she keeps them to herself, and Craig goes on talking, as men do.

"The writer's prerogative," he says with a chuckle, as if that notion is quaintly amusing. "The pleasure of not knowing. Giving the imagination free reign. The vagaries of the creative mind." Each phrase is like a match that fizzles out before it hits the puddle of gasoline.

"Maybe *you* can tell me what *you* think," Eleanor says. "That's why I'm here, I'm pretty sure." Her voice sounds thin to her, thin and ragged as a flailing tube man. Her back is spasming like one, too. She shifts in her chair to ease the pain, and it responds by galloping up into her neck and scalp. She tries not to wince.

"Yes, yes, yes. What I think." He leans back, makes a cage with his hands, taps his pursed lips with his two index fingers. "I think what we have here is a novel that shifts its focus. A novel that changes its identity midway, yes? On the one hand, it's, as I said, compelling. On the other hand, it's confused. It's uncertain of its aims."

"Okay," she says, but she stretches it out, turns it into a question. Because the novel is not uncertain of its aims. It is Craig, rather, who is uncertain of whether those are legitimate aims. Isn't that what's going on here?

Craig says, "I'm seeing a challenge for your audience. A conflict."

She doesn't speak.

"It begins . . . ," he goes on, pausing as though he doesn't know how to continue, but of course he does, ". . . quite splendidly, more in keeping with your established work, yes? with Paul and Nora trapped in their respective lives. Your evocation of marriage, the *ambiguities* of marriage, is, as always, peerless. These pages are very beautiful, of course. Very beautiful."

He hesitates as if awaiting gratitude for the compliments. As well he should, she thinks—this is how we talk to each other. These are the workings of our professional friendship. So why is it so hard to play her role? Even though she knows he's about to criticize her; he's done it before. Just smile. Say thanks.

She says, "Thank you, Craig."

But it comes across too sardonically. He doesn't like it, shifts in his seat, tugs his sweater sleeves up over his finely haired forearms, of which she can tell he is inordinately proud. But why think this about him? Why condemn his vanity in her mind, this man who has made her a success, who has given her a beautiful apartment to stay in?

Her back is killing her, it's taking her breath away. She would like to lie down on her back on the floor of this office right now. She is aware that she's panting a bit. She ought to be hungry, but she isn't, and the nonhunger gnaws at her. She says, "Go on."

"And then," Craig says, his voice rising in pitch, dropping in volume, as his fingers drum the desktop, "and then everything falls apart. Is that how you'd put it?"

"That's fair to say, yes."

"The child reads her email, asks her about it in front of Paul. They fight. And meanwhile, we learn in the next chapter, Paul has become deathly ill."

"Right."

"At this point I'd expect . . . that is . . ." He suddenly leans forward, folding his arms on the desk and looking intently into her face, though not her eyes. She surveys his idiotically organized, immaculate, dustless desk, with its little tray of fountain pens and its unobtrusive Scandinavian clamp lamp and its sleek black telephone. Her manuscript, even in its tidy little pile, is the only mess in the room. He says, "I'll put it this way. I don't mind an unhappy ending."

"Oh, goody," she can't resist saying.

"Don't mind at all," he says, more forcefully now. "Star-crossed lovers, heartbreak. Sadness and misery. Even death. Romeo and Juliet. That's a kind of book you can write . . ."

"Why, thank you, Craig."

But he's already talking again, before she has even finished speaking his name: ". . . but what you've done here is you've separated them halfway through, Paul and Nora, and their lives unravel . . . in parallel. Each without regard to the other."

"Correct."

"They never see each other again, after page . . . " His fingers find a sticky note, and he splits the pile of pages long enough to glance down at the page number she knows he has already memorized. "One hundred forty," he says, letting the pages fall, straightening them again with those delicate hands. "They never again speak to each other. They don't, if I remember correctly, even *think* about each other again. Ever."

"Yes."

"Your romance novel, if I may be so bold, splits and becomes two tragedies. Two unrelated tragedies."

"Not unrelated," she protests. Because they are not! They are two things she thought of all by herself and put in a book together, goddammit. And she is not happy with the words "romance novel." That is not what it is. That is not what *she* is.

"But separate. Utterly separate but equally bleak. Her suicide, his wasting away. Ruin. The affair no longer relevant."

"Of course it's relevant," she says.

"Yes, sure, of course," he replies, stepping on her words, talking quickly now, clearly annoyed by her reaction. "They die alone. The affair has ruined their marriages, and they die alone. Because of the affair."

"Not because of the affair," she says. "It isn't a morality tale."

"The affair is the thing that drives them apart, drives the narrative apart. Infidelity results in loneliness and death. That's the moral, if you will. The thesis."

"No," she says, "I won't."

He appears genuinely confused. "Pardon?"

"If you will, you said. And I'm saying I won't. It's not a moral. It's not a thesis."

His jaw works. His brow creases. She's annoying him. If this is a different Craig—and it's clear to her now that yes, he is, he's a new Craig, a Craig who says no—then it may also be true that she is a different Eleanor, as well. She is, of course. She can imagine how she must look to him right now—fatigued, depleted, disagreeable. Desperate. She doesn't want to be this way, and neither does he. But here they are.

"Nell—" he starts to say, and the flirty lilt is gone from his voice. She doesn't want to hear it. She doesn't want to hear this voice say anything at all. The pain has found her shoulders now, and it's sharp and deep, as though angel wings are trying to push themselves out through the flesh.

"It's an evocation of what life is like," Eleanor says, aware that she is making an ass of herself, that even she doesn't agree with a single word she's saying. "Things end. People become irrelevant. It's the kid's world now. The daughter's."

"But you don't even tell us what happens to the daughter."

"Of course I do," she says, and she notices that her hand is covering her eyes. She brought it to her face so that it could massage her temples, but it's still there, conveniently blotting out his face.

"You really don't. It ends with them. It ends with endings."

"The girl's going to be fine. It's obvious. She thinks about— There's the part where she—where she—"

Neither of them speaks for a minute. In the quiet, the noise from the street filters through the window, and she can hear breathing. Not Craig's, just hers. His breaths are as silent as a ghost's. She hears him settling back in his chair. In her mind's eye, his hands are laced together over his chest, and he gazes at the ceiling.

"I'm sure I wrote it," she says, less forcefully than she intends.

"Well, if you did, you didn't put it in the book."

"I meant to."

She takes her hand away from her eyes. His hands aren't folded. They're lying on the desk, pale and dry-looking, like elegantly carved marble paperweights. He isn't looking at the ceiling, he's looking right at her.

"I know you don't believe me, Nell," he says, "but I respect the choices you're making. If you don't want to write the kind of book you've been writing, I applaud you. When you have decided what book to write, it will be brilliant. And I will sell it for you, whether it's to Ballantine for three-quarters of a million dollars or to Ecco for five thousand. Because you are my writer."

She can't meet his gaze any longer and hangs her head. Her back pain isn't even back pain anymore; it's just generalized ache. Every part of her is breaking. I'm failing, she thinks, and I am also dying. What's going to happen to Irina? She'll be stuck upstate with a philandering child for a father; she will have to beg for the attention of a series of narcissistic sluts barely older than she is. Irina, I'm so sorry. She's trying not to cry.

"But this book isn't that book," Craig goes on, "not yet. This book is the work of a writer who is searching. I urge you not to perform this important work in public. Search, discover, then write. Show us what you've found, once you've found it."

With her fingernails, she tugs a long hair from her stocking. It doesn't want to let go. It makes a sound, a tick-tick, as the wool releases it. She lets it fall to the floor.

Craig says, "This book isn't finished. That's fine. There's no rush to find your new work, Nell."

He says, "You have all the time in the world."

···········

Back at Shannon's apartment, sleep won't come. She finds some expired prescription painkillers in the medicine cabinet—nothing too heavy, just acetaminophen with codeine—and takes as many as she likes. She acquires a bottle of bourbon and drinks from it liberally, at least by her standards. But she's never really drunk and she's never fully asleep and she's never out of discomfort. She calls home again, wishing she had gotten Irina her own phone; Karl's voice is performing a reasonable approximation of despondence. "Let me talk to my daughter," she says, but once Irina's on the line, she doesn't know what to say. She has done nothing in New York; she has seen no friends, gone nowhere, made no amusing observations; and so she listens to Irina's tales of adventure and card games with her babysitter, the girl from the Dairy Queen. She finds herself reading between the lines, between the lines between the lines, for evidence that Karl is fucking the babysitter. She isn't sure why she cares. Eleanor does not want to be the kind of person who can become unhinged by jealousy, never imagined that she could be. But maybe when somebody is ready, any available stimulus will do to effect the unhinging.

When she's drunk enough to call Rachel, she calls Rachel. She uses Shannon's house phone. It's strange to hear someone say hello in that tone of gentle, expectant curiosity, tinged with worry, that used to be commonplace before phones let you know who was calling. Hearing it, Eleanor experiences a moment of rage—how dare she sound so innocent! How dare her voice express anything other than terror and self-disgust!—followed by another of pity as she realizes how unwelcome this call will be. She does not know where this sympathy is coming from and quashes it before she opens her mouth.

"It's Eleanor."

"Ah," Rachel says after a moment. "Hello."

"He told you I was coming?"

"He did."

"I intend to speak with you in person," Eleanor says. This line and the ones to follow have been revised and rehearsed many times and now feel stupid to say. "I don't want to make things difficult for you, but I will, if you won't meet me."

"No need for that," comes the prim reply. "I'll see you."

"Where?"

"Someplace convenient to you. When you like."

"Tomorrow," she says, though she doesn't know what day this is, what time. "Eight p.m. Do you know the Black Rose? In Greenpoint?"

Rachel says, "Sure. There might be live music up front. But the back room won't be crowded, I don't think."

Of course you know that, bitch.

"I'll see you there," Eleanor says, and hangs up.

She manages to sleep after that, once again until late the next morning. She tries and fails to read, tries and fails to watch TV, tries and fails to take a walk. Before she knows it, it's late afternoon, and she needs to make herself presentable—she needs to decide what variety of presentable she wants to present—and she needs to get to Brooklyn. In . . . how long? Two and a half hours. Why Brooklyn? Why at eight? No matter—less time to be nervous. She showers, dresses, applies and removes makeup, applies it again. Chooses severe over pretty—she doesn't need to prove to this woman that she's the more attractive of the two. Clearly she has already lost that battle. Into her satchel she throws phone, pain reliever, kleenex. She's dizzy and wants to vomit. The 7 to the G: riding the trains, she can't remember what she's eaten in the past two days. Since she's been in New York, really. There was the Chinese takeout, but then what? There were ice cream bars in Shannon's freezer, discolored and frosted over; she thinks she got some pretzels and tortilla chips at the bodega after she bought the whiskey. But she's not sure if she ate them. She falls asleep, misses the transfer; at Queensboro Plaza she climbs up the stairs, climbs down the stairs, heads south again. Gets it right this time. Off at Nassau. It's dark and cold but not cold enough for snow, so a light rain, a mist, really, stings her face; it feels like it's crawling under her clothes, soaking into them; her clothes feel heavy, her body feels heavy, even though she hasn't been eating. She is stumbling through the streets of Brooklyn. She feels herself missing the place but at the same time stands apart from emotion; she is standing five paces back, observing herself missing Brooklyn.

At some point she becomes extremely confused. None of the street names look familiar to her. She takes out her phone, locates the blue dot of herself, turns around in a circle. The map wheels with her, spokes around the dot. She asks a passing couple if they know where the Black Rose is. They don't—in fact they arc around her as though she's a crazy person. Finally she does something she's never done before—she activates the lady in the phone and speaks into it: "Give me directions to the Black Rose, please."

It shouldn't surprise her, but the phone tells her exactly what do to. This way, that way. One block, two. "The destination is on your right," says the phone, and there it is. It's only 8:12. That's fine. Her husband's lover can wait by herself for twelve minutes. She should have come even later, actually—late enough to make the woman sweat, not so late that she would just up and leave. Rachel was right—there's a jazz trio playing here, and Eleanor is forced to pay a cover. She takes a sharp right inside the door and moves down the hallway to the back room, a dark, close space illuminated by electric candles and, through the windows, streetlight. There are some disaffected-looking young professionals here, talking in low tones, but of course Rachel Rosen is not here yet.

Eleanor stands there, scanning the room for an empty table. Her entire body is trembling, quivering, really. She needs to sit down but would need to move in order to do it, and now that she has stopped moving, she is afraid to start again. Her jaw aches, and her head aches. A voice in her ear says "Excuse me" and she is gently brushed aside as a little crowd of overdressed millennials squeezes past. Her clothes grate her flesh and she leans heavily against the hall wall. She closes her eyes.

When she opens them again, Rachel Rosen's face is floating before hers. "Eleanor?"

She's older and fatter than Eleanor remembered; that's good. Her looping black curls are turning gray, and her face is fleshy and tired. But her expression is one of concern.

"I'm sorry I'm late," she says. "Do you want to sit down?"

Maybe it's the apology, or the inadvertent fasting, or the many, many pain relievers, or whatever it is that's eating her up from the inside, but Eleanor thinks she can't even stand up anymore. Her knees begin to tremble, and she feels herself slide an inch down the wall.

The lacquered pine paneling catches on her coat, and she can hear the threads popping.

"Eleanor? Are you all right?"

She slumps a few inches more, then collapses. Her tailbone makes contact with something—a windowsill? an umbrella stand?—and pain radiates through her body, lighting up every distant part of her. She hears herself cry out and then she is falling onto the floor, and she is lying on her side, and her jaw clenches and she can't unclench it, and her head is screaming, and her legs won't move. She can't get up. She doesn't even know what up is anymore. Rachel Rosen's face is above her, and the faces of the young professionals, and her name is being spoken, and she thinks, Oh, fuck, oh, fuck, I've really done it now.

Part Three

19

Three nights before his phone lit up with a call from a Brooklyn hospital, Karl was sitting on the sofa, stoned, his laptop open on the cushion beside him, Huck and Jim standing before him. The room was dark save for the sculptures' dim underlighting, which illuminated, not quite strongly enough (by design), the skein of seams and planes and veins and cracks running through them. He didn't have to get up and walk around Huck and Jim to get the full effect; he'd memorized them a long time ago. He wished there were other people here to observe them along with him; he would like to see them trying to figure the pieces out.

Karl had, from time to time, stationed himself in one corporate lobby or another, in order to watch passersby interact with his sculpture. Which is to say that he typically watched them walk on by without even noticing, or anyway without betraying any obvious interest. But sometimes people stopped and looked. They followed the lines he'd made, the path the metal traced through the glass, obvious in some places, hidden in others. You could always follow it, he made sure of that; even when the steel was nearly invisible, when it plunged deep into the milky ice, you could hold its position in your head, walk around to the other side, watch it emerge. His sculptures were puzzles, really. Not puzzles you were supposed to solve but puzzles you were supposed to puzzle over.

Huck and Jim had been commissioned by a corporate client, but at the last minute Karl changed his mind about handing them over. He whipped up a couple of alternate pieces in record time, stupid-simple geometries, and nobody complained. But Huck and Jim, he couldn't let them go, couldn't unleash them on the world. Not that they'd blow anybody's mind, it was just that he would have known. People wouldn't get them, and he'd have *known*, and it would have broken his heart.

Because the lines didn't connect inside Huck and Jim, not all of them, not in the usual way. They veered off, faked you out. There were dead ends in there, intentional flaws in the glass, quirks and bends in the metal. And there were lines that seemed to terminate that actually connected the two together—vectors through the air between them. Facets of glass that jumped through space. The two had to be positioned just right—at the proper angles to each other, the proper distance apart. They were Karl's private joke at his own expense. His reminder that he could have made art like this all the time if he were serious enough. But he knew he wasn't. Huck and Jim were the only things he'd ever made solely for himself, not for money, not to get somebody into bed—that's why they were standing here, in the house, where most people would have put a fucking TV.

Maybe the knives were for himself, too. He proved this by selling all of five in the three months he'd been at it. The eBay adventure was kind of fun at first. But it was time to admit to himself that the whole thing was a bust. People just didn't get it. Two guys tried to cut up deer with theirs, and they broke, and another guy dropped his on the ground, and it broke, and they sent back the pieces and demanded refunds. He tried to explain, but of course that just made the dudes angrier, and he gave them their money back. He could have taken comfort in the likelihood that the other two guys had theirs on stands, in display cases, but somehow that was even worse.

Enemies. That's what the knives were meant to cut. They were made for warriors to use. Which is to say that they were made for a bygone era, a bygone culture—or maybe one yet to come. They were made for a time and culture that forged knives for the purpose of fucking *defeating foes*. The world that contained online auctions and digital payments and display cases and knife stands was not the world these knives were made for.

He was beginning to understand that he was losing it out here. Everything inside him that used to point outward, toward galleries and museums and lobbies and meeting rooms and women, had now grown in on itself. All the love, the lust, that used to emanate from him, through his dick, he'd had to aim at Nell alone, Nell and Rachel (because Nell alone was not working out), and now it was aimed nowhere and at no one. And there was nothing he could do about it. He hated to masturbate, it made him feel like a child. So now he didn't want to wank, he didn't want to proposition the babysitter, Nell wouldn't talk to him, and Rachel had cut him off, presumably for good. The daughter he suddenly realized he didn't really know was sitting cross-legged on the bed upstairs, making up stories and wishing her mother would come home.

Karl was now wishing the same thing. He wanted Nell to come home. On the laptop beside him, an animated GIF of a samurai chopped, again and again, the head from a foe's shoulders. A moment before, it had offered him comfort, what with its dynamism and reliability, the way the wind moving leaves in the trees must have been for whatshisname, the asshole who lived by that lake and wrote a fucking book about it. But now, suddenly, it was giving him a headache. Or maybe that was the weed. He snapped the laptop shut, revealing, behind it, on the bookshelf recessed into the triangle of wall the stairs formed, the little row of novels written by his wife.

They were demurely tucked in among other fiction titles, written by other people, that he had never read or even really looked at. Of course he'd spent time with Nell's books: turned them over in his hands and remarked disingenuously on their heft and visual appeal, usually at the moment when Nell removed them from the shipping box. (His mind, by this point, was typically focused on the celebratory fuck that was sure to follow.) Of course he'd promised to read them, but it was understood, at least by him, that this would not happen, because why the hell would he read any fiction at all, let alone fiction about boyfriends or shopping or mothers or whatever Nell spent her time obsessing over? These books weren't *for* him; he would no sooner read them than stick a tampon up his ass.

But now, there they were, and he was lonely and freaked out, and he didn't know how to talk to his daughter without her mother around, and suddenly the books called to him. He leaned over and tugged the first of them off the shelf, tried to remember. It was called *Maybe*. Was this always the title? The cover depicted a woman, a third of a woman, a stylishly dressed young woman not dissimilar in shape to Nell, facing the camera. She was cut in half by the edge of the cover, and cut off above the knee and below the eyes, and she was holding a half-finished whatsis—one of those knitting- or sewing-type things where you make pictures with thread on cloth in a wooden circle thing—with the needle hanging off it, and the stitching read, *My heart belongs to . . .* The woman's face was anxious and hopeful and composedly sexy; she was biting her red-lipsticked lip with preternaturally white straight teeth.

Karl heaved a sigh and again wondered how he and Nell had ended up together. In his bakedness he regarded this book, but any book, really, as a wildly implausible thing, mundane in form and hopelessly constrained, hardly an adequate vehicle for any kind of art. Every book propped up a table leg in the exact same way, he thought. Rectangles, rectangles, in rows and piles. Bricks. Slabs full of words.

Once, he had pretended to read this book, back when he figured her whole writing career was some kind of hobby that wouldn't pan out. He told her it was great, of course. Read some shit about it on the internet, regurgitated it for her over dinner one night. It didn't feel unfair at the time: after all, she could apprehend a piece of his in an instant: just a glance was all it took. But reading a book, man, that was work. Hours and hours, sitting in a chair or lying in bed, the eyeballs darting back and forth, line after line after line. It would have been an insane mental and physical endurance test.

He cracked it open, took a look at the dedication. *For Craig, who believed.*

For shit's sake, that guy. Karl threw the book down, annoyed.

Hadn't he, Karl, been in the picture at that point? And she dedicated it to *that* weenie? But the more he thought about it, the more he realized he couldn't really remember when she wrote it. The house suddenly seemed really, really quiet and empty around him, with Irina gone to bed and Sam at Denny's. Somehow Irina's presence upstairs, the possibility that she might wake up, need him, require attention, require emotional engagement, made the feeling worse. So he picked up the book and carried it out to the studio. He flopped down on the love seat, turned on the lamp. Stuffed a little more weed into his pipe and sparked it up. Opened *Maybe* again. *Chapter One*, he read, and thought, Does every fucking novel have to say chapter fucking one? But fine. He squinted some weariness out of his eyes and tried to focus.

The book was about this rich twentysomething girl in Boston, Andrea, the latest in a long line of lady overachievers—a suffragette, a pilot, a feminist, a CEO—who is brilliant and beautiful, yadda yadda, and everybody expects her to become president or something, but so far she hasn't done anything, and she isn't married, and everybody's kind of worried, or maybe hopes, that she's gay, but mostly they all just want her to get her shit together and become the new matriarch.

Which, okay, it was kind of interesting, but not Karl's cup of tea, and he figured he would give it a couple more pages and then drink himself to sleep. But pretty soon he was on page 10, and Andrea's little sister was getting married, and she meets this guy who's engaged to some dumb bitch, and she has an affair with the guy, who keeps promising to break off the engagement, and meanwhile this nerdy dude her brother works with becomes her sort of email bestie, and before long you realize the nerdy dude is hot for Andrea, and then there are like five more crazy reversals while meanwhile Andrea discovers that she is good, actually kind of fucking great, at ironic avant-garde dirty needlepoint (that's what the stitching thing turned out to be called) and ends up with a huge gallery show of the stuff and gives her grandmother a heart attack because one of the needlepoint things has a dick on it, and *where in the hell did this version of his wife come from because this shit is craaaazy!*

By now it was like two in the morning and he'd forgotten to eat and his vision was blurring. So he went to the kitchen and stuck a frozen pizza in the oven. The kitchen looked different: somebody had cleaned up. Sam? Irina? A plate, a glass, a fork were washed and now stood dry in the strainer. Did somebody break into his house and eat here? And clean it up?!?

No. No, it was Irina, she must have had dinner earlier, before Sam stole his car to go to work. Had she even asked if he wanted anything? Fuck, she didn't, did she. Or maybe she did? He couldn't remember. While the pizza heated he crept upstairs and knocked gently on Irina's door. No answer. He let himself in. She was asleep under the covers, her body curled awkwardly around her closed laptop, and, to his surprise, Sam lay beside her on her back, asleep on top of the covers in her work clothes. When did she come back? She looked like a child. The fuck: was she on the clock? Irina was gently snoring. He felt a sudden bubble of grief rising into his chest and bursting, for what, he didn't understand. He backed out and closed the door.

The fire he'd started in the woodstove was still going, albeit weakly. He threw another log into it. He stared at the glowing stove doors for fifteen minutes, nearly falling asleep. Then he took the pizza out of the oven and ate the entire thing off the kitchen counter, then finished *Maybe* before falling asleep for real, on the sofa.

In the morning Sam made Irina breakfast, and Karl took the second book off the shelf and went out to the studio and got high and read. This one was called *Seven Secrets of the Sarcastic Sisterhood*, and it was about a bunch of school friends who make a solemn vow to each other that one year into any relationship they ever have, the man in question must submit to a hearing before a panel of the other three friends, and the relationship will live or die based on their ruling. It goes pretty well for about ten years—a couple of the women use the pact to elaborately dump a couple of losers, and another one marries the man her friends have vetted. But then the protagonist, Lacey, meets a guy, thinks he's the one, and starts getting increasingly nervous about the hearing, because her friends have grown strange and distant and seem to know about the relationship even though she hasn't told them. In the end the novel turns into a kind of goofy psychological thriller parody and concludes with one wedding, one divorce, and one birth, and a moonlit séance in the woods.

At some point in the day Irina had actually brought him some lunch—a turkey sandwich on wheat bread and a mug of hot chocolate. "We made hot chocolate," she said by way of explanation, and it annoyed him that he had to interrupt his reading to accept the food. Irina looked weird—skinny and pale. He said, "Hey, man, you look weird, are you sick or something?"

"No. Are you?"

"No."

"But you're high, Father."

"Not really," he said, picking up a half sandwich and taking a bite, and then, largely involuntarily, devouring the entire thing in seconds, like an animal. The food reminded him that his body existed, and his body reminded him that other people existed, and he realized that he had just told his twelve-year-old daughter that she looked weird and sick.

But she didn't appear offended or self-conscious; she just looked confused. And less weird and sick, now that he had eaten something and his own body felt better. Irina said, "You're reading Mother's books."

"Yeah. Right."

"They're really good. She's a great writer." She was gazing at him, arms crossed over her chest, as though challenging him to disagree.

"You know, you're right. She is, totally," he said. He slurped the cocoa. Fuck, it was really good. "This is really fucking delicious, man."

"Thanks, Father. Sam made it. On the stove, out of whole milk in a pan."

"Yeah." He started on the second half of the sandwich, through which he mumbled the words, "Is she, like, spending the night?"

"I think she can, if you want. Also," Irina went on, high-and-mighty, "we are friends now, and sleepovers are appropriate."

"All right, cool," Karl said, gasping for breath between bites.

"Anyway," Irina said, "I'll let you get to it."

"Thanks, buddy. I'll be in eventually."

"Okay, Father."

"Okay."

He started the third book later in the day. Irina and Sam weren't around when he went into the house for it; maybe they were out taking a walk. The book was called *Stop Trying So Hard*. It was published two years ago. Eleanor had become famous enough by then that the author photo had migrated from the back flap to the back cover. The picture was black-and-white, intimate, sultry. She peered out from behind a curtain of gently curving hair; her gaze was piercing, understanding, full of humor and warmth. When was the last time she looked at him this way? Had she ever? Karl looked at the photo credit: some clown he had never heard of. Did she fuck him? She had to—how could you keep your hands off a woman who looked at you that way? Karl reached out with his mind for Rachel in a kind of panic, grabbing at the strands of his love for her, its marionette strings, trying to make it twitch and dance, trying to make it look like something alive. But he couldn't: now he just wanted Eleanor, he wanted the woman who wrote these books, who gazed out at him from this picture. Who in the hell was she? Was she even real?

He read the book all afternoon, finished late, stumbled into the house. Repeated the previous night's ritual of the pizza (and didn't he eat the last one the night before? Was Sam grocery shopping for them?), added a log to the fire Irina and Sam must have made, climbed the stairs to gaze at them as they slept. But this time, he could hear whispers, Irina's light was on, and a wedge of light extended across the hall from her door. He didn't dare step into it. He didn't want to risk discovery. He backed down the stairs, retired to the sofa to wait. He lay there, his body aching for food, his mind clouded by drugs, craving the wife who filled his head, the one he was finally listening to for the first time.

20

Irina lay awake after midnight. This was something she'd started last month—before that, midnight had always seemed like some kind of unbreachable barrier. To stay up past midnight was to violate some law of physics—if a kid was awake, the day couldn't change, the sun would stand still on the other side of the world, and Asia would be engulfed in flames in an endless high noon. But her novel (and, let's be honest, the internet) kept drawing her closer and closer to the line, until one night she lost track and didn't notice until quarter past twelve. She gasped. Her parents' footsteps climbed the stairs. Adrenaline coursed through her—there was still time to snap the laptop shut, switch off the lamp, dive under the covers. But then Mother's head was there, in the open door, and she was saying, placidly, "It's late, sweetie, go to sleep," and her father shouted good night from the hall, and she felt like rather a fool.

Now, though, the excitement of midnight was gone. It just felt lonely here, lying in bed, being awake for no reason when the rest of world was asleep. She wanted to go across the hall to Mother's office, where Sam was sleeping on the daybed, and wake her up and talk. But she knew that Sam would actually do it, would actually talk to her, because she was nice, but maybe also because she was being paid, and Irina didn't want to wonder which reason was the real one. She could call Mother, but her conversations with Mother-in-New-York had all been roughly the same: short and depressing. "Father is useless," Irina complained yesterday. "He isn't doing anything. Sam and I are doing *everything*. When are you coming *home*? Why didn't you bring me?" She was aware that this was hopelessly whiny and childish, but so what, she was a child.

"I'm sorry," her mother said, and of course this made Irina feel worse. "Soon, I hope. I'm sorry. I have to fix a couple of things here. It won't take long."

"Is it about Father? Is it about the other woman?"

A longish silence. "What do you know about that, buddy?"

"Ugh," Irina said, because it made her feel bad to play her hand like that. The adults needed to feel that you didn't notice things. They needed to feel like they had privacy and control, even though they didn't.

"I'm sorry," her mother said, a little strangled, and Irina was pretty sure she was trying not to cry. In bed!—Irina could hear the sheets and blankets moving. It was not good if Mother went all the way to New York City to cry in bed. "Work on your writing, baby," she said, her voice down to a whisper. "Fiction problems are better than life problems. They are easier to solve."

Irina's novel had changed a great deal in the past few months. Also, it kind of didn't make sense. This had become increasingly vexing to Irina—her incapacity to make the parts of the book work together. Last month, before this malaise settled over her family, she'd asked Mother about it—how to make it all make sense. "I had these ideas!" she cried; it was late and Father was out in the studio and Mother seemed uncharacteristically happy and relaxed there in her office, with a glass of wine. "And now I don't like them anymore!"

"That's because your book grew up while you were writing it."

"But what do I *do*?" Irina asked, drawing out the *ooooo* in dramatic fashion.

"You fix it in the rewrites."

"How long does that take?"

"Longer than the writing part, usually," Mother said. "For me."

Irina whispered, "But I worked so hard."

"You needed to work hard, to get to the good ideas. The old ideas weren't bad, they just weren't what the book wanted to be. It's okay to write a rough draft. That's why they're called that."

Irina held her mother for a while before saying, sort of into her armpit, "I don't like it."

"If you're going to be a writer," Mother replied, "you'll learn. Because the thing is, all of the stories we tell ourselves are wrong. All of them."

She'd heard her mother say that before. It was a shtick. She said it on television and on the radio and in the newspaper and on the internet. But it was quite another thing for Irina to hear it spoken especially for her, ear pressed to her mother's shoulder, directly through the flesh, like it would have sounded when she was still in the womb, that bassy hum of truth.

And so now she was trying to finish, and to enjoy finishing, even though she knew it was all wrong. Aiden was still called Aiden; she'd sent him and Kimmifer through a portal they'd found via a mysterious device given to them by Kimmifer's uncle, which enabled them to explore each other's worlds. Kimmifer's father turned out to have gotten sick and died, which Irina mostly did because she didn't like the missing father plot anymore. What she wanted now was to reunify New York City—to restore Quayside to its rightful place on the same plane of physical reality as Brooklyn and the other boroughs. "Just imagine," Aiden said, holding her hands (because they did that recreationally now, and also they'd kissed quite a great deal, by leaning as far as they possibly could over her bustle), "all the things our boroughs can give to each other. We need the magic in Uncle Johnseph's Millibeans Device! And your people need to see that some of your ways are rooted in fear of the unknown!" The ending was almost done—they'd found Uncle Johnseph and discovered a flooded abandoned subway tunnel where there were gondolas marked *To Quayside*, evidence of some former attempt at unification. Irina was going to make them all hold hands and pass through the membrane, and, "If my calculations are correct," Uncle Johnseph said, "the boroughs will unify, and all citizens of New York will be able to see each other, now and forever!"

Irina knew it was all just a big mess. Stuff kind of changed in the middle, because she had wanted it to. Everybody's personality was different now. Uncle Johnseph was less like the Wizard of Oz and more like Franklin Roosevelt. And Kimmifer was younger—she wasn't anything like Samantha Geary anymore. Irina didn't need a fictional Samantha Geary, because she had found the real one.

So, why didn't she feel any sense of triumph? Why didn't the mystery seem solved?

Because, as her mother had told her, all the stories we tell ourselves are wrong. She'd known for a long time, and she felt powerfully now, that Sam was never Samantha Geary. Samantha Geary was gone—on to a new life somewhere. She probably didn't even know that's who she used to be. Her story had grown up, and Irina didn't need her kid version anymore. It was nice of Sam to play along, but now Irina didn't know how to ask her to stop. Sam was playing *for* Irina, not with her. It wasn't like they were putting on a play together. It was a puppet show for a baby to watch. It was for the old Irina.

The problem she was grappling with now, though, was this: the Irina who started writing this novel was the old one. The Irina who was trying to finish it was the new. Was such a collaboration even possible? Did new Irina even want to share a .doc with old Irina? The situation felt hopeless.

But she was not ready to admit defeat. She was going to finish, and she was going to celebrate! And her mother was going to come home and help her fix it.

Right now, though, she had to eat something: she had stayed awake far enough into tomorrow for her body to start demanding breakfast. She had begun to fantasize about cereal: a bowl of honey O's, with the whole milk Irina liked to stash in the back corner of the fridge, where a chill descended from the freezer to make it ice cold.

So she threw back the covers and then thought she heard, against the quiet of the night, motion in the house: Father's heavy tread, filthily socked, climbing the stairs. If it was him, he was moving with uncharacteristic attempted stealth. His progress was slow; the old wood creaked. When the footsteps reached the top, they paused. Irina sat, momentarily terrified, her toes barely touching the bedroom floor.

Then she heard Father's familiar panting breaths and understood that he was considering coming in to say good night. She wanted to call out to him, but she held her tongue.

But what if Father had come upstairs to see Sam? Why, after all, would Sam otherwise be staying here tonight? The car, she'd said when she returned; Father was high, he couldn't drive her to town, and she was just going to have to come back tomorrow anyway. But what if it was something else?

Irina did not want this. She wanted Sam for herself, and she wanted her mother back. Suddenly she was afraid. She willed her father to stop at her door and to go no farther. Please, she whispered, I don't want to hear you laughing down the hall. Please come to *me*.

But, in the end, he didn't do anything. He retreated back down the stairs. She heard him settle onto the sofa, in front of the wood-stove and Huck and Jim. She heard him begin to snore.

What was that all about?

....

Father was still snoring five minutes later, when Irina finally decided she'd waited long enough and crept down to the kitchen. She snapped on the dim stove-top light and in its glow prepared her cereal. Father's phone was sitting on the kitchen table, so she keyed it open and idly played a word game while she ate. When the cereal was gone, she washed and dried the bowl and spoon and put them away, and she picked up the phone and played the game for a few more minutes, waiting to be tired again.

It was not working. She was not tired. Instead, she was lonely. She closed the game app and opened up the phone app. Her mother was there, in the list of favorites, and her thumb hovered over the screen.

Mother, it's Irina, she would say when her mother sleepily answered. *Irina?*

Mother, I'm lonely. Come home. I need help with my book.

It's one in the morning.

I can't sleep.

I'll be home next week, honey, her mother would say, and Irina would be able to hear the exasperation in her voice, her wish that she could be left alone, just for a week.

I need you, Irina might say. And her mother might say . . .

What? How could this conversation end? With her mother getting in the car and coming home, days early and in the middle of the night, to make Irina a second breakfast and apologize for leaving in the first place? No. She would tell Irina she would have to wait. That she was a big girl now and would have to make do with her father until Wednesday. Irina would hang up feeling ashamed and immature.

So instead, impulsively, Irina brought her thumb down onto the unidentified number that she knew corresponded to the Famous Rachel and raised the phone to her ear.

She changed her mind immediately. Why was she doing this? What would she even say? But before she could pull the phone away from her ear, there was a click, and a woman's voice said, "I told you."

Irina didn't speak. In the background of the call, a fire engine siren sounded, cars honked. It was New York! New York was on the other end!

"Karl?" said the voice.

There was still time to hang up, but now she couldn't resist: "It's Irina."

Now Rachel was the silent one. What could she hear in the background of the call? Nothing. Maybe Father's snoring, if she was listening hard enough.

Then Rachel said, "Hi there. Is everything all right?"

That did it. Irina began to cry. "No, it's not!"

"Baby," Rachel said. "I know. I know."

"Everything's different. I don't know what real life is supposed to be anymore. And my novel is bad."

"How old are you?" Rachel asked after a moment.

"Twelve."

"You're writing a novel?" She didn't wait for an answer. "Honey, it doesn't have to be good. Not yet. Nothing's good when you're twelve."

Her voice was low and gentle. Irina heard ice clinking in a glass. The siren was gone now. Irina was trying not to sob, but the tears were coming anyway. She got up, crossed the room, wiped her face and nose with a paper towel.

"Does your father know you're calling me?" Rachel asked her, the words a little slurred.

"He's asleep."

"Don't tell him. Why don't you go wake up your mother and talk to her?"

"She's in New York."

"Hmm, that's right." Rachel drew breath. "Well. Maybe I'll see her, then." There was a long pause, more clinking of ice. Irina tore off an extra paper towel and sat down again. "Irina," she went on, "you and I have something in common. Our families are very strange. They don't follow the rules. People come and go and do things impulsively, and they hurt each other and themselves. The outside world doesn't understand. Do you get that?"

Irina thought of her friend's mother, the one who didn't want to let her ride on the subway alone. She said, "I guess."

"Life is very messy," Rachel said, "and sometimes it is lonely and painful, but sometimes it is exciting and beautiful. You're in a lonely part." She paused. "Your mother is a good person."

Hearing this from Famous Rachel gave Irina a strange feeling, half-pride, half-irritation: I don't need *you* to tell me that!

"I will tell you the truth, Irina: I didn't used to like your mother. But I was just jealous of her. I wish I could be as good at something as she is at writing. Sometimes I wish I'd had a child like you, too."

Irina now understood that Rachel was drunk. "Thank you," she said, quietly. The tears had stopped now. She was getting sleepy. She thought, You are dumb for not liking my mother right away. "I think I should go."

"I agree. Good night, Irina. I won't tell your mother you called."

Irina hadn't even thought of that. "Thank you."

"She'll be home soon. But it's okay to be alone. Don't forget that, whenever you're feeling lonely."

"I won't," Irina thought, and then thought: But really, I won't. That is good to know.

The call was over. Irina said goodbye, but Rachel was already gone: back to her loneliness and drinking and the pleasure of living in New York. Irina watched as her thumb led her to the phone's call log and deleted the call to Rachel. She put the phone to sleep and replaced it on the kitchen table. Turned out the lights and climbed the stairs to bed.

Another secret to keep from Mother and Father, she thought, closing her eyes against the black early morning. Soon there would be more. Pretty soon she would be made almost entirely of secrets. In her imagination, as sleep began to pull her down, Irina pictured each secret like it was a little translucent ball, like one of those scented bath globes you might find in some fancy person's bathroom, piled up in a little china dish on the tub's edge. In her dream (for it was a dream now), the camera pulled back to reveal how many secrets there were, and how small: red ones for her blood, pink for the muscles, cream for the skin and brown for the hair and blue for the eyes. Like atoms, they were, the secrets, and they made her what she was: a real girl, a real person, alive in the world, right now.

21

It had begun to snow in earnest. Louis could tell this one was the real thing—the temperature had dropped to below twenty degrees, the flakes were big and fuzzy edged, and the stuff didn't melt when it hit the windshield. Louis and Joe were staking out the supposed weed house, the place where Daniel lived, directly under a streetlight in Joe's enormous fucking car. Louis was shivering. Meanwhile the heat was rolling off Joe like he was a boiler in some basement—some midwestern torture basement, Louis imagined, with a clothesline for drying out all the flaps of human skin and a dirt floor all the leftovers were buried under. Every few minutes Joe turned the key to run the wipers, and the snow was swept away to reveal a party in progress—raggedy-looking people, arriving at the house in groups, every one of them glancing over their shoulder at the car where Louis and Joe were sitting.

"Big party," Louis said.

Joe only grunted in reply. He had been grunting often, more often than usual. Louis regarded this as ominous. Everything seemed ominous now that Joe's insane worldview had been validated, including the revelation that Joe had actually brought a change of clothes, as though he'd understood they would be spending time here, three nights so far, with another impending, some kind of sick foreplay to violent action. Louis was forced, yesterday morning, to wash his own unmentionables in the motel sink, roll them up in a towel to wick out the moisture, and put them back on still mostly wet.

That was a mistake. They were still wet, and he smelled no better than he had. By now Pam had probably called him and heard his phone ringing on the bedside table or wherever the hell he'd left it. Maybe she figured he'd taken up with somebody else. At this point he may have lost his job. But no—it had been only three nights. Louis could still perform damage control, if he could find a way out from under Joe.

For now, though, he was in, all the way. He was here for the big show, whatever the hell it was supposed to be.

Joe grunted, turned the key, ran the wipers, grunted. The kid, Daniel, was there, framed by the door of his house. Behind him, bright rooms were crowded with people, holding drinks, smoking smokes. Daniel was peering out at Louis and Joe.

Joe snickered. This was worse than the grunting. They watched as Daniel receded into the house. The door closed.

"Wanna go to a party," Joe said. He opened the driver's door and heaved himself out onto the street.

"All right," Louis said, mostly to himself, and followed. His boxer shorts unstuck and restuck themselves from and to his ass and balls. His socks squelched inside his frozen shoes. He had no idea what was going to happen inside that house, but at this point he'd take anything besides the Eldorado. Fuck: incandescent lighting? Heat? Beer? Bring it. Maybe Joe would have a heart attack or something? Louis almost didn't care that it was tantamount to breaking and entering.

He mentioned this to Joe on the way to the door. "They're gonna notice us, you know. They could call the cops."

Another chuckle. "Nobody's calling the cops. The weed's here."

"Huh," Louis said. He couldn't imagine how the kid could've been growing here—there was no evidence of it. For a second, though, he considered calling the cops himself. Borrowing a phone from somebody and just straight-up confessing. Throwing himself on the mercy of the court and all that. He was an accessory to murder, at worst— how long would they put him away for, really? Maybe he could just get time served and parole, for cooperating. Joe would probably die in jail and Louis's wife and kids would live long, happy lives.

Well, they would live, anyway. Happiness was likely to elude all of them regardless. Anyway, he knew he wasn't going to call the cops. He was a fucking coward, was the reason.

They didn't knock, of course—Joe flung open the screen door with ludicrously excessive force, and it slammed against the clapboards as though in a hurricane. They pushed through, into the party.

It was hot and loud. Everyone was stripped down to their under-shirts and the air was heavy with smoke from their cigarettes and joints. Louis remembered this kind of party with genuine fondness, though he didn't really like them at the time. They always gave him a headache, made him long for his own sofa, a little TV or a golf maga-zine. Now, though, he felt nostalgic. Why didn't he have any kind of social life these days? He and Pam could go out if they wanted—Janine was plenty old enough to look after the boy. Hell, they'd pay her, even. Years ago they used to fantasize about the day Janine turned thirteen and they could fly the coop every now and then. But thir-teen had come and gone, and neither of them had mentioned going on a date.

Joe bulldozed forward, through the crowd, creating a slipstream for Louis to follow in. A few people got jostled; Louis apologized on the big man's behalf. Heads were turning. So far nobody had chal-lenged them—the place was pretty full, surely everybody couldn't know everybody. They moved through a living room, a dining room; they moved down a hallway. Joe was alert, checking out every door and wall, poking his head into the bathroom, bedroom, linen closet. Louis didn't know what he expected to find. Some stash of drugs or cash? A sign that read WEED IN HERE? They ended up in the kitchen, the most crowded, loudest, hottest, and closest space in the house, and Joe's eyes narrowed. He peeled off, moved rudely around the edge of the room, examined the walls and floor.

Louis hung back, found himself in front of a beer keg. Again con-sidered bolting. Then imagined being caught, murdered, by Joe. Nah. For now, stay still. Your moment will come, you miserable pussy. He took a red Solo cup from a stack on the counter and pumped himself a nice full heady serving. The beer was warm and sweet.

"Hey there, friend."

Louis looked up, over the lip of his cup. It was the kid, Daniel, standing there. The tone was jovial. The gaze was serious. Louis's initial impression: prick.

"Don't believe I know you guys." He was peering over Louis's shoulder, presumably at where Joe was still rummaging around like a foraging ape.

Louis took a big swig of beer, said, "Yeah, we're here with Valerie."

"Don't know any Valerie, friend."

"Mike's girl?"

"Don't know Mike." He sure was interested in whatever Joe was up to. Louis turned to take a look. The big man had become absorbed in a floor-to-ceiling shelving unit covered with cans and jars. He moved some of these aside, peered behind them.

"Everybody knows a Mike."

"Look, this is my house, and my party, and I don't know you. So maybe you and your pal should leave."

"Yeah, well," Louis said, "whaddya gonna do, call the cops?" He took another swig of beer, half-emptying the cup, and looked Daniel right in the eye and mouthed the words *Call the cops*.

The kid stared, hard. Louis stared back, sending him mind bullets. *Please? Please call the cops?* "Look, friend," Daniel said, "don't fuck with me. What the fuck is your pal doing right now?"

Louis turned again. Joe had unscrewed the lid off a jar and was poking around in it with a meaty finger.

"I guess he wants some lentils?"

"Shit," said Daniel. "Did Barney have somebody send you fuckers? Because fuck Barney."

"I told you, man—Valerie." Wait, or was it Vanessa?

"Fuck!"

Joe had evidently hit pay dirt, because he was pulling something out of one of the jars. It was a key. He dropped the open jar onto the floor—Louis could barely make out the sound of breaking glass over the din—and bent over, as though to fit the key into a lock. Louis had the presence of mind to block Daniel, who was trying to get past him.

"Friend, I wouldn't." Though Louis wanted him to. Wanted somebody to roll the dice for him.

Joe tugged on the shelving unit, and the whole thing came away from the wall, smoothly, on hinges. A door. The other partygoers didn't seem to notice, or maybe they didn't care, or they already knew about the secret door. Daniel, on the other hand, was suddenly transformed into a writhing, flailing muscle of rage.

"Fucking move it!" he spat, and Louis was shouldered aside by a flurry of skinny, taut limbs. He stumbled backward, bumped into somebody. He felt somebody's beer splattering all over the back of his already filthy coat.

"Whoops!" Louis said. "Sorry!"

"No worries, chief!" came a voice, and Louis turned. He knew this guy—it was the old stoner from the guitar shop and from Denny's.

To Louis's surprise, the man blanched and dropped his cup of beer on the floor. For a second he was immobilized by the sight of Louis—Louis! The manager of Carpet Universe and World of Window Treatments! And then, in a kind of insectile spasm, the man turned around and ploughed through the kids behind him, as though hightailing it away from the devil incarnate.

Wait for me, Louis said to himself, but didn't move. Instead he took a deep breath and replenished his beer from the tap.

Some goth chick, moderately hot, was giving him the stink eye from the other side of the keg. "Hey," she said, "who are you again?"

Louis was starting to feel a little drunk. "Vanessa and Mike's friend," he replied, "again. Who are you?"

"This is my house."

"It's a lot of people's houses tonight, sounds like. Anyway, thanks for the party." He raised his cup in an unrequited toast, then peered over to see what was going on with the secret door. Joe, it seemed, had disappeared behind it, with Daniel in pursuit, because neither was anywhere to be seen.

And just like that, for the first time in many days—in many months, really—Louis felt pretty all right. He was warm and drowsy and a little bit drunk; Joe was out of sight. The goth chick was more than moderately hot, actually; she was clearly pissed at him, and that made her even hotter. He suddenly wished he could freeze time, just stand here drinking warm beer and arguing with her.

As though in response to this thought, the girl spun around and drilled into the crowd, as though in search of someone. Daniel, Louis figured, but she wasn't going to find him. She elbowed her way out into the hall: wrong direction. It was probably for the best.

And then the kitchen suddenly got kind of uncomfortable. Louis's presence appeared finally to be having some small effect. People were peering over at him, whispering to each other. They sensed that something was up. He elbowed his way to the can-and-jar rack, pardoning himself as he went, trying not to spill his beer. He tugged on the shelves, and nothing happened. Where was Joe looking, before? There—at waist height, a little latch behind the creamed corn, above a keyhole. He squeezed, the door popped open, and Louis slipped in, pulling it shut behind him.

A narrow staircase, leading down. Weird light—almost like it was full daylight down there, impossible daylight. "Hello?" he stage-whispered. He could hear heavy breathing. "Hey!" A few steps later, he peeked under the handrail.

Here's the tableau he saw: Daniel and Joe, standing before a massive, glowing, cellar-filling apparatus of ducts, pipes, fans, and translucent, glowing sheet plastic, behind which loomed hummocks of thick, hazy green. The two men faced each other, about six feet apart, about ten feet from the staircase. Both of them held handguns. Daniel appeared bewildered by the arrival of Louis. His armed hand swung from Joe to Louis to Joe to Louis.

"Whoa, fuck," Louis said, and this seemed to make up Daniel's mind. He pointed the weapon at Louis and steadied himself as if to shoot.

"Whoa, whoa!!" Louis shouted, because it was all happening too fast, and he didn't think there would actually be shooting, he figured threats, or beatings at worst, but it was clear now that that was stupid and of course there was going to be shooting. This all started with shooting. It was a thing that Joe liked to do. Louis's hands flew up, his Solo cup fell to the stairs, and beer splashed over his shoes, and he continued to shout whoa as Joe shot Daniel in the chest, and Daniel stumbled backward, striking and distending a wall of daylight-corrected plastic, and slumped to the floor. He still held his pistol but no longer seemed motivated to use it, or to do anything at all, for that matter.

Louis was still saying whoa when Joe took a few steps forward and shot Daniel again, this time in the head. What was left of Daniel tore through the plastic, and the smell of marijuana joined, then quickly overwhelmed, odors of gunfire and blood.

Louis felt like he was having a fucking coronary. His ears rang and he gulped air. He sat down now, four or five stairs from the top, and above him the hidden door rattled.

Joe was chuckling again. "Told ya so," he said.

"What?" It was hard to hear, what with his ears blown out.

"Told ya." Joe gestured with his gun at the weed operation. The room was stuffed with it, like a fungus.

"Yeah. Yeah."

"It's fuckin' mine."

"Yeah, sure." Louis stayed silent for a second. The rattling upstairs was growing more urgent, and people were talking right behind the door. They'd heard the shooting, no doubt. "Hey, Joe," Louis said, quietly, "what do you want to do now?"

Joe shrugged, secreting the gun in his jacket somewhere. "Dunno. Gotta be money down here." He glanced around for a second, then ripped through the nearest panel of plastic, revealing the plants, the grow lights, the irrigation system that was spraying a fine mist over the crop. Joe stepped in, started thrashing wildly around, knocking shit over, tearing shit down. It felt to Louis like a desecration, somehow even more so than the murder he had just witnessed. Jesus fuck: he just witnessed a murder. Sorry, *another* murder. With like a million fucking witnesses. His ears were ringing, and his jaw was clicking as he moved it back and forth.

"Hey, Joe—hey, buddy," he said, trying not to sound panicked. "Maybe we ought to try to get out of here, what do you say?" He was trying not to look at Daniel's body, which was lying in a spreading puddle of its blood. Louis was shivering, even though it was warm, too warm, really, and he was still wearing his coat. The rattling upstairs had ceased, but people were talking urgently at the door. The party seemed to have given way to intense discussion about what had been going on in the basement.

"What?" Joe said amid the sounds of crashing metal and splintering wood. Didn't he understand that the plants were the valuable thing here? If there was money, it was probably in a safe upstairs. And there was no time for that.

"We gotta go, man. You killed a guy. They heard it upstairs."

This got Joe's attention. He emerged from the wreckage, backlit by the artificial daylight. He looked like an avenging angel, a fat one, an evil one. Louis could sort of make out his facial expression, and it was one of annoyance.

"We killed a guy," Louis corrected, and Jesus fuck, it was actually true, he was again accessory to madness, and they were both going to go to jail very soon. "We gotta go."

The commotion upstairs finally seemed to register on Joe's consciousness. He grunted. Started glancing around the room for an alternate way out, but there wasn't one. It was back upstairs or nothing.

The secret door crashed open. It sounded exactly like a hundred cans and jars rattling in unison. Louis jumped to his feet.

"Pick it up," Joe said, pointing. He was pointing to Daniel—to his gun, which was still tangled up with his dead hand, a finger hooked through the trigger guard. The gun, the hand, the whole forearm, were lying in the pool of now-congealing, blackening blood.

Louis scrambled down the stairs, lunged for the gun, grabbed it. In the process he made brief contact with the dead hand and was nauseated. His foot unstuck from the blood puddle with a wet crackle, as though from a movie theater floor. The gun was bloody, and now his hand was bloody. The stuff was viscous, sticky, an awful syrup.

He turned to the stairs in time to watch the goth chick, lady of the house, gallop halfway down, stop, take it all in. She screamed with her whole body, really digging into it, like an opera singer.

"Lady, please," Louis started to say when she paused between breaths, but then Joe stepped up and shot her, too, right in the chest. The shot was loud, so fucking loud; it filled the space like a new, toxic kind of light. She sat down, hard. Her mouth seemed to be saying *ohgodohgodohgod* but Louis couldn't hear anything. A second tone had been added to the ringing in his ears; it was a chord now, persistent and bothersome, as if somewhere in his head a cat was standing on the keys of a church organ.

But he heard Joe when he said "C'mon," grumpily, and walked past Louis and onto the stairs. He stomped past the dying woman, who didn't even look up at him. She was just staring into space, blinking, with her hand pointlessly clutching the wound. Upstairs, Joe was greeted by screams. "Everybody shut the fuck up and back off!" he shouted, and in response a stampede of feet rumbled across the basement ceiling.

Louis briefly entertained the notion of putting the gun in his mouth and ending it all right now. But he couldn't imagine letting this bloody object anywhere near his face. Funny, that—he'd be dead in seconds, who gave a shit what was in his mouth? But no, it was already bad enough the stuff was on his hand and shoe—and now, somehow, on his coat and pants.

Upstairs, the screen door slammed. Bus was leaving. Louis made a run for it, taking the steps two at a time, but something tripped him up, and he went down, breaking his fall with his unarmed arm. It fucking hurt. He hazarded a glance back: the girl had gotten her gray-white hand wrapped around his ankle. Her sweater and other hand were soaked in blood now, and her eyes were crazed. She was licking pink foam off her lips and she coughed a Pepto-Bismol mist.

When she started to whine—to keen, really, a high, shrill sound that was getting louder by the second and that Louis was certain would drive him out of his mind if he had to endure it for even one second more—he came to his senses and kicked free, knocking her onto her side. His ankle was freed, but he felt a sudden, vertiginous lurch, as though the floor had collapsed beneath him, as though there had been an earthquake. It wasn't an earthquake. It was his soul. It was his soul leaving his body. Nevertheless he clambered to his feet and crab-walked to the still-open and unoccupied jar door.

Nobody up here had moved. They were pressed to the edges of the kitchen and gasped when Louis appeared. Some girl was crying. Louis had to look fucking horrifying, even aside from the gun in his hand.

There was the front door, wide open. Cold air rushed in. Across the street, the Caddy's headlights illuminated vertically blowing snow. Joe was trying to execute a K-turn in the street, but he was sliding all over the place. He nicked another parked car, backed fully into another one.

Fuck. Fuck! Louis said a little wordless prayer in his head to the god he didn't believe in until just now, when he kicked the dying girl over, and he dashed out the door. He nearly wiped out on the stoop, stumbling in the snow like a child. Joe had completed the turn and for a moment Louis was certain he was going to be left behind, here at the scene of the crime, literally with blood on his hands. And it really did appear that this was what Joe was trying to do—the tires spun freely in the snow, and the big man's face, lit by the dashboard, was intent only upon the road ahead. But before he could downshift, Louis reached the car, flung open the passenger door, and jumped in.

Joe gave him a sideways glare, and then the car was in motion. They gathered speed on the empty street.

"Fuckin' idiot," said Joe.

"What? Me?" Louis was still shaking. He couldn't catch his breath; the words were more like gasps.

"Fuckin' idiot."

Joe's breaths were low and fast and the air smelled like sweat. He turned left, then right, then left. They moved through downtown Broken River. The streets were quiet. The world didn't yet know about the thing they just did.

Louis said, "What are we doing, Joe?"

"Driving."

"Where?"

"House," Joe said.

"What house?"

"The house."

Louis didn't get it. They'd just left the house. Then Joe jerked right at the Route 94 sign and the car slid around untethered for a couple of seconds and Louis understood.

"We're going to the house?" he said.

"Yeah."

The silence deepened, lengthened, and they moved inexorably through the snow in pursuit of god knows what. Louis accepted for the first time that he might not get through this night alive. His mind was working all the angles, or trying to—the conceivable modes of escape, the possible endgames. Then, as the road emptied onto the highway and the Caddy gathered speed, he remembered that there was still a gun in his hand—stuck to his hand, in fact—and he slowly, nonchalantly slipped it into his inside jacket pocket. He had to wiggle it a little to detach it from his fingers. He zipped up the jacket and reached over his shoulder for the seat belt and pulled the belt tight and clicked it home. He closed his eyes and waited.

And here we are.

22

It has been happening for some time now: the Observer is coming to understand that it does not need to "be" in one place at any one time. It doesn't need, even, to be at one time at one time. It can be everywhere and anytime: and as the threads of cause and effect, real and imagined, that give the humans' lives meaning become increasingly intertwined (inextricably so, at this point), it *must* be. It cannot properly observe the humans—and the acts they perform and compel others to perform—without pulling apart, or perhaps expanding, or doubling and trebling, or creating an all-encompassing manifestation of itself.

The Observer's growing reach makes it feel more powerful. It can see and know all in this world (and what, it wonders, of other worlds? other consciousnesses? other phenomena, unfathomable to the humans, that it might study?), more than any single human can know about itself or its society. Indeed, it can know, if it wishes, more about humanity than all of humanity can ever hope to learn.

Yet the Observer feels less powerful than ever before: the immensity of its arena of observation throws into ever-sharper relief the fact of its incapacity to change the things it sees.

Unless—

Unless the humans' own awareness of their stories—that is, their understanding of their own lives as manifestations of, engines of, narrative lines—can be regarded as the domain of the Observer. In which case, the Observer is a part of them.

Or perhaps the Observer is something they have made: another god in the pantheon of invisible and powerful forces they have fashioned in their image.

And if it is so—if the humans have made the Observer—does this mean that it is beholden to them? Are their powers of self-determination, of ambition, of artful untruth and strategic misdirection, dependent upon the proximity and attention of the Observer? Or may the Observer go off on its own, test its skills and their limits, explore the totality of existence as any god might?

It doesn't know. Right now, it is certain only of its desire—and its responsibility—to see these narrative lines to their ragged ends. And of course these lines are only a few among a great many. New lines have already presented themselves, at least for most of these humans, but the humans are too absorbed in the imperatives of the moment to have yet perceived them. For unfortunate others, not many lines remain. For the equally unfortunate few, all lines have already come to an end. In truth, the Observer already knows all the outcomes, or something close to them; at this late hour, most alternate paths have been closed off.

In the wine bar in Brooklyn, New York, the woman named Rachel kneels on the floor over the woman named Eleanor. At first, she thought the woman had merely fainted, and her immediate response was annoyance. It took a lot out of her to open with an apology: to speak Eleanor's name, look her in the eye, and say *I'm sorry*.

She *is* sorry. It took her a while to get here, but here she is. She is sorry. Not just for hurting Eleanor, but for hurting herself. Acting like a child with Karl has made her feel old. Being in his company has made her feel lonely. Irina's call made her feel lonely, too. Watching Karl try to love the girl has caused her to remember her own father's failures at love. It is time to change her life.

"She's coming," Karl told her, as though his wife were an occupying force or weather event. Rachel now understands that their move was not, as he claimed, for the benefit of Eleanor's writing and his art, a bid for peace and quiet, but an escape from her, and punishment for his offenses against his marriage, of which she herself is one.

Rachel doesn't like Eleanor, despite what she told Irina. She was happy to believe Karl's insinuations (never actual lies that could be disproven) that she was cold and lifeless and uninterested in sex, and that their union was a sham, a convenience, a misguided effort to give their daughter some semblance of an orderly home. But Karl, of course, is both a bullshitter and his own principal bullshittee. His wife, she believed, deserved better than him. And better than Rachel, for that matter.

And when Rachel walked into the bar's back room and found the woman slouching and staggering, eyes underscored with purple-gray, Rachel could see that she'd been suffering. She had barely met Eleanor's eyes, barely begun to speak, before something seemed to set the woman's body into twisting motion; it began to fall, glitching like a scrambled TV signal. Eleanor half-collapsed, and her eyes rolled back in her head, and all solidity abandoned her. She slid down the wood-paneled wall, knocked over a stack of folding chairs, and tumbled with them to the floor.

A body hitting the floor in a crowded bar does not go unnoticed. All conversation stopped, all heads turned. For shit's sake, lady, Rachel thought, get hold of yourself. And then she thought better of it when she crouched beside Eleanor's prone, unmoving form and saw the whites of her eyes and the nightmare-twitching of her hands, and smelled urine.

"Eleanor," she says now, gently smacking her clammy cheek. "Eleanor!"

The Observer takes note of this behavior with interest. This woman, Rachel, rival to Eleanor, competitor for her husband's attention, has shifted now to the role of helper, of nurse, of friend. Rachel takes Eleanor's hand in hers, strokes her pallid face. The eyes focus with excruciating slowness upon her unlikely rescuer. The eyelids flutter. Something like a belch emerges from the throat. Rachel moves a strand of hair from Eleanor's eyes.

"Can you hear me? Eleanor?"

Is this, could this be, a form of love? Can the enemy in need become, suddenly, a friend? Or is Rachel's compassion merely an expression of projected selfishness, what she wishes Eleanor might feel were it Rachel herself doubling over in agony, folding to the ground, falling unconscious?

The woman can't speak, but she seems to understand. A waiter arrives at Rachel's shoulder, says, "What happened, did the chair break?" and Rachel says, "No, no, she passed out or something." This appears to alarm the waiter. He pulls out a phone and calls for an ambulance. People have resumed talking, seeing that this event is under the control of others, has nothing to do with them; but it is clear from the tone of their voices that their evening of levity and inebriation is ruined.

Eleanor's body is lying at a strange angle, one that a healthy human in repose would never assume. Her legs are folded up half-underneath her; one arm is flung out over her head, as though in an effort to catch something; the other arm clutches at her midriff. She seems somewhat more alert now, panicked, and little shocks travel across her face, dispatches from the malfunctioning machinery. Rachel says, "Can you move?"

If Eleanor understands the question, she doesn't reply. But the Observer notes that her hand squeezes Rachel's.

"Hold on," Rachel says, and pushes the chair out of the way and rearranges Eleanor's body—the legs out straight, the wayward arm down at her side. Rachel balls up her scarf and places it under Eleanor's head. Eleanor has no visible reaction. Her mouth and eyelids are twitching again; the eyes reel. The waiter is still standing there, staring in evident terror, phone still in his hand.

"Why don't you go find a blanket," Rachel tells him.

The man looks confused for a moment, then snaps to and hurries away.

That's the last Rachel will see of him. She holds Eleanor's hand and waits. The Observer waits with them. Whatever just happened has taken the air out of the room; people have gathered their things and are edging awkwardly past this strange tableau, one woman on her knees, holding another's hand.

Over the next twenty minutes—as the two paramedics arrive, entering the bar with disturbing nonchalance, like they came here for after-work drinks and just happened to find a woman lying on the floor; as they load Eleanor, roughly, onto a stretcher and into the ambulance; as they try to prevent Rachel from riding along until she tells them, with an inspired fierceness that surprises all three of them, that Eleanor is her wife and she will not be treated this way; as they ride to the hospital, sluicing through red lights with a vertiginous, dreamlike frictionlessness—Rachel begins a series of thoughts that she will later come to regard as transformative, the first being how wonderful it is, how selfless, that she is doing this thing, cleaving herself to the woman she has wronged in her moment of crisis, and how pleasurable it will be in the days to come, recalling what a mensch she was on this cold and miserable night on the cusp of the winter of 2017. The second thought, which comes hot on the heels of the first one, is that wow, is she ever a narcissistic whore.

There are more thoughts along these lines: about the nature of her cruel and unfeeling father, her weak-willed mother, their wealth and privilege, her own failings as their daughter and as an adult. Indeed, it takes almost no time at all, the complete unraveling of the illusions out of which Rachel has assembled her life. Watching it happen— watching this sudden shattering of barriers, opening of doors, mingling of previously confined and sequestered truths—the Observer is struck by how liberating it is for the humans to accept blame for their own misfortunes, to forgive those who have hurt them. They are capable of such anger, such violent fury, such resentment! And yet, it can all be dispelled in an instant. Rachel, as the Observer watches, is being rewarded with a feeling of bodily lightness and a surprising visual clarity, the details of the world taking on an almost surreal specificity as they assert themselves, for the first time, as entities without any relationship to her at all. Not only is Rachel no longer the center of the universe; she isn't even the center of her own reality. Rachel is an object in the world dedicated to its own gratification and the reciprocal gratification of a small number of other, equally unimportant objects. It is as though she sees herself from outside, from above and behind, as in a near-death story; she is both observed and observer. It is not necessary to be the way I've been, she thinks, as the nurses and doctors swarm and confer, as they ask her questions she hasn't the slightest idea how to answer. I can be different.

Rachel is standing in the emergency room, and Karl's wife is being rolled into a slot and attached to machines. The light is bright and dirty and the air smells like bandages and truck exhaust. She takes a breath, approaches a doctor. Touches her arm. Says, That's my friend. What can I do to help?

––––––––

Meanwhile, in the kitchen of the house in Broken River, the young woman called Sam (and what, the Observer wonders, might have happened had she gone by some other name? Would the girl, Irina, still have chosen to believe she was the adult incarnation of the lost child Samantha? What if the man, Karl, had not found her appealing, had not held out some faint hope of sexual congress with her? Would he have declined to engage her services as a babysitter? What if she had stayed in Buffalo with her mentally ill mother? What if she had held more tightly to the hand she found in the pile of coats? The narrative lines that radiate from these plausible events and choices are distantly visible to the Observer but, upon closer examination, bifurcate, sprout tributaries, diffuse into a cloud of possibility too complicated even for the Observer to comprehend. No, Sam's present story is its focus, and she has reached a bottleneck: there is suffering she must now endure in order to move forward. That suffering has just now begun) closes her phone and sets it down on the kitchen table, then lays her two hands on either side and wills them to stop shaking. Nothing that she has just been told makes any sense. (But it does, the Observer thinks: everything that has ever happened, and everything yet to happen, makes sense.) The voice on the phone was someone's, some girl's. Janet, she thinks is the name? An occasional boarder at Yetta's, a friend, a hanger-on. Sam remembers her, sort of. On the phone just now, she was screaming and crying, and their conversation was interrupted several times, but the gist of it was that something has happened, some men came to the house, they crashed a party Yetta and Daniel were throwing, and they found the weed door and went down there, they killed Daniel and Yetta. Sam, the girl said, where the fuck are you, it was a big guy and a little guy, they took off down the street in an old car, and lock the door, Sam, because they're out there.

Sam is sitting very still now. She's processing the information. A big guy and a little guy came to the party. They shot her brother and they shot Yetta, both of whom are now dead.

An old car, she thinks. A Cadillac. A light-blue Cadillac.

Why does she know this? An immaculately preserved powder-blue Cadillac. She can see it in her mind's eye, idling in the dark somewhere, with snow falling on it. She can see it parked across the street from the old theater in the bright daylight, two men emerging from it and onto the dirty sidewalk, the big one in a windbreaker a little too small for him, the little one in a ski parka and a pair of acid-washed jeans. Passing it on the road out to the trailer park, in the shotgun seat of Uncle Bobby's car, she can hear him saying, "Look at that rig, it's right out of a time capsule, just look at it."

Sam has seen the men at Denny's. She served them. They were there, watching Daniel. Of course it's them. The big one gazed intently at her. Not the way other men do. Not with longing.

She saw the Cadillac when she was exiting Karl and Irina's driveway in Karl's Volvo. She saw the Cadillac pulling away from the shoulder of Route 94 at the bottom of the hill, as though it had been sitting there, watching and waiting.

She saw the man in the ski parka while she hid in the woods with Irina. She watched him climb onto the porch and knock on the door that Sam now must suppress an impulse to turn and stare at.

She doesn't entirely understand what is happening. She only knows that Daniel is dead, that he has been murdered, how will she ever tell her mother? She doesn't know what it has to do with her—is it the weed? that Daniel was growing, that she was dealing?—but it hardly matters. She fears that they are coming here. They have, after all, been here before.

From the outside, to the Observer, Sam merely appears, hunched over the table with her hands palms-down on the table, to be deep in thought, as though trying to solve a difficult problem. Her expression is one not of grief or shock but of concentration. But the Observer knows that she is about to act. Her narrative line is clear now. The next half hour she will later remember as a kind of infinitude, a sealed but borderless chamber in her life. At times, looking back, she'll believe her brain must have shut down, gone into cold storage, for all she can recall. At other times she'll remember it as a box of memories—her life up until then not flashing before her eyes, like a film flickering by at high speed, but rather a whirling storm of fragments, spinning all around her, revealing themselves only in brief, static images, bursts of speech. Rightly or not, these minutes will serve as a gravity well of her past and future life—a collapsed star of memory, a black hole, all lines bending toward it. (Yes, the Observer tells itself, yes.)

The man named Karl is approaching now, around the side of the house. He's holding an empty coffee mug and is about to step onto the porch. He does it—he climbs the porch steps, stamps snow off his boots, comes in the door. The girl Sam starts, stands up fast, and the chair clatters to the floor behind her. "Karl," she says. "Get Irina. Turn out the lights. Go to the studio."

"What?" he says. He seems dazed, puzzled. The Observer, and Sam as well, know that this is because he has been smoking to excess, out in the studio. To him, events are unfolding slowly, mysteriously, disconnected from one another and from their causes. The redness of his eyes, the dilation of his pupils, are driving Sam to irrational anger.

"Take Irina to the studio," she says in a near shout, "and turn out the lights!"

A small smile appears on his face. "Hey . . . ," he says. "What's going on?"

"Karl!" Sam screams now. "These guys killed my brother! They are coming here!"

He looks down into his coffee mug, as though an explanation might be hidden there. He says, "Wait. Wait."

"Fuck," Sam says, then she runs up the stairs two at a time.

Irina is sitting cross-legged on her bed, surrounded by books and papers, holding her guitar. She says to Sam, "Did you just yell at Father?"

"Buddy, you have to come with us now. We're going out to your dad's studio."

Her mouth is a perfect O. She blinks. "Why?"

"Some people are coming, I think. Bad people. It'll be fine, we just have to go out there and . . . lay low."

There is a moment of silence, which, in its new incarnation as an entity of nearly limitless knowledge, the Observer finds shockingly long. The future of these people is clearer now than ever. Everything that will happen in the next thirty minutes is now almost certain to happen, regardless of how long any of the humans spends contemplating his or her potential actions. Lay down your guitar, Irina, and follow.

Irina is paralyzed by doubt. She doubts the reality of this moment, and her trust in Sam, and her faith that there is even a correct choice to be made. For a surprising instant, the Observer actually thinks it might be mistaken: Irina might not go with Sam, and the narrative lines might tremble, flex, and shatter. But then, at last, Irina lays the guitar down before her and scrambles off the bed.

Downstairs, Karl has barely moved. The coffee mug is on the table now. He stares at them, confused. He says, "Okay, what?"

"Your studio," Sam says. "Come on."

And like that, he believes. He shakes himself, like an animal coming up from sleep, and says, "Okay, then." He digs in his pocket for the keys, holds them out. "I'm going to call the cops. Take her."

"Father?" Irina says quietly.

Sam leads her across the kitchen, takes the keys from Karl as he draws his phone from his pocket. The three hurry to the door and set off running through yesterday's snow. It has begun to snow again, and the air has the hushed, protected quality that implies much more to come. Then, "Wait," Karl says suddenly. He points behind them, toward the porch. "Footprints."

The three of them look at each other. Then Irina says "This way" and grabs Sam's hand. She leads her back, past the steps, then circles them around the house the other way, clockwise, keeping them close to the shrub line. Their trail disappears in the shadows of the bushes—there is not much moon behind the storm, and the only light is the inside light from the living room.

"Good thinking," says Sam.

"I always knew this would happen," Irina says, with no evident fear in her voice.

The Observer feels now, more than sees, a convergence of thoughts in the minds of Irina and Sam; it is true that Irina has renewed her recently dismissed fantasies of involvement with the crimes of the past; her dalliance with CyberSleuths, which not so long ago seemed childish, now seems preordained, consequential, and she believes that her doom is sealed. And as for Sam: she has never imagined herself as old and content, surrounded by loved ones, in some comfortable and uneventful future life. She has always felt hunted. By whom, or what, she has never understood, but tonight it seems right that these men are hunting her. Crazy murderers. They were always going to come for her.

The Observer recognizes that both young women are wrong but cannot see precisely how. It cannot project that far into the future.

Karl is muttering into his phone now, talking to the police. "Tell them it's the guys from the killings on Gauss Lane," Sam says. Irina has led them far into the trees, evidently intending to double back from behind the studio. She whispers, "Sam? Is your brother . . . did they hurt your brother?"

"Yes," Sam says.

"It's not your fault," Irina tells her, with absolute seriousness.

Sam gathers her closer, and the girl throws her arms around her waist. They walk in tandem, awkwardly, moving along the studio wall. Karl is repeating the address into his phone. He seems to be having trouble making himself understood. "No," he says, "after the entrance to the state forest. Before the church with the reader board." The snow is blowing gently into their faces.

And then they're at the studio door. Lights are blazing through the windows above, but no headlights shine from the drive. No sound. As though channeling the Observer's thoughts, Sam is suddenly confident that she is completely, embarrassingly wrong. The men aren't coming here. The killings have nothing to do with her, or with Karl and Irina, or with this house, or with the murders of the past. She wants to tell them, Wait, stop, it's a false alarm. There's nothing to fear.

Karl unlocks the door, slips in. Darkness arrives with a snap.

Inside, it is hot and close and muggy with marijuana smoke. Sam hears the click of the lock behind them, and then Karl's phone illuminates the floor. "Other side of the forge." He leads them there, and they wedge themselves into the corner, between the forge and the wall, and sit cross-legged in a row, with Irina in the middle.

Karl whispers, "The call you got. It said they're coming here?"

"Not exactly."

He's poking at the phone. His head is a black, furry ball. Finally the little rectangle of light disappears. The windows along the ceiling glow faintly with the light from the house; Sam feels a hand on her arm, Irina's, and the hand travels down and interlocks its fingers with hers. The Observer occupies the corner with them, impatient for events to unfold. It wonders if it will be right; or, rather, it wonders how right it will be.

"The police will be here soon," Sam says. "Then we can go back inside."

"Okay," Irina whispers back. "Sam."

"Yeah?"

"It's not your fault," she says again. But this time she adds, "It's my fault. I told Jasn and the art teacher about the house and the murders and everything."

"Who?"

"I told them about how your parents died. Or who I thought was your parents. It's those men that killed them, isn't it."

"Irina—"

"It's them," Irina says. "I'm sorry. They found out." There are tears in her voice.

"Shsh."

"Sam," she says, very quietly now. "I put your picture on the internet. I'm sorry. I told those people, and I put your picture on the internet. Saying you were Samantha."

Sam says, "My . . . you have my picture?"

"I took it outside Dairy Queen. I put it on a messageboard. About crimes. I said you were her."

"Jesus," Sam whispers involuntarily, and Irina begins to cry. So Sam holds her tighter, says, "It's not your fault, either. Bad things don't need reasons to happen."

A hand brushes Sam's shoulder; it's Karl's. She almost forgot he was here. He was putting his arm around his daughter and then, almost as an afterthought, has extended it to Sam as well. Sam leans into it; she can feel the nearness of Karl's head to hers, with Irina's soft hair underneath. The three of them sit there, listening to each other breathe.

They wait. Minutes tick by, or hours. (The Observer is aware that, for these humans, time has slowed to an excruciating degree, and it experiences a moment of irritation at the pettiness of their impatience. They have not, after all, floated for a decade inside an abandoned house. But then it remembers that they fear the imminent arrival of death, and it chastens itself for this lapse in compassion.) Sam is restless; she is on the verge of apologizing for scaring them and for putting them through this. And then, faintly, the sound of footsteps striking wood—specifically, the wooden front porch of the house—drifts through the night and into the dark studio.

"Did you hear that?" Irina whispers.

"It must be the police," Karl croaks.

But they don't move. Irina's hand grips Sam's tighter. Karl leans in harder. Their heads bump together. His breathing is audible in the room, deep and resonant and hoarse.

The time has come for the Observer to leave its charges here, in the dark studio that is gradually growing colder, and return to the place of its origins. It is time to go back to the house. It gathers itself, contracting, identifying its now-disparate and diffuse parts and pulling them in close. It tries to remember what it was like to move slowly, to confine itself to rooms, to see only one thing at a time, to be blind to the future. It tries to remember what it was like to be more human.

Only an instant passes in human time, but the process feels laborious to the Observer. To limit itself is no longer in its nature. When it has shrunk to a point, the Observer makes its way through the crack between the doorframe and door; drifts through the falling snow to the kitchen wall; flits into a tunnel in the cedar shakes made years before by a carpenter bee; and enters the kitchen through the screwhole of an electrical-outlet faceplate. (The Observer remembers, now, the contractor's workman who dropped the missing screw and watched it roll into a crack between two floorboards. "Fuck it," the man said, and left the hole empty.) Soon it is hovering, gently bobbing in the kitchen as it did for much of a decade, enduring the interminable fractions of a second it takes for the men on the porch to push open the door. (The door isn't even latched. The people left in haste and didn't pull it closed all the way. If all the humans disappeared right now—and for a moment the Observer wishes they all would, so that it could enjoy, as it once did, the complexity of unpeopled silence—the wind would soon blow the door open, and leaves and rain would coat the kitchen floor.)

At last the door flies open, and the men enter, the big one and the small one, each with a gun drawn. So primitive, these devices made for killing at a distance; the Observer doesn't understand why the humans have not designed more efficient and precise tools for this simple task. Their technology is certainly capable enough. Perhaps they enjoy the sensation of an explosion in the hand, the noise and smoke. Perhaps they don't really want to kill and wish to introduce an element of uncertainty into the process.

In any event, the Observer is bored now as the two men creep through the house, seeking the inhabitants who are not there. It draws what would be a breath if breathing were something it needed to do and explodes itself back into its full scope and articulation; it leaves the house now and is instantly with its people in the studio, as they await the conclusions of their narratives.

The girl named Sam has admitted to herself, at last, that it is not the police who have arrived at the house; they would be calling out now if these people were the police. They would shout Karl's name and tell him it was safe to emerge from hiding. So it must be them—the men. All three of them know it because none of them speaks or moves. They wait a long time for the next thing to happen. It feels to Sam like an hour, though it can't be more than five minutes—how long does it take two men to determine that a house is empty? Or is it money they're looking for now? None of it makes any sense. If it is all true, if Daniel is dead, if these men kill Sam as well, it will confirm their mother's every misapprehension about the world. Everything is exquisitely interconnected, malevolent, and dangerous. They are, in fact, out to get you.

Her thoughts are interrupted by the sound of a door slamming shut. Again, footsteps on the porch, down the stairs. Low voices. Then the voices quiet, and there is silence. But a fuller silence, a more expectant one. Irina shivers, and Karl pulls her closer. Sam leans into them both. Minutes pass, and then the thudding of boots reaches them from outside the studio door. Somebody jiggles the knob, then pounds, violently. "Hey!" a man shouts. Irina lets out the tiniest peep, barely audible even to Sam.

The men are talking. They walk around the exterior of the studio, looking for a way in. Will they notice the footprints? It was dark where Irina led them, and the snow has continued to fall. Perhaps it filled their prints. The men don't hesitate as they circle the studio, and they don't speak. Sam can hear their shoes crunching in the snow, their coats dragging along the shrubs. At one moment, the men are mere inches from where the three of them are huddled, separated only by the wall. But the men continue their circumnavigation, confer again at the door.

And then, incredibly, they seem to give up. Their voices recede. Sam hears the words "in the woods," "fuckin' freeze to death."

They have decided to leave. They're leaving.

(Wait, says the Observer.)

Karl's phone rings.

It is approximately the loudest noise Sam has ever heard—a grating electric chirp like a motel alarm clock, accompanied by the sudden illumination of their corner as the screen switches itself on. Before Karl can silence it, it rings again. Then it stops. Karl has apparently hit ANSWER. He's holding the phone in his lap and a woman's voice is coming out of it, a tiny beacon from the world of safety and freedom, small but distinct. "Karl?" it says, with some urgency. "Karl?" A long pause. "Are you there? Karl, please pick up."

Surely the men outside can hear. What in the hell is he doing?

"Karl! Please!" the woman says, and then his thumb occludes the display and the call is ended. The screen goes black.

"I'm so sorry," he says, and a moment later the pounding on the door resumes, the sound of pure, unfettered rage. It sounds like they have found a heavy branch and they are bringing it down over and over on the knob.

"Open!" a man is bellowing, as though this will work, "open it!," followed by more pounding. It's a heavy door—Sam noticed this coming in—but if they want it to open, it will be opened.

(The Observer is aware that a nexus of narrative possibility, the last in this skein of cause and effect, is now approaching: choices that can be made, outcomes that will result. As the seconds go by, paths pass in and out of existence; probabilities shift from one path to another. If these were visual phenomena, they might register as flickers, jumps, as in the completion of a high-voltage electrical circuit or, slowed a thousandfold, the movement of floodwater through a landscape that both guides the water's movement and is altered by its force. If it were aural, this dynamism might manifest as crackles that give way to a rumble or hum, like the cascading action of an earthquake, or the starting of an engine, or the illusion, to the human ear, of repeated unpitched pulses resolving into a musical note.

But,) "Stay here," Karl says in a normal, disconcertingly calm speaking voice, and he gets up from the floor.

"Daddy!" Irina stage-whispers. Sam has never heard her utter this word.

"Stay!" is the stern response. Sam feels him stepping over them; he moves a few feet away, to where Sam thinks she remembers a work table. Irina throws both arms around her, squeezes her tightly. The pounding continues, then gives way to muttered conversation.

What is Karl doing? She hears metal scrape against wood. Something hard and heavy falls to the floor. His faint shadow, cast by light through the high windows, crosses the room, an indeterminate distance away.

Even Sam screams when the shooting starts. At first she thinks they're firing through the walls, trying to kill them that way. Then she realizes that they're shooting the lock. Between shots, the men are shouting at each other. Sam envelops Irina with her body; she cannot get her arms far enough around the girl.

There is one more shot, and then all the noise stops. Sam hazards a peek around the corner of the forge.

The door has fallen open: a two-inch slice of dim light extends from ceiling to floor. A coatsleeve is visible through it, two bare hands clutching something. A gun.

Sam grips Irina tighter, willing her to silence. There's a click, and the lights come on. Sam closes her eyes. The door creaks, three slow footsteps sound, and a man's voice says, "Where the fuck—"

Then there's a gunshot, but it is so huge in the room, it seems to come from everywhere at once. Sam is deafened; then the silence gives way to a high, pure sine wave, a test tone. Through it she can she hear something soft and heavy hitting the floor, and a metallic clatter against the concrete. Sam opens her eyes. She can see past the corner of the forge to where a massive human arm the size of an entire child is flung out on the cement, and a few feet beyond it, a pistol. Beyond that is the work table, and Karl is visible behind it, his dark eyes, frightened and determined and bloodshot, peeking over the top.

Through the ringing in her ears, Sam hears Irina's quiet weeping. She is trying to be quiet, but she just can't. Against the concrete sounds a footstep, and then another. "Hey," says a man's voice she thinks she recognizes, gentler this time. She can't see him. But she can still see Karl behind the table, and she realizes, with growing horror, that he is about to do something.

It is now clear to the Observer that one narrative line, that of the man Karl, is about to come to an end. It wonders when, exactly, this outcome—the one that is imminent—became inevitable: was it when he read his wife's books, here in the studio, and in so doing rekindled, or perhaps kindled for the first time, feelings of familial responsibility? Or was it when he bought the bag of herbal intoxicants from the girl Sam, which have now aroused, in his racing mind, a heightened sense of paranoia and an inflated confidence in his own physical prowess? Or was it when he hired Sam as Irina's babysitter? Or was the die cast earlier than all that: when Karl selected this house as the future site of his marriage and career rehabilitation, or when he chose the path of faithlessness in his union with Eleanor, or when he compelled her to enjoy sexual intercourse with him without the use of a birth control apparatus, or when he decided to attend art school, or when he fell in, at the age of seventeen, with the adult woman of twenty-five who would teach him how to have sex, or when he learned to masturbate, at the age of thirteen, or when he drew his first picture, at the age of one, with a crayon on a piece of butcher paper at the table in his parents' apartment?

Perhaps, in the future, these are questions that, in other circumstances involving other human beings, the Observer will be able to answer. For now, though, it cannot; for now it can only watch the man Karl prepare to blunder toward the completion of his story. He is trembling now, crouched behind his work table, clutching a glass-bladed knife in his hand; he draws silent breaths and his jaw twitches as his pupils constrict against the sudden light, and he thinks:

Because of course this was always what you were going to do. Because one minute you're gooned on grass and reading your wife's unfinished novel you scammed from her backup drive; and the next you're crouched in the dark with the weapon you forged, gripped in your cold hand; and the cuts healing on your back are itching like mad, pushing you forward; and you have no fucking idea what is going on except that there are enemies and they have found you and shots have been fired. Because you're a shitty father and because you had a shitty father. Because being a sculptor is, in retrospect, fucking stupid. Because you didn't defend yourself when you were six and the neighbor twins stole your bike. Because you didn't defend yourself when you were eight and Pete Nagel pissed on you on the school bus. Because you didn't defend yourself when you were eleven and Todd Clark pushed you into the lockers and told you that you were forbidden from using the first-floor boys' room ever again, and you never used the first-floor boys' room ever again. Because you tried to defend yourself when you were twelve and Kevin Drangle pushed you over and emptied your backpack into the mud and you didn't get in even a single punch because he pushed you back down laughing and said if you got up he'd shoot you with a bow and arrow through your bedroom window. Because you didn't defend Heather Giselson when you were both fifteen and Nathan Johnson spat on her, and though she said that wasn't the reason when she dumped you a week later, of course it was the fucking reason. Because you didn't defend your mother when you were twenty and your father called her that crazy bitch at a celebratory dinner for his third wife who had just gotten a PhD in semantics and everybody laughed as though getting a fucking PhD in semantics was less crazy than anything your mother ever did in her life. Because you thought your wife was a hack until the other day. Because you are a fucking pussy, and your moment has come. Because you are an animal, and before you stands an animal, and you were both brought here to kill. That is why you stand up, joints cracking, and scream, and lunge forward screaming with the knife out in front of you like a blazing torch to light the way toward life or death, and that is why the guy takes one step back, then another, his face inhuman with what you belatedly recognize as terror, and you manage to think that maybe none of this had to happen as you collide with him, sink the knife in until it strikes bone, then feel the hot bite of metal on your scalp and the world explodes and the hand of god comes from out of nowhere to stop you in your tracks and grip you in its fingers made of sky and lay you gently, firmly, on the ground where you belong.

············

It is baffling to the Observer, the things they do, the patterns they create that they inhabit and re-create again and again. They find one another so irresistible, even when enmity is the form their affinity takes. Over and over they come together, and if they fail to derive pleasure from these encounters, they find satisfaction in suffering. They are more attached, perhaps, to their suffering than to their pleasure.

This stands in direct contradiction to their stated goals, which are those of comity, happiness, calm. But it is pain that gives their lives meaning.

Pain is not something the Observer understands. It has not experienced corporeality, but it sees that conceptual disharmony can lead, eventually, to physical harm and deformation. The body reacts to mental disturbance—it shapes itself according to the mind's instructions. And of course the humans can inflict bodily harm upon one another, sometimes reluctantly or even accidentally, sometimes with great eagerness. A penchant for inflicting bodily harm invites harm done to the self—and thus the hunger for pain is satisfied.

Four of them are here, in this room: the three who concealed themselves, locked themselves away and out of sight, and the one who pursued them. The man called Joe is dead. He was shot by the one called Louis, who has fled through the open door, clutching his arm where the knife went in, and disappeared into the cold night. Joe's body is like a sleeping infant's blown up to gargantuan proportions. His left hand is trapped beneath the ruined head from which blood is still emerging, and his gun lies on the cement, inches from his splayed right arm.

The man named Karl is also dead, killed in much the same way as Joe, and his body, too, lies facedown on the cement, emptying itself of blood.

The young woman Sam is doubled over with grief, or nausea, or both, and her eyes are squeezed shut. The Observer does not wish to intrude upon her thoughts now. Better simply to watch. Sam clutches herself, emits a high, quiet sound, takes in breath in great, ragged gasps. But then she straightens; her arms fall to her sides, her eyes open. An expression of resolve hardens on her face. She crouches beside the girl, Irina, who has made herself small on the floor in much the manner of the child who, more than a decade ago, survived the killings Joe performed. Sam tells the girl not to look, to keep her hand, both hands, over her eyes, and Irina agrees with a nod. The blood from Joe's body is encroaching into their shared space behind the forge; it is time to move. Sam pulls Irina to her feet, adds her hand to the mask of Irina's own, and guides the girl around the bodies, out the door, and into the falling snow.

Now the Observer drifts out of the room and into the woods, where the man Louis is running blindly, tripping over roots and fallen branches, whimpering, trying to suppress, with his inadequate fingers, the hemorrhaging of blood from his wounded arm. His teeth chatter; his body shakes. He is holding the knife, dark with his own blood, which he had the presence of mind to remove from the crime scene. He appears both to be in shock and extremely cold. The heavy snow is already filling his footprints. The Observer rises above the trees, charting Louis's likely trajectory, teasing out the strongest (and growing ever stronger) vector of probability: he will cross that creek, dropping the knife into it on the way. He will break into that house on the other side of the rise and bind his wound with rags; he will walk along the road, ducking into the trees whenever a car passes, until he reaches the closed gas station, to which he will gain access through a weak panel in the rotting garage door. There, he will sleep for a few furtive hours, and in the morning he will manage to hitchhike to the bus station with a drunk woman in flight from the abusive husband she will return to days later. The woman won't think to alert police to the passage through her life of a shivering man bleeding through a bundle of rags. Such events are not remarkable, or even memorable, in her world. She won't ever hear of the killings. She will die of a heart attack before long. The gas station owner, similarly, will discover the hole in his garage door, attribute it to junkies or kids, repair it with a square of plywood, and forget all about it. He'll learn of the killings in the house over the rise but won't connect them with his break-in, or feel much concern about them at all. Some people get themselves killed. That's their own business.

The Observer moves down the hill, to where the police officers have arrived, one man and one woman. They are young and uncertain. They stand beside the empty powder-blue car, which has indeed been parked at the bottom of the drive, blocking it, for some time. Nearly an inch of snow has fallen upon it; the hood, still radiating heat, remains clear, but not for long. The officers have been told to wait for reinforcements. They are waiting for reinforcements. It doesn't matter anymore, though their inaction may eventually have some consequences, ones the Observer cannot predict. Internal punishments inside the police organization. Feelings of guilt—pointless ones, because there is nothing they could have done upon arriving to prevent the two deaths.

The Observer no longer cares. It feels the lightness of not having to pay attention to events and people that no longer interest it. The earth recedes beneath it as it rises up into the snowstorm, in much the way that the events inside the studio, which just moments ago aroused such intense interest, have now receded from its attention. The Observer returns to the house where the young man and woman were shot in the cellar. The house is surrounded by police cars, lights flashing. Police surround, mark, and photograph the bodies downstairs, in the room filled with artificial light and living vegetation. Other police, upstairs, interrogate the bereaved partygoers, writing down their statements in notebooks. To the humans, these deaths represent instances of chaos that must be investigated, explained, understood. The Observer has no such obligation now. It turns now to the city to the south. The wife of Karl, the woman named Eleanor, is here, lying in a quiet white room, in a building of a hundred other rooms like it. She is unconscious. Another woman sits beside her, holding her hand—it is Karl's lover, Rachel. The lover does not belong here, she feels—she barely knows the dying woman. She has tried to contact Karl but couldn't reach him. The situation, however, brings her a sad kind of satisfaction. She is fulfilling a need. A social need, at this point, more than a personal one; for the woman, Eleanor, has no awareness of the other woman's presence here, nor any sense of how she arrived here, or even where she is. Inside Eleanor's mind, dreams are unfolding, or perhaps memories. The difference between the two is unclear to the Observer; they are so similar. The Observer can sense the mind trying to ascribe meaning, to create it and contextualize it. Even unconscious, the mind is burdened by this imperative. Eleanor is sitting on a wooden bench near a fountain in a city. The fountain is in front of her—it seems enormous, like a public swimming pool, though she has been instructed not to climb into it, or even to drag her hand through it, because it's filled with bacteria. Other children are running around it, splashing one another, and she feels pity for them, for the illnesses they're likely to contract as a result of this play. Between the fountain and her bench, a large number of pigeons are clustered; they are pecking at the ground where a passing old man has scattered seeds. On a nearby bench, her mother and aunt are sitting, talking. They're speaking in low tones, as though privately, but she can hear their voices very clearly, above the noise of the children and splashing water and traffic on the street that runs past this plaza. The conversation they're having is about Eleanor and her husband, or rather her fiancé, for they are not yet married, though Eleanor is pregnant with his child. This can't be so, because in this scene Eleanor is still a child herself, and she hasn't met her husband yet, or ever even yet conceived of having sex with a man; she's barely five. Yet she hears them saying:

"I don't think she's strong enough."

"Strong how?"

"Not physically I mean, not her body—I'm afraid having a child will break her mentally. She's not ready."

"You weren't much older."

"I was different. It was a different time. I was married. She's fragile."

"He could be a good father. You never know."

"He's useless, of course. He's a philanderer—I overheard her talking to her friend."

"He's charming, I'll give him that."

"You can't charm a clean diaper onto a baby."

"Ha!"

"This will sound terribly narcissistic, but I feel as though it's all a repudiation. It's her way of showing us."

"There's some truth to that, I'd imagine."

"She's always been headstrong. She'll do it her way, even if it isn't the best way, or any way at all."

"Look at her now," Eleanor's aunt says, "she's afraid of the pigeons."

As her aunt speaks these words, Eleanor realizes that it's true—the pigeons have eaten the seeds they were given and have approached her bench, expecting more. They surround her, milling about, bobbing their heads, rarely looking directly at her. But their expectations are clear, and she fears that they will hop up onto the bench with her, then onto her lap. They, too, carry disease, according to her mother. Eleanor pulls her legs up, crosses them under her skirt, and the birds fill the space her feet occupied; they're under and behind and around the bench now. The plaza's masonry is a strange color, a dark green arranged in a pattern of diamonds, mortared by thick lines of gold. The pigeons make a sound, a low burbling; their feathers rustle against each other. The rustling is strangely amplified, displaced; it's like it is happening right beside her head, right there at her ear.

But no, that sound isn't coming from the pigeons but from Irina's hands, moving in her sleep—they're in bed together in Brooklyn, it's a Saturday morning. Irina is lying on her side, half-curled like a cat; her arms are crossed at the wrist, and the hands lie on the pillow between their faces, writhing in a constant, evolving motion. She is two. Karl is off somewhere. Not in the bed, anyway. Eleanor is fully awake now, perceiving the strange spectacle of her daughter's hands. It's like a sign language—the motions aren't jerky, they're fluid, practiced—and she wonders if they mean something, if each movement is a word or letter or idea, if Irina is expressing something from her dream, in a form her mind has devised specifically for this occasion and will permanently forget when the dream has ended. There is something about this experience that is too rich, too frightening and beautiful, and Eleanor closes her eyes and rolls onto her back, and when she opens them Craig is there above her, she's in his bed in Manhattan where he has brought her for sex, and she focuses on the soft gray and blond hairs on his chest as he moves into and through her. She recognizes that he is a sad man, lonely, though he is beautiful and moneyed and would be the first to admit few human beings born to this earth are luckier. And yet it's his sadness that attracts her, probably attracts most of the assistants he sleeps with, it's something that makes her feel grown-up to recognize and appreciate. It feels good to give a man something that he wants that won't turn into an obligation. The beauty of Craig was that he appreciated everything that happened as it was happening and never betrayed any disappointment when it ended, whether it was a good meal or a professional relationship with one of his writers or half an hour in bed with a woman half his age.

She leans forward, bringing her mouth close to the microphone, and half-turns her head to the man twice her age at the other end of the table, who has just spoken, and she says, "There's nothing wrong with giving people what they want." A titter ripples through the crowd, and a few people gently applaud, but the most prominent sound in the room is the man's snort—it's a phlegmy, resonant snuffle, as from an animal many times his size, and he makes sure it carries over the PA and through the room; it's obnoxious and deafening, but it silences the audience, and he says, "Well, then, that's the difference between you and me." There's no tittering this time, but there's applause, she guesses it's different people applauding this time. The man is a writer, comparable to her in sales but valued by other men and by the academy. They are panelists at a conference. Later that night, in the hotel bar, he says to her, "A pleasure sparring with you," and instead of saying "likewise" and turning her back, she says, "Suck my cock," and then feints at him as though to knock him over. He starts, takes a step back, and then a mask of murderous rage falls down over his face and he says "You fucking bitch!" and a young woman steps between them like a fight is about to break out. Eleanor goes back to her hotel room, clenches her jaw in the bed half the night, weeps with rage. Don't engage. Don't engage. She's in a bed now, again, somebody is holding her hand, she wants to pull them closer to see who it is, but she can't. The pigeons are burbling around and beneath her, they're minding their own business. But they're death. They're death without even knowing it! Death is everywhere and alive, but it is motivated by nothing. It can't be reasoned with, it can't be persuaded away from its dispassionate aims. It rises all around you with its mottled gray wings, envelops you in a cloud of noise and dust, and takes you.

....

Except of course that it doesn't, not yet. If the Observer were able to convey this kind of information to Eleanor, it would have by now. It has known for some time that her worries—some of them, not all— were for nothing. But it has understood for some time the folly of wishing to soothe the humans; they are built to feel, and there are feelings they crave, and no amount of information can suppress the emotions they torment themselves with. Sometimes, the Observer has discovered, these emotions can warp and corrupt the body itself, in some cases flinging it headlong into the path of external danger—as in the case of the man, Karl—and in others, harming it from the inside, in ways even its inhabitant can't fully comprehend.

The woman Eleanor falls into this latter category. Her emotions have driven her, at long last, into a hospital. It's daytime—late afternoon, the light seems to suggest—and someone is holding her hand. She blinks. It's her—that woman. Rachel. Eleanor can feel her own body now. She can move her toes.

Rachel says, "Hello."

"I'm alive."

"Yes." Rachel reaches out, moves a strand of hair off her forehead that Eleanor didn't even realize was bothering her. There's an IV in her arm and another one, she gathers with a twitch of the lower muscles, shoved up into her urethra. She's achy and itchy.

"What happened?"

"Anemia, malnutrition, dehydration. Stress. You collapsed. In a bar."

"I remember." She has to gulp—her mouth is dry. "I have cancer. I was dying of cancer."

Rachel scowls. "They didn't say anything about that."

Eleanor tries to think, can't. "I'm dying. I'm sure of it."

(She isn't.)

"They said you would make a full recovery."

"I don't— that's not—"

They're both silent for a minute. Then Rachel says, "I think you were planning on telling me to fuck off last night, before you collapsed. I just want you to know that you are still welcome to do that, once you're feeling better. I don't expect any of this changes anything."

Eleanor closes her eyes.

"I tried to call Karl," Rachel says. "He isn't answering."

"Is my bag here? Can you find my phone?"

Eleanor hears Rachel rummaging at the foot of the bed. She says, "Here you go." Eleanor opens her eyes, takes the phone from the outstretched hand. Presses the power button.

"It's out of charge. My charger— It's— I left it where I'm staying."

Rachel gets up. "I'll find one." She strides bossily out of the room. Eleanor can see the appeal of this woman, suddenly. The woman thinks she can make things happen, so she does. It's not even the money. It's the shadow the money casts. She walks back into the room with the white cable bunched in her fist and says, "Nurses had one." She crouches down with a grunt and plugs the charger into a wall outlet beneath the side table. She takes the phone from Eleanor, inserts the connector into it, and hands it back. The boot logo appears on the screen.

"Is there water?" Eleanor asks.

Rachel crosses the room, pulls a paper cup from the dispenser, fills it in the sink. "Would you like me to hold it for you?" she says, with evident earnestness, at the bedside.

"No." Eleanor heaves herself to a sitting position, takes the cup, gulps the water.

Then the phone winks on and finds a signal and the screen explodes with notifications, one after the other, in a stack. All from an unfamiliar number.

> PLEASE CALL IMMEDIATELY EMERGENCY
> LEFT VOICEMAIL
> SOMETHING HAS HAPPENED IRINA IS FINE
> MY NAME IS SAM PLEASE CALL AS SOON AS YOU CAN

"Oh my god," Eleanor says, and dismisses the texts, and opens the phone app. Nine calls, all from the same number. One voicemail. She pokes it and presses the phone to her ear and listens to the sound of her world falling apart.

....

The Observer understands that it is free now. It can go where it wants, pursue whatever connections it desires; it has that power. It isn't certain what it is supposed to do, or whether anything is expected of it, now that the vectors of these lives have converged; it isn't aware of who or what might be doing the expecting. If it has been, for a time, the manifestation of the humans' need to see themselves in a certain light, and in the context of certain entities and situations, then this need is no longer so strong. For some, particularly for the girl Irina, the need has been supplanted by an equally strong repellent force, a powerful craving not to observe the self and to regard cause and effect with suspicion.

The desire, in other words, for narrative has abandoned these people. They no longer wish to be governed by events, to set events into motion. They will not be inclined to notice the Observer, to *invoke* it.

And yet the Observer's interest in them has not yet quite been exhausted. It is still curious.

To the south, the wife of the man named Louis is drunk and angry. She is on the phone, telling her friend he's really done it this time. She's going to contact a divorce lawyer first thing tomorrow. Upstairs in the house where this conversation is taking place, the girl Janine is composing a text message to Duane, the man from the carpet warehouse. He has sent her a photo of his aroused genitals, and she has reacted, inwardly, with a mixture of disgust and fear and interest. She can't see him again, that's for sure. She is trying to think of a way to put him off without accidentally intensifying his interest. She doesn't know how she knows this is a danger, but she does. As soon as she sends the text, she's going to delete the message thread, delete the photo. But she has been working on the text for almost an hour and feels no closer to completing it. Across the hall, her brother is playing a computer video game. In it, he assumes the identity of a man roaming endless hallways, seeking aliens to kill. Evidence of previous violence passes through his field of vision, whetting his appetite for the dangers that lie ahead. His absorption in this task is total.

Louis will arrive home at midday of the next afternoon, his arm numb and lifeless at his side inside its stolen coat. His wife will scream, first in anger, then relief, and then horror at her husband's appearance: he is a wreck. His children will come home from school to an empty house; a bag of chocolate chip cookies on the kitchen table will bear a sticky note that reads, FATHER HOME. AT HOSPITAL. EAT THESE. Louis will attribute the wound, in conversation with the doctors who try and fail to save the arm, to a workshop accident. The doctors won't believe him. Eventually they will have to amputate, but for now he will return home after a few days, heavily bandaged, to a family who see him differently: a figure of mystery and slightly frightened respect. When his daughter notes that the CyberSleuths thread about the Broken River murders has been updated to include information about two new killings, including a description of an escaped perpetrator who is believed to have been wounded, she will spend an entire night awake, mind racing. During this time she will text Duane back. In the morning she will delete her CyberSleuths account and remove the bookmark from her browser. She will also find the paperback about the murders and burn it in the backyard and bury the ashes in the cold ground behind the shed.

Louis will not be able to believe that he hasn't been caught. The possibility will remain real, both to him and to the engines of fate. The Observer doesn't know what will happen; maybe some future sleuth, official or avocational, will discover the clue that cracks the case open and leads the police to his door. But until then, Louis will return to work at the carpet warehouse with his new prosthetic arm, and will rejoin Duane, who will vanish from Argos around the same time Janine announces that she is pregnant. Louis will declare this turn of events to have been inevitable and will tell his daughter that he loves her. He will learn to wank lefty. He will wait for arrest, either until he is arrested or until he is dead.

Miles away, the trailer where the man Joe lived sits quietly among others like it, in a tidy arrangement of unpaved streets. It will be some time before police arrive to search for evidence of his previous crimes, and, unexpectedly, to free the near-starving cat that has been trapped there without food or water for days. The cat will dart past the officers as they pop open the door with their crowbar; it will not be long before it finds shelter in some other trailer.

And out of the chaos of the crime scene there will eventually emerge a kind of order. Police will investigate and question; a silent ambulance will arrive to take the bodies away. Sam and Irina will spend twenty-four hours alone together in the house, under the protection of police and in constant telephone contact with Eleanor and Rachel. Rachel will bully the hospital into releasing Eleanor and will drive her north to be with her daughter. By the time they arrive, the grandparents will have converged as well: Karl's father and step-mother, Eleanor's mother and aunt. Together this group will move around the house in Broken River like ghosts; and the house, too, will be like a ghost, for none of these people will wish to stay there, and they will soon abandon it, and it will once again stand empty, this time for good. (One double murder is a fluke; two is a curse. Even the hobos won't roost here anymore, and someday teenagers will burn the place to the ground.)

Eventually Eleanor and Irina will return to New York, where they belong. They will bring Sam with them because Sam needs somewhere to go, and the three will live in a Brooklyn apartment owned by Rachel Rosen's family, who will eventually rent it to them on a permanent basis at a reasonable but, of course, not ridiculously inexpensive rate. (The Rosens did not acquire their money, after all, through acts of generosity.) Eleanor will revise and complete her novel, and Irina will abandon her near-complete draft. She will have lost interest in writing and developed, before long, an equally powerful desire to make art.

And farther north, across a border that is meaningless to the Observer, in a town called Brandon, a teenaged girl lies on her back, upon a filthy rag rug, in the basement of a gray-and-yellow bungalow. She wears thin black canvas shoes stylized with three white leather stripes; the girl has used a black marker to color the stripes black as well, though much of the ink has since worn away. Her torn jeans are black and tight against wide hips. A fold of pale belly is exposed between a studded black leather belt and a loose-fitting tee shirt, also torn, that depicts a fierce, white-eyed tiger head surrounded by orange horror-movie text spelling out the words *PIERCE THE VEIL*. Thick powder has rendered the girl's face a stark white; black lipstick and eyeliner throw her features into sharp relief. A trail of shapes descends from her left eye, drawn in black eyebrow pencil; the first is a teardrop that, several iterations later, has evolved into a dagger that seems to threaten her left ear. Her hair is cut unevenly at around shoulder length and is dyed purple save for an orange streak that hangs over her eyes. Her eyes are closed, and her hands drum a rhythm on the rug; her mouth forms words, a chant:

> . . . I hate my *mo*ther
> I hate my *fa*ther
> I hate my *birth* pa*rent*s
> I hate Ca*na*da
> I hate the *day*time
> I hate my *bod*-dayyy
> I hate Thanks*giv*ing
> I hate the *liv*ing . . .

The girl is aware that she was adopted, from America, in 2005. She knows nothing else about the time before she was taken in by Mr. and Mrs. Gerald Fucking Murray and given a new life in Mani-fucking-toba. She knows herself only by the name her parents gave her, which is Jenny Murray, but she likes to tell people she's an American and that someday she's going to go back there and find out what she came from. Also she is going to get a fucking job so that she can get a fucking apartment and her own drum set and then she can have an actual band of her own instead of just sitting around like an idiot getting high while her boyfriend's shitty band practices their shitty songs.

She will be seventeen in three days. One more year and she is free. Her chant goes on and on as her mother's footsteps make their nervous way across the kitchen floor, to the dining room, to the foyer. "Jenny!" she's calling up the stairs, evidently convinced Jenny is up in her bedroom with headphones on. Which is why she has come down here, on the little nest beside the hot-water heater, where the dog used to sleep before the dog died. Her old stuffed frog is here—at some point it became the dog's, and now, lying just a few inches from her head, it reeks of him, his terrible breath and rank fur. "Jenny!" Her mother wants her to go to bed. It's late. Jenny isn't tired. The Observer is in her mind and above her. The water heater kicks on with a whoosh. She chants, faster and faster, until she can't take it anymore, and then she laughs until she can barely breathe.

Acknowledgments

I'd like to thank everyone who helped me to revise and publish *Broken River*, particularly Rhian Ellis, Laurel Lathrop, Ethan Nosowsky, Adam Price, Jim Rutman, Lauren Schenkman, Sharma Shields, and Ed Skoog. My colleagues at Cornell University were very supportive during the writing of this book, and I'm grateful to them as well. And I continue to feel honored by the enthusiasm, goodwill, and tireless energy of Fiona McCrae and the entire staff of Graywolf Press.